THE
ORPHANS
OF MIRNA

LINDA B. WHITE

Harrigan Creek Press
Denver, Colorado

Harrigan Creek Press
Denver, Colorado
www.lindabwhite.com

Publisher's Note: This is a work of fiction. Names, characters, places, and incidents are a product of the author's imagination. Locales and public names are sometimes used for atmospheric purposes. Any resemblance to actual people, living or dead, or to businesses, companies, events, institutions, or locales is completely coincidental.

Cover Art: Shannon Faber, www.ink-and-tea.com

The Orphans of Mirna / Linda B. White. — 1st ed.
ISBN 978-0-9973300-0-7

An excerpt of *In Blackwater Woods,* a poem by Mary Oliver, appears in Chapter 24.

To Alex and Darcy,
who have loved, inspired, and encouraged me
their whole lives.

We are stardust, we are golden
We are billion year-old carbon
And we got to get ourselves back to the garden.

—Woodstock, Joni Mitchell

PART I

GRAVITY

ONE

Reilly Landreth tugged his cap over his cold-nipped ears and gazed out the observation window of the *Remus*. The planet Cinnabar practically filled the entire view. A large, ocher-colored continent reminded him of a woman's back. A mountain range ran like a sash diagonally across the shoulders. According to his studies, the white tops were snow, the purplish areas vegetation, the lavender splotches lakes. White clouds shrouded the hips of lowland jungle. The smooth orange waist was a vast desert. The *Remus* was supposed to land in the middle of it, as close as possible to the first colonists' coordinates.

Had all gone according to plan, the ship would have swung into orbit around the planet. Then a small scouting party would have shuttled down, set up temporary shelter, and reported back. Instead, the entire crew was stuck on the ship, trying to stay warm, trying not to panic.

So close, Reilly thought. He had spent his entire life traveling here. The crew had survived near annihilation. To fail this close to their final destination, to be shut down by a meteor seemed tragic, preposterous, and downright unfair.

For fifteen years, the *Remus* had outmaneuvered every meteor that had come its way—until seven hours ago. Reilly and most of the others had been on the observation deck, harnessed into their seats for the entry into Cinnabar's atmosphere.

The alarm had blared, eclipsing chatter about this final phase of the journey. Captain Baca's voice came from the speakers, "Meteor aft."

Reilly's father said, "Don't worry. Oren's got it." Ensign Oren Rabin was their best pilot.

Captain Baca spoke, "Ten seconds to impact."

Impact? Reilly glanced from one parent to the other. They were looking at each other.

Thrusters thundered; the ship, already under the sway of Cinnabar's gravitational force, lurched. *Eight seconds. Seven. Six.*

Gravity hitched meteor to ship, ship to meteor, tugging them like blood cells toward the planet's molten heart. Outside the observation window, the air went from black to red. The ship shuddered. The planet framed in the observation window appeared to pitch sideways. Reilly shut his eyes. The screech of rending metal outmuscled human screams. The stench of burning plastic, molten metal, and fear thickened the air.

Silence. The ship groaned, then seemed to stand still.

A child cried. Keid. His forehead was bleeding. Where was his helmet?

Reilly's mother brushed pieces of ceiling tile from her lap, unclipped her harness, grabbed a bandage from the first-aid kit on the wall, and pressed it against Keid's forehead. His mother said something, but Reilly couldn't hear. Keid nodded and closed his eyes.

Ensign Morten removed his helmet and checked the video monitors. "We're screwed," he said.

Reilly's dad shook his head. "Don't worry, pal," he said to Reilly. We're now orbiting Cinnabar. Soon we'll be on the surface."

The meteor had raked the *Remus'* starboard side. For the first few minutes, it seemed the damage was mainly cosmetic—a few more dings and a blackened scrape. Then the computer diagnosed errors in the climate control system. The levels of oxygen and carbon dioxide remained within normal limits. But, within five minutes, the temperature began to plummet.

Ever the positive thinker, his mother said, "Well, we can try out our cold-weather gear sooner than later."

Captain Baca ordered immediate mass evacuation to the shuttle. They would have to skip the scouting and exploration trips. After all, they had the first colonists' reports. The crew of the *Romulus* had landed over a year ago. Reilly liked to imagine that the first colonists would, by now, have established buildings, bounteous crops, and thriving livestock.

It was impossible to know whether that dream was a reality; the *Romulus* and the *Remus* had been out of radio contact for many months. Reilly's mother maintained that mechanical failure of the first colonists' radio was a more likely explanation than their wholesale extinction on an eminently habitable planet. His father didn't weigh in—not in front of Reilly.

As the crew prepared for the descent, fear iced Reilly's gut. For weeks, he'd secretly dreaded leaving the only home he'd ever known. But this new angst gripped him harder. *Something else is wrong,* he thought. *Don't be silly. You'll be on Cinnabar sooner. That's all. Get a grip before Tab notices.*

But something else was wrong. The captain announced that the meteor had warped the shuttle's undocking system, which meant the ship wouldn't release the shuttle, which meant they couldn't leave.

His mother said Commander Shen and Ensign Morten would fix the docking coupler. Then his mother went to inspect the climate control system.

Reilly watched at the observation window with his father and a half dozen other crew. Shaped like an outsized grain of rice, the shuttle lay snug in its bay under a wing-like projection from the ship. Two figures dressed in silver space suits and helmets clung to the shuttle's side. The smaller, more agile figure was Lian Shen; the larger was Harlan Morten. An umbilical cord of titanium mesh connected them to the ship. Strong magnets affixed their boots to the metallic surface and made each step look herculean. Every few seconds, the welding gun in Commander Shen's gloved hand emitted a red glow. Beside her, Ensign Morten wielded various tools tethered to his belt.

The door whisper-slid open, and Reilly's mother entered. Her blue eyes stood out in her cold-blanched face. "How's it going out there?" she asked.

"Nothing has budged yet," her father said. "Any progress with the heating system?"

"Oren hasn't made much progress. And I wasn't much help."

"Anika," his father said, "you're a biologist, not an electrician."

Alarm tightened Reilly's stomach. Ensign Rabin was the ship's mechanical engineer and all around electronics wizard. He was supposed to be able to fix anything.

"Oren took off his gloves to work," Reilly's mother said. "I'm worried he'll get frostbite. The temperature's already near zero."

Zero degrees centigrade, Reilly thought, *the temperature where water changes from liquid to solid state.* Until now, the ship had been kept at a pleasant 22 degrees centigrade, a temperature where you felt perfectly comfortable in pants and shirt, a temperature that raised neither sweat nor goose bumps.

"I'll go check on Oren," Reilly's father said.

"Wait a bit, Skyler. When I left, the captain had just called him to the control room to monitor the undocking system. Oren said he'd buzz you later."

A vitro girl named Maia sidled closer. The cap pulled low on her forehead flattened her wild hair and accentuated her stubborn jaw. Reilly braced himself for the usual torrent of questions.

"What's going on, Lieutenant Bergen?" Maia asked Reilly's mother. "Will it get warmer soon?"

"Ensign Rabin's working on it," his mother said.

Snot glistened at Maia's nostrils. "Meaning he hasn't been able to fix the problem?"

Reilly's father nodded. "Not yet."

Maia frowned. "If we can't undock the shuttle, we can't descend to Cinnabar. And if we remain on the ship—" she frowned, as though working out a complicated physics problem. "Well, we'll become hypothermic and die, won't we?" She sounded very cause and effect. Reilly could practically see the vector diagrams in her head. Cold exposure → hypothermia → death.

Reilly's father cleared his throat and glanced at two other vitros, Tab and Nova, who stood a few meters away, watching the shuttle repairs, their foreheads practically touching the icy observation window. Nova looked thoughtful. Tab gestured animatedly. He looked downright excited. Of the six surviving in vitros—Reilly mentally referred to them as "vitros"—Tab and Maia were least likely to exhibit fear. Reilly had long surmised they'd been bioengineered for bravery.

Aside from the advantage of desirable genetic traits, the vitros obviated the inconvenience and risk of pregnancy for the adult females. Plus, the vitros didn't come of age till later in the trip, which meant they ate relatively less, yet would be strong enough to work when they reached Cinnabar. Even though Reilly was born five years before the vitros graduated from their incubators, they were nearly his biological age—about fifteen. At maturity the growth factors wore off, which meant, Reilly and the vitros would age at the same pace.

"Well," his father said, "I'm sure we're going to be able to get off the ship before anyone freezes." His breath puffed tiny white clouds that hung in the frozen air, then vanished.

"I heard we only have a little over an hour before people start to become confused and drowsy. From what I've read, we'll basically fall asleep and die." Maia pursed her lips. "I guess it's better than dying from a virus, or a fire, or—"

"Thanks, Maia," Reilly interrupted. In truth, he'd gone through a similar thought process—short of the comparative death scenarios. He'd seen people die from the Dagnar virus. He'd nearly been one of them.

"Is it true that all the greenhouse plants have already frozen?" Maia asked.

His mother sighed. "Yes. I just heard from the captain."

"Fyce," Maia said.

The kids weren't allowed to swear; Reba, the android, shocked them with the Electroprod if they did. The vitros got around the rule by making up words—grot, radge, fyce, minjen, preme. Stupid words, Reilly thought.

"So what will we do now for food if—when we land," Reilly said. He pictured the rows of trays of seedlings of drought-resistant greens, beans, and berries. The seedlings were supposed to provide a head start on their crops.

"We'll start from seeds," his mother said. "The first colonists probably have stores and can show us which native plants are edible."

"And we'll have the animals," Maia said.

"But we can't eat them," Reilly said. "Not yet. And never the dogs."

Maia shrugged. "People on Earth ate dogs."

"In some cultures," Reilly's father said. "Anyway, if Talitha has her way, we won't eat any of the animals—goats, turkeys, and chickens. Maybe not even the eggs." He glanced over his shoulder.

"Tally's not here. She's helping Lieutenant Schuler," Maia said. "She mostly loves the goats. Plus, we'll need the proteins in their milk for textiles." She wiped her nose, leaving a silver trail on the backside of her glove. "Tally told me the animals are getting cold stressed," Maia said. "Nova and Keid already have frost-nipped fingers."

Reilly's mother looked over at Nova, who stood nearby, hands in jacket pockets. "Are they wearing their gloves?" When Maia only shrugged, she said, "They should get inside their sleeping sacs for extra warmth. I need to go check on everyone." She tucked her blond bangs under the band of her thick red cap.

"Weird hat," Maia said. Everyone else wore blue caps. "Where'd you get it?"

"My mother."

"It was Captain Bergen's?" Maia said. "That's preme." She pulled off a glove and touched the hat. "It's not as soft as our BioSilk caps. What's it made of?"

"Wool," Reilly's mother said.

"Sheep's hair," Reilly added. "Sheep were Earth ungulates." He flinched at his pedantic tone. And what were they doing nattering about wool at a time like this?

"I *know*," Maia said. "There are supposed to be ungulates on Cinnabar."

"Yes," she said and turned to gaze at the planet looming in the observation window. She emanated a blue coolness that Reilly felt in his chest. He often felt other people's emotions. His parents insisted he was simply empathetic. Yet no one else talked about the color and temperature of other people's feelings. The few times he did, the vitros' taunts quickly silenced him.

Reilly knew his mother was thinking about her dead parents. They had died during the Dagnar virus epidemic, along with ten other adults, two womb-born children, and four *in vitro* kids. Now they were down to seven adults, six vitros, and Reilly, the only womb-born child.

Reilly stepped back, his arm bumping some soft part on Maia's torso. Heat warmed his frozen cheeks. He said, more abruptly than he'd intended, "How much time do we have?"

His mother checked her wristwatch. "One hour and forty minutes."

Reilly shivered, and wrapped his arms around his torso.

"Are you two packed for the descent?" Reilly's father asked.

"I've been packed for ages, Lieutenant Landreth," Maia said and flashed her white teeth.

Reilly wondered how anyone could smile at a time like this. A combination of cold and fear had paralyzed his own face—and his sense of humor.

"Hey, Maia," Tab called, pointing out the window at the shuttle. "Looks like they're finished." Tabit, "Tab" for short, was the biggest, brawniest, meanest kid on the ship.

They hurried to the window. Maia inserted herself between Tab and Nova. With a grudging look, Nova moved aside. Of the three girls, Nova was the prettiest—glossy black hair, golden skin, large wide-set eyes, full lips, and newly acquired curves now hidden beneath her jacket.

Outside, Ensign Morten was passing through the portal into the ship. Commander Shen was no longer visible. The portal closed.

Nova stopped chewing the tip of her long braid. "Now what?" she asked.

"I think they're going to start the shuttle," Tab said excitedly. "They must have got her unstuck."

For a few minutes nothing happened. Then a light came on in shuttle's cabin, illuminating the head and shoulders of Commander Shen and Ensign Morten sitting in front of the control panel. Ensign Morten raised a gloved hand to helmet in an irreverent salute, probably in response to an order from Captain Baca. The shuttle shimmied in place, then lurched forward. A rear thruster flared briefly.

"What if they can't redock?" Nova asked. She pushed back her cap and rubbed the birthmark on her forehead, a nervous habit. Reilly thought the birthmark resembled a large comma, but his mother, who had named this girl, said it was like starburst. The other vitros were named after particular stars—Tabit, Maia, Keid, Talitha, and Nash. They sometimes called her 'Supernova,' which Nova liked, even though a supernova was a collapsing, burning star.

"I'm sure they will," Reilly's father said.

"But what if they can't?" Nova said. Her eyes glazed with tears—either that or the cold simply made her eyes water.

Maia put her arm around Nova. "Just watch," she said. "Forget the what-ifs."

Nova pressed her lips together and looked obediently out the window. After a moment, she touched the glass with bare fingers and said, "What is this white stuff?"

Reilly looked. Tiny white crystals were spreading along the surface of the clear polychiton.

"Frost," Reilly's mother said. "Water in the air is collecting and freezing there."

Reilly had never seen the entire shuttle, except in illustrations on the computer, which showed the shuttle as a capsule-shaped object alongside the disc-shaped ship. His view from the observation window had always been limited to the craft's rounded nose. Now, as the shuttle moved out of its bay, he could see that the rear segment flared out, so that the whole thing looked like a giant saltshaker lying on its side. The wider end contained the landing gear. Reilly hoped it would soon touch down on the planet.

"They're coming right at us," Nova exclaimed. Darting around Maia, she clutched Tab's arm.

Tab kept his eyes on the shuttle. "Minjin' astral," he breathed.

Commander Shen and Ensign Morten were now so close their faces were visible. The ensign waved. Tab waved back. A thruster pulsed red on the shuttle's elongated portside and the craft moved sideways, away from the ship. Another pulse and the shuttle turned ninety degrees.

"Where are they going?" Maia asked.

"They're going to circle the ship, nannobrain," Tab said, rubbing at an inflamed pimple on his neck. "Wicked phenomenal. Everything according to plan, just like Harlan said."

The kids were supposed to address the adults by their titles, but the vitros used Ensign Morten's first name. Reilly had never called him Harlan, and the ensign had never invited him to. While other adults mainly treated the vitros like work—things to be managed, Ensign Morten seemed to enjoy them. In fact, he seemed like an older version of Tab—strong, fearless, and endowed with the sensitivity of a hammer. Reilly had wondered whether they'd come from the same batch of frozen embryos. He once asked his mother whether Ensign Morten was himself a vitro, but she said "no."

The shuttle arced around the ship and disappeared from view. Floating in the background, Cinnabar looked like the florid face of a bald, furious man. Reilly remembered that cinnabar is also the name for a red Earth rock composed of mercuric sulfide, which is poisonous. He felt the planet tugging at him, as though its gravitational force were already weighing him down. If the shuttle could redock, he would soon know the heft of that force. And the heat. According to their data, desert days were nearly 38 degrees Celsius, then dropped to zero after sunset.

It seemed ironic that the crew of the *Remus* had left Earth because it had gotten too hot. Images from his history lessons haunted him—flooded towns with people perched on rooftops, swollen rivers clogged with the bloated bodies of dead fish and humans, bombed-out buildings, flaming forests, crops withered in cracked soil, emaciated people holding out bony hands. But there were beautiful pictures too—a cactus blooming red in a desert, jagged mountains stabbing a blue sky, turquoise waves breaking on a white beach, cities with tall, gleaming buildings. His favorite was the planet photographed over two hundred years ago during one of the first trips to Earth's moon. The gauzy white clouds, the blue ocean, the yellow-red desert, the brown-green forests and grasslands.

That photo made him think of his grandfather, who had taken his own photos of Earth as they rocketed away. Sometimes he would show them to Reilly on the computer. Sometimes he would take Reilly on the observation deck and help him find other planets in the telescope.

"Does that one look like Earth?" Reilly would ask. And his grandfather would explain how it was drier, wetter, bigger, or smaller.

"Will we ever go back to Earth, Granddaddy?" Reilly had once asked.

His grandfather had smiled and cupped the back of Reilly's head with his huge hand. "Heck, Reilly, I'm old. I won't live long enough to make another fifteen-year trip."

Reilly had started to protest, but his grandfather had added, "You'd have to drug me comatose to get me back on another ship. I want to drink water and breathe air that hasn't been recycled a million times. I want to hear the wind and smell dirt and feel the sun on my old hide. I want to want to walk for hours and see something new with each step. Heck, I know every stain in the carpet of this ship by heart."

Now, a hand waved in front of Reilly's eyes. It belonged to his father. "Hey, buddy, are you going hypothermic on me?"

Reilly blinked. "No," he said. "I was looking at Cinnabar and thinking that space shots of Earth look, well, more inviting."

His father sighed. "A long time ago, Earth was a nice place to live."

Reilly recalled lectures about the apocalyptic twenty-second century. Lots of wars over water and food. Bioterrorism. There'd been a news bulletin about terrorist groups seeding ventilation systems in government buildings—he couldn't remember the country—with a virulent virus. Because of the time it took radio waves to travel, that news was, in real time on Earth, five years old. For all he knew, humans might now be extinct on Earth.

Reilly looked his father in the eye, something he'd only recently grown tall enough to do. "What if this place isn't any better than Earth?" His teeth banged together as he formed the words. He clamped his hands over his jaws to still the movement. The muscles in his back shivered involuntarily, which embarrassed him.

His father gently bumped his shoulder against Reilly's and said, "It has to be. It's habitable and not overrun with humans."

"It's not like we have other options," Maia muttered.

Reilly hadn't realized she was listening. Then again, she always seemed to be hanging about, watching, listening.

Reilly's mother said, "If we're successful on Cinnabar, other people will be able to leave Earth and join us."

Reilly had heard it hundreds of times. But now the "if" seemed more ominous.

"Where's the shuttle?" Nova piped up. "Why's it taking so long?"

"Back side of the ship," Tab said.

"The colonies on Riona have been doing well," Reilly's mother continued, more brightly now. "And probably the colonists on Cinnabar—"

Maia butted in. "We'll either succeed and live, or fail and die. No point worrying about it now."

Reilly checked his mother's face for sign of reproach, but she just nodded.

"Yeah," Tab said. "We're out of fuel, hume."

"My hands hurt," Nova said. "I didn't realize cold caused pain."

"Eventually," Maia said, "your hands will go numb."

"Stick your hands in your armpits, Supernova," Tab said. "That's what Harlan said to do." He didn't look at all cold.

"Just don't stick them in Tab's armpits," Maia said, deftly dodging the boy's elbow. "Not unless you want to stink."

"Where are your gloves?" Reilly's mother began.

Tab whooped at the sight of the shuttle's nose reappeared under the ship's wing. "They're about to dock," he said.

There came a faint clanking sound as the shuttle butted against the side of the ship. No one spoke. Commander Shen and Ensign Morten unbuckled their harnesses, stood, and passed from view. The lights went out inside the shuttle.

For a moment, everyone on the observation deck remained silent.

Nova turned her large, dark eyes toward Reilly's father. "They undocked and redocked. That means we can leave, right, Lieutenant Landreth?"

For the first time in many hours, Reilly's father smiled. "Looks that way, Nova."

Nova beamed.

"So when do we get off this hunk of junk?" Tab asked.

The door into the observation deck slid open. Lieutenant Erik Schuler entered.

"They made it!" Tab announced.

Lieutenant Schuler's craggy face cracked into a smile. He began to move around the room in slow circles, swaying, humming. Reilly blinked. Stolid silence was the lieutenant's usual mode of operation around people, though he became almost clownish with the animals. Laughing, Nova ran up to him, took the lieutenant's hand. He pirouetted her, his other arm clamped across his middle.

Something squawked and the lieutenant's jacket rippled across his belly.

TWO

Lieutenant Schuler let go of Nova's hand and unzipped his jacket partway. A yellow beak stabbed the air, red wattles tossed, and auburn wings fluttered.

Tab laughed. "It's a minjin' chicken. You're going to have chicken shit in your jacket, Lieutenant Schuler."

Lieutenant Schuler, the ship's veterinary specialist, had raised six chickens, six turkeys, four goats, and two dogs from embryos. All the animals had just reached maturity in time for the landing.

The lieutenant grinned and clamped the chicken's wings to its sides. "I was trying to warm her," he said. Bobbing her head, the hen clucked and regarded them, pupils round and irises rust red.

"Looks like you succeeded, Erik," said Reilly's mother. "And, Tab, don't say shit, okay?"

Tab smiled. "Okay, Lieutenant Bergen. How about chicken feces? Chicken droppings? Chicken poop—"

Nova giggled.

"Those will all do, Tab," said Reilly's father, suppressing a smile.

The vitros still found fecal material, farts, and belches humorous, confirming Reilly's premise was that, for at least some of the kids, mental maturity trailed their accelerated physical growth.

Maia darted into the hall, calling over her shoulder, "Nova and Tab, go tell the others. I'm going to the control room."

Nova and Tab tore out the door and turned left. Reilly and his parents took a right, following Maia. The windowless corridor ran in a 350 meter-long loop down the middle of the donut-shaped ship. To stay in shape, they were

20

all supposed to run 10 laps a day, plus work out 30 minutes in the cramped gym. Each lap took him a minute and a half, and by the third Reilly usually felt nauseous from running in circles. From the observation deck, the control room was a quarter of the way around the loop.

At the entrance, Reilly's father said, "Open," and the door slid into the wall. The room was pie shaped. The curved wall was interrupted with two large windows and a hefty oval door. A computer screen occupied the other wall. The console table in front of it also had held a second, wafer-thin computer and a few switches and levers.

Ensign Rabin sat at the console, frowning at the monitor and giving orders to the computer. His cap flattened his curly black hair, giving the impression his head had shrunk. His untucked shirt hung below his jacket and the beginnings of a beard darkened his jaw.

Maia stood behind the ensign, peering over his shoulder. Captain Baca waited before the oval door that led to the docking center portal, presumably waiting for Ensign Morten and Lieutenant Shen to step through. The captain studied the computer monitor area that displayed the gauges indicating the atmospheric pressure and oxygen levels on the other side of that door.

"Computer," Captain Baca said, "open inner portal." The wheel-shaped handle on the door should have revolved counterclockwise, but it didn't.

Ensign Rabin stood and began tapping and manipulating various functions on the screen. A few seconds later, the captain repeated the order, louder this time. The portal didn't budge. A message flashed on screen in red letters. *Maneuver failed.*

Reilly's father went over to the ensign. "What's the problem?"

Without taking his eyes from the screen, Ensign Rabin shook his head and mumbled something about trouble with the docking coupler.

The door to the control room slid open and Reba advanced, metal exterior gleaming, parts whirring as her head swiveled to get them into her sights. After the Dagnar virus killed the three members of the childcare team, the android's sole job had changed from running the mess hall to monitoring the vitros. There simply weren't enough adults left to maintain the ship and raise kids.

A monotonic voice came from the oval speaker placed mouth-like in Reba's lower face. "Clearance not granted. You are out of bounds, Maia."

Maia's eyes went flat and watchful.

Reba's three-fingered hand rested on the butt of the Electroprod, which was clipped to its thigh. Reilly didn't think Reba would use the Prod for such a minor infraction. Then again, androids didn't tend to split hairs when it came to protocol, nor was this model programmed for compassion.

Maia edged closer to Reilly's mother, who drew a protective arm around the girl's shoulders.

"Desist, Reba," Captain Baca called. "Maia has permission to remain. See that Tabit, Nova, and Nash are in the dorm. Have them double check the packing list. Send Keid to help Lieutenant Schuler and Talitha crate the animals for transport."

"Affirmative, Captain." Reba rotated a hundred eighty degrees and rolled out of the room.

Maia blew out her breath. "Thank you, Captain Baca."

The captain grunted.

"Captain Baca," Reilly ventured, "will we transport to the planet soon?"

"Let's hope so," the captain said.

Reilly felt his spinal fluid freeze.

"Hope?" Maia said. "The docking system's okay, right? We saw the shuttle undock and redock."

"Well," the captain said, "do you see Commander Shen and Ensign Morten?"

"No, sir," Maia said.

"That's because the inner door won't open."

The wall clock usually displayed the time, but now was running backwards in some sort of countdown. 52:39. 52:38. 52:37… Reilly checked his watch and recalled what Maia had said—that after an hour, they'd begin to suffer serious hypothermia. So this was a countdown. His chest felt hectic, as though Lieutenant Schuler's hen were trapped within his ribs and trying to escape.

Reilly's mother leaned toward Maia and murmured, "Not a good time to bother the captain."

Maia pursed her lips, nodded.

Reilly went over to where his father and Ensign Rabin sat before the console.

"Dad," he whispered, "what's wrong?"

"The inner door is stuck," his father said, not taking his eyes off a display that showed a schematic of the interface between shuttle and ship. "The impact of the meteor must have deformed the seal."

"But the inner door opened when Ensign Morten and Lieutenant Shen left to test ride the shuttle."

Ensign Rabin rubbed the bags under his eyes. "It wasn't easy to open or to shut it after them. Now, it won't open at all."

"So Commander Shen and Ensign Rabin are in the pressurized chamber between the doors?" Maia said.

Reilly gave her a quick, irritated glance. The girl dogged his every step.

"That's right," Ensign Rabin said. He blew on his fingers, which were so white that every black hair stood out, then went back to flipping switches and typing computer code.

"What's that noise?" Maia whispered to Reilly. Then she looked him full in the face. "Oh, it's coming from you."

Reilly turned away. "My teeth," he muttered, jaw hammering. "I can't stop it."

"My teeth are chattering too," Ensign Rabin said. "Muscles shiver to generate heat. It's involuntary and entirely normal." He blew on his fingers, reset a series of functions, manipulated data on the screen, frisked his hands together, commanded the computer to run another set of diagnostics.

"Oren," Reilly's mother said in exasperation, "please put on your gloves."

"Gloves slow me down," Ensign Rabin muttered.

"So will frostbite," Reilly's mother said. "And, Reilly, you should go to our chambers and wrap up in your sleeping sac."

Reilly said nothing. Maia hadn't been told to leave. And why wasn't she shivering?

"Oren," Captain Baca cut in. "Oren, put on the damn gloves."

"No time. We have to get off the ship before the cold locks up the oxygen generator."

The captain opened a drawer, pulled out a packet, tore open the wrapping, and unfurled a two-by-three-meter rectangle of thin silver fabric. He wrapped the fabric around Ensign Rabin's shoulders. The ensign thanked him.

Reilly knew that unfolding the thin fabric activated a heat-producing chemical reaction. But the warmth only lasted two hours. Then what? Which would come first, death by hypothermia or death by asphyxiation?

Commander Shen's voice came thinly from the speakers. "Any luck at your end?"

"Negative, Lian," Captain Baca said. "We're going to have to force it open."

"Great," came Ensign Morten's voice. "Let me know when to start."

Reilly whispered to his father. "But if we force it, then it might not open and close later."

His father stood. The skin under his eyes was so dark it looked bruised. "It'll be okay for at least one more trip."

According to the original plan, it would take at least two trips to transport humans, livestock, and gear to the planet. What would they leave behind? Reilly wondered. They couldn't leave the animals. Or the people. Or the gardening implements, tools for constructing dwellings, computers. At least they didn't need to bother transporting the trays of frozen seedlings.

Reilly's parents and Captain Baca took turns trying to turn the metal wheel in the middle of the door to the shuttle.

Ensign Rabin typed something on the horizontal computer in the console, then called, "Any change?"

Captain Baca yanked again on the wheel, but it didn't budge. "No," he said, "switch to manual override."

"All three of us at once," the captain said, and Reilly's parents added their hands to the wheel, which was about a half meter across. "One, two, three," the captain said, and they all strained.

Manual override, Reilly thought. Manual labor. He had grown up with the computer performing almost every function; he told it to open a door, raise or lower the temperature, make new clothes, prepare a meal. The desired effect occurred. He'd taken it for granted. If they made it to Cinnabar, they would have to do a lot of manual labor. It was one the reasons for the daily weight-lifting.

Ensign Morten's voice came over the radio speakers. "Come on, over there! I can't do this by myself. Put your backs into it."

The space between the two doors would be extremely cold and nearly airless. Ensign Morten and Commander Shen wore spacesuits, which supplied oxygen and insulated from the cold, but they weren't impenetrable.

"Can I help?" Maia asked.

"Not enough room," Reilly's father grunted, a vein bulging in his neck.

Reilly glanced at the clock. 47:24. Just over three quarters of an hour. He flexed and extended his cold fingers. The inside of his nose stung with each inhalation.

The wheel budged. "Yes!" his mother cried, and the wheel began to revolve more quickly.

There was a dull repetitive thud from the other side of the door. Reilly's parents and the captain tugged the door toward them. It groaned open, and Ensign Morten tumbled into the control room. Commander Shen followed, sedate even in her spacesuit.

Ensign Morten's helmet was fogged. He tugged it off, rubbed his flushed face, got to his feet. "That operation wasn't as slick as I'd hoped."

Sudden relief wetted Reilly' eyes and clogged his throat.

"For once, I'm glad to see you, Harlan," Captain Baca said, the corners of his mouth twitching upward.

"Aw, shucks." Ensign Morten clownishly batted his eyes and grinned, exposing his strange front teeth. When he was a teen and still on Earth, he'd lost them in a fight. He had jammed the two incisors back in the sockets, but had accidentally reversed them, so that the right was where the left should be. He declined cosmetic dentistry because he preferred his "unique look."

Commander Shen removed her helmet and smoothed her black hair off her forehead. Though drawn, her oval face retained its relentless composure. She glanced at the clock. "Less than forty-five minutes," she said. "Time to get off this dying ship, wouldn't you say, Captain?"

THREE

Reilly's father stayed with Ensign Rabin to make some final adjustments to the docking system. His mother went with Maia to the vitros' dorm to make sure the kids were ready for transport. Reilly returned to his chambers—an eight-foot-long space with a tiny desk, chair, and a pull-down bed. As instructed, Reilly sorted the packed duffels, daypacks, and crates belonging to him and his parents. Because all the crew was now evacuating at once, they could only bring essentials. Reilly switched out some of his parents' personal goods for scientific instruments. His dad was specific about leaving his flute in his duffel. His mother insisted on traveling with a few old-fashioned family photos, just in case computers should ever fail.

Then Reilly gazed at his own crate of books—books that had belonged to his grandmother. He shouldn't take any. But what if he never made it back to the ship? These books were as precious to him as his father's flute was to him. His mother kept paper photographs in case the computers failed. The same rationale applied to books. No one else owned any. His grandmother's authority as the ship's captain at the start of the voyage was able to exceed the cargo weight restrictions. Now Reilly swapped a pair of pants and for a couple of slim books. Then he moved the three duffels and three packs to a neat pile by the doorway.

He checked the time. Thirty-one minutes. Shivering violently, he looked about and wondered what to do. His skull had become a zero-gravity chamber of floating, randomly colliding neurons. Brownian motion. Dust in an airshaft. A computer game sounded about right; he'd played all the games so many times he could do them in a hypothermic stupor. He slid his computer from a pocket in his pack—a palm-sized plastic sheet that rolled into a compact tube. His cold-clumsy hands fumbled the clasp. Once unscrolled, the screen illuminated and emitted an unusual high-pitched hum, as though it too felt the sting of the cold. He pulled the bed down from the wall and sat.

A moment later, the door slid open and his mother entered. "Hi, buddy," she said. "Seven minutes till we board the shuttle. Ready?"

"Ready as ever," Reilly said.

His mother sat beside him on the bed. "We're all nervous, Reilly. For a lot of reasons."

Reilly held up his gloved hand, fingers pulled into his palm. "First, allow me to point out, I'm shaking from cold, not high anxiety. Next, let me count those reasons. Lieutenant Bhatia is long dead and no one else has had half his experience with planetary entries." He uncurled his thumb. His words were coming out with annoying slowness, as though he were ice-picking each one free.

"None of the adults has set foot on a planet for fifteen years. None of us kids have ever been on a planet." He extended his index finger.

"We haven't heard from the first colonists ss-since their fourth week on Cinnabar." His third digit went up. His fingers were so cold, he needed the assistance of his other hand to move them.

"Reilly, you're starting to slur your words."

"Yeah. Well, your lips are blue."

"Yours too."

"Sooo. On to point four." His forth finger was so cold stiffened, he had to straighten it with the other hand. "We know ss-Cinnabar can sh-sustain life, but that's about all we know. And now, we won't be able to do any exploratory trips to gather more data."

"Right."

"If we don't like sh-Cinnabar, we'll have to stay until we find a fuel that can, you know, blast us back to Earth." His pinky wouldn't quite straighten, the result an old run-in with Tab. "Am I forgetting anything?" He looked longingly at his bed. Sleep seemed a warm and irresistible idea. He started to lean away from his mother and onto his side.

His mother's pulled him upright. Her free hand tapped her chin. "Ah, yes. Number six: Earth may no longer be a place anyone in her right mind would want to live."

"I rest my case." Reilly plopped onto his side, crossed his arms, snugged his hands underneath. "Sleep now."

His mother shook him. "Later, my son. Keep listening to my voice. You've watched too many old movies. Anyway, we'll be fine—better off the ship than on it. And, don't forget, we have information from space probes and the colonists' initial reports—all of them positive."

Reilly squinted up at her, annoyed that she kept talking. "But sk-sketchy. The colonists hadn't yet discovered the things like predators."

"When did you become so gloomy?"

"Shhh," he whispered.

"Reilly!"

"Recent events have chilled my perspective." He giggled.

His mother wrapped her arms around him. "Reilly, keep talking to me. It's unlikely a predator killed all the colonists before one of them could radio. A broken radio better explains a sudden loss of communication."

Reilly didn't agree, but didn't have the energy to talk anymore. "Whatever."

"Anyway," his mother continued, her breath warm in his ear, "all the data suggests the planet is habitable. There's water, plant, and animal life. The air's breathable, the temperature range reasonable. Ideal real estate."

"Hmm," Reilly said. He tried to open his eyes, but only got so far as seeing his own dark lashes.

The intercom speaker emitted Captain Baca's blunt voice. "Attention. All personnel report immediately to module D. Repeat. All personnel to module D for shuttle boarding."

∞

The shuttle's interior was dinged, dingy, dank, and ripe with the scent of humans, domestic animals, and food.

He and his parents were among the first to board. Others filed in, took their seats, and murmured to each other. Behind a closed door to the rear, crated animals bleated and cheeped in muted distress. All of them— humans and animals—were aboard. If the Dagnar virus hadn't killed fifteen adult crew and the other two womb-born children, it would have taken at least two trips to just to transport all the humans to the surface, another for the livestock. More trips to ferry equipment. Reilly fleetingly wondered what they would have done, given that only one shuttle trip was possible. Probably some of the animals would have been abandoned. Beyond that, he didn't want to think of the choices that might have to be made.

It was warmer here than on the ship, in part due to the proximity of mammalian bodies, in part because of the flight suit's insulation. It took long minutes for him to stop shivering. His fingers fumbling with the harness felt alien, and the returning circulation made his hands ache.

From the row ahead came the sound of Nova sniffling, and he wondered whether she was experiencing similar pain. His thawing brain awakened to the realization of the fact that he had indeed become hypothermic.

Commander Shen stood in the center aisle, helmet under one arm. Set against the androgynous flight suit, her egg-shaped face, with its blown-glass cheekbones, looked incongruously elegant. In a brisk voice, she reminded everyone to test the oxygen flow to his or her helmet, a feature that would come in handy if shuttle's pressurization system failed. Reilly inserted a mouth guard that had been hanging from a string around his neck and pushed the helmet onto his head. It made him even warmer and made him aware of the staleness of his breath. The helmet and suit would also protect against the heat of the descent.

He remembered the blazing meteor that had hit the ship. That's what meteors did when entering a planet's atmosphere: they ignited and shattered. Shuttles were basically manmade meteors, kept from combusting by a layer of protective tiles. He hoped the recent collision hadn't loosened any of them.

Commander Shen's voice sounded from a small speaker inside helmet. "Take a look at the display on your flight suit."

Reilly looked down at the palm-sized pack in the chest of his suit. The flashing green light indicated that the system was normalizing gaseous pressures. The solid blue light signified normal bodily temperature.

While Ensign Rabin sealed the door, the commander reminded them what to expect on this last leg of the journey. The thrusters would turn the shuttle so that it entered the atmosphere tail first. It would fall backward for a while, then descend at a 40-degree angle. When they entered the stratosphere, the shuttle would start flying, slowly dropping through the troposphere until they reached their target destination. About 600 meters above the ground, she would pull up the shuttle's nose to slow their descent and prepare for landing. The symptoms they might experience weren't pleasant. Yet Commander's Shen voice was so calm, her face so composed, her bobbed brown hair so neatly hooked behind her ears that the words nausea, vomiting, dizziness, headache, blood clots, and ruptured capillaries carried little emotional impact. Plus, it would all be over in half an hour.

In the cockpit, Commander Shen secured her helmet and took the pilot's seat. Ensign Morten sat copilot. Reilly could only see the back of their helmeted heads. Their gloved hands flipped switches on the instrument panel.

There were four rows of four seats, two on each side of an exit aisle. Reilly's mother sat on his left. His father was across the aisle, seated beside Ensign Rabin, whose eyes looked even more shadowed inside his helmet.

At the end of every other row, there was a porthole in the wall. The one in Reilly's row showed the gray side of the ship. He had rarely seen the exterior, except on their refueling stop, when they'd been allowed to roam the refueling station, a desolate, dimly lit place staffed by a dozen unshaven, grimy, smelly men. A trio of adults had herded around Reilly and the other kids on the creaking, groaning, station. He had looked out a porthole at the *Remus,* tethered alongside. If his memory from seven years ago served, the density of dents and scrapes had tripled. But still, the view filled him with longing. Home. That was his home.

Reilly's mother reached over and slipped a hand under his seat harness to verify its snugness. He was glad the other kids were ahead of him and couldn't see.

"Mom," he mouthed, "I'm fine." He didn't speak aloud, because she wouldn't be able to hear him without his switching on his microphone, and then everyone would hear him.

The overhead lights reflected off the clear bubble covering her face. She nodded and smiled, her lips stretching around the clear molding of the mouth guard. He knew she was worried about the undocking procedure, worried whether the shuttle would release properly.

"Undock," Commander Shen said to Ensign Morten. The ensign's hand moved to a button on the adjacent wall.

A single, lonely clank rang out, then the shush of a thruster. No movement. Reilly held his breath. The thruster fired again, and the shuttle drifted away from the ship. His mother looked at him, her eyes glistening with relief. The portal framed the black of space. The shuttle revolved, which made Reilly queasy. The rear thrusters rumbled down to his bones. The shuttle floated a moment then started falling. The acceleration gathered strength. Reilly's spine threatened to bisect the back of his seat. The skin on his face felt like it had stretched to the back of his skull.

The body is approximately 60 percent water. A human physiology lesson made suddenly, explicitly meaningful. He pictured fragile cell membranes trembling, viscous fluids jiggling. The pressure rose in his eyes and lungs. His jiggling eyeballs felt ready to pop free of his skull, and he squeezed his eyelids shut. As his teeth clacked against his mouth guard, he clenched his jaw, hoped his teeth wouldn't break.

He looked at the vibrating porthole, which framed only blackness. He glanced at the time display by the shuttle's console, but couldn't make out the jiggling numerals. He closed his eyes, thought about deep sleep and hibernation, two conditions where the brain hummed along, dreamless and unaware of time. He'd never hibernated. None of the kids had because the process slowed metabolism, which would have arrested their growth and development. For the adults, retarding the aging rate had kept them from being entirely decrepit upon landing. Decrepit was his grandfather's word.

Reilly's parents took turns in hibernation, so that one was around to raise him. The first time he witnessed hibernation, his mother was inside the pod and the barely perceptible rise and fall of her chest and her failure to respond to his touch and his voice had terrified him. His father had spent hours convincing him everything was okay. Now, he pictured the electronic monitor with its languid green tracings of heart, respiratory, and brain-wave activity. He tried to imagine the steady and slow rhythms of his own heart, lung, and brain.

In a sort of trance, he opened his eyes and watched the sky outside the portal, which changed from fresh-bruise purple to the blue of freeze-dried blueberries, to the azure of his mother's eyes. He had heard that, from the ground, the sky looked blue. That meant they were almost there. The seats shimmied harder. The shuttle rotated, but he had no idea in what direction.

Inexplicably, the sky turned an opaque orange. The shuddering shuttle began to toss side to side. The speakers inside his helmet crackled.

"We've hit a dust storm," Commander Shen announced.

"Wild ride ahead," Ensign Morten added, his voice jerky.

The shuttle rattled and pitched. A child's cry penetrated his helmet. He thought he heard the muted squawking, bleating, and yelping of the animals in the aft cargo area. Then the clinking, clattering, and jangling of assorted manmade materials drowned out all other sound.

There was a roaring. Reilly felt a jolt, then the drag of the forward thrusters brake-ing their final descent. His harness tightened automatically, constricting his chest. He gripped the armrest.

The shuttle thudded, bounced, slid, then stopped. There followed an uncanny stillness.

Reilly opened his eyes. In the sudden silence, his heartbeat rapped beneath the harsher sound of his breathing. Sour breath filled his helmet. His jaw ached. He tasted iron and his tongue was sore where he must have bitten it through the mouth guard. His shoulders felt bruised from the harness.

The dim cabin lights flickered. Reilly looked out the porthole. All he could see was darkness—not the clear black of space, but an impenetrable murkiness. He'd been told they'd land in the day, and he knew day was when the planet faced the sun. There hadn't been any clouds over the desert when they left.

Captain Baca stood in the aisle, helmet tucked under his arm. "Everyone okay? You can take off your helmets. Plenty of oxygen down here." His fine brown hair was plastered to his scalp, his flushed face smiling.

For a moment, no one replied. Then there came the clunk of helmets being stored and the click of harnesses being released. When Reilly pulled off his own helmet, he smelled vomit, acrid sweat, and animal feces. Someone was crying.

"Shut up, Keid. We're here. We made it, hume!" Tabit's voice.

A couple vitros cheered, then everyone joined in. His father held out his hand across the aisle. Reilly slapped his palm, then his mother's.

"Nash puked," Nova complained.

Other kids made noises of disgust. A goat bleated forlornly.

"Shut it," Nash said. "Captain Baca, can we go outside?"

"Not until this dust storm passes," Captain Baca said. "What's the wind speed, Commander Shen?"

"One hundred thirty-six kilometers per hour."

Reilly became aware of a rasping hum enveloping the shuttle.

"The sand flying around out there would take the skin right off your face," Ensign Morten called from the cockpit.

The two dogs barked hysterically. Lieutenant Schuler stood and moved toward the rear of the craft, bending his long frame to avoid hitting his head on the ceiling. When he opened the cargo door, the cabin filled with a cacophony of animal noises and the heightened stench of manure.

In a deep voice, Lieutenant Schuler called, "No bark, Beau. No bark, Xena." The barking gave way to piteous whining. The lieutenant switched to German, his mother tongue, and gentled his tone. Reilly knew enough of that language to translate a few random words: *ruhig* – quiet, *ja* – yes, *gut Hund* – good dog. The dogs began to make grateful, throaty noises, and Reilly suspected the lieutenant had stuck his huge hand into the crates to pet the dogs' shaggy heads.

The chafing, hissing noise abruptly ceased. Just as suddenly, it grew lighter inside the shuttle. The sky outside the portholes turned a pale blue. On Earth, the sky was blue. Reilly had seen the pictures, but he had never before witnessed a planetary daytime sky.

"Is it over?" Tally called.

"Looks that way," Ensign Morten said.

Maia's voice asked, "Captain Baca, can we go out now?"

Speaking in low tones, Captain Baca and Commander Shen studied the positioning-system screen. It had grown uncomfortably warm. The commander's bobbed black hair clung damply to her forehead and neck.

Finally, the captain straightened and turned to face the crew.

"For now, you can remove your flight suits," Captain Baca said, and a couple kids began chattering excitedly and moving into the aisle. "Hold on. You're not going anywhere yet." He glanced at a computer screen. "The data out there looks good. Wind speed is down to three knots. And it's a balmy 37 degrees Celsius outside."

Several people clapped. Reilly's attention stuck on the ambient temperature, which was the same as normal body temperature, which was hot.

"But first," the captain said, "Ensign Morten will scout the immediate vicinity. The rest of you please stay in your seats a few minutes more."

Ensign Morten had already shed his flight suit, which he left crumpled on his seat. He slapped on a broad-billed cap, put on his sun goggles, clipped on a holster, and slid in his *yridium* gun. The shuttle door slid up. Sunlight lifted the shadows from his face, glinted off the gun. The ensign strode down the ramp to the outside and the door shut behind him.

For five long minutes, everyone waited in tense silence, broken occasionally by whispers from the kids. Commander Shen watched a video monitor, murmured something to the captain, and pressed a button. The door once again slid up.

Ensign Morten hopped inside, flushed and grinning. "All readings reflect previous data. No sign of predators. No sign of any life forms, save for some scrub and a few trees." He paused. "Damn, but it feels good out there. Downright hot."

The crew cheered.

"Can we go now?" Tabit shouted over the rest.

The captain did something he hadn't done in ages. He laughed. "All right, all right. Bring your canteens, hats, and sun goggles."

The vitros immediately stood and began hauling out their gear from the overhead storage units. Tally stood on the seat to reach into that space, accidentally treading on Nash's hand. Nash cursed and swatted at her leg with his free hand. She fumbled the pack she was trying to unload and it fell on Keid's head, eliciting a volley of yelps. His forehead already bore a laceration, the edges neatly BioGlued together, from the ceiling tile that had come unmoored during the meteor strike.

The captain put two fingers to his lips and whistled shrilly. "Listen up. Before we get to work, we'll take a few moments to get our bearings. Ensign Rabin and I are going to scout out a site for our base camp. During that time, none of you kids will wander more than ten meters from the shuttle. That goes for you too, Reilly." A couple kids chuckled.

The captain continued, "If any of you encounter a life form, don't touch it. I repeat, do not touch it. We have little data about the fauna and flora of this planet. If you see anything of interest, report it to an adult. Understood?"

Yes, yes, yes, the vitros called.

Life form, Reilly thought. He'd read that the colonists on Riona found their planet inhabited only by edible plants, protozoans, and animals with four appendages coming off a central area studded with eyes. The photos made the creatures look like disembodied hands walking on fingertips. The reports said they stood as high as a man's waist, tasted great, and had no defenses against the colonists.

The captain issued a few more commands. "Lieutenant Schuler will monitor the animals. It's going to heat up inside the shuttle. We'll get them off as soon as possible. Lian," he said to the commander, "run the climate control system if you must, but keep in mind we need the fuel to return to the ship later."

Reilly wondered how that would work, unless someone fixed the portal between the shuttle and the ship. An hour ago, it had taken crowbars and several adults to open it, then close it behind them.

Captain Baca continued, "You other adults, keep tabs on the younger generation. Oren, activate Reba. Maybe she can help herd."

Reilly frowned at the word "herd," balked at being lumped in with vitros. Then, he went back to thinking about life forms. Some could be dangerous.

He had read about Earth's extinct predators, had seen images of lions, wolves, bears, and alligators, had watched videos of such animals attacking their prey.

What exactly would the creatures of Cinnabar be like? Before radio transmissions ceased, the first colonists had reported that the desert flora and fauna appeared meager but generally benign: a dozen botanical species, three avian species, and several types of insects. Unknown was the threat posed by a large arachnid, many-legged reptile, and four apparently mammalian species. None had yet attacked the humans, though someone had been bitten when putting on a shoe a juvenile arachnid had been sleeping in. The bite reportedly wasn't fatal, though it had produced a great deal of pain and inflammation.

What particularly worried Reilly were the things you couldn't see with the naked eye—toxins and microbes. After watching his grandparents die, he especially dreaded viruses. They could kill you before you had a chance to fight back.

Reilly heard his father whistling "Oh, Susannah." He was rummaging in his pack. He pulled on his sun goggles and adjusted the head strap. His mother, who was mopping her sweaty face with her sleeve, caught his gaze and smiled at him. Were they nervous and not showing it? Reilly wondered. He felt his own anxiety squeezing through his pores, swimming out with his sweat.

There was a beeping sound. The captain tapped a tiny disc-shaped radio pinned to his collar. Reilly heard Ensign Morten's voice, but couldn't make out the words. Then the captain faced the others and grinned, displaying near-forgotten dimples. He clapped his hands for attention. "Everyone ready to check out our new home?" he called.

A volley of yeses followed. Reilly had never seen the adults so animated. The front row rose and filed toward the door. People raised palms to shield themselves from the sun, pulled goggles over eyes, tilted their heads back and smiled. Lieutenant Schuler opened the cargo door, releasing two leashed and yipping dogs. He pulled back on the leash and ordered the dogs to sit, which they did reluctantly. The two rows of vitros surged forward.

Reilly's mother squeezed his clammy hand. "Our turn, buddy."

FOUR

As Reilly descended the ramp, a blast of heat assaulted him. He felt as though he wore ankle weights, despite the fact that the gravity aboard the ship had been set to simulate Cinnabar's. Letting go of the handrail, he stepped out onto orange ground. His heels sank into loose granular material. So this is sand, he thought. He squinted against the harsh light. The black sky of space had been replaced by an azure dome, featureless save for a solitary, blazing sun. The dry air carried a pungent smell that reminded him of an herb from the ship's greenhouse.

His mother tapped his shoulder. "Keep moving, Reilly. There are people behind us."

Ankles wobbling, he sloughed forward. Once out of the way, he rummaged in his backpack for his sun goggles. He slid them on, straightened, and turned in a slow circle, swaying unsteadily on the shifty soil.

In three directions, a flat orange desert stretched away from him, curving slightly downward at the horizon and contrasting dizzyingly with the upward tilt of the floors on the ring-shaped ship. He had the stomach-lurching feeling that, if he kept walking, he would fall off the planet. The soil appeared barren, save for scattered lavender clumps. He assumed the clumps were some form of plant life. Aside from their general bushy shape, they didn't resemble any of the species that grew in the ship's greenhouse.

In the distance, a bluish mountain range stuck up like a row of broken teeth. A flat-topped mountain hunched before that range. Its steep sides were swirled with shades of red and slashed with an occasional, garish yellow, and he guessed he might reach the nearest rock face within a half hour's walk. At a recent briefing, he had learned the name for this type of geographical feature. Mesa? Yes, that was it. Mesa, Captain Baca had told them, meant table in Spanish. Reilly squinted at a black oval on the cliff face, and judged it was a hole. Some animals lived in holes, he recalled. The larger holes were called caves; the smaller holes were burrows. Larger holes suggested larger inhabitants, or perhaps a community of animals.

This particular cavity was high off the ground. How would the animals get there? Walk up a nearly vertical surface? Smaller animals such as Earth insects could do that. Larger creatures would have to fly, wouldn't they? Or did they have tools—ladders and ropes and such—to climb with?

His eyes scoured the landscape, then the sky. Nothing moved. All the adults held *yridium* guns, even his parents. The weapons were silver and fit inside an adult's palm, the muzzle extending three centimeters beyond the grip. When the index finger depressed a button, a red beam of *yridium* extended 25 meters. A dial increased the laser's intensity. On the ship, guns had been restricted to the target-practice area. Like everyone else, Reilly had learned to use a gun. He had reached level 5 of proficiency, which meant he could reliably hit stationary objects, whereas Tab had just hit level 9, which meant he could hit an object 20 meters away traveling 35 kilometers/hour. Tab and Nash both had the bulk to shoulder the LR-50, so named because of its 50-meter range. Now, standing visible to any alien eyes tucked into burrows and caves, Reilly wished he'd devoted more time to that skill, less time to reading books and studying his computer courses.

A dark shape skimmed over the top of the mesa. His stomach flipped. He blinked, and the thing disappeared. Maybe he had imagined it. Maybe the illusion was a product of the heat, the exhaustion of the trip, the vastness of the landscape.

The six vitros ran past him, kicking up sand.

"Come on, Reilly," Maia called over her shoulder. "Why are you just standing there?"

"Prince Reilly isn't up to playing with us," Tab said. His face glistened with a sheen of oil and sweat. He drew himself up, accentuating the two centimeters he had on Reilly's height. "How'd you enjoy the ride, Rye? Did you piss your pants again?" He looked meaningfully at Reilly's crotch.

Tab, who couldn't remember historical dates, seemed incapable of forgetting the day, years ago, when Reilly had wet himself when a comet sped uncomfortably close to the ship. Reilly felt grateful that he hadn't leaked more than a string of spit during the descent. He almost pointed out the patch of yellow vomit crusting Nash's collar, but figured he'd only egg Nash into harassing him too. Not a good idea, given that Nash, though shorter than Tab, was nearly as muscular and recently bore the traces of a moustache on his upper lip. Reilly fell back on his usual strategy: Look disinterested and say nothing.

"Oh, no!" Nova shouted, "Reba's coming."

All eyes turned toward the android. She stood at the top of the ramp, sun glaring harshly off her white exterior. In the place where eyes should be, two concave discs rotated left, right, up, down. Her eyes at last focused on the kids. "Children, stop," her voice commanded. "I must accompany you."

Tab swore softly. Keid shifted his feet and gingerly touched the cut on his forehead. Maia looked toward the mesa, as though she were thinking of running for it. On the ship, Reba could travel faster than any human, as long as the terrain was smooth and firm. Now, Ensign Rabin had replaced the rollers at the end of Reba's legs with foot-like objects. The legs now moved independently.

"This should be interesting," Reilly said, thinking of the response of his own body to the loose, uneven footing.

Reba stepped forward and walked stiffly down the ramp, metal parts clinking. Ensign Rabin was now visible behind her, arms folded over his chest. Reba paused at the junction of ramp and sand, then stepped forward, tottered, stepped again.

Her eyes on the android, Maia backed away. Grinning defiantly, Tab followed suit. As though pulled by magnets, a couple of other kids shuffled with him.

"No. Stop, children," Reba intoned. She attempted to increase her pace, but caught her foot in the sand. She teetered, regained her balance. Nash guffawed. No one had ever laughed at Reba. The android, being a machine, didn't react with indignation or any other emotion. She merely resumed her efforts to reach the children. Gears whirred as Reba increased power to her legs. She charged forward, lost her footing, and pitched forward.

"Someone assist me. I must resume vertical positioning." Sand muffled the android's words. The lean mechanical arms flailed at the ground.

Tab hooted with laughter. "Skinny chance of that," he said.

"Come now," Reba commanded, "or you will all receive the Electroprod."

Reilly's eyes flicked from Reba to Ensign Rabin, who was now striding down the ramp toward Reba.

"Okay, kids," the ensign said. "I'll trust that you'll stay within ten meters of the shuttle."

Maia jerked up her chin at Reilly, almost as though inviting him. Reilly shook his head. She probably didn't mean it. Tab certainly didn't want him around. Maia shrugged and strode away. The other kids tagged after her—except for Tally, who approached Reba and stopped within two meters of the struggling android.

"Come on, Chicken Chic," Nova called. "Reba's just a machine. You don't need to feel sorry for it."

Tally wanted to rescue everything, even the spider that had crept aboard during a refueling stop. It had spun a web and hung up an egg sac on the ceiling, just above her bunk. Reilly only knew about Tally's spider because Tab had eventually found and crushed the arachnid and her unhatched offspring, sending Tally into such hysterics she'd been dosed with Harmonal till she slept.

Now Tally smiled sheepishly, then scampered to Nova's side. The two girls walked off, hand in hand, heads bent toward a secret. The sunlight made Nova's black hair gleam and transformed Tally's from brown to amber.

Reba struggled onto hands and knees, then swiveled her head in Reilly's direction. "You, Reilly Landreth, assist me."

Reilly took a step toward the android, then hesitated. Though he had never gotten the Prod, he had always disliked the android. When he was little, the sight of the android made him run for the closest parent.

"Stay cool, Reba," the ensign said. "You've got great legs. They just need a little work." Reba's head revolved toward the ensign as he aimed a tiny remote and pressed a button. The android froze, still on all fours. The ensign chuckled. "Once we set up camp, I'll replace the legs with a tractor module. Help me carry her back into the shuttle, Reilly."

As they hoisted the android back inside, a side panel on the shuttle levered open. From the dark interior, an engine rumbled, then hummed. The pointed nose of an airscouter emerged, then the whole thing. Visible within a clear dome, Captain Baca sat at the pilot's seat.

Once he had cleared the shuttle, he halted the scouter, raised the dome, and stood. "Play with the robot later, Oren," he said. "Time to locate a camp site."

After Reilly and Ensign Rabin set down the android in the entry, the ensign hurried toward the airscouter, elbows pumping with the effort of treading sand. Blinding silver in the sunlight, the scouter was six meters long from nose to tail, and 3.5 meters across at the triangular, swept-back wings. There had been room on the shuttle to transport four of the six scouters. Each dart-shaped crafted seated two people, one in front, one behind.

Ensign Rabin took the co-pilot's seat, a position Ensign Morten referred to as "riding shotgun." Recently, Reilly had asked his father what the term meant, and his father had answered that, back before the invention of motorized vehicles, when people traveled in horse-drawn coaches, the person sitting beside the driver was supposed to shoot attackers—usually other humans— with a shotgun, a weapon that propelled lead pellets. Despite many history lessons, Reilly had never been able to comprehend humans killing humans. After all, the continued existence of the crew depended on everyone surviving. Each death was a horrible tragedy.

Ensign Rabin waved to Reilly, then lowered the clear dome that sealed the cabin. The engine hummed, the craft lifted straight up, the needle-shaped body swung ninety degrees, then shot forward. Reilly knew that, at Cinnabar's gravitational force, a scouter could accelerate to 100 kilometers per hour in 1.4 seconds. During the voyage, he had learned all about the construction and operation of the craft. The adults had all trained on airscouters at the International Space Academy. Reilly had practiced in the flight simulator on the ship and couldn't wait to fly the real thing.

In a few seconds, the scouter grew so small that Reilly could obliterate its outline with his outstretched thumb. The craft stayed that size, which meant it was hovering; maybe they'd spotted a suitable site for their base. He couldn't estimate the distance between himself and that spot. The ship had traveled so fast that huge expanses—the distance between stars and planets—were hard to fathom. And he lacked the experience of judging objects separated by kilometers. Short distances he could gauge. For instance, he knew that the ship's diameter was 120 meters, his room had measured 8.2 by 9.3 meters, his arm span was 178 centimeters, just short of his height.

The airscouter touched down near a line of trees, or rather, shapes that resembled photographs he'd seen of trees. The blue-gray trunks were thin and tall. The sparse foliage at the top was magenta. Lavender shrubs fanned out from the trees. The pattern of flora suggested the presence of a creek. Riparian growth, Reilly said to himself. The repetition of scientific fact somehow grounded him. He felt cheered at the promise of water in this desiccated landscape. The plan had always been to land near a creek and build their compound near its banks. If there was enough water, his mother had promised to teach him to swim.

Now, Reilly thought of aquatic creatures from Earth zoology courses—sharks and whales, stingrays and crocodiles. From where he stood, the thin ribbon of plant growth didn't suggest a body of water large enough to camouflage predators.

Reilly shifted his attention to the area between the airscouter and the mesa. Massive rocks studded the sand, as though slabs of the mesa had fallen, then migrated outward. It looked as though a giant sculptor had been working on these boulders. One had a narrow base and saucer-like top. One looked like a standing man in profile, his hands clasped at his waist. He seemed to stare into the shadow that pooled invitingly at his feet.

Caught in the sun's blaze, Reilly could practically feel the light quanta pulsing against his skin. The heat of the sand penetrated the soles of his shoes. The pleasurable escape from the ship's deadly cold had worn off. He had never felt so hot, not even when he exercised, not even when the virus had fevered him. The uniform—lightweight blue-gray pants and matching long-sleeved shirt—had an inner membrane. This membrane contained pores that were supposed to open to allow heat loss and close to keep heat in. The outer surface contained UV reflectors to keep them cool and nanovoltaic cells for powering digital devices. Reilly wiped at his sweaty neck. Clearly textile technology was no match for the star that had caught Cinnabar in its orbit.

The mesa and its sculptured rocks broke into jagged lines. He turned his head. The lines remained, now fracturing the trees. He closed his eyes. The image reversed—white jagged lines against the black of his eyelids. What was wrong with him? Heat stroke? He'd learned they would have to guard against this malady. He crept into the shade of the shuttle and sat, first extracting his space suit from his backpack and using it as a cushion against the scorching sand. After a minute, his vision cleared. He took out his canteen and sipped water.

His father squatted in front of him. He was wearing one of the weird hats Lieutenant Schuler had distributed to everyone—beige with a long bill in front and a curtain-like flap that covered the neck. Sweat dotted his flushed face. "Isn't this amazing, Reilly?" he said. "A bit arid, but there's supposed to be plenty of water in the creek."

"I guess," Reilly said. He wasn't sure why he expected something more beautiful, more inviting.

His mother walked by, a blue specimen bag hanging from her shoulder. She pulled on a thin pair of gloves and, using a pair of scissors, snipped a tiny plant from the ground and dropped it into a clear bag, which she sealed and slid inside the satchel.

"Already collecting specimens, Anika?" Reilly's father asked.

His mother beamed. "I've waited fifteen years to do this." She frowned at Reilly. "Are you okay? You look weirdly pale."

"I don't know. My head's starting to hurt. One minute ago, these squiggly lines made it hard to see."

"Sounds like a migraine headache," his father said. "My mother had them."

Rubbing his face, Reilly muttered, "Great. *Mi*-graine. Why not *your*-graine? Better yet, *Tab's*-graine."

"Fortunately, it's not contagious," his father said. "As soon as we unpack the meds cabinet, I'll get you some Anaral. In the meantime, drink plenty of water and put on your hat, okay?"

His parents walked away, their outlines shimmering in the heat. No way was he putting on that ridiculous hat. Not until the vitros donned theirs. He looked toward where they had gathered near a scraggly bush about 3 meters away. They were jabbering and laughing and not looking overheated or nervous about their strange surroundings. Only Keid looked ill at ease. He stood apart from the others, chewing on the cuff of his shirtsleeve.

Maia turned a cartwheel and fell on her backside. Laughing, she got up and tried again. Her shirt came untucked and slid toward her upside-down head. Reilly glimpsed a pale blue bra cupping her breasts. Breasts. When had she grown those?

"Hey, Nash, look," Tab called. "Maia's showing off her boobs."

"Shut up, radge brain," she said. She stood and jabbed her shirt into her waistband.

Nash tossed a handful of sand at Tab, who ducked behind Keid, who yelped and clapped a hand to his cheek.

Reilly's mother strode over to them. "No throwing sand," she said. Tab opened his fingers, releasing a stream of red dirt. "Don't touch anything. Did you already forget what the captain told you?" She took Keid's face in her hands. His right cheek was red. With gloved hands, she brushed sand from his pale skin and fair hair.

"Good thing you had on your goggles," she said.

"Why is his skin red?" Maia said, moving closer to Keid. "The sand didn't hit him very hard."

Reilly's mother pushed back her own goggles and squinted at the pink patch of skin. "Looks like an allergic reaction." She pulled her water bottle off a clip on her belt, angled Keid's face, and poured water down his cheek.

Keid stood meekly still.

Maia looked at her upturned palms. "Are there toxins in the sand?"

Reilly stood and, resisting the urge to brush off his backside, approached the others.

"The first colonists never reported such a thing," Reilly's mother said. "I suspect that some of the substances on this planet will provoke immune responses, at least until we get used to this environment. Later, I'll run a sand sample through the Chemalyzer."

"Are you saying we might be allergic to this planet?" Reilly said.

His mother only laughed, then tousled Keid's blond hair. "Come with me to the shuttle, young man. I'll give you an Allersan patch." She surveyed the group and added, "All of you put on your hats. You, too, Reilly."

They all did as told.

Nash chortled. "You look mug in that hat, TabMan. Major mug."

Tab scowled. "Mute it, Nashkin."

"Lieutenant Bergen?" Tally called. "May I come with you?"

Reilly's mother nodded.

Tab looked at his beefy palms, which were bright pink. "Minjin' grot. My hands sting," he said. He spit onto his palms, wiped them down his pants.

Maia checked her own hands, curled them into fists, and jammed them into her pockets. "It's not that bad," she said.

"If you hold out your hands, I'll pour water on them," Reilly said, looking from Tab to Maia.

"Nah," Tab said. "We're fine."

"Whatever," Reilly said. "You kids should be more careful."

Maia, Nova, Tab. and Nash stared at him.

"Kids?" Maia said. "You kids? What does that make you, a grownup?"

"He isn't even human," Nash said. "He's a minjen android."

"A royal minjen android," Nova added.

"Right," Tab said, his big slab of a face flushed and glistening. "Hey, sorry, Prince Rye. Stupid me to be touching stuff. Good thing we have Your Lordship to set us straight."

"Piss off," Reilly said. His head throbbed and he felt nauseated. He started to walk away.

Maia squatted and stared at the ground. "What do you call this grade of pulverized rock?"

Reilly turned. "Sand." Clearly Maia had already gotten over his unintended insult. His feelings, on the other hand, still smarted from the slap down.

"Yeah," Maia said. "Maybe, if it scratches your skin, a toxin is released into the tissue, and from there into the circulation. Who knows? Maybe enough of it would kill you."

"That's scary," Nova said. The heat had darkened the starburst birthmark on her forehead.

"Don't listen to her, SuperNova," Tab said. "She's just making stuff up. We'd know if the sand was toxic. The first colonists would have said."

Pain jabbed Reilly's left cheekbone. He turned away and crept back into the shuttle's meager shade. Nearby, Commander Shen inspected the white tiles covering the exterior. She called to Ensign Morten, who joined her.

"What is it, Lian?" Ensign Morten said. A splotch of red marred the white of one eye. Probably a burst capillary from changes in cabin pressure, Reilly thought. The commander had described this very thing before they descended.

"Wind shear damage," Commander Shen said. "Here." She pointed. "And here."

Ensign Morten let out a long whistle. He was a head taller than the commander, tall enough to run his fingers over the damaged tiles.

Commander Shen removed her hat and fanned her face with the bill. Her dark hair clung helmet-like to her head. "We'll have to repair these tiles before we make another run to the ship."

"Yeah. That and the warped docking coupler."

So, Reilly thought, they were stranded. He thought of stories he had read about shipwrecks. He saw himself wandering the planet in tatters, his tongue swollen with dehydration, his brain addled with fever. Before he could get very far into this rumination, one of the girls let out a shriek.

FIVE

It was Tally. She was squatting several meters away and pointing at something.

"Come look! It's so cute," she called.

The other vitros dashed over, half stumbling through the sand, and clustered around her.

Ensign Morten got there before Reilly. "Move away," he commanded. His silver *yridium* gun glinted in the sun.

Everyone gawked at a hole in the sand at the base of a big rock, but Reilly couldn't see what had caught their attention.

Tally pushed her sun goggles atop of her head, which caused her bangs to stick straight up from her wide forehead. "It looked harmless."

"So did poison dart frogs on Earth," Ensign Morten said.

"What did you see, Talitha?" Commander Shen asked. She had her gun out too.

"A little animal. It's pink," Tally said happily. "When I spoke, it ducked back inside its burrow." She pointed to the hole, which was about sixteen centimeters in diameter. "Everyone be quiet," she whispered. "Maybe it will come out again."

A couple minutes passed. Reilly heard a faint snuffling, like the breathing of a kid with a cold. A few grains of sand fell across the mouth of the burrow. Something grayish pink and glistening appeared at the entrance. Nova giggled, and Tally held a finger across her lips.

A conical shape protruded. A hole in the center quivered. When the entire head came into view, Reilly realized the pointy thing was a long snout, the hole at the end a single nostril. Gradually, the whole animal slowly emerged

47

into the light. Small ears clung to either side of its head. The two black eyes opened wide, then narrowed against the light. The creature's configuration fit the basic model of most Earth mammals—head at one end, tail at the other, four legs extending from a central trunk. Except it had dusty pink scales rather than fur. The torso was long and lean, the tail short. It stood on all fours, but after a hushed moment rose onto its muscular hind legs, its more puny front legs dangling in an oddly casual manner. It was about knee high.

"Wow," Maia exhaled.

A second pair of ears unfurled from the top of the creature's head like tiny satellite dishes.

Tally took a step toward it. The animal hunkered down.

"Get back," Commander Shen snapped. Her gun pointed at the animal's chest.

"You're not going to shoot it, are you?" Tally squeaked.

"Not if I don't have to."

Tab toed sand toward the creature, and Commander Shen yelled, "Stop!"

The sand fell short, but the animal startled. Some of its scales hinged outward to become short spikes, instantly transforming the lithe, cute creature into a breathing ball of barbs. The kids jumped back, jostling against each other, and the commander stepped in front of them, finger on the switch for the gun's laser beam.

The animal dove for its burrow and disappeared.

"Tab, you grothead," Maia said.

Tally socked Tab in the arm, but he didn't take notice.

"Did you see how it took off?" Nash said. "Total phenom."

"Right. And did you see how it got all spiny?" Tab said. "I wonder if it attacks. Maybe it sort of throws itself at you."

Ensign Morten grabbed Tab by the collar and leaned into the boy's startled face. "That was stupid, Tabit." He kept his voice low. "What if it had leapt into your face? Maybe its barbs are venomous. Maybe hundreds of its kin are under our feet right now, planning retaliation."

Nova looked anxiously at the ground and took a step back.

Commander Shen cleared her throat and the ensign let go of Tab.

Tab loosened the sweat-darkened fabric at his neck and muttered, "Sorry. "I was just trying to protect Tally."

"Tally was not in apparent danger," the ensign said, biting off each word. "Not until you provoked the animal."

Tab looked at his shoes.

"You've heard the lectures," the commander said. "Leave the native animals alone. Do not antagonize them. And," she added, looking at Tally, "don't try to make friends with them."

"I don't want any of you children to so much as move without an order from an adult," Commander Shen added. "They're only fourteen of us. We can't afford to lose anyone."

Several kids mumbled assent. Nova sniffed back tears.

Lieutenant Schuler came toward them, preceded by two white and brown collies that strained against their leashes.

Talitha ran forward. "Beau! Xena!"

Tails wagging, the dogs lunged toward her and licked her lowered face.

"What has happened?" Lieutenant Schuler asked.

"Talitha has located our first native animal," Commander Shen said.

Lieutenant Schuler asked what the animal looked like, and Tally rattled off a description.

The lieutenant nodded. "A few minutes ago, I saw an avian creature flying in and out of those trees." He pointed.

Everyone looked that way. The air around the trees looked lifeless.

Xena sniffed the ground and lowered her rump to urinate. Beau snapped something off the ground and the lieutenant growled "Drop!" and the dog let a slender object fall from its mouth.

Nash bent and reached toward the object.

"Nash, you idiot!" Ensign Morten said. "Don't touch that stick. What part of the order 'do not touch anything' has failed to penetrate your thick skull?"

Nash looked ashamed. His short black hair shone in the sun, and his face seemed to have already gone a shade darker.

Lieutenant Schuler moved closer. "It's a bone," he corrected. "Probably from the limb of a small animal."

"Listen up, kids," Ensign Morten said. "I understand you all want to explore. You've been cooped up your whole lives. But please pay attention to what you're doing. We adults simply want you to survive the first day on this planet, ideally longer. We could use your help."

All the kids smiled, except Maia, whose face remained neutral.

"Here's what I suggest," Commander Shen said. "Why don't you all go back in the ship and put on your gloves."

Nova whined, "But it's so hot."

"Either wear the gloves or keep your hands in your pockets," the commander said. "As soon as the captain gets back, we'll get to work. You'll need gloves then to prevent blisters."

Nash, Tab, and Nova ran to the ship.

"The dogs are sure panting hard," Tally said, a hand on each of their shaggy heads. "And what about their paws? Will they get burned, Lieutenant Schuler?"

The lieutenant checked the dog's paws. "Their pads look okay. But perhaps I should take the dogs back to the shuttle."

Ensign Morten jerked his head in the direction of the creek. "The captain and Oren are flying back."

The approaching airscouter flew low to the ground, the sleek outline shimmering.

"Why do things in the distance look—I don't know, quavery?" Tally asked.

"The heat waves rising off the sand cause visual distortion."

Reilly was relieved that the illusion wasn't caused by his headache.

His mother and Keid walked up. Keid's cheek looked less florid.

His mother looked around. "So beautiful." She sighed. "I wish my parents were alive to see this day."

Reilly touched her back, and she tilted her head onto his shoulder. Suddenly self-conscious, he glanced at the other kids. Nova, Nash, and Tab were scampering back, carrying several pairs of gloves. Keid and Talitha were talking to Lieutenant Schuler.

Maia stood apart, watching Reilly and his mother with an odd expression on her face. Suddenly, Reilly knew what she was thinking, almost as though her thoughts were in his brain. She wanted a mother, wanted his mother. Was the migraine making him hallucinate? He dropped his arm, frowned at Maia, and shut his mind to her. Maia's face darkened, and she gave him her back.

The scouter glided toward them, slowed, hovered, then set down, sending out an apron of sand. Once the dust settled, everyone clustered around the craft. The dome opened. Captain Baca stood, stepped onto the short wing, and hopped down. Ensign Rabin followed. Both men looked sweaty and pleased.

"We found a site," the captain said. "Close enough to the creek to run a water line, far enough away to avoid animals that also use the water."

"When do we leave?" Reilly's father asked, a bit breathless from hurrying over to the group.

"Now," Captain Baca said. He glanced at the sun, which was now directly overhead. "We have time to erect at least one building before sunset."

He patted the airscouter's wing and, looking at Reilly's father, said, "Skyler, I know you're dying to fly one of these again."

"You bet," Reilly's father said.

"May I go with him?" Reilly asked.

"Up to you, Skyler," the captain said.

Reilly's father nodded.

"Not fair," Nash said. "Why does Reilly always get to do stuff?"

"Because he's special," Tab said. "Haven't you figured that out by now, nullskull?"

Captain Baca's look silenced him. "You will all have plenty to do in a few minutes. And as soon as we set up our base camp, all of you will learn to fly airscouters."

Nash whooped, and Maia grinned. Tab's face remained sour.

The captain clapped his hands once. "Back to the shuttle. Within the hour, you'll all get to fly in an airscouter. We have to taxi everyone in from here to our new base."

∞

Heart pounding with excitement, Reilly slid into the copilot's seat. He didn't care that it was like an oven inside, didn't care that his headache had so enlarged it seemed impossible his helmet could contain it.

"Can you see over my shoulder?" his father asked.

Reilly said he could. His father reviewed the console and monitor display. During practice sessions in the simulator, Reilly had memorized every lever, switch, and dial. The left side of the dash contained the engine controls; the right displayed the flight instruments.

As though reading his mind, his father said, "The simulator is helpful, but it's not the same as actually flying. It's been over fifteen years since I've flown a scouter." He laughed. "Let's hope I remember how."

He depressed the ignition button. The engine sounded rough for the first couple seconds, then evened to a purr, then nothing.

"I can't hear the engine," Reilly said.

"Unless the scouter is accelerating, the *yridium* engine switches off. The electric engine is nearly silent. Okay, put your left hand on the control column, your right on the throttle. Lightly. I'll fly. You just follow and get a feel for the mechanics."

His father reviewed the controls. The left hand manipulated the control column, which was a curved stick between his legs; the right hand let out the throttle, which controlled the speed. To fly forward, the control column was pushed ahead. Left and right movements controlled the ailerons on the wings. A pedal moved the tail rudder. By coordinating the movement of the ailerons and the rudder, the pilot could make the craft pitch, roll, or yaw. Reilly hoped he would remember how to put it all together, hoped that someday these movements would become automatic.

His dad flipped a lever that directed the engine nozzles downward, and the craft lifted off the ground amidst a vortex of dust. In two seconds, they were twenty meters off the ground. Down below, Reilly's mother looked tiny as she stood in the doorway of the shuttle. She waved. Beaming, Reilly lifted his hand.

When instructed, Reilly swiveled the engine nozzles for forward thrust and engaged the throttle. Thrumming, the scouter accelerated over the planet's surface. Reilly's pulse popped in his neck. His back pressed into the seat, but with a pleasant pressure, not the horrible bone-rending force he'd experienced on the shuttle.

The altimeter read 23 meters; the air-speed indicator read 50 kilometers per hour, less than a third of the maximum speed. Purple shrubs became blurred dots on the orange sand. The lavender-blue ribbon of the creek passed underneath, lined by the magenta-leaved scrawny trees.

After standing on the endless desert, the containment of the cockpit restored some of the security he'd felt in his small sleeping room on the ship.

"Based on our coordinates, this is the spot," his father said. "We're ahead of the other three scouters. Want to take over the controls till they catch up?"

"Yes!"

"I'll keep my hands on the controls, in the off case you get into trouble. Go ahead, Son."

The control column and throttle felt slick under Reilly's damp palms. The mesa's cliffs of mottled auburn and lavender loomed large. He throttled back slightly, pressed the control stick left, and depressed the left pedal. The scouter first rolled then yawed, just enough to make Reilly's stomach contents do the same.

"Ease up on the stick," his father said, sounding as though there was no big rush, even though too much roll could cause them to lose altitude and crash.

Reilly compensated, completed a relatively smooth turn, and headed toward the three approaching scouters. He waved at Commander Shen and his mother, who shared a scouter, and they waved back. Ensign Morten was in the cockpit of another scouter with Tab riding shotgun. The ensign saluted him. Tab gave him the finger. Captain Baca was flying with Maia, who grinned maniacally at him.

"Turn her around, Reilly," his father said.

As he did so, Reilly's gaze caught a vaguely familiar form, like a huge grain of rice come to rest on the ruddy sand. It looked like a shuttle. The image wavered, even after he blinked. Was it real or an effect of heat on sand?

"Dad, do you see that?"

"What?"

"The white thing at two o'clock. Looks like a shuttle."

"Could be. Let me take the controls, Reilly."

It was a shuttle. The first colonists' shuttle. To the right, closer to the creek, stood a cluster of domed roofs surrounded by a high wire fence. There were two wind turbines, a guard tower, a barn and corral, four small buildings and one large one. A net sagged over a rectangular plot with several rows of withered plants. Nearby a shovel lay across the orange dirt. Reilly held his breath, hoping people would come out of the buildings. Nothing stirred.

"Where is everyone?" Reilly whispered.

His father didn't answer. He flew past twice. No one appeared.

"Can we land?" Reilly said. "Maybe they're inside."

"They would have heard the scouter."

If they were alive, Reilly added silently.

"We'll investigate later."

"Why not now?"

"Don't argue," his father snapped. "Precautions have to be taken. We have to notify Carlos first."

They flew to the site of their new base in silence, the initial euphoria of the ride deflated. The shuttle had landed and people had begun exiting the craft, carrying armloads of gear.

As Reilly climbed out of the scouter, his mother hurried toward them. "Where'd you two go?" Her smile flattened. "What's wrong? What's happened?"

"We found the first colonists' camp," Reilly blurted. "I think they're all dead."

SIX

Reilly's announcement chilled the collective mood. Conversations halted, smiles vanished, and worry lines creased brows. The captain demanded an immediate report, and Reilly's father complied, though there wasn't much to say. Nova and Tab kept shooting Reilly reproachful glances, as though he, the bearer of bad news, had somehow contributed to this misfortune.

Ensign Rabin fanned his face with his hat. "Well," he said, "that explains why they didn't answer their radio."

"We don't know for certain that they're dead," Captain Baca said. "No bodies were seen." He kept gazing toward the first colonists' base.

"Right," Tab said. "Maybe they just, you know, moved."

"Maybe so," Ensign Morten said. His eyes flicked to the captain, then back to the vitros. "Once we get settled, we'll send a couple of adults to inspect the site. In the meantime, none of you kids will go anywhere near the place."

"That's right," the captain said, gazing in the direction of the first colonist's compound. He touched a green stone that always hung from a cord around his neck, most often hidden beneath his shirt.

∞

After a quick lunch of water and Sustabars inside the shuttle, they began unpacking. The buildings would be constructed of a BioFuerte fabric and stretched over inflatable beams. Embedded within the tough fabric were solar cells.

The hopeful act of constructing a new home buoyed moods. Chatter resumed. A recurrent theme was the beauty of this site, but some of the praise and cheer sounded forced. Reilly thought the place looked pretty desolate, though not inconsistent with the first colonists' reports. Maybe he had daydreamed too much about Earth landscapes of rivers, oceans, lush fields, and verdant forests.

Reilly's job was to carry a textile tube to the air pump and hold it steady while Commander Shen inflated it. Each thump of the air pump jarred his aching head, and, despite the sun goggles, the bright light stabbed clear to his brain. Once filled, the tube became a taut arc. The air beams varied in size, the longest forming the central arch of each building. Progressively shorter beams ran in parallel and were held in place with steel cables and staked to the ground.

As they were finishing their new mess hall, the last stake kept slipping loose. Ensign Morten jammed it in hard. A pocket of sand opened at the stake's base. A second later, two pointed objects projected from the spot, then the whole creature—an arachnid big as a human head, purple, hairy, with about a dozen legs, and a half dozen yellow eyes on stalks. Sucking air, Reilly hopped backward, but the ensign held his ground and drew out his gun. Four similar, but smaller creatures emerged behind the big one. For a moment, both species froze. Then the five arachnids scurried toward the humans. In rapid succession, Ensign Morten shot the small ones. Commander Shen hurled the stake she held in her hand. The point buried itself smack in the large creature's middle. It sagged to its belly, the legs wobbling, then going still.

A pain jolted in Reilly's left cheekbone, as though a stake had pierced him too. With gloved hands, Commander Shen removed the stake. A viscous yellow fluid dripped from the pointed end onto her pant leg. Seconds later, she dropped the stake and rubbed frantically at her leg.

"What is it, Lian?" Ensign Morten asked.

"Some of its body fluid got on me." Commander Shen grimaced. "It burns a little, no big deal."

There was a small hole in the fabric of her pants. Ensign Morten pushed up her pant leg, opened his canteen, and irrigated the small patch of blistered skin. Nash approached, an uninflated airbeam clamped to his chest. As his boot grazed one of the dead creature's legs, Ensign Morten yelled at him and he stumbled backward.

Barking excitedly, Beau bounded up, dragging his lead. Ensign Morten hollered at Reilly to grab the dog. He trapped the purple webbing under his foot just as Beau's quivering nostrils made contact with a fragment of an arachnid. Reilly pulled him back. The dog's tail stopped wagging. He licked his nose, then lowered his head and swiped at his muzzle with his front paw. Whining, he swiveled and thrust his nose against Reilly's leg. As Reilly attempted to drizzle some of his water over the Beau's nose, the dog's pink tongue lapped at the stream. Ensign Morten told him to stop wasting water. The others gathered around, wanting to know what had happened.

"Order," Captain Baca called, the word cutting through the chaos. Even Beau went still. With a glance at the lowering sun, the commander assigned the kids jobs toward getting dinner ready.

As Reilly turned to go, movement caught his eye. One of the baby arachnids appeared to be inching sideways. He lifted his sun goggles and squinted. A swarm of iridescent green insects—each one the size of a lentil—had latched onto the dead creature and were dragging it toward a small hole in the ground. Reilly watched as the arachnid disappeared into the ground. Sand cascaded over the entrance, and within seconds, the hole was invisible. Reilly shivered. What if a person fell asleep on the ground? Would he awaken with sand filling his nostrils and eyes, with a thousand tiny, ravenous mouths nibbling his flesh?

∞

By twilight, they had erected the mess hall and one of the barracks. The animals had been fed, crated, and installed in the barracks—a temporary measure until they could build a barn. There was some joking about who would later inhabit this barracks—some of the adult crew or the vitros. Reilly doubted there was much question.

Now, Reilly, his parents, and a couple other crewmembers were standing outside the mess hall, shaking sand out of their clothes. Some people had broken out in hives from the sand. So far, it hadn't bothered Reilly.

"Well," his father said, "we made it through the first day fine."

Reilly frisked his arms. The day's heat had faded with the setting sun. He became aware of a low, pounding noise. For second, he thought it was the pulsing headache. "What's that?"

"What?" his father said.

The sound intensified; the ground vibrated.

"Over there." Reilly pointed.

In the gathering shadows at the mesa's edge, four dark animals galloped. They were enormous—about six times the size of a dog. Four short legs supported a bulky body and a wide head. At this distance—a kilometer or so—it was hard to make out much else. The creatures disappeared into a dark crevice in the mesa's side.

"What were those?" Ensign Rabin said hoarsely.

"Don't know," Ensign Morten answered. "Remind me of rhinos.'

"They're bigger than that," Ensign Rabin said. "Did the first colonists describe such beasts?"

"Yes," the captain said. "Or something like them. We'll learn more soon enough." He spoke louder. "Everyone, let's go inside."

As though they'd be any safer there, Reilly thought. The fabric was tough—it took a special knife to cut through it. But could it stop behemoths like that? Did the animals have sharp appendages—teeth, claws, horns? Did they exude gases or liquids that dissolved woven metal?

Now that the sun had sunk behind the mesa, the temperature plunged from a searing 41 degrees Celsius to just above zero. Anxiety hitched a ride on the cold air that managed to penetrate the fabric's pores. It seemed they'd been transported back to the freezing, dying ship.

Everyone—even Tab and Ensign Morten—looked exhausted. Those gym workouts on the ship hadn't quite prepared them for physical labor performed under a harsh sun.

By the flickering blue light of telsar lamps, they ate a meager meal of flatbread spread with a nutritional paste, water, and dried fruit. They hadn't yet assembled any furniture, so they sat on sleeping mats, which made Reilly worry about the green insects. The building's fabric released a sharp, synthetic smell. The lamplight cast eerie shadows, exaggerating facial lines and hollows and making the air beams resemble the ribs of a huge animal. Reilly tried to eat, but his headache seemed to have poisoned his appetite. He felt light-headed and queasy.

Conversation returned to the first colonists. Where they alive? If so, where were they? If they had relocated, why hadn't they radioed their whereabouts? Radio failure explained some things. But if the colonists had moved, why would they have left behind their building materials? If they were dead, what might have killed them?

The captain cut in. "There's no point speculating until we have more information. Tomorrow, I'll take someone with me to investigate."

A sudden nausea gripped Reilly. His skin went cold and clammy. His stomach contracted, and he clamped a hand over his mouth. If he puked here, he and everyone would have to smell it all night, and the vitros would razz him for months.

Without a word, he bolted from the mess hall, nearly knocking over Ensign Morten, who was standing sentry at the door. He managed to run a few paces before he vomited. The ensign asked if he needed help, and, wiping his mouth on his jacket sleeve, Reilly said he didn't.

He straightened and blinked at the night. The black of the sky wasn't the deep black of space, but more of an indigo. Also the stars glittered silver, whereas in space, they had shone steadily and more brightly, their colors vivid shades of blues and reds, rather than the washed out white caused by Cinnabar's atmosphere. Nevertheless, the sight of a dark, coruscating sky soothed him.

Straight overhead hung a pale blue moon. He saw the blinking light of the *Romulus* in its orbit. The *Remus* wouldn't pass overhead for another few hours. A strange glow limned the horizon. Transfixed, he watched as it grew steadily brighter until the second moon—this one larger and marbled with orange—climbed into the sky. Although he had long known that two moons orbited Cinnabar, this view of them stunned him.

From overhead came a shushing sound, a stirring of air. A dark shape moved across the blue moon. Head at one end, tail at the other, and, in between, a slender body bisecting broad wings. It looked huge, but Reilly wasn't sure how far above him the thing was—fifteen meters, maybe less. One beat of the wings, and the creature vanished into the night.

He scanned the sky, but detected no bodies other than the celestial kind. Strangely, he didn't feel afraid, merely curious. He thought the animal was similarly curious about him, had regarded him benevolently. No, he thought, that's crazy. No way could he have divined the creature's intent. He shivered, but only from the cold. The headache had miraculously evaporated.

"When I was a kid in Florida, the heat sometimes made me spew. But usually only after putting away some Cuban rum."

Reilly jumped. He had forgotten all about Ensign Morten, on sentry duty, who had moved to stand behind him. "Did you see that?" he said, looking at the now vacant blue moon.

"See what?"

"Something flying up there." Reilly described what he saw. They both scanned the empty air.

"I'll keep my eyes peeled," Ensign Morten said. He zipped his jacket to his neck, sat on a crate, and leaned his back against the mess hall.

Reilly felt grateful he didn't have to stand guard alone in this wilderness. Even though the sentry shifts lasted only two hours, 120 minutes would stretch long on this first night. He pushed open the flap-like door to the mess hall and nearly struck his father in the chest.

"I was looking for you," his father said, concern creasing his tired face. "What were you thinking, going outside by yourself?"

"I had to throw up," Reilly said. "If I'd tried to tell you, I would have puked on you."

His father put a hand on Reilly's shoulder and peered into his face. "The migraine. Damn. We forgot to give you some Anaral. I'll get some now—"

"No," Reilly said. "Now that I vomited, I feel fine." He stifled a yawn. "Just sleepy."

"Makes sense. Migraines often follow that pattern." His father smiled. "Next time, we'll medicate you at the first sign."

Reilly smiled. "Nah, just put me in the hibernation chamber. Wake me when it's over." He remembered that the hibernation chambers were orbiting the planet.

A few people were looking their way, including his worried-looking mother. Reilly smiled reassuringly. "Dad?" he whispered, turning his back to the others.

"What is it, Son?"

"I saw something out there."

His father tensed. "What?"

"I don't know. It was flying. Ensign Morten was on sentry, but he didn't see it."

"Probably a bird. Your mother saw some by the creek earlier."

Reilly shook his head. "I didn't look avian. It was big. And it had legs."

"Birds have legs."

"Not four of them."

His father's eyes cut to the other people huddled in the center of the room, some of them engrossed in conversation, some of them still eating. Maia looked over her shoulder at them and arched an eyebrow.

"I'll mention it to the captain. We'll make sure everyone stays inside all night."

Before they lay down, the crew covered the ground with a large sheet of the BioFuerte, to protect from emerging arachnids and any other subterranean surprises. On top of that, they positioned sleeping mats and bags. The vitros lined up like a row of batteries in a pack. There followed a few moments of pushing and grousing, but there was no reason for them to be so close together, so Reilly figured they either liked proximity or were too used to the absence of personal space to seek it out.

The adults split up with women on one side of the vitros, men on the other. Except for Reilly's parents, who slept side by side, and Reilly, who lay on his mat a meter away from his mother. During the day, the sleeping sacs had been hung over the airscouters so the embedded solar cells could charge. Now the stored power heated stainless steel fibers that threaded through the polypropylene fill. Reilly adjusted the temperature setting on his sac and settled himself.

For a moment, there was silence, then Nash muttered, "Quit it, Tab."

"Quit what?" Tab said. "I didn't do anything. That's Maia making her moves."

"Shut up," Maia said.

"Enough!" Captain Baca barked.

The vitros quieted.

Reilly lay on his back, staring up through the darkness at the barely visible ribs of the ceiling. His arms and shoulders ached from the work he'd done. To his left, his mother's breathing became slow and regular. One of the men began to snore. From some distance away, there came a faint lilting sound, a sound that raised goose bumps on Reilly's arms. It was almost like human laughter, or, more precisely, like the sound a person makes who can't decide whether to laugh or cry. Halfway through the trip, one of the adults had made such noises. First she'd had insomnia that didn't respond to the usual drugs. Then, came the radio news that her mother had died. Then came the laughing and crying that seemed to stretch for hours. The doctor put her into hibernation for a few weeks. Afterward she was better, but then she died in the viral epidemic. Reilly could scarcely remember what she looked like, only the sounds she made.

Outside, the eerie laughter stopped.

Nova whispered, "What was that?"

"The birds that nest by the river, I think," Reilly's mother said.

A few minutes later, there came a shrill chirping, at first one voice and then a dozen, all of them close. A sudden shriek bolted Reilly upright. The chirps became mournful, then diminished to a murmur.

Someone lit a telsar lamp, and Commander Shen appeared within its blue glow, *yridium* gun in hand. Captain Baca stood beside her, head cocked as though listening intently. The commander moved silently to the flap-like door, unzipped it, and disappeared outside. Reilly could hear her and Ensign Morten speaking, but Reilly couldn't make out their words.

When she returned, she and the captain talked, their heads close together.

"What's going on?" Maia demanded.

Captain Baca turned and raised the lamp, casting a ghostly glow over the crew, most of whom sat in their sleeping sacs wearing startled expressions. "Just the natives communicating," he said. "Clearly, many species are nocturnal. Nothing to worry about. Anyway, they're gone now."

"What if they come back?" Keid wanted to know.

"BioFuerte is tough as steel. And Ensign Morten is guarding us." Captain Baca walked closer to vitros. "It's okay," he said gently. "Everyone back to sleep."

"Is Harlan okay?" Tab asked, pushing up on his elbow. "I can go take guard duty with him."

"That's Ensign Morten to you," the captain said. "He's just fine. Sleep now."

Tab lay down.

Clutching his sleeping sac to his chin, Keid continued to sit. "Lieutenant Landreth," he said, "would you play your flute?"

Reilly's father looked at Captain Baca, "I don't mind," he said. "Not sure if everyone wants me to play or not."

"Go ahead, Skyler," the captain said.

"Yes, do," said Commander Shen.

Reilly's father slid out of his sleeping sac, crossed to the pile of personal gear, and pulled a slim black case from his duffel. In the dim light, he assembled the silver flute, stood, lifted the instrument to his lips, began playing Brahms' Lullaby.

Talitha tapped Keid's shoulder and whispered something. He curled on his side, facing her, and she took his hand. Nova, who was on his other side, hummed the melody and stroked his hair. Reilly wondered whether any of the vitros would comfort him if he needed it.

Reilly's father played the song twice and put away the flute. The lamp was extinguished. The space filled with sleeping noises—snuffles, snores, mutterings. Before long, exhaustion tugged Reilly into oblivion.

SEVEN

Over the next two weeks, the colonists constructed more buildings: a barracks for the adult crew that contained a separate room for Commander Shen, a small barracks for Reilly and his parents, a shower stall, latrine, and a rough barn that the animals crowded into at night. True to Reilly's prediction, the structure they raised on their first day—the one the animals had stayed in the first night—became a dormitory for the vitros.

After tests showed the creek water potable, they ran a line from the creek to the mess hall, barn, and a washbasin outside the latrine. Ensign Morten drank the first glass drawn from the pump. He wiped his lips on his sleeve and said, "That sure as hell beats drinking the ship's recycled piss."

The colonists next surrounded the compound with a high-voltage fence. Although the native animals had not overtly threatened them, the rhino-sized creatures galloped past most nights, and a couple of people had spotted large canine-like animals skulking near a pile of boulders a half-kilometer away.

They planted beans, peas, zucchini, carrots, and leafy green vegetables and installed a drip line. The tools they'd brought were deliberately primitive, just old-fashioned hoes, shovels, rakes, and trowels—reliable and durable implements that could easily be repaired.

In addition to weeding and watering the garden, there was a seemingly endless list of daily chores: cooking meals and cleaning up afterward, feeding the animals, mucking out the barn and corral, building wind turbines and solar panels, and cataloging the growing list of native plants and animals.

Some of the jobs were relatively pleasant: Ensign Morten's survival class and shooting practice sessions, Lieutenant Schuler's first-aid and animal-care classes, and airscouter flying lessons. Reilly again flew copilot with his father. The other adults took turns teaching the vitros to fly.

His mother hadn't yet taught Reilly or anyone else to swim; she wanted more information about the riparian fauna. She'd mounted a video camera in one of the trees. So far, it had captured only the birds that nested in the trees lining the creek. One evening recording caught them squawking at something below the camera's range.

The clay banks tinted the water a murky-lavender, making it impossible to see what lay on the bottom. Ultrasonic readings showed animals morphologically similar to fish, surface insects, and worm-like creatures at the bottom. The creek was a little over a meter deep. In Reilly's opinion, the fact that you could easily wade diminished motivation to learn to swim.

As the colonists went about their work, they learned more about the animals. For instance, before bending close to the ground, it was a good idea to probe carefully with a long-handled hoe, an action that flushed any arachnids. Also, if you paid attention, you could spot the arachnid nests, which were marked by a small hole in the ground and a nearby pile of gluey sand.

As suspected, most animals were nocturnal, making daytime relatively safe for the humans. At least two species appeared harmless: the pink murine creatures that burrowed at the base of rocks and the creek-side birds. The rat-like animals didn't bother the humans and only raised their spines when provoked. At dusk, they began to pop out of their burrows, stand on their hind legs, clasp their short front legs before their chests, and watch with inquisitive dark eyes. If the humans ignored them, one or two of the more adventurous creatures might take a tentative hop or two forward. If the dogs saw them, they would bark and strain at their tethers. The children were under strict orders not to approach the animals, and so far, they had obeyed—even Tally, who liked to watch them through binoculars.

Tally's observations provided them with an invaluable piece of information. The rodents' behavior predicted sandstorms, which had recurred three times since the landing, always during the day. What Tally noticed was that the rodents would sometimes awaken during the midday heat to seal their burrows with stones. A stone was pushed from inside the den and wedged into the opening. This action occurred a good quarter hour before the humans could detect the stirring of air and distant low red clouds that heralded a sandstorm became visible in the distance—more time than the five minutes their instruments signaled the sudden drop in barometric pressure. Paying attention to the rodents gave them a better chance of making the shelter in the mess hall before a storm peaked.

The other innocuous species—the birds that nested by the creek—also had a pre-storm repertoire. First they let out a long, two-toned whistle: high sliding to low. One avian species, which Reilly's father dubbed the town crier—*sang bee-yo, bee-yo,* then the others joined in. Just before the storm hit, they seemed to have more trouble flying. Lieutenant Schuler theorized that a drop in air pressure made it harder to create lift under their wings. These birds gathered on low branches near the tree's trunk. Seconds before the wind rose, they flipped their long tails up to their chests, tucked their necks, raised their shoulders, and pulled their wings around themselves. They looked zipped up. His mother said they resembled outsized cocoons.

Reilly liked these birds, which appeared not just harmless, but friendly. Occasionally, first light would find one or two of them perched on various structures, most often the barn, where they would wait for the door to open and the chickens and turkeys to come out. Long purple tail feathers draped over the roof, they would cock their teal heads, watch the domesticated foul flap their nearly useless wings, and cluck sadly. Flight was about the only advantage they held over the turkeys and chickens. Superior intelligence was unlikely, given their small craniums.

A more sinister avian species began to hang about morning and evening. Compared to the creek birds, they were twice as big and three times as ugly, with gray scaly bodies, curved orange beaks, and a two-meter wingspan. They had a single saucer-shaped eye set above the cruel beak. These cyclopean eyes coldly appraised the barnyard animals, as though determining relative vulnerability. They didn't blink when the dogs lunged and barked. In fact, they seemed incapable of blinking. Reilly's mother said they probably had a nictitating membrane, but no actual eyelid. When they arrived, the other birds scattered and, beating their short, rounded wings, sought refuge in the trees' meager canopy.

Reilly detested the creatures. He discovered one of them hunched atop the compost bin, trying to open the door with its talons and only giving up when Reilly yelled and hurled rocks. He was surprised how much he wanted to hit the thing. But, mindful of orders not to injure the natives unless necessary for survival, he only threw the rocks near enough to scare it off. Only after the third rock skimmed a scaled shoulder did the bird lift off, soaring above Reilly and eyeing him balefully.

∞

The kids helped with all tasks save one: investigating the first colonists' camp. In fact, Captain Baca made it very clear that any child caught anywhere near that compound would be in serious trouble. The adults went to the site in pairs.

Captain Baca and Reilly's mother were the first to enter the buildings. As Reilly watched their scouter disappear from view, he felt a painful tug in his chest, as though the invisible tether that connected him to his mother had grown taut.

The fact that Reilly had to hoe beans with Maia did nothing to lessen his unease. She had unfastened the sleeves from her shirt, something Reilly didn't dare do with his fair skin. Like the other vitros, her skin had gone from pale to deep brown within days of arriving on Cinnabar—a genetically engineered feat Reilly envied.

As she worked the hoe, the long, lean muscles of her arms flexed.

For a long hour, she alternately chatted and badgered. "You missed a weed there… They must be there now. At the first camp, I mean… You should pump some water for that row… I wonder if the first colonists left a message. You know, like told us where they've gone… Minje but you're so slow. I hope you don't think I'm going to help you with your half… Reilly, are you listening to me?"

Reilly mostly didn't respond, and when he did, it was in monosyllables. Even when she wasn't speaking, he could hear her in his head, her thoughts rootlets piercing his brain. Between Maia and the heat, he felt exhausted. He pictured building a wall to keep her out, mentally piling rocks higher and higher. Finally, his mind cleared. The peace was fleeting. Something else entered, a blue coolness.

He stood, dropped his hoe, and scanned the eastern horizon. "They're coming back."

Maia straightened, her shirt soaked from her armpit down to her waist. "I don't see them."

Reilly couldn't either, not yet. But he felt a relaxation in his chest that told him so. He had fixed his attention on his mother until he sensed her approach. The sensation was mixed—a relaxation in his core, sapphire visual shimmers, vague and undecipherable thoughts in his mind.

"Oh! There they are," Maia said, pointing.

Reilly wondered whether Maia's vision was better than 20/20. In a moment, the silver glimmer of the scouter wavered on the horizon. Inexplicably, his heart quickened and his breathing went shallow. Something bad had happened. He dreaded the details, knew he could not avoid them. He walked slowly toward the landing area, as though into a strong wind.

Maia ran ahead of him. "Come on, Reilly," she called over her shoulder. "Snap out of it."

Everyone clustered around the scouter as it landed. The dome slid back. The captain and Reilly's mother both looked grim.

"What is it?" Tally said. "What's wrong?"

Captain Baca jerked his head toward the mess hall. Everyone followed him there. He kept his hat pulled low over his face and let Reilly's mother debrief the others.

"The yard was lifeless," she said. "There were only three airscouters, and they all looked as though someone had taken a huge blowtorch to them. The cockpit domes were blistered, the metal blackened."

"What could have happened?" Ensign Rabin asked. "Did you see signs of fire elsewhere?"

Reilly's mother shook her head. She went on to describe the plates and utensils still on the mess hall tables, the scatterings of bones and feathers in the barn and corral. Strangely, the perimeter fence was locked and secure. One barracks was empty, save for articles of men's clothing and a makeshift desk.

"In the other barracks—" she paused, and Reilly felt anxiety grip his throat. "There were twelve futons."

"No people?" Lieutenant Schuler asked, though he didn't sound hopeful.

"Atop each bed, save one, lay a single skeleton."

"What happened?" Nova asked, her voice thin with fright.

His mother cut through the gasps and murmurs. "The cause of death was not apparent. We took samples of bone, hair, and nails. We also collected samples from the air and surfaces inside the barracks."

Keid looked pale. Tally moved closer and took his hand in hers. They stood there, petite and perceptive.

Commander Shen spoke up. "Anika, please describe the position of the skeletons. That is, does the arrangement of the bones suggest a struggle?" Her elegant hands were blackened with engine grease. As she tucked a loose shaft of hair behind her ear, she left a dark smear at her right temple.

Captain Baca remained silent and still, save for the hand that strayed to the green stone hanging from a cord around his neck.

Reilly's mother drew a long breath. "The bones appeared intact, undisturbed. The skeletons lay on either their backs and or their sides. I saw no sign of trauma, save for an old fracture of the fifth metacarpal in one male."

Ensign Morten removed his cap and rubbed his forehead. "That man likely was in a fist fight," he said. "Sounds like the entire crew died in their sleep."

"But why?" Ensign Rabin asked. "Could it have been an infection?"

Lieutenant Schuler ran a hand over his craggy cheekbones and said, "The agent would have to be swiftly lethal to cause everyone to lie down and die en masse."

"It's possible though," Maia said. "I mean, think about some of the nasty Earth microbes, like the Ebola virus. People dropped quickly."

"Maybe so, Maia," Reilly's mother said. "But the skeletons looked so—"

peaceful. Like there wasn't agony in the death."

Reilly remembered the effects of the Dagnar virus—the rigors, the wracking cough, the labored efforts to breathe. He remembered standing outside the window of the sick bay's quarantine area. On the other side, his grandfather was propped up in the bed, looking exhausted with the effort of breathing. Reilly visited several times a day, holding up pictures he had drawn, each one with the caption: "Get well, Granddaddy." At first his grandfather would smile and wave, maybe mouth some words, or give him a thumb's up. Later he smiled wanly and wiggled his fingertips. Later still, there was no response, just the rise and fall of his chest, interrupted by long bouts of coughing. Next time Reilly had visited there had been an empty bed, which was soon occupied by a new victim.

"What about poison?" Nash asked excitedly. He was a fan of detective movies.

Reilly's mother nodded. She looked tired, as though gravity tugged harder at her face and shoulders. "Also possible," she said, "especially if everyone took the poison simultaneously, and if the poison didn't cause muscle spasms, agonizing belly pain—symptoms that would have distorted the posture."

Clutching herself, Nova said, "Grotty."

"At any rate," Captain Baca cut in, "we'll screen the specimens for infectious agents and toxins."

Reilly's mother added. "The tests will take more time than they would on Earth, given our lack of familiarity with microbes and biochemicals on Cinnabar."

"Twelve people landed," Commander Shen said, thinking aloud. "You said one of the cots was empty. That's eleven skeletons, right?"

Captain Baca nodded.

"Maybe one of the crew died earlier of another cause," Ensign Rabin said. "Perhaps the others had already buried him or her."

"Her," Captain Baca supplied. He looked at his hands and picked at a callous. "Anika and I counted eight men and four women. Five women made it to the planet."

"How could you tell them apart?" Tab asked. "I mean, they were just bones."

"The female pelvis is wider," Maia said. When the other kids, including Reilly, goggled her, she added, "I learned that from the anatomy archives."

Reilly's mother studied Captain Baca, who was gazing toward the mesa. "Maybe," she said, "the twelfth member of the *Romulus* is still alive."

∞

That night, after everyone had turned in for bed, Reilly overheard his mother and father talking. He lay sleepless on his inflatable futon, his back to his parents' larger futon three meters away.

"Something's up with Carlos," his mother whispered into the dark.

His father yawned, then mumbled, "He looked distracted tonight. But this news about the *Romulus* crew has upset everyone."

"No. It's more than that. When we entered the barracks containing the skeletons, he started frantically checking the foot bones. I had to remind him not to touch anything."

"What do you think he was doing?"

"Looking for someone."

After a moment's silence, his mother added. "Remember that woman Carlos had been in love with?"

"Right. She was assigned to the *Romulus,* Carlos to the *Remus.* "

"Remember her name?"

"No. I never met her."

"Me neither. But I heard about her, saw her and Carlos together a couple times when we were training at the Academy. She was short and compact with wavy brown hair. Carlos told me her name once. Something Hawaiian. Ona? Lani?

"Did she have a club foot or something?"

His mother laughed. "No."

"Shhh."

Another pause.

His mother whispered, "I just remembered seeing her coming out of the flight simulator with a magnetic cast on her foot. Maybe she had a broken a bone."

His father yawned. "Another of life's mysteries." There was the wet sound of a kiss. "Goodnight, Anika love," he said.

"Sweet dreams, Sky."

Reilly had the strange feeling his mother's mind was reaching out to his, silver tendrils threading his neurons, accessing his level of consciousness.

"And sweet dreams to you, my big-eared son," she murmured.

∞

A week later, Reilly got his chance to see the remains of the first colonists. No one yet knew what had killed the *Romulus* crew. So far, the screening tests hadn't turned up an obvious pathogen. Captain Baca assigned Ensign Rabin and Reilly's mother with the task of returning for further investigation and to seal off the area. He said he wanted to keep animals from tampering with the site, but Reilly suspected he wanted to make sure curious kids stayed out.

After dinner, Reilly approached the captain and asked permission to help, promising right off to wear protective clothing and stay close to the adults. Captain Baca granted him a reluctant okay, which, once the word got out the next morning, raised a predictable round of grousing from the other kids.

Reilly was excited to see the area, but also nervous. Death scared him—the discomfort leading up to it, then the oblivion. As opposed to life, it was permanent. Confronting corpses made any delusions of immortality impossible. Like every other human, he would die. So would his parents. Thinking of them dying made him sadder than imagining himself dead. And if they didn't know what killed the first colonists, how could they protect themselves from the same fate?

The day was, like every other day since their arrival, hot. It was already pushing 40 degrees Celsius. No wind, blue skies, the sun a spiteful ball of fire. Reilly and his mother took one airscouter, Reilly sitting in the pilot's seat and his mother co-piloting, which entailed giving him more advice than he thought he needed. It was his fourth time in an airscouter, his second with his hands on the controls. He loved flying—the exhilaration of controlling the liftoff and landing and the speed, the eerie detachment of rising above the ground and watching the rest of the crew shrink to dots.

Ensign Rabin flew a second scouter packed with tools and construction materials. After they landed, they donned their gloves, goggles, and masks, and zipped up their flight suits. Booted feet shushing through sand, they approached the perimeter fence. Many of the fence's wires had been severed and the bent gate yawned open. Passing the three airscouters, Reilly wondered what had burned them. Lightning? Space probes had long ago shown that electrical storms developed in the mountains. So far, the storms he seen had brought windblown sand but no lightning.

There were four buildings—barn, mess hall, and two barracks, all made from BioFuerte stretched over inflated tubular supports. The first three buildings were nearly empty. The barn contained a few feathers, desiccated droppings, dried plant stems, and a lingering musky smell. The remaining bones and hide had already been taken for analysis, which hadn't turned up anything unusual.

Reilly and his mother held a swath of BioFuerte over the barn door and Ensign Rabin tacked it down with a glue gun.

When they reached the mess hall, Reilly asked if he could peek inside. His mother frowned, but, after first checking for dangerous animals, Ensign Rabin said, "Why not?" It looked much like their own mess hall—a long table with a dozen folding chairs dominated the center. There was a kitchen area and a sink with a faucet. Strangely, there were still plates and sporks on the table and in the sink—as though something had interrupted the meal. Something had long since picked the plates clean of food. The pantry contained dusty bags of dried beans, bags of unidentifiable food matter, a box of salt, a few spice jars.

Reilly poked at one of the bags and two green insects as long as his thumb scrambled out from behind the bag, unfolded iridescent wings, and flew at his face. With a scream, he blindly batted the air in front of him.

Both his mother and the ensign ran toward him.

"What's happened?" Ensign Rabin asked. "Are you okay?"

Reilly straightened his mask with a trembling hand. Sweat ran in rivulets down his sides. "Yeah, fine. A couple of those green bugs just startled me."

"I told you not to touch anything," his mother snapped. "Come help me cut some BioFuerte for the windows."

Cutting the tough textile required a laser scalpel set on high. Reilly measured the windows and called the dimensions out to his mother, who wielded the laser scalpel, while Ensign Rabin held the material taut.

They repeated the same procedure at the smaller barracks. It was empty save for a desk littered with lab equipment and a computer scroll, a pair of large work boots, and a couple men's shirts lying on the floor. Reilly wondered if the captain of the *Romulus* had used this building.

As they approached the larger barracks, Ensign Rabin said, "So, Reilly, you've been told about the skeletons, no doubt."

"Yes, sir."

"You don't mind seeing them?"

"No," Reilly lied. In truth, he felt a mixture of dread and morbid curiosity.

While the ensign and Reilly sealed the door, his mother measured the window dimensions. Reilly edged closer to the window and peered in. As his mother had described, twelve sagging futons were arranged in a haphazard circle. In the middle of the circle was a pit. Someone had cut a hole in the BioFuerte floor and ringed it with rocks, which were covered in ashes. What had they burned? Surely not the scarce trees.

He let his eyes move over the beds. On the ship, he had seen freshly dead people. They still looked, aside from an ashen waxiness, much as they had in life—and much different from the desiccated, bony remains of the first colonists. He stared now at their rag-covered skeletons. Some lay on their backs, some on their sides. He remembered that some were men, some women, remembered Maia saying the width of the pelvis distinguished between the two sexes. From where he stood, Reilly really couldn't discern much difference. Maia had also said that, in a dry climate, the flesh might have been preserved for years. But it hadn't been (except for some leathery patches on the skull, hands, and feet), which raised the clammy question of what had consumed it. Stringy hair clung to the scalps and long fingernails jutted from the sinewy fingertips and toes.

"Mom," he whispered hoarsely. "Why are the men and women all in one barracks?"

"Don't know," she said. "Maybe they got lonely. Maybe they wanted to build just one fire pit." She stretched the measuring tape, then let the thin metal reel back into the case with a loud clack.

Reilly swallowed. "Why are their nails so long?"

"Hair and nails continue to grow for a time after death." His mother called out the dimensions in centimeters to Ensign Rabin, who began cutting a piece of BioFuerte. She turned back to Reilly and said, "Why are you whispering, Reilly?"

Reilly shrugged. Using his glove, he wiped away dust from the window. "You said all the internal organs were gone, right?"

"Yes, why?"

"There's something in that skeleton's pelvis."

"What do you mean?" his mother said, leaning closer to the dusty window. "Hmm. Almost looks like a nest." She knocked on the window, which caused the fabric of the wall to ripple.

"Nobody home," Ensign Rabin joked nervously. He had joined them at the window. Suddenly he gave a short shout, startling Reilly.

Within the bony cradle of the pelvis, something stirred. The ensign went for his gun. Reilly clapped his hand to his mouth, but didn't quite capture a yelp. A nose poked through what appeared to be shredded bits of sleeping sac.

Reilly's mother laughed nervously. "It's one of those pink rat-like things."

"Looks like more than one," the ensign said as a half dozen smaller heads pushed up into the air. Tiny black eyes blinked at the humans. The mother— if it was female—stood on her hind legs, short forelimbs pulled to her chest, and began chattering, her tiny rectangular teeth moving up and down.

"We're probably frightening her," his mother said.

"Glad it's mutual," Reilly muttered.

"Let's cover the window," the ensign said, stowing his gun back in its holster. "But how will they ever get out?" Reilly said.

Ensign Rabin finished cutting the square of fabric. "Same way they likely got in," he said. "They probably tunneled in through the fire pit."

Fire pit, Reilly thought. He picked up the glue gun and ran a line of adhesive around the fabric's edge. "What do you think they burned?"

"That, my boy, is the mystery," the ensign said.

"Not a complete mystery," his mother added. "We've been analyzing samples from the ash."

"What have you found?" Reilly asked.

"Mostly carbon. Also nitrogen, oxygen, some trace elements as oxides. It's fairly characteristic of a plant-based fuel. Something denser than wood, more like coal. Some of the elements, however, I've yet to identify."

"You mean they're not like elements found on earth?" Reilly asked.

"Correct," his mother answered, then knelt beside Ensign Rabin and, careful not to touch the strong glue, lifted the fabric and pressed it over the window, blotting from view the skeletons and the creatures that now inhabited their bones.

When they finished, Reilly's mother went into some of the outbuildings—the latrine and the solar showers—to collect more samples. She told Reilly to help Ensign Rabin, who was examining the first colonists' wind turbine. He had already set up a stationary turbine for their base, and now wanted to launch a high-altitude generator. He had the essentials, but extra supplies would remain on the ship until they fixed the shuttle. He said he may as well recycle the first-colonists' materials.

Reilly stood in the slim shade offered by the wind turbine and waited for the ensign to give him orders. The turbine was near the fence. A stone's throw away stood a pole about seven meters high. What purpose could it serve, Reilly wondered. While the ensign muttered to himself and wrenched loose various bolts, Reilly sidled over to the pole. There wasn't anything hanging from it or mounted on it. It was just a pole. Feeling hot and bored, he kicked at the sand. The toe of his boot jammed painfully into something hard. He jumped back and waited breathless for some new species to rise from the sand. Nothing. Again, he nudged the area with his foot. He squatted and dug with his gloved hands. He felt square corners—something box-like. Using both hands, he grasped it and pulled. It was a video camera attached to a flexible neck that ended in a broken clamp.

EIGHT

Back at the base, Ensign Rabin repaired the videocam's solar battery. Reilly, his parents, and Captain Baca stood by as the device quickly recharged. The power light blinked on. The captain pushed play. Any kind of motion triggered a recording. They fast-forwarded through several clips of dust storms and a few clips of the river birds. Then, a nighttime shot caught a dark lean body, tail, and wings. Reilly's breath caught.

"What was that?" Ensign Rabin asked.

Another clip showed a dozen of the creatures flying overhead.

"Jesus," the captain muttered.

One of the creatures circled back and paused in front of the lens, looking with interest. It's face filled the view—gray, smooth, with a small whiskered snout below large amber-colored eyes with diamond shaped pupils. One eye was smaller than the other, as though the eyelid didn't quite open fully. Off camera, something snarled, and the outsized feline face ducked out of sight. A second head appeared—larger, with yellower eyes. Its mouth opened, exposing pointed teeth. It roared. Two fingers ending in sharp nails reached out, obliterating the lens. There was a wrenching noise, then nothing.

The captain powered off the camera.

"Wow," Ensign Rabin asked. "Why haven't we seen those yet?"

"I saw something like that the first night," Reilly said. "Just one."

"I remember," Reilly's father said. "Wonder why they've stayed away since then."

"They seem to be nocturnal," Reilly's mother said. "Maybe they don't want to be seen."

Reilly shivered. "Did these creatures kill the first colonists?"

"Well," the captain said, rubbing the bags under his eyes, "if they killed the first colonists, they did so indirectly. Otherwise, we would have seen evidence of trauma."

"We need to tell the others," Reilly's father said.

∞

After the rest of the crew saw the video, tensions increased. Commander Shen mounted the second colonists' camcorder atop the mess hall. They had already attached two video monitors to the fence. The captain ordered that no kid could venture out alone after dark, even within the perimeter of the charged fence. Reilly hated being escorted to the latrine, but at least the vitros had to abide by the same rule. Ensign Morten had everyone—adults and kids—doing target practice each day.

Days passed without incident. No flying creatures passed near the base, aside from the usual avians. The nighttime videos showed the usual scaly rodent, the large canine-like animals (including a segment showing three of them tearing apart a rodent), and the enormous rhino-like ungulates, which seemed to be herbivores. The colonists' domestic animals grew fatter, except the two dogs, who ran within the confines of the fence until the heat sent them to seek shade. Some of the crops withered in the heat. But the erection of a shade canopy allowed the rest of the plants to inch taller. And so, the colonists breathed a little easier.

During a break from chores the next afternoon, Reilly and his father made a weathervane for their barracks. Because compass needles swung wildly on Cinnabar, the rising and setting of the moons and sun determined east and west respectively. In honor of Cosmic, his grandparents' black cat, Reilly and his father cut a feline shape out of scraps of polychiton and stood him on the north-south line. When his grandparents had died, Cosmic had moved in with Reilly, slept at the small of Reilly's back, curled into his lap when Reilly read, occasionally batting the computer screen. Then Cosmic's kidneys began to fail. He peed on the carpet, lost weight, and eventually clumps of silky black hair. While Reilly and his parents wept and stroked the cat's bony body, Lieutenant Schuler euthanized Cosmic.

As Reilly worked on this two-dimensional feline representation, his mind streamed with these remembrances of Cosmic and also of his grandparents. When Reilly was little, he had a habit of escaping his chambers and toddling into the ship's control room. His Nanna, as he called her, would look up from her work and say sternly, "What are you doing here, young man?" Then a sly smile would crack the façade of military discipline. Sometimes, she would crouch and run toward him, holding her hands up like claws, and he would scamper away, shrieking with delight. She always caught him, which was what he wanted her to do, and lifted him into the air, saying, "I got you, you little rascal."

He remembered playing cards with his grandfather: Go Fish and War, when he was younger, then on to Cat and Mouse and Double Solitaire. If they could recruit other players, they'd play Poker and Hearts. There were other games: Beazique and Oh, Hell and I Doubt It. Reilly accused his grandfather of making these up, but his grandfather swore he'd learned them from his own father. When Reilly was small, his grandfather would let him win, smacking his brow with his palm and exclaiming, "How'd you manage that?" Later, they played in earnest, betting with biscuits and SoySnax. His grandfather said that, on Earth, people bet money. The concept of currency at first stumped Reilly since they had none on the ship.

"Hey, buddy," his father said. "I'm going to get a ladder. Then we can mount this beast atop our abode."

Reilly dragged a scrap of polychiton into the shade, sat, and drifted back to thoughts of his grandparents. His grandfather was one of the first people admitted to the sickbay, and one of the first to die. Again, the image of his grandfather smiling wanly at him from the clinic bed surfaced. He saw his grandfather's body jackknife into the spasm of a cough that brought pink and frothy sputum to his bluish lips.

When his grandmother had begun to cough, Reilly became hysterical. He screamed and tried to push past the medics into sickbay. He got far enough to see her. At the sound of his voice, she struggled to sit. Short silver hair framed her lean face. Her eyebrows arched neatly over eyes the same blue as Earth's oceans, her lips curved in a faint smile, and she said, "Don't worry, Reilly. You have to stay well and take care of your parents. Go with Amelia."

But Reilly pulled himself free of Amelia's hands, and the other medic, Kito, had to carry Reilly out—not easy with a struggling, rangy nine-year-old—and sedate him. While he slept, his parents were roused from hibernation. Usually only one of his parents hibernated at a time. But, just before the Dagnar virus outbreak, his mother had joined his father in the hibernation chamber because she had developed acute arthritis in her hands, an affliction Doctor Mbaake had treated with medication and a month's rest. When Reilly awoke, his father was at his side, holding his hand and whispering reassurances that belied his worried eyes. His mother was at the sickbay's observation window.

Eight hours later, his grandmother died. Reilly's mother sobbed during the cremation ceremony. As the body slid into the incinerator, Reilly had closed his eyes, which did nothing to block the sounds of ravenous flames and sorrow. He had never known his mother to cry more than a few tears. His father stopped playing "Danny Boy" on his flute to comfort her. After the ceremony, Reilly held his mother's hand and hugged her and cried with her, but she remained inconsolable. When the tears refused to stop, one of the medics gave her a dose of Harmonal. Her drugged sleep looked so like death that Reilly lay beside her, middle finger on her wrist, obsessively counting her pulse.

During his vigil, he noticed that his own skin felt hot and that his heart rate was nearly double his mother's. Then his memories fractured, leaving only random shards snagged in his memory. He remembered waking up shivering, his pajamas and sleeping sac drenched with sweat. His first fear was not of death, but of being quarantined, of being separated from his parents. He remembered his father's cool hand on his brow, the worried look in his blue-green eyes. Cosmic snuggled against him, his purrs vibrating his hip. There was the pressure of the drug gun against his upper arm and the dull pain of liquid forced through skin as a medic injected him with the antiviral agent. He remembered waking up one day and realizing his fever was gone. He had marveled at the sharpness of his hipbones, the bagginess of his clothes.

Reilly remembered standing at a ceremony with the other sallow survivors and hearing the roll call of the twenty-one who had died. So many names, his grandparents, his two best friends, Phillipe and Sara, and their parents. Dr. Mbaake had died too. She had married Captain Baca during the flight. The captain had stood rigidly during the service, as though he might crack if he displayed any emotion. Commander Shen had officiated. While she spoke, Reilly silently begged that his parents never die. If they did, he would be lost.

Reilly became aware of movement. Nova and Nash approached, both of their faces as brown as tree bark. The two paused to look at the small barracks where Reilly and his parents lived. Nova and Nash apparently didn't see him sitting cross-legged in the shade.

"It's not fair he doesn't have to sleep with us other kids," Nova said. "He never has."

"Yeah," Nash said. "And his father and mother don't have to sleep in the adults' barracks. Like they're special or something." He hawked up spit.

Reilly bit his lip against a retort. Idiots, he thought as the kids walked away, leaving a wake of orange dust. They haven't a clue what it means to be a family. He'd rather be left naked in the merciless midday sun than to live in the kids' barracks.

Although he'd never liked Reba, he half wished Ensign Rabin, the only one who felt affection for androids, would fix her. The ensign had redesigned the android's lower body to better navigate the sand, but the central computer kept mysteriously fritzing out. Reilly's mother thought they'd all be better off without Reba, though Reilly wasn't sure why.

His dad returned with the ladder, and they spent a half hour affixing the weathervane to the top of their dwelling, a process that involved glue, ropes, and pulleys. Then they stood back and admired their work, but the weathervane stood motionless in the evening breeze.

His father chuckled. "It'll take a gale to move that thing." Then he ducked into the barracks, returned with his flute, and, facing the weathervane, played an Irish reel called "The Wind that Shakes the Barley." It was a simple, joyous tune, and one of the first tunes Reilly had learned to play. His mother appeared, clapping her hands in time. She hooked an arm through his and together they spun, smiling.

It had been weeks since Reilly had heard music. For much of the voyage, Reilly's father had played flute in a trio with Lieutenant Shen, who played oboe, and Ensign Kito Higashi, who played violin. Until Kito died five years ago from the virus, the trio would set up on the observation deck, their backs to the large window with its ever-changing views of planets, moons, and suns. Other times, the crew would simply access music from the computer archives.

Raucous music began streaming from the vitros' dorm. Reilly found himself wanting to go inside and listen, which seemed a betrayal of his parents, whose tastes tended toward classical music and jazz. On the ship, when Reilly wanted to hear something edgier, he had to wear earphones.

But now, outside in the waning sunlight, Reilly became aware that he and his parents had attracted some of the crew. Commander Shen walked over with her oboe and started a new piece. Tally sauntered over, trailing the two dogs and a goat. The door to the mess hall opened, and Keid emerged carrying an empty crate and two cooking spoons. He set down the crate upside down beside Reilly's father, kneeled, and started percussing the crate with the spoons. Reilly laughed. For the first time, he felt like he could be happy on this planet.

∞

The following day, the crew met to discuss construction needs. They lacked a lookout tower and a laboratory, but had exhausted the building supplies shuttled from the ship. Until they determined what caused the first colonists' deaths, they couldn't recycle materials from their base.

After much—and, in Reilly's mind, tedious—discussion about conservation, the crew voted to cut two of the trees that grew along the creek. Reilly's mother explained that the birds depended on the trees for habitat and that, quite likely the trees had other functions, such as the canopy shading any organisms living along the creek, the roots maintaining the banks, and the trunk housing as yet unidentified species. As the vitros started fidgeting and whispering, Reilly wished his mother would sit down and stop talking.

Ensign Morten and Ensign Rabin volunteered for the tree-cutting job. As their laser saws shook the russet branches, several of the resident avian creatures took flight, trailing their extravagant lavender tail feathers.

Inexplicably, Ensign Morten drew his gun and shot one of them. The bird paused; wings outstretched, then plummeted to the ground. As Ensign Morten loped the short distance to the body, Ensign Rabin shouted a string of curses.

Reilly and Talitha had stopped milking the goats to watch the felling of the trees. Tally cried out. Captain Baca ran out the gate, shouting and waving his cap. Reilly was too far away to make out the ensuing conversation, but the captain's gestures were angry and the ensign's posture was strangely defiant. Half a dozen birds resettled themselves in nearby trees and watched, repeating the same three-note, sorrowful call.

When Ensign Morten strode back to camp, holding the bird by the tail feathers, the rest of the crew gathered to see—except Ensign Rabin, who sat a reproachful distance away, cleaning under his fingernails with a screwdriver. The bird was a meter long, beak to tip of tail. The purple tail feathers were as long as Reilly's arm. The wing feathers shimmered green and black. The red breast was scaled, not feathered. Curled lash-like feathers fringed the glassy green eyes. The long yellow beak was tube-like; even when shut at the sides, a hole remained open at the end. Reilly's mother remarked that the beak's configuration must allow it to suck up small animals from the creek's muddy banks. Tally kept stroking the bird's back, as though her actions might actually offer solace.

"The thing's dead, Tally," Tab said.

"I know."

"Can I have some of the feathers?" Keid asked.

Nova pouted. "I want the feathers."

"But I will make something with them," Keid said.

"So will I," Nova said.

"Right," Maia said, "you'll probably put them in your hair. Keid will make art."

"I create art," Nova said. "Fashion is art. Just because the rest of you are happy wearing ugly uniforms—"

"Enough!" the captain said. "We'll distribute the feathers equitably."

A flicker caught Reilly's eye. One of the gray, vulture-like birds had alighted on one of the fence posts and was eying the dead bird. Lieutenant Schuler jumped up and waved his arms. With a screech, the bird leapt into the air, spread its colossal wings, and flew toward the creek. The lieutenant scooped up the dead bird and took it into the barn for a more thorough examination and toxicology testing. Reilly's mother followed.

That night, they roasted the bird. Everyone got two bites. Ensign Morten thought he should have more since he downed the bird, but the captain said no. Nash and Tab split the morsels Tally refused to eat. The meat tasted gamey and sinewy, but was the freshest thing they had eaten since the plants in the ship's greenhouse froze.

At the meal's end, Captain Baca re-emphasized that no one would harm any native species unless defensive actions were required. Lieutenant Schuler proposed a moratorium on killing more avian creatures until they better understood the local ecology. Reilly's mother added that they couldn't cut more trees for the same reason. As all other hands rose in favor of a temporary hunting and logging ban, Ensign Morten bent his head to a delicate thigh-bone and gnawed sullenly.

∞

In the middle of that night, the alarm sounded. Pulling on jackets, Reilly and his parents tore outside. The animals were making a racket—goats bleating, chickens and turkeys squawking, dogs howling. Commander Shen was on guard. When Reilly and his parents emerged into the yard, she stood facing the northwest corner of the fence, her gun arm hanging at her side. Beau was barking hysterically and dashing up and down the fence.

Tally and Lieutenant Schuler called to him, but he wouldn't come. Tally started shouting, "Xena! Xena! Where's Xena?"

After the entire group had gathered, she explained that the dogs had begun frantically barking. As she raced toward the small barn, two dark, winged shapes rose into the sky. A wriggling dog—Xena—dangled from one, a goat from the other. She estimated the predators' size to be on par with a horse.

Reilly thought of the flying creature he had seen that first night. How close had he come to being carried off? He felt cold and tucked his hands into the sleeves of his jacket.

The captain looked at him. "Does this sound like the animal you reported, Reilly?"

"I think so," Reilly said. "It was pretty far away. But it was large and winged. Did these animals have four legs?"

Commander Shen nodded. "Tails, too. They definitely weren't avian."

Ensign Morten rubbed his stubbled jaw. "We should have installed a mesh over the animal enclosure."

"But all the animals were inside the barn," Commander Shen said. "Xena ran out the dog door. But the goat was inside."

"You're sure of that?" Captain Baca asked and the commander nodded.

"Prehensile digits," Lieutenant Schuler mused.

Nose to the ground, Beau began running tight circles. He stopped, tail swaying uncertainly. Tally went to him. Reilly followed and watched her gather tufts of black and white dog hair, press her face into the mass, and weep. Whining now, Beau resumed his search for his mate. Reilly put a hand on Tally's shuddering shoulder. She pressed her wet face into his neck. Just as Reilly put his arm around her, she jerked up her head and called, "Commander Shen, which goat was it?"

"I don't know," Commander Shen said.

Tally raced toward the barn and returned moments later, crying, "It was Betty! She was pregnant." As she sobbed, Maia took her hand and led her toward the kids' dorm.

Captain Baca ordered the other kids to follow, adding, "Stay inside. Wait until an adult comes in the morning."

"What if we have to pee?" Nash asked.

"Use the bucket," Lieutenant Schuler said.

"It stinks," Nova said.

"Back to your dormitory!" Captain Baca said, and they went.

Reilly's father nudged Reilly. "You too, buddy. We'll be there soon."

As Reilly walked, he scanned the sky, but saw nothing other than the indigo sky, a spangling of stars, and two moons—the blue one half full, the other a crescent. The idea that something might, at any moment, dart down and snatch him froze his spine solid. As he turned toward his barracks, he thought he saw something skim the top of the mesa. He blinked and the object—if it was there at all—vanished.

∞

After the attack, there was much discussion about how to safeguard the base from aerial attacks. Using the roseate wood from the two felled creek trees, they erected a lookout tower, which made it easier to spot approaching predators and also protected the sentry. Ensign Rabin designed a modification to the electric fence that would arc current over the entire compound. To make it, he needed more wire, a generator for when the photovoltaic cells ran down, and a fuel to power the generator. In addition to the photovoltaic cells embedded in the textile covering the barracks, the crew had already assembled a solar panel and a wind turbine. But so far, these energy sources only produced enough power to light up the buildings at night.

Ensign Rabin and Commander Shen had nearly finished assembling a high-altitude wind turbine, which was basically a huge kite equipped with eight small turbines that would harness the power in the strong, steady winds 300 meters above the surface. The electricity generated would travel back to the ground in the strong tether. The trick was getting the kite, which had a wingspan of 10 meters, off the ground. Ensign Morten had already volunteered to trail the kite behind an airscouter till the wind caught the wings. But that maneuver was weeks away.

Meantime, they needed to find a combustible compound to heat the barracks, power the protective force field, and—if all went well—build a hydrogen engine. The airscouters ran on solar power, except for liftoff and rapid acceleration, which required combustible fuel. The same went for the shuttle and the ship. A reliable fuel would allow them to fly the first colonist's shuttle back to the *Remus* to transport the rest of their gear—including the remaining photovoltaic cells—to the surface. Until they had more power, they lacked an adequate defense against aerial attack.

As it turned out, they didn't have that much time.

Within a span of ten days, the winged creatures attacked twice more, always in the middle of the night. The first time, two chickens and a turkey were carried off. The colonists increased their night guards from one to two, with one person positioned at the barn door and the other in the tower. But the winged animals' dark color camouflaged them, blending with the night sky.

In the second attack, a flying creature landed silent and unseen on the barn's roof. Beau's barking alerted the guard at the barn, who fired at the creature, grazing it with *yridium* beam and sending it away. The third time, a half dozen creatures attacked—too many for that night's guards—Ensign Rabin and Reilly's mother—to fend off.

When the alarm sounded, Reilly tore outside, heedless of his father's orders to the contrary. The night reverberated with the sounds of people shouting, goats screaming, fowl shrieking. About ten meters overhead, six animals flew, all of them facing the northwest. They each had four legs, two wings, the inside edge of which was scalloped. And tails, Reilly now saw. One creature lagged behind, clutching a writhing, yelping Beau in its forelegs. The light of one moon caught the white fur on the dog's belly.

Reilly closed his eyes and clapped his hands over his ears, but the horrible noises penetrated and he couldn't take his eyes off the scene. Where was his mother?

Thin red beams of *yridium* slashed the sky. Reilly saw his mother crouched near the barn, firing. One shot connected and the creature let out a horrible yowl but did not drop the dog. Another animal roared. It was not a single rumble, but an angry torrent of noises. This second animal circled back and bore down on the humans. Reilly could see its head, which formed a large triangle with two smaller triangles at the top that must be ears. It opened its horrible mouth, releasing a plume of fire. Someone screamed. A *yridium* beam leapt from the top of the guard tower, where Ensign Rabin stood, bracing his gun arm atop a beam of wood. Again it roared, but this time it retreated. All six creatures formed themselves into a diamond and moved westward. Beau's yips became fainter.

Someone moaned. The sound was male and came from the guard tower. Reilly looked up. Ensign Rabin doubled over and Lieutenant Schuler scrambled up the guard tower ladder toward him. Reilly turned and zigzagged through the dazed-looking crew, looking for his mother.

"Mom?" he called. "Mom!"

"Over here, Reilly."

She was standing a few meters away; scanning the sky, moonlight silvering the tracks of her tears. Reilly hugged her hard, and her face wetted his cheek. He felt her trembling. "Beau," she said. "I couldn't save him, Reilly."

"It's okay, Mom," Reilly said, blinking away tears.

Tally tore from the kids' dorm into the yard, screaming, "Beau! Beau!" After a pause, she howled, "Noooo!"

She ran to Captain Baca who stood, watching the animals disappear into the western sky. Tally snatched his gun from his hand and raised it.

"Tally!" the captain shouted.

"I want to shoot them," she sobbed.

"They're out of range," the captain said, gently removing the gun from her hand.

Tab punched the air. "Go after them with the airscouters!" he exhorted. "Do something!"

Ensign Morten stood beside Tab. "I'd like to, champ," he said. "But it's too late and too risky. And we don't know how many others there are."

Keid appeared. He was crying, his face blanched and his lips twisted. He made no sound, save for an intermittent ragged inhalation. Reilly's father came up to him and spoke in a low voice. Keid nodded mutely and allowed himself to be led back to the dorm. Reilly's father called to Tally to join them, but she shook her head and followed Lieutenant Schuler into the barn.

The good news was no other animals had been taken. Captain Baca ordered everyone to the mess hall for a briefing. Inside, everyone sat except the captain, Reilly's mother, and Ensign Rabin. Reilly felt light headed, and gulped air to clear his mind. In his head, he could still hear Beau's barks. He covered his ears, but the sound increased.

His father put a hand on his knee. Keid sat hunched on the other side of him.

"I'm okay," Reilly said, and his father removed his hand.

"What the hell happened to your hands, Oren?" Ensign Morten asked.

Ensign Rabin pulled his hands to his chest, holding the palms up, fingers curled, as though he were cupping water.

"And your scalp? It looks burned," Lieutenant Schuler said.

Ensign Rabin gingerly touched the area on the back of his head where his hair had been singed away. The remaining tufts stood out from his head like solar flares. The backs of his hands were red and blistered. There were holes in the blackened fabric of his jacket cuffs and his gloves, which lay on the table in front of him.

Lieutenant Schuler went to the tall medicine cabinet, which stood in one corner of the mess room. There was a door on top and another below. The top door to the pharmaceuticals was locked, and only the adults knew the code to open it. Behind the bottom door, which was always unlocked, were the first-aid supplies. The lieutenant knelt and pulled out bandages and ointments. He also took a drug patch from the top cabinet.

"Have a seat, Oren," the lieutenant said.

Ensign Rabin looked at the captain, who nodded, then sat and allowed Lieutenant Schuler to apply the patch, which Reilly figured contained Anaral, to his inner arm and dress the wounds.

Captain Baca looked at Reilly's mother and said, "Brief us, please."

In a frayed voice, she said, "Oren was in the guard tower. I was stationed just outside the main barracks. I thought I heard voices over near the barn."

"Voices?" Commander Shen asked.

"Yes. They were more guttural, lower pitched than human voices."

"Anika, why do you say voices, and not animal sounds?" asked the captain.

"They seemed to have a cadence," Reilly's mother said. "There was a give and take. Like a conversation."

"But you couldn't understand what was being said," the captain said.

"No."

Captain Baca nodded, "Continue."

"I approached the barn, but didn't see anything. The sounds came from the west. I looked up, and there they were. Six large animals flying toward me. I radioed Oren in the guard tower. The animals hovered over the barn."

"What did you see, Oren?" the captain asked.

Ensign Rabin spoke up. "The same thing Anika saw. A half dozen winged, four-legged animals." He flinched as Lieutenant Schuler took up a pair of scissors and began clipping away hair at the margins of the ensign's burned scalp.

Commander Shen nodded. "That's what I saw—the night of the first attack. They were big as horses."

Lieutenant Schuler tore open a silver packet, squeezed gel from it, and applied to Ensign Rabin's scalp. The ensign shut his eyes a moment.

"But the head wasn't at all equine," Reilly's mother added, her voice oddly mechanical. "It was more feline. The wingspan was huge. At least six meters. The inside edge was scalloped like a bat's. But, unlike members of Earth's Chiropteran, this animal has four free limbs that function independently of the wings."

"What do you mean?" the captain asked.

"I mean they must have six limbs—two of which contribute to the wings. The scapulae must allow for articulation in two places... Anyway, I can't tell you more about the anatomy without seeing them at closer range."

"Cat-bats," Ensign Morten said. "So what did you two do?"

Ensign Rabin took up the story. "I readied my LD50. One of the creatures began calling in a low voice. Beau tore out the dog door, barking. I fired. The beam hit the creature's hind end. It shrieked and dove behind the barn.

The other five animals rose and scattered. I got in a couple shots, but didn't do more than graze one of the animals. They flew out of range so quickly."

Ensign Morten shook his head, as though to express frustration at this missed opportunity, as though to say he would have brought down the whole lot.

"And what about the animal you hit?" the captain asked.

Reilly's mother spoke up. "I saw it. It landed on all its hind legs. Turned its head and licked the wound. Then it crept to the barn door and opened it."

"How?"

"It was hard to see, even with the night goggles. But it seems to have long digits on the forelimbs."

"So these animals really can open doors," Lieutenant Schuler said in awe. "They must have an opposable digit and the brains to think through such an operation."

"Apparently so," Reilly's mother said. She rubbed her eyes.

"What happened?" Ensign Morten said. "The suspense is killing me."

"I fired my gun, connecting with a shoulder. The animal crouched and sprang into the air, beating its wings. I thought it was flying away. But then, it growled and wheeled toward me." Reilly's mother took a breath.

"Then what?" Nova called.

"Beau ran over, barking," Reilly's mother continued. "I had ducked behind the water trough. As the creature came toward me, Beau leapt at it. The animal snatched Beau with its forepaws—" She stopped, pressed her lips together. Locks of blond hair had escaped her ponytail and limply framed her exhausted face.

"What happened next?" Ensign Morten prompted.

Reilly wanted him to stop badgering his mother.

Ensign Rabin rose and stood beside her. He looked even worse for wear, with his bloodshot eyes, bandaged hands, and singed hair. "That creature rose into the air," he said. "The other five animals had reassembled above the base. I was firing with the LD50. One must have gotten behind me. Suddenly, there were flames—around my head. I batted off my hat, tried to keep firing."

"Where did the fire come from?" Commander Shen asked.

Reilly's mother cleared her throat. "The animal's mouth."

Astonished murmurs followed.

"Holy shit," Ensign Morten said. "Not cat-bats. Cat-dragons."

"Major rad," Tab said.

"I hate them!" Tally said. "We should have boarded up the dog door after Xena died."

"The dogs' job was to guard the other animals," Lieutenant Schuler said. Sadness shadowed the hollows of his craggy face.

"Well, now we don't have any dogs," Nova said dolefully.

Tally began crying again. Nova, who sat beside her, stroked her hair.

Discussions continued for another half hour. Reilly's adrenaline had ebbed, leaving him exhausted and yearning for his bed. Later, when he was back in his barracks, he couldn't sleep. He kept seeing the flying creatures, the flames, Beau's twisting shape. He heard muffling weeping from the kids' dorm. Tally. In the distance, a lone bird made a burbling sound, heralding the approaching dawn.

Reilly tried to think about pleasant things—Cosmic purring on his chest, soft black fur under his fingertips. He listened for his parents' breathing, but he couldn't make it out. One of them turned restlessly, rustling the sleeping sac's shell. His father whispered something. Reilly almost asked him to play his flute, but it was so late and his father was probably exhausted. He remembered how, in the midst of the Dagnar virus epidemic, he had believed that, once they got to Cinnabar, everything would be fine, better, maybe even wonderful. But if this life was an improvement, he couldn't imagine what worse looked like.

∞

"Catdragons," Maia said with a sage nod, as though she knew all about them.

It was a few hours later. Everyone was eating a late breakfast in the mess hall. The collective mood was tense. People sat in groups, rehashing the event, discussing defense, planning new ways to protect the animals. Reilly was standing in line, waiting to wash his bowl. He hadn't realized Maia stood next to him till she spoke.

"What did you say?" Reilly said, turning to look at her.

Maia held her bowl in her palm. It looked as though she'd licked it clean. Maia and her clothing, on the other hand, looked grubby. Orange dirt clung to her clothes, dusted her hair, lodged under her nails.

"Catdragons," she said. "It's a good name for creatures that look like huge, winged cats and breathe fire."

"I know what they look like," he said. When Maia stiffened, as though he had sounded like some know-it-all, he added, "I mean...I saw one our first night."

"Me too," she said. "In the middle of the night, before we had to have a guard chaperone us, I went out to the latrine and one flew over me." Her voice was calm, matter-of-fact.

"What happened?" He worked the water pump and, while a cool violet-tinged stream ran from the tap, rinsed his bowl.

She shrugged. "I went into the latrine to pee, and when I came out, it was gone."

"Oh." Reilly paused, then pumping water for Maia. "How do you know about dragons?" He had read about these mythical creatures in one of his grandmother's books. But the vitros weren't exposed to fiction, aside from videos. Their computer texts dealt mainly with math, science, and technology. The computer databases stored literature classics and some genre fiction, mainly mysteries.

Maia silently scrubbed her bowl.

Normally, Reilly would have accused her of unauthorized book borrowing. But he didn't want to send her huffily away. "Did the animal seem aggressive or anything? Did it swoop at you? Breathe fire?"

Maia shook her head. She glanced over her shoulder. Ensign Morten was behind her, picking at his weird front teeth with the end of his spork. Behind him stood Tad and Nash. Nash had turned to shout something at Nova. Tad's gray eyes watched Maia and Reilly.

Maia looked at Reilly and jerked her head toward the door. She left and Reilly followed a bit hesitantly. Outside, it was already hot. Maia led them to a panel of shade behind the mess hall.

"I didn't want to talk about it in front of the others," she said.

"Why?" Reilly said.

"I don't know." Maia frowned. "I think I wanted to keep the experience for me. Hard to explain."

"I think I understand."

She looked him in the eye, as though reading him. Unnerved, Reilly finally looked away.

"Anyway," she said, "it flew pretty close. It could have harmed me, if it wanted. I mean…I wasn't carrying a gun or anything. But it seemed—I don't know—friendly. You probably think that's naïve." She narrowed her eyes and lifted her chin as though anticipating ridicule.

Reilly, however, had no intention of teasing her. Besides, he knew she'd punch him if he did. "Something like that happened to me our first night on Cinnabar."

"So you said."

"I mean…I had the same feeling about the creature being benevolent."

Her face relaxed. "Really?"

"Yeah."

"But then, last night—well, those catdragons clearly weren't here to welcome us to the planet."

"I know."

"And what about the fire? How do they do it? Why doesn't it burn their mouths? How do they ignite the flame?"

Reilly shook his head. "No idea. It seems cliché. The fire-breathing dragon."

"Tell that to them."

Reilly laughed. He'd never felt so relaxed around one of the vitros.

"So, Reilly, why did the creature you and I saw seem benign? Did we encounter the same animal? Why are the others so brutal?"

The stream of questions reminded Reilly that Maia normally annoyed him.

"Carrying off our animals," she said indignantly. "Why'd they do that? Did they attack out of hunger? It's not like there isn't native prey."

Reilly shrugged. He suddenly felt tired and hot.

"Poor Beau. I loved the dogs. But not the way Tally did. When they were pups, she would wake up during the night to feed them formula. She won't get over this loss easily."

"I know," Reilly said. "Maybe the natives want to get rid of us."

"Do you think they're that sophisticated? Neurologically speaking, I mean. Can they intend good and evil—"

"Maia." Reilly held up his hands. "How would I know?" *Neurologically?* How far had she gotten into her medical studies? Clearly, he hadn't given her enough credit.

"Don't you wonder too?"

"Of course. But you're asking too many questions."

"They're good questions."

"You're—overwhelming."

Maia sighed. "And here I thought you were making progress. Just forget it. I don't know why I bother talking to you." She turned to go.

Reilly blinked. "Sorry—"

"Is that sweet," Tab called, his voice pitched high. "Reilly's started mixing it up with the test-tubers."

"Fuck off," Maia said and hurried past Tab. "Both of you."

"I could report you for swearing," Tab said.

"Feel free," she said over her shoulder.

His back to the sun, Tab stopped uncomfortably close to Reilly. Reilly fought an urge to step back.

"Did you enjoy last night's skirmish?"

"No," Reilly said, squinting against the glare. "Why? Did you?"

Tab frowned. His sungoggles had left white rings around his eyes. He didn't tan as readily as the other vitros. His nose was peeling. "No. But now we know what we're up against."

"What do you mean?" Reilly said.

"Now we know that these catbats mean war. We have to go after them."

"Go after them?"

"Yeah. You know, make a preemptive strike."

"Sorry, Tab, but the creatures already preempted that strategy."

Tab rolled his eyes, as though Reilly were the one who had said something stupid. "Whatever. So we retaliate." he said. "Before they hit us again. That's what Harlan was talking about at breakfast."

"Is the captain in agreement?"

"Not yet."

"Well," Reilly said. "I wouldn't get your hopes up, Tab. Good talking to you. But I have work to do."

Tab grinned. "See you around, Reilly."

∞

Ensign Rabin wasn't the same after that attack. His sense of humor, which had started off strong then dwindled over the long voyage, now evaporated. He developed nervous tics. His hands were never still. They tugged at the beard he had recently grown, plucked at the bandages on his hands, and patted the bald, reddened spot on his scalp. His dark, curly hair appeared to have been cut in a friar's tonsure. The skin under his eyes looked bruised and puffy. When outdoors, he glanced skyward every few seconds and startled at noises.

And it wasn't just Ensign Rabin who was on edge; everyone was nervy and short-tempered. Arguments erupted over petty things. Adults berated kids for even minor offenses—neglecting to put away the gardening rake or forgetting to switch off a telsar torch.

In meetings and smaller gatherings, the crew endlessly discussed the threat of repeat attacks from the winged creatures and hashed out strategies for defense. Lieutenant Schuler and Tally compulsively monitored the health of the surviving livestock: four chickens, five turkeys, and three goats. Everyone fretted about losing so many animals. They needed the foul for meat and eggs. The goats were not just a source of fur and milk, but the milk's genetically engineered proteins could be spun into textiles and made into medicines.

The dogs' chief functions were to defend the other animals and, later on, to help with hunting the native animals. But they also provided companionship. Everyone—especially Lieutenant Schuler and Tally—missed them. Lieutenant

Schuler mourned in a stoical quiet way. Tally made no attempt to hide her grief. She cried easily, awoke screaming from nightmares (Reilly could hear her from his barracks), and picked at her food. Reilly's mother said if the girl didn't start eating soon, they might have to sedate her and put in a feeding tube. Fortunately, it didn't come to that. Maia began letting Tally sleep in her bunk, which had helped chase away the nightmares. The bunks were so narrow; Reilly couldn't imagine two people, even two skinny girls, fitting.

"What a big heart that girl has," his mother said.

Reilly added, "And a big mouth too." He immediately regretted the comment, because of his mother's disapproving look, because he knew she was right, and because he worried that perhaps his heart, or whatever body part governed empathy, was, by comparison, cramped.

At one meeting, Lieutenant Schuler suggested bringing the remaining animals into the barracks at night, but Commander Shen questioned whether that wouldn't further endanger the humans. Until they came up with a better plan, they fortified all entrances and locked the animals in at night.

More than once, Reilly wondered why the catdragons hadn't carried off any humans. Granted, the animals were smaller and therefore easier to carry off, but the catdragons looked big enough to hoist a human into the air. Ensign Rabin weakly joked that maybe the animals smelled more appetizing.

These days, the humans stank. On the ship they misted themselves with a solution containing a bacteria that metabolized ammonia in the skin, reducing odor. And once a week, people stepped into an ultrasonic booth for additional cleansing. Now, they took weekly showers under a solar tank Ensign Rabin had set up.

Reilly wondered whether the catdragons simply hadn't gotten around to abducting humans. Maybe they wanted to instill as much terror in them as possible first. Or maybe they had other means of getting rid of the colonists.

He visualized the first colonists' camp. No sign of domestic animals other than feathers and excrement and a few bones. The colonists lying dead in their cots, as though they'd fallen asleep and never awakened. Clearly the catdragons hadn't killed the humans. Not directly.

NINE

During an evening meeting the following week, Reilly's parents asked permission to go on a scouting mission. "Prospecting for fuel," was what Reilly's father called it. Analyses of the ashes in the fire pit never did pin down the substance the first colonists had been burning. His father wanted to bore into the mesa's rocky cliffs for samples.

With sidelong glance at Reilly, Captain Baca thanked Reilly's parents for their offer, but said it wasn't a good idea for them both to go. Reilly let out the breath he'd been holding. The thought of them venturing away from the relative safety of the base terrified him.

In the distance, an animal made a sound between a bark and a laugh. Another answered, then another.

"How 'bout I go with Anika?" Ensign Morten said, flashing a grin at Reilly's mother.

Sitting beside his parents, Reilly felt his father stiffen. Reilly liked the idea. The ensign, the best marksman of them all, would protect Reilly's mother, and his father could stay with Reilly.

With a cool glance at Ensign Morten, Reilly's mother stood, faced the captain, and said, "Skyler and I make the ideal team for this mission."

Reilly knew what she was getting at. His mom was the ecology expert; his dad had the geophysics and biochemistry training. They would be the best duo to search for and analyze the planet's raw materials.

The captain opened his mouth to speak, but Reilly's father rose, stood beside his wife, and said, "The rest of the adult crew, particularly Ensign Morten, have assignments that make the departure from camp more difficult."

The ensign had permanently taken the post of night watchman—a schedule that suited his increasingly nocturnal tendencies and his craving for vengeance.

Outside, a gust of wind riffled the domed walls of the mess hall. The telsar lights, which now ran off the solar chips in the textile roof, wavered. Shadows danced on his parents' faces.

"The solar batteries have already run low," Commander Shen said with a sigh. "I think we ran too many electronic devices this evening.

Reilly's father chuckled. "Thus emphasizing our need for a power source."

"Captain Baca," Reilly's mother said, "we'll only be gone three days, max. Plus, we'll wear tracking buttons and keep in radio contact."

It struck Reilly how handsome his parents looked standing together. The sun had given their skin some color and made his mother's hair even blonder. His father had let his brown hair grow out a bit, which suited him.

"Uh huh," Ensign Morten drawled. He tipped back in his chair and laced his fingers behind his head. "Let's say we get a distress call from you and pinpoint your location. But you're so far away, we can't get there in time—"

Ensign Rabin interrupted. "Even if they were a few meters away, we might not be able to get there in time." With a reddened and peeling hand, he rubbed the shiny pink patch on the back of head where stubbly hairs were finally springing up.

"Ensign Rabin is right," Reilly said. "Being in radio contact wouldn't be much protection against a catdragon attack." He recalled the way the creatures soared silently through the night, invisible unless backlit by the moons.

Reilly's mother glanced at Reilly, then said, "The flying creatures are clearly nocturnal. We'll sleep in the scouter."

"Yeah," Tab said. "Bring a piss bottle. A person can die just going to the latrine at night."

A couple of the kids snickered. Tab, aware he'd been unwittingly funny, grinned.

The lights flickered out completely. Moonlight shafted through the mess hall's one window, illuminating Captain Baca's tanned hands, which were clasped together on the table top, laced fingers kneading the knuckles of the opposite hand. He cleared his throat and said, "All right, Anika and Skyler. Permission granted. Don't make me regret this decision."

∞

Reilly's parents left early the next morning. When Reilly walked outside to see them off, the sun hadn't yet pushed above the horizon, hadn't yet banished the night's chill. Feeble predawn light illuminated the mesa and its satellite of rock formations. To the west, the blue moon had already set and the marbled red one squatted along the flat line of desert.

While Ensign Morten checked the scouter's engine, Reilly helped his parents load their gear into the small cargo hold of the airscouter. They had food for four days, water bottles, a water purifier, a small backpack for the specimen bags and tools, a duffel containing a change of clothes and two sleeping sacs, and a first aid kit.

"Bring you back a souvenir," said his mother. Her artificial gaiety only heightened Reilly's apprehension.

"I wish I could go with you," Reilly said miserably.

His father ruffled his hair. He reached into the duffel and pulled out the rectangular black box that contained his flute. "I think I'll leave Lola with you," he said.

Lola was the name his father had given his flute. He played almost daily and knew tunes from every era and from all parts of the Earth. Except for the periods when his father was hibernating, Reilly had drifted to sleep nearly every night to the strains of flute music.

The instrument had been handed down through generations of Landreths. Why would his father give it to him, unless he thought he might not return?

"But you play it every day," Reilly protested.

"There isn't enough room," his father said. "Besides, how can you practice if I take it?"

Reilly almost said he probably wouldn't practice anyway, not without someone to bug him, but his father looked oddly vulnerable. Reilly mumbled,

"Okay," and the case passed from his father's hands to his, which Reilly noticed were now not only the same shape as his but the same size.

Three large, gray birds appeared in the sky overhead and began circling. The skin at Reilly's nape tightened at the sight of the hooked orange beaks.

Reilly's mother frisked her arms. "They remind me of vultures."

Ensign Morten slammed shut the engine hood, which elicited a grating squawk from one of the birds. "Yeah, they act like vultures too. A couple days ago, I saw one disemboweling something. The dead animal had hooves."

"An ungulate," Reilly's mother mused. "Maybe we'll see more on our trip."

Reilly waved his arms and yelled, "Go away!"

One of the birds responded with a belligerent shriek.

"Carrion eaters serve a purpose, Reilly," his father said. "Remember what happened on Earth after the vultures disappeared?"

"Yeah, yeah," Reilly said. "Infectious organisms thrived on the carcasses and people got sick and died. Doesn't make me like these ugly birds any better."

The scaly avian trio flapped to a cluster of low boulders on the other side of the fence and hunkered there. Three cyclopean eyes watched the humans.

Captain Baca emerged from the mess hall. "I just checked the monitor," he said. "Your tracking buttons are working fine."

"See?" Reilly's mother said, smiling too brightly. "You'll know where we are every minute."

Ensign Morten stood, wiped his hands on his dirty pants, and said, "The *Kestrel's* all ready for you."

"Thanks, Harlan. Well," Reilly's father said heartily, "time to go." He clapped Reilly on the shoulder, stepped onto the airscouter's wing, and climbed into the copilot's seat.

His mother hugged Reilly and took the pilot's seat. The clear dome slid shut.

Don't go, don't go, don't go, Reilly thought. His mother lifted her hand to her mouth and blew him a kiss.

"Ooooh, isn't that sweet?" a voice jeered.

Tab stood just outside the kids' dorm, arms over chest, pimpled chin thrust forward. Maia pushed out the door, stood behind Tab, her expression inscrutable.

Reilly started to tell Tab to piss off, but Captain Baca, who had been standing close by, said in a low voice, "Let it go, Reilly. He's just trying to get a rise out of you."

The airscouter's engine whirred on, and the silver craft lifted straight up. Reilly's father looked down and waved. The scouter swiveled and accelerated toward the sun, now a red ball on the horizon. The light bleached Reilly's vision. He blinked and the silver craft disappeared around a camel-shaped rock.

∞

Reilly tackled the day's chores with zeal, as though ceaseless activity might blot out the anxiety he felt about his parents. His assignment was helping Commander Shen work on the generator.

As the sun neared its merciless zenith, Reilly twisted the wrench so hard that the head of the screw he was tightening sheered off.

"Take it easy, Reilly," the commander said. She mopped her brow with a dusty sleeve. "Time for a break?"

"I'm fine," he insisted. He almost pointed out that she had smeared dirt across her forehead. But why bother? Everything they owned was now filthy. A shower granted about five minutes of cleanliness before the orange dust settled. With a sigh, he fished in a box for another screw.

The day dragged on, interrupted by a lunch of Sustabars and baby greens, which had managed to grow under a shade cloth. Finally, the sun sank back toward the horizon and the dinner bell sounded. During the meal, the radio cracked and his mother's voice issued from the speaker, *"Kestrel* to base. *Kestrel* to base. Come in. Over." Reilly leapt from the bench, knocking the table, and sloshing water from cups. Humiliatingly, his voice cracked with emotion as he spoke into the microphone. "Mom? Dad? How are you? Where are you?"

His parents swore they were doing well. They had set up camp atop the mesa, in a small depression about 50 kilometers due west of the base. Captain Baca strode to the radio and turned up the speaker volume.

Conversation in the mess hall stopped. Reilly turned and realized everyone was listening to the radio.

"Anything noteworthy to report?" the captain asked.

"In terms of the geology, yes," Reilly's mother said. "The cliff face of the mesa makes it easy to examine the various rock strata."

"Easy for you to say," his father interrupted. "You hover the scouter while I hang out into space and take samples."

"Your arms are longer." His mother laughed.

"Anyway," his father said, "we've found a layer roughly ten meters above the desert floor that contains about seventy percent carbonaceous material."

"Which suggests this area was once more dense with vegetation."

"If that's true, this strata—"

"—which is a deep purple—"

"—might burn like coal. It could be what the first colonists had been burning."

"And who knows?" his mother said. "If there's coal, and coal comes from compressed plants, maybe animals have been compressed in deeper layers to form— What, Reilly?"

"Oil!" he said, feeling instantly like an overeager student.

Behind Reilly, Tab muttered something unintelligible, his tone derisive.

"But what if this rock is toxic?" Reilly said.

"The ashes in the first colonists' fire pit were clean," his mother said. "And I've sealed the sample in a specimen bag. I'll test it when we get back."

"Have you seen any new animal species?" the captain asked.

"Yes," his mother said excitedly. "A half dozen two-toed ungulates atop the mesa fifteen kilometers northwest of the base. They're larger than North American mountain goats but about half the size of the three-toed behemoths that have been thundering past the base at night."

Ensign Morten had bounded up, his mouth full of food. "That's what I was telling you about this morning. That's what I saw the vultures working over."

"I figured as much," Reilly's mother said.

"What do they look like?" Tally was now crowding the radio.

"Hello, Tally," Reilly's mother said. "Is Lieutenant Schuler within earshot too?"

"*Ja,*" called the lieutenant. He slid his long legs free of the bench and approached the radio.

"Good. So get this. Whereas most of the mammals we've seen have scales, these ungulates have silvery fur."

Ensign Morten nodded. "Those pelts will come in handy."

"That's not all," Reilly's mother continued. "Between the two black horns atop their heads they have a third eye."

"Fascinating," Lieutenant Schuler said. "Makes sense, when you consider that at least one of their predators flies."

Reilly's father said, "Also there are simian creatures by the creek, about ten kilometers north of our base. I don't know why we haven't seen them before. They're far from secretive."

"Right," Reilly's mother said in a delighted voice. "When we flew past, they hung from branches by their tails—they have two—and tried to hit the scouter with some sort of seed pod."

A couple of the vitros laughed and exclaimed, using words like, "Minjin,' preme, and major rad, and astral."

"We also flew over some of those canine creatures we've seen before," Reilly's father said. "I saw one leap to the top of a three-meter tall boulder."

"What about the flying creatures, the catdragons?" Maia, who had silently come to stand beside Reilly, asked.

"Hello, Maia," Reilly's mother said. "No sign of them, thank goodness,"

"Well," his father said, "that's it for now. We've eaten and are safely ensconced in the scouter, though I'm not optimistic about sleeping much in this position."

"Don't worry about us, Reilly," his mother said. "I love you all."

Reilly turned down the volume.

"Love you," his dad echoed.

Tally giggled, but stopped when Reilly glared at her. Straight faced, Maia looked away. The rest of the vitros remained at their table, vibrating with poorly contained laughter—except for Keid, who looked forlorn.

He wanted to answer, "Yeah, me too." But he was embarrassed and, besides, the radio had gone silent.

∞

Once the meal was over, Reilly went straight to his barracks in hope that sleep would make time pass more quickly. His futon felt uncomfortably hard, as though over-inflated. His nerve endings were on hyper-alert, jangling at the slightest sensation. His mouth still tasted of dinner—texturized protein and rice, the whole thing loaded with powdered garlic, which Lieutenant Schuler swore protected you from all manner of microbe, even the as-yet-unidentified species on Cinnabar. Light from the two moons glared through the window, and even when he put his mother's pillow over his head to block the light, he could feel the cold glow. His mother's scent made him long for her.

Sounds seemed exaggerated. Each time he rolled over, the material of his sleeping sac crinkled. His breathing sounded weirdly loud. Some distance away, an animal howled. Another answered. A chorus of them yipped. The large canines. He pictured them bounding up rocks, tongues lolling, fangs listening. He thought of Beau and Xena —their soft fur, trusting eyes, laughing mouths, wagging tails. A sob rose from his lungs and caught painfully in his throat. Outside, a harsh call—low and grating, like two boulders grinding together—silenced the yips.

He wished he were back on the ship in the relative comfort and safety of his pre-meteor-strike chambers. When he left the door ajar, he could hear his parents' nighttime breathing. The regularity their breathing had reassured him on Cinnabar, too. Now he regretted ever teasing one or the other parent for occasionally snoring.

He curled on his side, slid his mother's pillow under his head and clamped his father's pillow over his ear. Enveloped in their familiar smells, he finally fell asleep.

Some time later, he awoke to a howling that sounded like no animal he knew. He sat, pillow clutched to his chest. His barracks' walls rippled. He wanted to cry out, but his heart was in the way, ballooned to twice its usual size and thumping the breath right out of him. With a groan, the entire structure slid a half-meter. The stakes must have worked loose. Overhead, the airbeams flexed, and the fabric covering them flapped.

He looked for his parents, then remembered he was alone. He got to his feet, stumbled to the door, began to unzip the flap, then froze. The wind shrieked through the opening, blasting sand into his face. Eyes tearing, he yanked the zipper shut and wiped his face with his shirt. No sandstorm had struck at night before.

Above, the airbeams undulated like tentacles. The barracks slid forward again—a whole meter this time. The wind jacked up the back end of the dome-like structure. The telsar lamp hanging from the roof beam swung crazily. He burrowed inside his sleeping sac, and closed his eyes. Nothing to do but wait out the storm.

He thought of his parents. He hoped they had parked the airscouter in a sheltered spot. Reilly remembered when the shuttle landed in such a storm, the air so full of sand you couldn't see out the portholes. Ensign Morten had said *the sand flying around out there would take the skin right off your face.* Reilly buried his face in the pillow and thought, *please be in the scouter. Please come back to me.*

A thumping noise overhead made him peer out of his sleeping sac. The airbeams writhed. The wind shrieked. The barracks skittered sideways. He leapt onto his parents' futon and pulled his own atop him. He waited, listened to his breathing, smelled his own acrid sweat, felt his bladder fill, felt the foam that covered the inflatable futons press against him. Finally, after what seemed like an hour, the wind dwindled to a low moan, then nothing. Everything went still.

He crawled out from between the futons, drenched in sweat. Early morning light shafted hazily through the grit-scoured window. Orange sand layered everything. Fortunately, the stuff no longer irritated his skin, unless it got into his underpants. He dusted himself off, shook his pant legs, blew orange snot from his nose. To exit the barracks, he had to step over a half meter of sand piled against the entrance.

To the south, a huge dust cloud swept away from the base toward the deeper reaches of the desert. The base looked awry. The outhouse had tilted. Someone's shirt and a few uprooted bean plants now twined the electric fence.

His barracks had also blown up against the electric perimeter fence. Did BioFuerte conduct electricity? Unsure of the answer, he stepped a few meters away the barracks. The point of one of the useless stakes had apparently lacerated the outer layer of the textile wall. The weathervane had moved a full ninety degrees such that the cat's forepaw pointed north. He remembered his father saying, "It'll take a gale to move that thing," and he wished he were here to see it, here to crack a joke about the situation, to emphasize that the event was now in the past, to celebrate their survival. Had they survived?

Other people ventured out of the buildings, some of which had shifted, but none of which had migrated as Reilly's had. The animals were sounding off. Half the corral had blown down, and the barn door yawned open. A goat wandered the yard, bleating forlornly.

"Hey, Reilly!"

Reilly turned and Maia raised a shovel. She was dressed in a filthy skirt— one of Nova's creations made from scrap material—including what appeared to be a man's undershirt. Reilly felt he'd been alone for ages. For the first time, he was glad to see her. He raised his hand in greeting.

"You traveled," she called, her demeanor unaccountably cheerful. "Pretty incredible, huh?"

"Yeah," he said. He almost crossed the short distance to her, but his thoughts went back to his parents. "You okay?" he called.

"Never better," she returned. If there was a note of sarcasm, Reilly missed it. She went back to shoveling sand away from the door to the kids' barracks.

Reilly hurried to the three airscouters. Usually parked in a straight line, they were now slightly askew. The wind had not flipped any of them, which Reilly took as a good omen. Maybe the weight of two humans had further stabilized the *Kestrel*.

Captain Baca called his name. He was standing outside the mess hall. Reilly walked over to him.

"Are you all right?" the captain asked. Stubble shadowed his jaw. His short brown hair lay flat on one side of his skull and bristled on the other.

"Yes, sir," Reilly said. "Do you think my parents are okay? I'd like to radio them."

Captain Baca nodded. "I was just waiting for you."

The captain wore a small disc-shaped radio clipped to his collar, but it wasn't nearly as powerful as the main radio inside the mess hall. He kicked aside the drift of sand piled in front of the door, unzipped the fabric, and pushed through.

They sliced through the dusty air to the small table that held the tracking screen and the radio. The captain swept sand off the computer cover, opened it, and turned the machine on. The monitor sprang to life, displaying a topographic map of the area. A red dot in the center designated the base. Concentric circles extended from the dot; the distance between each represented 10 kilometers.

As the captain zoomed out, two blinking blue dots appeared 45 kilometers to the northwest, at the mesa's edge. Maybe, Reilly thought, the storm would drive them back early. If so, they could arrive within the hour.

The captain spoke into the radio microphone, "Base to *Kestrel*. Base to *Kestrel*. Come in, *Kestrel*. Over."

Reilly's father answered right away. "*Kestrel* to Base. We read you loud and clear."

"Hi, Dad," Reilly said. "Is Mom there too?"

"We're both here," his mother said. "We're in the scouter and were just about to radio. How did you all make out in that dust storm? Are you okay, Reilly?"

"I'm fine," Reilly said, trying to sound nonchalant. *I'm scared,* he thought. *Please come back. When you're here, I'm not afraid.*

"The gale relocated your barracks," the captain said.

"What?" his father said.

On the tracking screen, the blinking lights moved southwest. Reilly's heart jumped. They were heading back to the base.

"The stakes came loose, and the wind pushed the barracks clear to the fence," he said.

"Oh!" his mother said. "Reilly, you shouldn't be in there alone."

You're right. Come back. The two blinking lights now moved north, away from the base. *No,* Reilly thought, *don't leave me alone another night.*

"Yeah," his father added, "not enough ballast."

Reilly tried to play along. "Come back and throw your weight around."

"Don't worry about Reilly," the captain said. "He won't be alone tonight."

"Thanks, Carlos," Reilly's father said.

Reilly cleared his throat. "So, how are you two? Where were you when the storm hit?"

"In the scouter," his dad said.

"Last night, we parked in a canyon," his mother added. "So we were nicely protected."

The radio crackled.

"You're breaking up," the captain said.

"We're flying above the mesa," his mother said. "The radio doesn't seem… here. Not…canyons either."

"…camera… acting up…" his father's voice stuttered. "bring… pictures."

"…beautiful." This last word from his mother was buoyant with awe.

"Bye," Reilly shouted, as though they might hear if he spoke loudly enough. Anger pricked beneath his breastbone. Why? Because his parents sounded like they were having fun? Because they had left him behind? Because they weren't worried enough about him to return ahead of schedule? Yes, yes, and yes. He felt ashamed of his weakness.

The captain scraped back his chair, raised a hand, and smoothed his hair. It was getting thin enough on top to reveal the brown, shiny scalp. The adults were aging before Reilly's eyes, yet he felt childish and vulnerable.

∞

The rest of the morning, Reilly and Commander Shen relocated and repaired Reilly's barracks. Other people worked to right the latrine, clean sand out of the animals' water trough, clean off the solar arrays and the communications system receiver, and sweep out the buildings.

In the afternoon, Reilly worked with Lieutenant Schuler on the high-altitude wind turbine. A lightweight version of BioFuerte covered a frame made of FeatherSteel. Once sprayed with a resin, it would be able to withstand winds up to 180 kilometers per hour—significantly higher than the peak wind velocities in the upper troposphere.

The fumes from the resin combined with the punishing heat made Reilly lightheaded. The edges of objects shimmered. Every time his peripheral vision caught a bird in flight, his heart lifted in the mistaken notion that the *Kestrel* had returned ahead of schedule.

That night, as Reilly slid into bed, his leg brushed something cold and moist, releasing a fetid odor. He bolted upright, unzipped his sleeping sac, and saw a handful of goat turds. There were brown streaks on the liner of his sleeping bag and on one of his legs. *Tab. Fat-necked, pixel-headed, moronic, pimpled, slab of sludge.*

He carried the bag outside, slid out the liner, and shook it. In the vitro's barracks, a light illuminated the dusty window. The silhouette of a head ducked out of view. Then window went black.

Hot with rage, Reilly tossed his sleeping sac inside and strode toward the dorm. He saw himself pushing through the door flap—and doing what? It would be six against one. And even if the other kids didn't rally around Tab, Tab would easily best Reilly. A fistfight was probably what Tab hoped for.

Reilly remembered that, since the catdragon attacks, an adult usually spent the night in the vitro's dorm. That meant fighting wasn't a viable option. Another was to tell the adult on duty what had happened. Tab, or whoever had played this trick, would be punished. Except…later, when no adults were looking, Tab would exact revenge and the other kids would tease him.

There was a faint shushing sound overhead. Reilly's head jerked up in time to see the dark underside of a catdragon. He barreled into his barracks and stood there, clutching his sac and trembling. Something was wrong—and it wasn't just that a catdragon had scared him. It was more like the creature was telling him something.

A moment later, Ensign Morten was at his door. "What the hell were you doing?"

"Uh," Reilly said, "I had to go to the latrine." He sat on his hands to hide their shaking.

The ensign shone his torch on the plastic urinal in the corner. "That's what those are for," he said. "Don't tell me you have to take a crap in the middle of the night."

"No."

The ensign wrinkled his nose, "Smells like you already took one in here."

"No, sir."

Ensign Rabin chuckled. "Guess tonight's beans got to you too."

Reilly smiled weakly.

"Well, if you have to go to the latrine, radio me for an escort."

When the ensign left, Reilly cleaned himself and his liner as best he could with water from his canteen. He thought wistfully of the ultraviolet clothes cleaner on the ship. All you had to do was open the door, toss in the soiled item, shut the door, turn a switch, and wait a couple minutes. In the same manner, a cylindrical version cleansed their bodies.

Reilly went back to bed. A short while later, he heard the door's zipper being worked. Tab? He bolted to his feet, fists in front of him.

Captain Baca pushed through the flap, sleeping sac slung over his shoulder.

"What are you doing up?" the captain said.

"You startled me."

"I told your parents you wouldn't sleep alone."

∞

When he entered the mess hall the next morning, Tab, who was already sitting at the vitro's table shoveling cereal into his mouth, called cheerfully, "How'd you sleep last night, BioBoy?"

Reilly felt the heat rise in his neck and cheeks, but said nothing.

"Yeah, BioBoy," Nash said, "how'd you sleep without mommy and daddy to hold your hand?"

"That's enough, kids," Ensign Rabin chided. His black hair curled over a strip of blue cloth tied across his forehead. Aside from the kindly expression, he looked like a storybook pirate. He went back to scouring a pot with sand.

The grating sound made Reilly want to clap his hands over his ears. Lips pressed together, he scooped himself a bowl of oatmeal and took a seat beside Lieutenant Schuler, who greeted him then returned to silently spooning down breakfast. Reilly appreciated that he didn't have to make small talk.

His father said they were on the far side of the mesa, a location confirmed by the twin blinking dots on the tracking monitor. They would fly back part way today, spend the night, take a few more samples, and return to the base by midday.

Before dinner, Reilly hurried to the mess hall. Ensign Rabin was measuring grain into a pot. Without speaking, Reilly went to check the tracking monitor. The screen was blank. He rebooted the system. Nothing. He tried the radio. Dead. The red light glowed above the on switch, which meant the solar battery hadn't run out.

"What's going on?" he said agitatedly. The vaporous premonition from the previous night condensed to ice in his gut.

Ensign Rabin called, "All the electronics are down. Computer systems. Radio. Radar. Everything."

"Why? What's the matter?"

"Dunno," the ensign said. He glanced at Reilly, then quickly away. "I'll do an analysis later." He poured water into the pot.

"But I can't see where my parents are."

"They're probably on their way. They said they'd be back tomorrow. Give me a hand, would you?"

After dinner, Reilly waited around while Ensign Rabin checked the system. Nothing worked—not the tracking monitor, the communications transmitter, or the receiver. "Solar flare," he muttered.

"What?"

"Electromagnetic surges are common in this solar system. I think a big flare—a coronal mass ejection—on Phoebus scrambled our electronic systems." The ensign's large, bloodshot eyes held Reilly's gaze. "A coronal mass ejection is a—"

"I know, I know," Reilly snapped. "A huge discharge of plasma." He felt furious with Ensign Rabin, as though the malfunctions were his fault. He jabbed at a switch on the small black radio and leaned toward the microphone hole. "Base to *Kestrel,*" he said urgently. "Base to *Kestrel*. Come in. Over."

The speakers stood as silent and impassive as stones.

Reilly tried again.

"I'm sorry, Reilly," the ensign murmured.

"Base to *Kestrel*. Base to *Kestrel*. Base to *Kestrel*."

The ensign laid a meaty palm on Reilly's shoulder. "Give up for now, Reilly."

Reilly threw off his hand. He expected a reprimand, but none came.

"The radio might start working after the electromagnetic radiation abates," the ensign ventured.

"The first colonists' radio never worked again," Reilly said savagely. "My mother said it was totally nonfunctional."

He punched the power button to the tracking monitor, but the screen remained a dull gray. His palms were cold and damp, and his fingers shook.

"Reilly," Ensign Rabin said, "you're going to break the equipment."

"I want to see where they are," Reilly said, his voice high.

Ensign Rabin stared at him.

"I'm sorry," Reilly said, looking away. "Later you'll be able to repair the radio, right? You can fix anything."

The ensign's thick, black eyebrows met in the middle. "Sure," he said.

Reilly pictured the first colonists' skeletons, the long nails and scraggly hair, the ratty creature stirring within a pelvis.

"Something's happened to my parents. We should take an airscouter and go look for them."

The ensign shook his head. "They're okay, Reilly. They'll be back tomorrow morning."

Reilly's lungs filled to bursting with a volatile mixture of fear and frustration. "You're always saying things are okay. Things are definitely not okay. Things have not been okay since we set foot on this hellish planet." He stormed out, hating himself for behaving like a toddler.

TEN

When, by late afternoon of the following day, Reilly's parents had failed to return, Captain Baca sent Commander Shen and Ensign Rabin searching. Their airscouters returned at nightfall. Reilly was waiting outside, his eyes strained from peering through binoculars. A vacuum formed in his chest when he counted only two scouters, but he held to the hope that his parents' were riding copilot. But the copilot's seats of both crafts were empty. The commander and the ensign strode past him, largely ignoring his frantic questions, and cloistered themselves in the men's barracks with the captain.

Reilly waited in his barracks, expecting one of the adults to come speak to him. But the only person to push through the door was Maia.

"Dinner started," she told him. "Why aren't you there?"

"Not hungry," Reilly said.

"They didn't find your parents," Maia said, her gaze direct but not unkind.

Reilly nodded, blinked away tears. A high-pitched whoosh startled him.

"The adults are setting off flares. Maybe your parents will see them. They have flares too."

"I know that."

"Look, I know you're worried."

"You have no idea."

Maia sighed and left. A short while later, she returned with a bowl of brown stew and a canteen of water. Reilly knew he should thank her, but his vocal cords felt petrified. Also, the food's leguminous aroma made him queasy. He just sat on his futon, his back to her, and stared out the window till he heard her stand, sigh, and let herself out. Then he continued to sit.

Hours later, the captain arrived.

"Why are you sitting here in the dark?" he said and switched on the telsar lamp.

Reilly held a hand to his eyes. He felt stiff with sitting, brittle with angst. "Please tell me what Commander Shen and Ensign Rabin found."

"Nothing." The captain sat heavily on the other futon.

"What do you mean?"

Captain Baca lay out his sleeping sac. "They didn't see the *Kestrel*, nor any sign of your parents." He began inflating the inner core of his pillow.

"How far did they go?"

"They paralleled your parents' presumed return flight path."

"Did they check the area around their last campsite?" Reilly thought of his last look at the tracking monitor, pictured the two blinking dots that signified his parents' location near the mesa's far western rim.

"They didn't have time to fly that far."

"They should have kept going—"

"Not after dark, Reilly. I am not going to risk losing any—" The captain pressed his lips together.

"They're not gone," Reilly insisted. "My parents aren't gone."

"Right. Most likely, their scouter broke down as they returned to the base." The captain just sat on the futon, motionless except for the tapping of one forefinger against his thigh.

Reilly stood. "Can I go?"

The captain frowned up at him. In the bluish telsar light, the lines across his brow looked as broad and deep as furrows. "Go where?"

"Out in a scouter. What if their scouter did fail? What if my parents are walking back? What if their scouter crashed and they're hurt?"

"Too dangerous."

"More dangerous for them than for me. I'll bet Ensign Morten would come with me. I'd be safe with him."

"No."

"But—"

"I'll send another pair to scout at first light."

"That's hours from now!" Reilly's lungs felt like sails filled with a howling gale. He pictured sandstorms, imagined he could blow down the barracks, spew red dust from his mouth, blast the skin off Captain Baca's adamant face.

The captain exhaled wearily. "I'm worried too, Reilly. Go to sleep. By the time you wake, someone will be out searching. Or maybe your parents will be back." He said this last without a hint of optimism.

Reilly stepped toward the door. He didn't know where he was going; he just needed to move.

"Lie down, Reilly."

Long used to obeying orders, Reilly lay rigidly on his futon. The captain extinguished the lantern. Reilly promised himself he wouldn't sleep, as to spend even a moment unconscious seemed a betrayal of his parents. He wanted to keep his senses trained so that, if they called out, even from a distance of a kilometer, he would hear them. He wanted to be the first to see them come through the gate, tired but happy to be back.

Once he thought the captain was asleep, he groped for the cool metal of the picture frame on the nearby table and depressed the button that turned on the digital photo display. Nothing happened. Normally, a slide show of family scenes played: his dad teaching a six-year-old Reilly to play the flute, Reilly playing cards with his grandfather, his grandmother beaming from the captain's chair with a newborn Reilly in the crook of her arm, Reilly as a toddler asleep with Cosmic curled between his shoulder blades, Reilly's mother presenting a birthday cake with six candles to Reilly, who sat at the head of a long table with Sara, Phillipe, and the vitros.

Reilly shook the frame, pressed the on button. The screen remained black. Nothing, it seemed, worked. He wanted to hurl the photo display, but feared permanent loss of the images. He collapsed onto the bed and wetted the pillows with silent tears.

∞

When the sun warmed the room, he awoke, his face tight with dried salt. The computers still weren't working, and the radio remained silent.

That didn't stop Reilly from trying to radio his parents hourly. No one knew when the electromagnetic maelstrom would subside, and when it did, he wanted to be sure his parents heard from him. Besides, he didn't know what else to do.

The search for his parents continued all day. The captain refused to let Reilly fly with one of the adults and sent him to work in the barn with Lieutenant Schuler. The lieutenant didn't comment at Reilly's hourly trips to the radio, or the distracted way Reilly fed and cleaned up after the animals. One of the ewes followed Reilly around. At one point, Reilly found himself sitting in on the musty floor, absently petting the ewe, which, in turn, nibbled Reilly's shirt collar. He blinked and the ewe stared at him through her weird slit-like pupils. The lieutenant nodded at Reilly, then returned his attention back to checking chicken nests for eggs. A tom turkey poked his head in the barn door, turned one baleful eye on Reilly, shook its red wattle, and withdrew.

Ensign Morten and Captain Baca had taken the afternoon search. At the whooshing sound of their landing, Reilly stopped raking up animal droppings and tore out of the corral. His palms were damp and his heart knocked against his ribs.

"Did you—?" Reilly began, but the captain shook his head.

Ensign Morten clapped Reilly on the shoulder. "Next time we'll find 'em, Ryeman."

Reilly kept his eyes on the captain, who silently strode to the mess hall and let the door flap shut behind him. Ensign Morten followed. The alarm sounded the two-tone drone that called the adults to a meeting. When Reilly tried to enter, the captain told him to stay out.

Reilly stood in the twilight, heart beating in the fragile bowl of his chest. Despite the fact the temperature had passed into the ideal zone that caused neither sweating nor shivering, he felt chilled.

Maia passed by. Sand stains had mottled her once blue T-shirt with orange. She stopped and turned. "Come inside, Reilly. You know it's not safe out here once the sun goes down."

Reilly nodded stiffly. With one backward glance, Maia disappeared inside the barracks. The sky darkened to the color of a fresh bruise and the heat slipped away. Maia pushed open the door and called to him. Reilly slunk around to the backside of the mess hall.

To the west, a sweep of mauve limned the mesa. Just above that, a scarf of greenish light wavered. Reilly blinked. The green remained. It shimmered, then became more distinct. Reilly rubbed his eyes. The three migraines he'd had since they landed had distorted his vision, but had never caused colorful hallucinations.

He watched the green light ripple, occasionally fractured by a bolt of red. A dot of black specked that electric curtain. The black dot grew larger, became a shallow triangle, grew wings and a long body. Reilly watched transfixed as the catdragon glided closer. Just outside the fence, it hovered, lazily fanning the air with scalloped wings. A long tail snaked behind. Reilly thought he heard it make a noise, but it seemed the noise came from inside rather than outside his head. The sound repeated, whispery with a high-low-high lilting tone. It seemed to him a message. He felt that, if he only concentrated, he would understand, perhaps learn something about his parents.

"Reilly!"

He wheeled.

Ensign Morten sprinted toward him, yelling, "Get down!" He raised his arm, *yridium* gun in hand.

"No!" Reilly said. He craned back to see the catdragon, which had wheeled toward the north.

Ensign Morten fired, but the red beam petered out many meters behind the creature. Reilly felt an odd relief.

The ensign berated him for being outside after sundown, asked him if was stupid or suicidal.

"What's that green light?" Reilly interrupted.

The ensign turned. "Well, I'll be dipped in shit. Wow. I think it's an aurora, a natural light show. On earth, you could see the lights at high latitudes, the aurora borealis in the north, and the aurora australis in the south. I never saw the real thing, only videos."

"What causes it?"

"You should ask Erik. He did some kind of research at the Arctic Circle. Some do-gooder crap like trying to save the last polar bears. Anyway, I think the lights have to do with solar flares."

"How does it work?" Reilly kept his eyes on the light. The movement reminded him of shirts on the clothesline fluttering in the breeze.

"The flares electrically charge the atmosphere. Don't ask me why that creates colors. Ask Erik."

Reilly heard exclamations. Everyone had come outside and was staring at the sky. After a moment, Captain Baca ordered everyone into the mess hall.

Reilly took one more backward look. He wanted to hate the light, which was a reflection of the phenomenon that prevented him from speaking with his parents. But it was too beautiful. It was like hating the sunrise for heralding the midday heat.

∞

On the fifth day following his parents' departure, Reilly was crouched in a sliver of shade, repairing a hole in the side of the barn. While the morning search party was out, Tally saw a bird dive into the water and come up with something in its beak, which it dropped onto a rock. She reported this news to Lieutenant Schuler and together they ran to investigate.

Weighted down with lethargy, Reilly remained at his task, gluing a Bio-Fuerte patch in place. He had already quizzed the lieutenant about the aurora and found out that, yes, they had to do with solar flares, which, yes, could interfere with all kinds of electronic devices.

Minutes later, Tally and Lieutenant Schuler panted back, cradling pieces of slimy, yellow shell and trailing Keid, Nova, Nash, and Tab. The lieutenant explained to the assembled kids that this shell had probably housed a soft invertebrate.

"So it's a mollusk?" Keid asked.

"Seems likely," the lieutenant said. "Though it's hard to know how to categorize the animals on this planet. That will take time. Once we get the lab set up, genetic mapping will tell us a lot."

Reilly thought about his mother. She had planned to help Lieutenant Schuler catalogue the plants and animals. He pressed his knuckles into his sternum to counter the pain deep inside.

"Can you eat it?" Tab wanted to know.

"*Ja*. On Earth, people eat such creatures," Lieutenant Schuler said. He smiled and half closed his eyes. Reilly hadn't seen him smile since the dogs disappeared. "With a sauce made of garlic, lemon, and white wine, they taste delicious."

Nash licked his lips. "How do you catch them?"

The lieutenant shook his head. "On Earth, you usually scrape them off the rocks, to which their shells attach. But we won't put them on the dinner menu— not until we analyze the flesh and rule out toxins." Nova pouted and Lieutenant Schuler added, "And not until we have fully identified all the complex organisms living in the creek."

∞

During that afternoon's work break, the adults were all resting in their barracks—all except Captain Baca and Ensign Rabin, who were out searching for Reilly's parents. Reilly slouched in a folding chair in the shade of his barracks, where a slight breeze made it marginally cooler than inside. He wondered why his parents hadn't sent out a flare or made a fire or done something to show their location. By now, they could have walked back to the base from where their last campsite was.

Unless they couldn't walk. Or couldn't use their hands to make a fire. They could have fallen into a crater atop the mesa. Maybe his parents were now in the bottom of one, bones broken, lips cracked with thirst.

Harsh whispers made him look up. Three of the vitros were sneaking toward the gate. Tab balanced a shovel over his shoulder. Nova's hand dangled a trowel. Nash was trying to balance a plastic bucket atop his head.

Idiots, Reilly thought, they're going to dig along the creek for mollusks. He stood to get their attention. Tab turned and glowered, hands on hips. Reilly thought of the goat turds and the brown streaks that stained his sleeping sac liner, despite several washings. He sank back into his chair.

Nothing moved down by the creek. Even the raucous, long-tailed birds had been stunned to stillness by the heat. Well, Reilly thought, predators didn't really come out until night. Still, he should probably go tell an adult. But he felt so tired and apathetic. Also, he was fed up with being called "squealer" and "goody snipe." Maia had recently called him "sanctimonious prig." Where she had picked up such an insult was a mystery. Her more sophisticated insults stung the most.

So Reilly stayed where he was. Shading his eyes with his palm, he watched Tab open the gate in the fence, watched the three kids slink through the opening. Then they disappeared behind the creek bank.

Reilly closed his eyes. Sometime later, screams startled him awake.

Nova tore into the yard, crying, "Help! Come quick. Nash is hurt."

The adults rushed out of the barracks. Between sobs, Nova told them an animal had dropped out of a tree onto Nash and bit him. She said it had a long and skinny body, yellow head, orange eyes, "millions" of little legs. Lieutenant Schuler grabbed a first aid kit and took off in the direction of the creek. Ensign Morten snatched up a gun and followed. Commander Shen started scolding Nova for leaving the base, but Nova ran, her boots spraying sand, back toward the creek. The commander stared at Reilly.

"What did you see?" she demanded.

Reilly shook his head. "I was asleep. Shouldn't we go help?"

They both looked toward the creek. Lieutenant Shuler was running awkwardly, carrying Nash in his arms. Nash let out a high-pitched shriek. Behind him, Tab walked head down. Nova hooked her arm through his elbow. Ensign Morten came last, dragging what looked like a piece of hose from a rope.

"Come, Reilly," the commander said. "Help me set up the first-aid station in the mess hall."

Within seconds, Commander Shen had opened the medical cabinet and thrust a tray of instruments at Reilly.

"What should I do?"

"Set it on the counter. Clean off a table, then spread out the surgical drape."

Lieutenant Shuler burst through the door, Nash writhing in his arms.

Tally, Keid, and Maia appeared.

"What happened?" Tally asked. Her hair was mussed and she looked sleepy. Her eyes widened. "What's wrong with Nash? What's happened?"

Maia stared at the thing dangling from Ensign Morten's rope. "What is that?"

Reilly tore his eyes from Nash, who bucked and kicked as the lieutenant tried to settle him on the table, to the thing tied to Ensign Morten's rope— not a hose, but a limp serpentine creature about a meter and a half long. He hoisted up the animal, its narrow, head was level with his own and the tail swung back and forth at his knees. The body was striped vertically with yellow, orange, and purple. At least a hundred short legs ran down each side. There was a hole in the flat head, presumably made by the ensign's laser.

Nova, who stood in the corner, looking ashamed and terrified, made a gulping noise.

"Dispose of that, Harlan," Commander Shen said. "Then escort the children back to their dormitory."

Lieutenant Schuler said, "We might need to create antivenin. And I need to examine the animal."

"Okay," the commander said. "Bag and crate it for now."

"Right," the ensign said and left.

∞

The commander pulled on a pair of surgical gloves and jerked her head toward the door. "All you kids, everyone but Maia return to the dorm. Maia, I could use your help."

Maia nodded and pulled a pair of gloves from the closet. Out of everyone— kids and adults—only she looked composed. Not immune to the pathos, but somehow detached from the turmoil. Her gaze flicked to Reilly, and her steady hazel eyes made him feel transparent. He felt she could see through his veneer of self-control to the despair and fear that roiled like molten rock within.

Reilly hesitated, paralyzed by a morbid curiosity, unsure whether the order to leave applied to him. Nash quivered on the table, making inhuman yelps. Lieutenant Schuler peeled off the boy's shirt. The skin of Nash's right arm was spotted with tiny bruises. Commander Shen pulled a drug gun and several vials from the pharmacy cabinet. Ensign Morten, now free of the horrible creature, grabbed an oxygen mask and jammed it over Nash's face. The boy stopped screaming. His body went rigid. Then his back arched and his arms and legs rhythmically pounded the table. Blood dripped from his nose. Commander Shen loaded the drug gun with a vial and pumped it into Nash's neck.

Then she noticed Reilly and ordered him out. He stood outside the door, unsure which was worse—being alone in his barracks or sitting in the dorm with Tab, Nova, Keid, and Tally.

Two airscouters touched down and Captain Baca and Ensign Rabin stepped down.

The captain looked around at the empty yard, fixed his eyes on Reilly, and called, "Where is everyone? What's going on? What's happened?"

Mortified, Reilly shook his head dumbly and pointed toward the mess hall. How could he explain? *I could have prevented this,* he thought.

Captain Baca ran inside, the ensign on his heels.

Reilly put his ear against the hot fabric of the mess hall wall. He listened to the adults talking and moving about. At first the voices were loud and frantic. Then they grew quieter. Ensign Rabin said, "Oh my God. No. No." Then all was silent.

Reilly heard breathing behind him, turned, and saw that the other kids were behind him. Tally and Nova leaned, weeping, against one another. Keid chewed anxiously on his shirt cuff. Tab looked stunned.

Maia stepped out of the mess hall, her expression grim. Her eyes found Reilly's and, in that moment, he understood that she had also known about the outing to the creek, that she also blamed herself for not aborting that excursion, blamed herself for Nash's death. He wanted to express that recognition, wanted to point out that Tab, Nova, and Nash, himself, bore some responsibility, but Nova threw her arms around Maia's neck.

The mess hall door parted and Captain Baca emerged, his face drawn and gray. "Nash is dead," he said flatly.

Crying, Keid sought comfort under Tally's arm. Tab stood tall and alone, tears coursing his cheeks. For a second, Reilly felt moved to touch Tab's shoulder, maybe even hug him. But, even in grief, Tab intimidated him. He would likely push Reilly away. Reilly glanced again at Maia, but she had turned away.

∞

Hours later, after the kids had temporarily run out of tears, Commander Shen gathered them for a talk. Reilly was relieved that she didn't yell at them, assign blame, or highlight the stupidity and tragedy of their rebellious act. Instead she took questions. Captain Baca stood in the background, arms folded across his chest. Ensign Morten sat in the corner, cleaning his knife on a rag.

Nova wanted to know why Nash was jerking.

"The animal's venom contained a neurotoxin, which caused seizures—those jerky motions," the commander said. "We think the venom also contained a hematoxin, which caused the red blood cells to burst."

"If Doctor Mbaake were alive, she would have saved him," Tally said and lapsed into fresh tears. Nova put an arm around her.

At the name of his dead wife, Captain Baca looked down at his hands.

"The rest of us know basic emergency medicine skills," Commander Shen said calmly. "And medical expertise wasn't really the issue, because only antivenin would have saved Nash. We haven't been on the planet long enough to develop such medicines."

"That means," Ensign Morten said, "you all should stay clear of the creek. Don't walk under those trees, not without looking up first. I hovered over the trees in an airscouter. I think those serpents take over old bird nests. My guess is they stay in the trees, except to drop down on prey. "

Reilly shivered at the thought of one of these creatures landing on his shoulders and biting his neck.

Nova sobbed. She and Tally folded together and cried into each other's shoulders.

The captain ran a hand down his face. "I hope you kids now understand the rule about not leaving the base. Not without an adult. Not without proper authorization. Not if you want to live. There aren't enough of us to—" He pressed his lips together and his brown complexion paled, as though the effort to control his fury drained away blood and pigment. He shook his head and sighed.

Tab stuffed his hands in his pockets and stared at his shoes. Though his eyes were dry, his eyelids were red and swollen. His face looked mottled.

Reilly pictured Nash—the glossy black hair, caramel skin, and eyes the color of strong coffee. The round face that dimpled when he smiled. Maybe, given time, they might have become friends. Now he'd never know. If only he'd alerted an adult.... He glanced at Maia, who nodded grimly.

ELEVEN

In the subsequent days, the search parties for Reilly's parents went from two scouters to one. Captain Baca said they were conserving fuel. Reilly worried the change reflected a waning hope that his parents would be found alive. The whole rationale behind two scouters, each flown by a single pilot, was to leave the copilot seats empty for his parents.

Again, he requested permission to go as co-pilot, and this time the captain said yes. He went out in the morning with Commander Shen, and in the afternoon with Ensign Morten. There was no sign of the *Kestrel* or Reilly's parents. They had now been gone eight days. In the aftermath of the solar flares, the radio had come back to life, but not the radar.

Back in his barracks just before sunset, Reilly paced the small space, touching his parents' things. He pulled long blond hairs from his mother's hairbrush and wound them around his finger. He picked up his father's shirt and fingered a hole in the sleeve. He put the shirt on, rolled up the cuffs, which were only a little too long. A crate had been turned on its end to serve as a bedside table. Atop it was a photo of Reilly and his parents. Not the digital kind, which solar flares had rendered useless, but an actual print. His grandmother had taken the photo and printed it, back before they had run out of paper. Reilly must have been ten. His mother and father kneeled on hands and knees, side by side, so that their backs made a flat surface upon which Reilly balanced on all fours; Cosmic crouched on his shoulder. They were all smiling—except Cosmic, who appeared annoyed. His father looked at his mother, and his mother looked over her shoulder at Reilly. Reilly grinned at the camera. He was missing a first molar and his front teeth looked too big for his face.

Reilly longed for the happiness and security caught on camera. Why could no one find the *Kestrel* or his parents? Were they hurt and hiding? Images flashed in his mind: the serpent that had killed Nash dangling from Ensign Morten's rope; the purple arachnids filled with corrosive yellow fluid; the huge lumbering animals that occasionally thundered along the base of the mesa at dusk; the carrion-eating birds with the cruel curved beaks; the flying creatures that breathed fire like dragons. His parents had radioed about a canine species and a new ungulate. Were they dangerous too?

The call-to-dinner tone rang, but Reilly ignored it. Night fell and he curled on his parents' futon and listened to the usual assortment of animal noises, which sounded louder and more menacing than ever. Whenever he let his eyes close, he saw various creatures harrying his parents. He saw his parents cowering as a catdragon plunged, a serpent dropping from a tree onto his father, an arachnid poised to bite his sleeping mother's neck. Each time, the visions vanished when he opened his eyes. He tried to keep them open, but couldn't. At intervals, he lapsed into nightmares where he saw his parents bleeding, burned, pocked with tiny bruises, convulsing. More than once, he awoke gasping and drenched in sweat.

Finally, he sat, arms wrapped around his knees, and whispered into the darkness. "I'll come find you," he said. "I promise."

∞

The next afternoon, Reilly received permission to accompany Lieutenant Schuler on another search. The computers were still down, and the captain had drawn a map of the region on the back of an empty seed bag, partitioning the mesa so that each search covered another section. He shaded in the areas search parties had already covered, and assigned a section to Lieutenant Schuler.

As Reilly stepped up on the scouter's wing to climb into the copilot's seat, Maia called, "Reilly!"

She was standing in the garden performing the seemingly futile act of watering the wizened beans. She removed her sun hat and, waving it over her head, shouted, "Good luck!"

"Thanks," Reilly called. A couple of years ago, he'd concluded that there was no such thing as luck. Things happened a certain way because of the events that had led up to that point. He believed in cause and effect. Now he clung to the idea of luck. Even the notion of divine intervention appealed to him. Had he known how, he would have prayed. To no one in particular, he thought, *Please. Please let me find them.*

He took his seat, put on his helmet, and snapped the safety harness over his shoulder, the metal buckle scorching his fingertips. The dome hissed as it slid shut. The engine hummed on, and the craft lifted. Reilly yearned to take the controls. Since the big solar flares, the scouter's instrument panel still flickered uselessly. But, like the adults, he knew how to fly manually.

He had the irrational feeling that intuition would guide him to his parents. And yet, he'd been trained to make decisions based on accumulated data rather than speculation, not to mention sheer whimsy. He'd been taught that such objectivity was especially important when high emotion threatened rationality. Now, look at him, banking on luck and intuition. Before long, he'd believe in magic.

At any rate, Lieutenant Schuler wasn't likely to let Reilly fly. All Reilly could do was attend to every detail in the landscape. With the computer systems down, they were unable to use the Doppler and infrared mapping systems. Now, their eyes were their best sensors for seeking two lost humans.

While the lieutenant flew the craft low to the ground, Reilly peered through the sand-pitted dome. His eyes swept the desert landscape, the murky violet of the creek, the skinny vermilion-leafed trees that lined it, the carmine cliff of the mesa pocked with caves inhabited by who knew what, the purple saw-tooth pinnacles of the mountain range far beyond. The thing he longed to see—his parent's scouter coming toward him, smiling faces visible through the dome—did not appear. A weight bore down on him, as though he'd been transported to a planet with greater gravity. His stomach fought the viscous stew he'd forced down at lunch, and his face felt slimy with sweat.

The scouter ascended to the top of the mesa and flew parallel to its flat top in a southwesterly direction for 40 kilometers, west for 10 kilometers, then northeast for 40 kilometers, at which point they reached the mesa's edge. They worked their way back and forth. On the fourth lap, they skirted a side canyon. The canyon floor rose gradually, so that it ended only a few meters below the mesa top. It had also narrowed by half, to about 20 meters across. The lowering sun cast the lavender rocks of the canyon into shadow.

Off to the right, amongst the shadows, came a flash of light. Reilly blinked. There it was again. A metallic glint.

"Lieutenant Schuler," he cried and tapped the man on the shoulder. "Look to starboard. About two o'clock. At the end of the canyon."

The lieutenant banked the scouter in that direction, and the harness dug into Reilly's shoulder. Squinting against the setting sun, he concentrated on the shiny object. The glint resolved into the silver wing of an airscouter, then the entire machine.

"It's their scouter!" Reilly said.

"*Ja,*" Lieutenant Schuler said, throttling forward. "I see it."

Reilly strained against the harness for a better look. His eyes searched. No sign of his parents. His pulse throbbed in his throat, and his breathing quickened. His stomach felt like he'd swallowed the head of a hammer.

They hovered directly above the downed scouter. The word *"Kestrel"* was visible on the right wing. The canyon bottom was flat enough for a landing.

Reilly's hands went cold and sweat trickled down his side. His heart flopped against his ribs. His parents had to be down there. Where else would they be? Even if the scouter had malfunctioned, they wouldn't have gone far. The rule was stay put and wait to be found.

The lieutenant put the craft into a descent. When a scouter went straight up or down, the engine thrummed. It was loud enough to alert anyone on the ground. No one appeared.

There were a couple boulders near the *Kestrel*. One was wider at the top than the base, creating an overhang that could shelter two people, if they sat side by side. From the scouter's position, he couldn't see anyone. Maybe his parents were on the far side, the shady side, seeking refuge from the afternoon heat. He pictured the way his mother drew her feet underneath her, so that she could practically spring to her feet. He pictured the way his father waved, hand level with his shoulder.

Dust rose as they neared the ground, obscuring Reilly's view. He felt the touchdown in his belly. He stabbed the button that opened the dome, unclipped his harness, tossed his helmet onto the seat, stepped onto the short wing, and sprang to the ground. The balls of his feet crunched into the coarse sand. He ran toward the *Kestrel.*

"Mom!"

The scouter was empty, save for a blue duffle of chemical analysis gear. Reilly circled the craft.

"Dad!"

A hand gripped Reilly's shoulder, and he whirled.

Lieutenant Schuler shook him with one hand; the other held a *yridium* gun. *"Halt,* Reilly. We must stay together." He looked down and shook his head. "Acht, you are going to ruin the tracks."

Reilly tried to catch his breath. Why was he gasping? He hadn't run that far. His thoughts whirled like sand in a dust devil. Focus, he told himself. His parents were big on focusing. Maintaining focus, they often told him, was critical to survival. In his head, his father said, *Take slow, deep breaths. Keep a cool head. Review your options. React methodically.*

Reilly peered at the ground, noted a scattering of dimples and indentations, some the size of a human foot, others bigger. But the scrambled pattern didn't tell him anything. Lieutenant Schuler, his long frame bent double, had begun to follow a line of shallow depressions. Reilly followed, overwhelmed by how vivid everything looked. He noticed the blond streaks in Lieutenant Schuler's hair, the sunburned skin of his neck, the reddish cast of his short beard, the chomping sound of boots on sand, the scurrying small ruddy insects disturbed by their feet.

"A big animal was here. Maybe two." Lieutenant Schuler pocketed the small gun and pointed to depressions in the sand. "I can barely make out the tracks. Look there. See the suggestion of a claw? Could it be avian? Here, the claw marks are gone. Perhaps the claws are retractable, feline. Or the wind has erased them. It lands, takes a few steps, then disappears. *Acht.* Either it flew away or the wind took its tracks." He looked up, hand shading his eyes, as though he might yet catch a glimpse of it.

"Catdragon," Reilly whispered. For a second, he again saw Beau struggling in the forearms of a flying catdragon, heard the dog's pitiful yelps. He wanted to scream at Lieutenant Schuler to hurry and find his parents. He tried to speak, but his chest felt rigid and his tongue stuck to the roof of his dry mouth. *Don't lose control,* he told himself and took ten jagged breaths.

The lieutenant walked toward a big boulder at the end of the canyon, and Reilly followed. They stopped at a small pile of purple rocks covered with ashes. Some of the rocks were blackened, as though burned.

Reilly put out his hand to see if the rocks still held warmth, but Lieutenant Schuler knocked it away, saying, "No. Might not be safe." He donned gloves, crouched, and scooped a chunk of rock into a specimen bag. A breeze kicked up cinders. Lieutenant Schuler pulled up the neck of his T-shirt to cover his nose and mouth and mumbled something about wearing a mask.

Reilly remembered the ashes in the first colonist's fire pit. "I think my parents found what the first colonist's were burning in that fire pit."

Three meters away, a strip of foil scuttled against the boulder. Reilly leapt forward and pinned it under his foot. It was a meal wrapper. He picked it up and read the label. *Cajun rice and beans.* The inside was empty, save for a faint spicy smell. The top corner had a ragged tear. He saw his father ripping open the top, heard his mother joke about farting in the confines of the airscouter.

Reilly tucked the foil into a pocket and bent to look under the boulder's rocky overhang. Two sitting people could fit snugly in that space. His spine tingled. He looked at scrapes in the dirt and imagined his parents huddled from the chilly nighttime wind, eating dinner out of this bag. Where had they gone? A white canteen lay half covered in dirt. He picked it up. Tiny holes punctured one end. Bite marks? The owner of those teeth couldn't be big enough to kill a human. Unless the bite contained venom.

"Mom!" Reilly called. "Dad!" Despair serrated the words so that their edges scraped his throat and jangled off the canyon walls.

"Reilly," Lieutenant Schuler said sharply. "Not so loud." His gun was in his hand again.

Reilly circled the rock, careful not to trample any tracks. There was about a meter's clearance from the side walls of the canyon, which were only about three meters tall at this point. He began walking toward the canyon's entrance, his eyes raking the ground. No footprints led away from the canyon.

Lieutenant Schuler called, "Reilly, better that we continue searching from the air." He was standing on the wing of the *Kestrel*. He had raised the dome and was looking at the instrument panel.

"Will it start?" Reilly asked when he reached the scouter.

"No charge," Lieutenant Schuler said. "Otherwise, she's fine."

When the lieutenant climbed down, Reilly stepped on the footrest to peer inside the dome. A chill ran down his spine. "Their sleeping sacs are spread over the seats."

"Yes," the lieutenant said and hefted a backpack from the tiny cargo area.

"That's my parents' scientific equipment bag," Reilly said.

The lieutenant nodded.

"What about the duffel?"

"I don't see it."

Reilly looked into the small hold and saw it empty, save for a few Sustabar wrappers.

"Reilly, help me open the solar panels. If enough light penetrates the canyon, we can fly it back tomorrow afternoon."

With shaky hands, Reilly unfastened the clip that held the solar panels snug to the wings during flight. "If nothing's wrong with the scouter, why did my parents leave it? And why didn't they open the solar panels? Why would they leave behind their gear?"

The lieutenant shook his head. He didn't meet Reilly's eyes, and Reilly was glad because tears had thickened his vision.

After they climbed back into their scouter, Reilly said, "Which way should we go?"

"Well, they might have climbed up from the canyon's end onto the mesa. The rise is not too steep. We will circle that area. Next, we can cover the opposite direction—out onto the desert."

Up on the mesa, Reilly suggested places to check. The lieutenant worked the controls silently, only refusing to comply when Reilly proposed they drop into a neighboring canyon that cut a deeper, longer gash into the mesa. The canyon's bottom was lost in darkness.

"But how else will we find out if my parents are down there?"

"Too dangerous," the lieutenant said. "If we descend into that canyon, catdragons could fly overhead and trap us. It's near dusk. Time for them to come out. For all we know, they live in that canyon."

"But—"

"No." The lieutenant glanced over his shoulder at Reilly, then back to his instrument panel. "We will skim the top. Two passes. If Anika and Skyler are down there, they will hear us and perhaps fire one of their flares."

Reilly stared into the shadowy depths as they twice passed over the canyon. Nothing but cliffs swirled with purples and reds. A few caves. No living thing stirred.

As the sun squatted atop the distant mountains, Lieutenant Schuler cleared his throat. "Reilly, we must return to camp."

"No," Reilly said. He was wound so tightly he felt he could fly of his own accord.

Lieutenant Schuler turned in the pilot's seat. Although he had removed his sun goggles, his glacial eyes were inscrutable, and his mouth formed a straight expressionless line in his square, stubborn jaw.

"Please, Lieutenant Schuler. We can't give up. Not yet. It's getting dark, yes. That means it will soon be cold. My parents are out there, away from their scouter, possibly without shelter, food, or water." He saw his parents huddled together, shivering, their lips cracked with thirst. He tried to moisten his own lips with his tongue, but his saliva had turned to paste.

"We don't know where to look," the lieutenant said. "We covered the obvious places."

"But they're somewhere," Reilly insisted. "They didn't vanish."

Lieutenant Schuler pointed the scouter toward camp. "The battery is low," he said. "And captain's orders were to return by nightfall. Someone will return to the site in the morning."

"But—"

"It won't help anyone if we die."

Reilly wanted to scream at Lieutenant Schuler to turn around, wanted to grab his helmet with both hands. An ingrained respect for superiors stopped him. Plus, the crew would judge him emotionally unstable and bar him from further scouting missions. So he breathed through the tight bands encircling his chest and tried to slow his skittering heart.

After a half hour's silence, Lieutenant Schuler gave a forced chuckle. "Reilly, do you see that *dummkopf* bird? It is hanging upside down from the branch."

They were flying along the creek. Reilly said nothing and didn't look down. He had seen the river birds hang upside down, exposing their red-scaled breasts, their long purple tail feathers flopping over their backs. So far, they seemed to be the only harmless creatures on this horrid planet.

Lieutenant Schuler flew over rock formations that appeared to have budded off the mesa. Rock babies. Some were as large as spaceships. Reilly remembered a scouter ride he had taken with his mother. It was his first time in the pilot's seat. They had made a game of finding the shapes of Earth creatures among the formations—a giant camel, a cat's head, a hawk with folded wings. He knew those animals only from pictures. His mother had said that someday they would see the forms of animals native to Cinnabar in these rock sculptures. Then she had instructed him to turn around and fly low, looping his way amongst the rocks. A test of his ability to maneuver, she had said. Reilly asked why bother, given that there was nothing but open space. *You never know when you'll need such a skill. It's the same reason I taught you to thread a needle.* That's what she had said.

Reilly blinked. The scouter banked over the capsule-shaped shuttle that had transported Reilly's group and, minutes later, the shuttle belonging to the first colonists, the white tiles grimed orange and glowing in the dusky light. To starboard huddled the low buildings built by the first colonists, now so many skeletons reclining upon their cots, sheltering insects and rodents within the hollows of their bones. After Reilly and his mother and Ensign Rabin had sealed the doors and windows, Captain Baca had said that, once the crew determined the cause of death, once they knew it was safe to move the remains, they would bury them. So far, the tests hadn't provided a single clue. Maybe the same mysterious entity had killed his parents. Maybe it would kill him too. Right now, he didn't care if it did.

Straight ahead lay his people's camp, the domed roofs dulled with dust. The damn sand sifted under doors and got into everything. Reilly glanced down at his shirt and pants, blue veneered with orange. He ground his teeth and felt grit between his molars. Why had the Earth scientists ever targeted this horrendous planet for colonization?

We've got to make this mission work. His father's words. The two of them were on the ship's observation deck. How long ago? At least two months. His father was practicing a Mozart concerto while waiting for Commander Shen to show up with her oboe. His father had set down the flute and gone to the telescope. He called Reilly over to look at Cinnabar. While Reilly squinted at the vermillion planet—too far away at that point to see landmasses and oceans, his father had said *we've got to make this mission work, Reilly.* Now Reilly heard the unspoken words, *or die trying.* From where he stood now, staying on Earth seemed the lesser risk.

TWELVE

The next day, Reilly awoke late. Dust textured the light coming through the window. The sun had been up long enough to warm the room. He closed his eyes, then remembered why he had been allowed to sleep late. His parents had disappeared. Everyone felt sorry for him—at least the adults did. For some reason, their pity enraged him. He didn't want to see anyone.

He got up and paced, but the cramped space only allowed three strides in any direction. Reading usually quieted his mind; he would try that. He reached under the cot and dragged out his duffel. With the computers down, he felt justified in having smuggled a few books onto the shuttle.

On top of his duffel lay his father's flute in its scuffed black box. He recalled the fond, almost wistful look on his father's face when he had handed it to Reilly that last morning a week ago. His father had wanted him to practice. Guilt needled Reilly's heart.

He released the metal clasp and opened the case. He said, "Hello, Lola," to the three silver cylinders nestled into the faded red satin. He picked up the smooth, cool pieces and fitted them together. He raised the instrument and pursed his lips over the air hole. The shriek he produced reminded him of the sound the mono-eyed birds with curved orange beaks and gray scaly bodies made, the birds that had hung about the morning his parents departed.

They remind me of vultures, his mother had said, hunching her shoulders as though suddenly chilled.

Vultures. Earth birds with heads devoid of plumage. Animals that feasted upon carrion. The word *carrion* echoed in Reilly's mind, and he pictured the grey birds perched on his parents' motionless bodies. He put the flute away and snapped shut the case, as though the black box could confine ugly thoughts.

Closing his eyes, he conjured an image of his parents alive. He saw his mother sitting at her desk in their chambers on the *Remus,* reading something on her computer tablet. His father played the flute, switching from something classical to a bouncier tune that made his mother look up and smile. Springing to her feet, his mother began singing in her spritely soprano, "Oh, Susannah, now don't you cry for me, 'cause I come from Alabama with my banjo on my knee." Reilly had laughed at the line, "A buckwheat cake was in her mouth; a tear was in her eye." A woman crying with food in her mouth sounded unattractive. By the time his mother got to the third stanza, Reilly added his alto to the refrain. That was a good two years ago, before his voice had started to break unpredictably to a higher pitch.

Reilly felt a pain behind his sternum, and eased it with a sigh. He thought of the times when his father had stopped playing the flute to ask if Reilly wanted to learn the piece. Too many times, Reilly had said no. He was busy playing solitaire on the computer or reading a novel or studying astrophysics or enticing Cosmic to attack a ball of string. Now, with the cat long dead, the computers kaput, and his parents missing, he wished he had said yes more.

Reilly shook his head. What was he doing? He should be out searching for his parents. He looked out the dusty window. Off to the right, Commander Shen and Tally hoed the garden, while Tab, bare to the waist, pumped water through the irrigation hose. Once they had a fuel, the generator would pump water. The muscles in Tab's arms and back flexed and relaxed, flexed and relaxed. Why not wear his UV-blocking shirt unless he wanted to show off his muscles?

Maia appeared and began moving the hose around the garden, then turned to Tab, her big mouth moving. Reilly guessed she was giving orders. With a twinge of guilt, he realized she was also doing Reilly's work. For all their faults, Maia and Tab were doers. If they were in Reilly's shoes, they wouldn't sit around moping.

Off to the left, two parked airscouters gleamed in the sun. Ensign Rabin had his hands deep in the engine of one of them. With a jolt, Reilly caught the word *Kestrel* along the tail. Someone must have flown it back early this morning. If nothing was wrong with it, why had his parents abandoned it?

What if something awful was happening to them right now? Panic gripped his guts.

No point in scrambling into the other scouter. The ensign would obstruct him. He'd have to wait for an opportunity. He used to be good at waiting, as long as he had a something engaging to read.

Turning back to his duffel, Reilly fished out one of his favorite novels. On the first page, his grandmother had written *Twyla Bergen, February 2, 2149.* She would have been 25 in that year. She had loved paper books, even though the rest of the world had switch to e-books over 150 years ago. And she had brought her favorites onto the ship—fairy tales, myths, fables, poems, plays, old leather-bound classics, short story anthologies, contemporary novels, mysteries, essays, a few science books.

Reilly had managed to jam eight books into his duffel—six novels, one poetry anthology, and a collection of Shakespeare plays. He'd nearly ripped the duffel's zipper trying to fit in the Shakespeare. Now he wondered whether he should have brought something more practical—maybe a text on navigation or weapon making or first aid. Had he known the shuttle would make only one trip, known the computers would go down, he would have figured a way to transport more books.

The door flap opened and Maia walked in. She pushed up her sun goggles, wiped sweat from her eyes, and appraised him.

Reilly frowned. "Haven't you ever heard of knocking?"

"The door's made of fabric, nannobrain."

"Go away."

"I just—" Maia hesitated, chewed the tip of a black, untidy braid. Her grimy shirt strained over the breasts she seemed to have grown overnight. He forced his eyes down to her boots. They were damp from watering the plants and encrusted with sand.

"You didn't come to breakfast," she said. "Are you sick or something?"

"No. Listen, I want to be alone, okay?" Actually, he hated feeling alone, but it was his parents' company he sought.

"It's almost time to go to survival class."

"I'll pass."

Maia pursed her lips. Reilly had never seen her look so tentative, almost timid.

"Go on. Go play with someone your own age," Reilly said.

Maia put her hands on her hips, which made her breasts even harder to ignore. "I am your age—biologically, if not chronologically." She paused. "What are you reading?"

Reilly held the book to his chest. "None of your business."

The soft, almost vulnerable expression vanished, and her usual truculence reasserted itself. "Whatever," she said.

"You wouldn't understand anyway."

"I can read, bean breath. Quit acting so superior."

"Why?"

"Because it makes you unlikeable. Why do you think none of the other kids stopped by to check on you?"

The comment stung. To hide his reaction, he opened the book on his lap and tracked his eyes left to right. The words ran together, but he turned the page anyway.

"Also," she said, "you've made yourself the librarian, the godlike guardian of the books. Why don't you stop being so selfish and share the books with the rest of us?"

Reilly's head jerked up. This uncomfortable thought had occurred to him. His grandmother wouldn't have wanted him to hoard the books. Yet, he hated the thought of dirty fingers riffling the pages, bending the spines. What would he do if they became damaged or, worse, lost? Without computer databases and printers, the books were irreplaceable.

"Get lost," he said and turned another unread page.

"I know what happens in the end."

"Yeah, you probably saw the movie on the ship."

"I did not. I read it."

"Liar."

"You are such a— Okay, listen. At the end, the young cowboy—you know, the main character—is alone. He returns home, but his father is dead and someone else owns their ranch. The guy stands there, uncertain of his place in the world. The author writes that the sky was the color of blood. That wasn't in the movie."

Reilly's eyes widened. She *had* read it—without his permission.

Maia picked up speed. "My favorite part was when the two guys tamed all those wild horses. Also when the main character heated the muzzle of his gun in the fire and cauterized his gunshot wound."

"This book wasn't on the computer system."

Maia shrugged.

"Thief!" Reilly stood, and the book fell from his lap to the floor. "I knew it. Books would disappear then reappear on the ship and even since we landed. You've been putting your grubby hands all over my books!"

Maia looked at her palms, then rubbed them down her pant legs. "Well, I've already read all the e-novels. Besides, now I can't download anything onto my notebook, can't even get my minjin' notebook to work."

"I don't care. That doesn't give you the right to come in and filch my things." Reilly scooped up his book, shook out the dust, smoothed the bent pages, blinked away maddening tears.

"It's not filching. It's borrowing."

"Borrowing implies first asking permission."

"Quit acting like such a filthin' prince. At least you have things worth borrowing."

Anger rushed up Reilly's spine and filled his head with a flammable fluid. "Get out," he said.

"Hey, I was trying to be nice. I came because—"

"I don't care. Just go away."

"Pish on you," she said, her voice suddenly taut with rage. "Your parents are dead. I was feeling sorry for you. Not any more. Now you have a clue what it's like—"

"MY PARENTS ARE NOT DEAD!"

For a second, Maia looked sad. Then her lips pressed into a line and her eyes narrowed. "Yes they are, Reilly. Everybody says so. The sooner you accept it the better."

Reilly took a step toward her, but she held her ground. "You little shit," he said. "How can you—they were always nice to you." Rage vibrated his body. He tried to shove her toward the door, but she blocked him with crossed forearms.

"Right," she said. "But they were nicer to you. Always so special, you and your parents. The little biological family. No sleeping in the ship's nursery, not for you. No being crammed into the dorm here. Well, guess what? That's all about to change."

Reilly punched, felt the plush wetness of her lip, then the hardness of enamel. She hit back. He was bigger and angrier, but Maia's speed and greater fighting experience enabled her to duck, twist, throw in quick punches, then dart back out of range.

Commander Shen burst into the room, wielding a gardening hoe. She slid her hands down to the middle of handle and wheeled the tool through the air, separating the two kids without striking them.

For a moment, the only sound was that of three people breathing loudly.

Commander Shen set the hoe business-end down. "What is the meaning of this?"

Reilly and Maia locked eyes. Reilly broke first and glanced at Commander Shen. Her face was flushed, hard, and beautiful.

"Sorry," he said. He tasted iron. He touched his tender nose and his fingers came back bloody.

The commander drew a deep, composing breath. "Do you think I have nothing better to do than to interrupt childish brawls?"

"No, Commander," Maia mumbled through swollen lips. "That is, I know you have better things to do."

Commander Shen sighed. "Look at you two. Reilly, you should know better."

"Yeah, Reilly," Maia said in a low voice. "I'm just an ignorant vitro. But you— you're practically royalty—"

Commander Shen took a step toward Maia. "That's enough, Maia," she said quietly.

Maia lifted her chin. For a moment, Reilly saw them not as a female officer and a girl, but as two women, both of them strong, both of them fierce when necessary. He held his breath. Defiance flickered in Maia's eyes.

"Go to the dormitory, Maia," Commander Shen said evenly. "Remain there until I decide which extra chore to give you."

Maia groaned, but a sharp look from Commander Shen stifled further comment.

"You are dismissed, Maia."

As soon as Maia clumped out, Commander Shen ordered Reilly to sit on his cot. He did. The commander remained standing, forcing Reilly to look up at her.

"Now," she said, "tell me what happened."

Reilly shook his head. Though not in physical pain, his vision glazed with tears. He blinked them away.

Commander Shen exhaled loudly. "Let me guess. Maia came in here and said something insensitive about your parents. You gave in to your anger and hit her."

"Not a bad summary," he said. He rubbed the sore bones in his right hand.

"You usually master your emotions better than this."

Reilly nodded.

Commander Shen sighed, smoothed her hair off her forehead. "You children must become more disciplined. It's part of being a warrior. And to survive on this planet, we must become warriors."

Reilly remembered how Tab and Nash had scuffled in the yard. Was this play fighting a warm-up for the real thing? Tab must miss Nash. Reilly missed him too, but they hadn't been best friends. Who had Tab to spar with now? Maia? His physical strength intimidated all the other kids. Reilly thought of the enemies they might have to fight: catdragons, the huge rhinos, the chuckling canines...

The commander spoke. "Let me tell you something about Maia."

Reilly studied his chafed knuckles and waited.

"Two things motivate her behavior toward you."

"Let me guess. Loathing and sadism."

Commander Shen sighed. "Jealousy and affection."

Reilly gaped. He had suspected the jealousy, but affection? "What?"

"She likes you. Poor girl."

"Why?"

"Good question."

Reilly hung his head. He felt like a walking blister. His parents were gone and social skills stunk.

"I expect better of you. So would your parents."

Salt stung his eyes. *Would. So would your parents.* As though they were already hazy figures from the past. "You think they're dead," he mumbled.

"I hope they aren't."

Reilly's throat hurt. It felt like one of the spiked desert fruits had lodged there.

The commander stepped closer, rested a hand on his shoulder, and looked into his eyes. Reilly dropped his gaze.

"Reilly," she said softly. "I love your parents. I've played music with your father for years. Your mother is my best friend. She and I are the only women left. If she doesn't come back—"

Reilly looked up, but it was Commander Shen's turn to avert teary eyes.

The commander cleared her throat, wiped her sleeve across her face. "Well," she said. "Hanging about and brooding won't help. There's work to be done, and I could use your help. Take a moment to collect yourself, then come to the greenhouse. We have to transplant some seedlings before it gets any hotter."

THIRTEEN

Alone again, Reilly pressed his fists into his eyes, but mutinous tears leaked around the blockade. He held his mother's pillow to his face and sobbed. *They're not dead, they're not dead, they're not dead.* He silently repeated the mantra till he convinced himself his grief was premature. He blamed the adults for giving up on his parents, equating an abandoned airscouter to the death of its occupants.

Reilly caught his breath, dried his eyes on his sleeve, reviewed the facts. The *Kestrel* was parked in a canyon, battery dead. Why hadn't they opened the solar panels? Were they anticipating another sandstorm? Did they choose a canyon campsite for better defense? Had some creature threatened them? There were no obvious signs of struggle. Why then hadn't his parents opened the solar collectors? Was it already too dark in the canyon? Or had something distracted them? Had they set off on foot to investigate? Had they been chased away from the scouter? Might they have gotten lost? After all, the positioning system was down. The probability of spatial disorientation depended upon which direction they went. Out on the desert, as long as the mesa was in view (and the only time in didn't loom large was during sandstorms), you couldn't get too turned around. But if they'd ascended the canyon, that high plateau spread for nearly a hundred meters. Still, the distant mountain range marked west. And, if you were near enough to the rim, you could see the desert stretching eastward. However, had they headed toward the mesa's center, they might have trouble relocating the canyon. There were so many canyons cut into the mesa's edge. Maybe they'd ended up at the wrong one at dusk and taken refuge in a cave. Maybe one of them had twisted an ankle and couldn't make it back to the scouter. They would be low on food, of course, but they could have killed a small animal—one of the prickly rodents or one of the ungulates they'd described. They hadn't left behind their *yridium* guns, so hunting remained an option. And they could defend themselves.

One thing was certain: he wasn't going to believe they were gone until he saw their bodies.

Out in the yard, Keid shrieked in unintelligible anger. Tab cackled.

Ensign Rabin hollered, "Tab, that wasn't funny."

"Sorry, sir. I didn't mean to knock over his rocks."

"It was a sculpture!" Keid said.

"Whatever."

"Apologize to Keid."

"Sorry, Keid." Tab said flatly.

"Okay, boys. Both of you get back to work."

Back to work. Reilly would have to go out there with them. They'd all be watching him. They'd be hoping that, with a bit of goading, he would break down and cry. Well, he wouldn't. In his head, his grandmother said, *never let them see you suffer.* "Them" referred to anyone hoping to intimidate you. His grandmother swore that this philosophy, plus a lot of hard work, powered her meteoric rise to the rank of captain.

Reilly wiped his face on his sleeve. He would show Commander Shen and everyone else that he was a man. He gathered his hat, work gloves, and sun goggles and   marched into the relentless heat, eyes focused onto the dust-dulled plastic panes of the greenhouse.

All the greenhouse windows were open. A photoreactive material within the panes turned them gray in the sunlight, making the inside somewhat cooler than outside by day. At night, the windows shut to insulate the seedlings from the cold.

Commander Shen had unzipped her pant legs, converting her pants to shorts. Her sleeves were rolled up past the elbows. Sweat darkened the material under her arms and down her back. She glanced at him, seemed to gauge his fragilely contained emotions, asked no further questions, and spoke only quiet instructions. They loaded trays of bean and corn seedlings into a cart and pushed them to the garden. Reilly was relieved to see Maia on the far side of the compound, helping Captain Baca form bricks from creek mud and dried plants. Nova, who had been digging holes for the seedlings, eyed him darkly, but said nothing.

Back in the greenhouse, Reilly and Commander Shen readied the next batch of seeds, soaking them in an antimicrobial solution, rinsing them, filling trays with fertilizer-laced sand, poking in the seeds, watering them. Reilly worked silently, concentrating on the ripe smell of the fertilizer, the yellowed wrinkles of the corn seeds, the brown smoothness of the bean seeds, the warmth of the water pumped from the creek.

∞

After lunch, Captain Baca followed Reilly to his barracks and said they needed to talk.

The captain removed his hat and rubbed at the crease it had made across his forehead. "Reilly, I don't think your parents are coming back."

Reilly's ribs turned to iron and his heart beat within that cage like a wild bird. "No," he said. "That's not right."

"We've sent out numerous search parties. We've combed the area."

"But, sir, we don't have proof that—" a spasm in his throat cut short his words. He put his hand on his neck, inhaled, continued. "—No proof that they died."

"We haven't heard from them in five days."

"That's because they can't radio."

"The magnetic storm is over. The radio started working again this morning."

The news forced a sharp, audible exhalation. Why hadn't anyone told him? He pressed his hands against his thighs to stop them trembling. But his legs were shaking too. So was his back. He felt his body might fly into a million pieces, as though he'd been ejected into the vacuum of space. He sank onto his futon.

"What about the positioning system? Do we know their location?"

"The tracking system isn't working yet," Captain Baca said.

Reilly felt oddly relieved. It seemed far worse not to know where they were than to see their location on the screen, go to that spot, and find their lifeless bodies. He licked his dry lips. "They just got separated from the scouter. Maybe they removed their radios or turned them off, thinking they weren't working anyway."

"We've searched the area within a 200-kilometer radius. We've set off flares."

"Maybe they're injured and can't travel."

"They have their own flares. They could also use their *yridium* guns as beacons."

"Maybe they're being held captive."

Captain Baca arched an eyebrow. "By whom?"

"The catdragons?"

The captain blinked at Reilly.

"Well," Reilly said, "it's possible. They're intelligent. Also mean."

Silence. Captain Baca sat on a stool and looked at his hands.

Reilly bolted to his feet. "We haven't found their bodies." His voice came out strangled.

The captain took a deep breath, blew it out. "I'm sorry, Reilly."

Reilly pressed together his lips in a vain attempt to control the quivering. It seemed disrespectful to stand while the captain sat, but his knees didn't seem capable of bending. He felt rigid, as though someone had flash-frozen him. His chest seemed too rigid for normal breathing.

"I'm not saying we're giving up. We'll continue to look for Anika and Sky—for your parents. Ensign Morten and Lieutenant Schuler went out this morning."

Reilly searched the captain's face for the result, read the futility there.

"Ensign Morten's going out again with me in a few minutes."

Reilly clenched his jaw and perched at the edge of his bed. No one spoke. Reilly wished the captain would leave so that he could weep without shame.

"While I'm away, Ensign Rabin is going to help you move to the kids' dorm."

Reilly looked up. "What?"

"I can't keep spending nights here. And you can't stay here alone."

Reilly took in a frayed breath. "No. Please. I'm fine here."

"You'll have company."

"They hate me." Reilly shook his head. "I'd rather sleep in the barn."

The captain frowned.

"Look, I'll stay inside at night. I'll be fine." Reilly's voice shook.

Captain Baca tapped the wall and the fabric rippled. "You're living in a glorified tent, Reilly. Less than a week ago, a sandstorm blew your structure halfway across the base."

"Couldn't one or two of the crew move in with me?" Reilly said. "You know, weigh this barracks down a bit. Or we could use longer stakes." Any minute and he'd start crying.

Captain Baca looked away. "Maybe later."

"Okay."

"We could really use this space as a laboratory."

Reilly bit his lip and tasted iron. He thought of the bed frames being folded and stacked, the air mattresses being deflated and rolled into a corner, his mother's things being packed away, her smell replaced by the sour scent of chemicals. "I could move into the men's barracks. Sir, I'm almost fifteen. I can—"

"The men's barracks is too crowded as it is. Once we build more permanent structures, I'll move you, Tab, and Keid in with the men."

Tears leaked down his cheeks. He pressed his lips tightly together, but couldn't control the muscle spasms in his face.

"It's only temporary."

"What's temporary? Living with the horrid vitros? Being an orphan? The latter sounds pretty permanent."

The captain crossed his arms over his chest and stared at Reilly. On his brown wrist, a pale band outlined the place his watch usually occupied. He put his hand over his eyes.

"Sorry," Reilly whispered, wiping his face on his shirt. "I was rude."

The captain lowered his hand. Reilly thought he saw a film of tears, the captain blinked them away.

Reilly lowered his head and dug his hands into his hair, which felt stiff with oil and dust. The futon shifted beneath him, and Captain Baca's arm rested on his shoulder. Reilly allowed himself to lean his head on the captain's shoulder and weep.

After a time, Reilly sat up.

The captain pulled a cloth from his pocket. "It's pretty clean," he said.

"Thanks." Reilly dried his face and started to hand the cloth back.

"Keep it." The captain spread his work-hardened hands on his thighs. "It's possible they're still alive."

"You really think so?"

"There's no way to be sure. But I will keep looking for them."

"Thank you," Reilly whispered.

"I still want you to move to the dorm."

Reilly took a deep and jagged breath.

"There are just six of you kids left. Six. A small number. I don't want to hear you refer to the others as 'vitros' or 'in vitros' anymore. We are all humans. And we must band together like never before." Captain Baca stopped and watched him a moment. "Understood?"

"Yes, sir."

"Stay in the kids' dorm for a few nights. We'll see about moving you, Tab, and Keid in with the men. Commander Shen and the girls can have the dorm. It's time we separated the boys from the girls anyway."

Reilly kept his eyes on the floor. A tear dropped from his face, darkened the reddish-orange dust that coated the polymer flooring. He hoped the captain didn't notice.

"Captain?" It was Ensign Morten's voice coming from just outside the door.

Captain Baca slapped on his cap, and tugged down the bill. "Coming," he called.

FOURTEEN

R eilly? Reilly?" A hand shook his shoulder.

Struggling to awaken, Reilly blinked up at Ensign Rabin's benevolent face. Reilly had read about mythical divine beings. If such things existed, the ensign would make a good angel, albeit a hirsute one.

"Too early," Reilly mumbled. "Sleep more."

"All right, buddy. Get up, now. Time to move to the dorm."

Buddy, Reilly thought. His mother and father always called him that. When he didn't budge, the ensign squatted in front of him. A line of sweat that began at each temple disappeared into his black, curly beard. Corkscrews of hair showed at the opening of his shirt and tufted from his ears. He smelled of old sweat and scouter grease. Maybe not an angel, Reilly thought, but a faun.

"Sorry," Ensign Rabin said, "but we need to get you packed." The man radiated sympathy, empathy, and commiseration. And something else. Anxiety. The ensign was afraid. Captain Baca, too, Reilly realized. All of them were, with the possible exceptions of Tab and Ensign Morten. They were going to die, maybe not en masse like the first colonists, but one by one.

The ensign had brought him a Sustabar and water and hovered until Reilly had taken a few bites and swallows. Then, with an irritating solicitude, he helped Reilly pack a few things to take to the dorm. More than once Reilly said that he didn't really need help. The ensign responded with apologies and allusions to the captain's instructions. Lately, the word "sorry" had become a nervous tic. Reilly wanted to shout at him to stop.

Reilly packed a few clothes and books into a duffle. Also his father's hairbrush and flute. He knew he would never play the flute in the dorm, but he wanted it with him. In a smaller bag, he stuffed his sleeping sac and his mother's pillow.

Outside, in the afternoon glare, Nova and Tab were playing two-square. The court was scratched into the dirt. The ball was half flat and made a thunking sound each time it struck the sandy ground. Both kids were hatless, and only Tab wore sun goggles, probably because his pale eyes were sensitive to the sun.

As Reilly passed them, Tab caught the ball. He wiggled his toes, which protruded from the rough holes cut from his work boots.

"Hey, radge head," Nova said. "No holding."

Tab jerked his head at Reilly.

Both kids stared unabashedly at Reilly. Nova's sun-darkened skin now blotted out the starburst birthmark on her forehead.

Tab spun the ball on his extended middle finger, the other digits curled down. Reilly suppressed an urge to return the obscene gesture. "Moving into the ghetto with us, eh, BioBoy?" he spoke low enough that Ensign Rabin, who was several paces ahead of Reilly, might not hear.

Reilly pressed his duffle to his chest and kept walking.

"Yeah," Nova drawled, tucking a stray lock of black hair behind her ear. "Poor Bio Boy. Joining the menials." She rocked her skinny hips side to side.

"Bitter," Tab said with mock sympathy. "Total filthin' bitter."

Reilly's shoulders stiffened. Apparently, Captain Baca hadn't given them the lecture about fraternity, about how they must all band together.

"That's enough, kids," Ensign Rabin called over his shoulder.

Reilly pushed through the dorm's door flap. Whereas Reilly's living space had been dome-shaped, the footprint of the kids' barracks was rectangular with an arched roof. The ground had been covered with carpet cut from the shuttle in a vain attempt to keep the dirt out. Bunk beds stood perpendicular to the long walls, two bunks of two on one side, two on the other. An adult slept in one bed, leaving, until Nash's death, only one vacancy.

Had Reba still been functioning, the adults could have stayed in their own beds. Also the room would have been tidy. Reba would have seen to that. Given the frequency of solar flares, Reba became a relic of the past.

Reilly hoped he wouldn't have to occupy Nash's old bed. He scanned the room for a bunk that was obviously unused, but all of them were similarly heaped with bunched sleeping bags, discarded clothing, gardening gloves, a trowel, bits of rope and wire. Detritus cluttered the floor as well. The air smelled of sweat, oily scalp, and some funkier musk.

A dingy green tarp had been hung to divide the room into a boys' half and girls' half. Just now, the tarp was pushed aside, and the cord that supported it was draped with laundry, none of which looked particularly clean. The sand had stained everything orange, even undergarments. Reilly avoided looking at the girls' panties. Weren't the kids embarrassed? No way would he hang his shorts out to dry in view of the other kids.

On the boys' side, Keid was lying shirtless on the floor, arranging pebbles in geometric patterns in the dirt underneath the bunk. On the girls' side, Tally sat on a lower bunk bed gluing a patch over a hole in the knee of her pants, which were still on her legs. Wisps of honey-colored hair that had escaped her ponytail hung over her eyes.

Maia sat cross-legged before one wall, her back to Reilly. A Xylar patch kit was open beside her. Reilly figured she was mending a tear in the wall's fabric. Small, unseen animals had been nibbling at all the barracks. Though Maia kept her head bent to her task, Reilly felt watched. She glanced his way, and Reilly glimpsed her puffed lips and the swollen purple skin under her right eye. He felt both ashamed and satisfied.

A neon-green insect the size of a man's thumb buzzed in, and Ensign Rabin shooed it back out with his hands.

Tally looked up. "They mostly come in at night."

"What?" Ensign Rabin asked.

"The green bugs. That's why Maia is fixing that hole. Other animals make the hole—probably the pink rodents, but the bugs come in that way. They don't bite or sting or anything, but it's creepy to find them under the covers in the morning."

Reilly wondered whether anyone would bother to tell him what to do.

"*Bon jour,*" Commander Shen called as she ducked through the door. She was fluent in French and sometimes used it, even if no one replied in kind.

Reilly blinked. The commander was wearing a gray-blue shirt and bright pink shorts that hung low on her narrow hips. The shirt was part of the regular uniform. The shorts were not. The regulation pants had removable legs, so that they could convert into shorts. Until recently, everyone had worn the lightweight pants as protection against the ultraviolet rays. Most of the vitros had been genetically engineered to tan quickly. The adults and Reilly also wore sunblock patches. Stealing another glance at Commander Shen, Reilly wondered whether she'd given in to comfort or doubted she'd live long enough to develop skin cancer.

Nova and Tab pushed into the dorm. Tab held the ball under his arm.

"Wow!" Nova said. "I love your shorts."

The commander smiled in an oddly shy way that made her look girlish. "I've been saving them. Thought they'd cheer me up."

"They make me happy," Tab said. His grin fell under the commander's frosty look.

"Are you staying with us tonight, Commander Shen?" Nova asked.

"Yes."

"Goody," Nova said.

"Did everyone welcome, Reilly?" the commander asked.

Tab and Nova rolled their eyes at each other.

"Oh, right. Welcome, Reilly." Tally said. She pushed a lock of honey-colored hair behind her ear, then winced as some stuck to her glue-sticky fingers.

Keid continued his pebble project. Maia kept her eyes on her patchwork.

Fingering the tarp that separated the boys' side from the girls' side, the commander leaned toward Ensign Rabin and murmured, "We really need to enlarge the men's barracks and move the boys in with you. Meantime, we need a dividing wall."

"Why?" Ensign Rabin said.

"Puberty," Commander Shen whispered.

Nova and Tab slipped out through the door flap.

They were a little late, Reilly thought. Since they landed, he'd seen Tab and Nova kissing. Who knew what else they'd done? Reproduction was, of course, part of their survival plan. Now didn't seem like a good time to have babies, given the fragility of their survival. Plus, they—the kids—were too young, weren't they? For a moment Reilly imagined himself lying entwined with a girl like those he'd seen on the ship's movies—long limbs, long blond hair, clean and unblemished skin. He couldn't picture her face. His face warmed and his balls prickled. He banished the image. If his only options for sex were Maia, Tally, or Nova—well, he'd rather go without.

Commander Shen cleared her throat, and Reilly realized he'd been staring at her slender legs.

Ensign Rabin said, "We need more buildings."

"The captain has nearly perfected his adobe bricks," Commander Shen said. She smiled. "All it took was a little goat manure to hold things together."

Tally looked up from her patchwork and laughed. "Goat poop. Won't the bricks stink?"

"Not after they dry in the sun," Keid said, poking his head out from under the bunk. "I got to help the captain. Building with them will be fun."

"Oh, joy," said Nova sarcastically.

Keid nodded at Reilly. "Commander Shen, what's he doing here?" A fresh bruise bloomed on his upper arm. Reilly figured Tab had something to do with it.

Commander Shen and Ensign Rabin looked at each other.

"He's moving in with us 'cause his parents are gone," Tally said to Keid.

Reilly wished he could drop through the floor and disappear.

"How do you know?" Keid asked her.

"Maia told me." Tally went back to her mending. "Minje," she said. "I've stuck the filthin' patch to my skin."

Keid laughed.

"Shut up," Tally said, as she slipped a hand up her pant leg and attempted to peel the patch off her knee.

Keid looked expectantly at Reilly.

After a moment, Reilly looked away, but not because Keid was intimidating, but because he looked so alarmingly vulnerable—the thin face, the skin around the lips chapped from nervous licking, the blue eyes perpetually wide with anxiety, the assorted nicks and bruises.

Reilly remembered a conversation he'd had with his parents as they approached the planet. They'd insisted he scroll through the entire roster of the adults and children aboard the *Remus*. For each person, there was a photo followed by a text description of areas of focus, hobbies, and other interest. His parents had wanted him to understand the roles each person, especially the vitros, might each play on Cinnabar. For most of the kids, the key talent was obvious. Tab was strong, skilled in martial arts, a promising marksman, and well versed in military strategy. Tally had excelled in basic sciences, with an emphasis in veterinary medicine. Nova inclined toward psychology, with an emphasis in child development and a passion for fashion design. Maia had studied human physiology and pathophysiology and had passed a course in emergency medical training.

As for Keid—Reilly didn't see how Keid's artistic talent was any more useful than his own love of literature. On the other hand, Keid was also good at math and physics. Recently, he'd helped Ensign Rabin improve the design on the wind turbine. Now, Reilly considered he was the one who lacked useful skills. He wished his parents were there to remind him. He wished his parents were here, even if all they did was reproach him for being an indolent snob.

Ensign Rabin and Commander Shen left. The kids went variously back to patching, peeling, and playing with rocks.

Reilly wondered what he was supposed to do—make hand puppets from their filthy socks? His grandmother had taught him to do that. The memory, usually a happy one, made him sadder. He shifted his feet. Dust rose then settled across the tops of his shoes.

"So, Keid," he said, "where should I put my stuff?"

Keid looked at him, his face as blank as the pebbles he arranged. "Dunno. None of us has much stuff."

"What about under a lower bunk?" Reilly suggested. "Which bed should I take?"

Tally stopped peeling her patch away from her skin to point. "That one," she said. "Under Tab's bunk."

"That's Nash's old bunk," Keid added.

"I figured," Reilly said. He pushed aside the detritus of wadded clothes and tools to stow his things under the plastic frame. The thought of Tab turning above him made his stomach clench.

Keid piped up. "Tab says he doesn't want anyone sleeping there. Especially you. Tab says he'll wait until you're asleep and then—"

Maia slapped her hand against the wall, and Keid startled. "Shut up, pixelhead." She sighed. "Sorry, Keid. Can Reilly sleep under your bunk? That's the only other free spot."

Keid chewed on the collar of his shirt a moment, then ventured, "Okay." He looked at Reilly. "You won't kick my bunk or anything will you?"

"Of course not," Reilly said.

Keid stood and patted the lower bunk with a dusty hand. "Here you go. And please don't mess up the mandala."

"The what?"

"Under the bunk. I'm making a design with pebbles and sand, like the ancient Buddhists and Hindus did."

"Keid," Tally said, "you're so weird."

With a shrug, Keid went back to his work.

Reilly leaned down to see. A circle of pebbles was divided into quadrants and colored in with sand. "Nice," Reilly said.

Keid beamed at him.

Reilly heard the faint vroom of an airscouter setting down and ran to the window. The dome slid back, and Captain Baca and Ensign Morten emerged. As they walked away, the captain paused and looked toward the kids' dorm. Then he turned, his shoulders sloped in exhaustion, and followed the ensign.

Someone behind him sighed. It was Tally. "Guess they didn't find 'em."

Maia glanced up, then went back to her work patching the wall.

Reilly tried to sniff without making a sound. He wrapped his arms around his chest, as though he might hold himself together.

"Reilly?" Tally asked. She took a step toward him.

No, Reilly thought, holding his elbows. *Don't talk to me. Don't touch me. Leave me alone.*

"Tally," Maia said, "why don't you finish mending that hole in your pants."

"I already did. I think Reilly's crying."

"He is?" Keid asked.

"Mend something else then," Maia said. She still hadn't looked directly at Reilly.

"My socks all have holes in them, Tally," Keid offered.

"Fix them yourself," Tally said.

The dinner gong sounded. Tally and Keid hustled out the door. Reilly watched Maia out of the corner of his eye. She smoothed the glue with a fingertip, capped the glue, wiped her hands on her pant legs, and left.

Reilly sank onto his bunk, bumping his head against the bottom of Keid's bunk. He wept, in spite of his fear that Tab would come in and make fun of him. He rolled onto his side, his back to the center of the room, and cried, wetting the cover of the sour-smelling, inflatable mattress. Finally, he fell asleep.

∞

Reilly woke to a pain in his hand. He tried to jerk it away, then, after a confused and terrified second, realized someone was standing on it. He yelped. The foot lifted. A big face leaned toward him. Tab.

"Hey, sorry," Tab said. "Didn't know you were there. I was climbing into my bunk."

Like hell you didn't, Reilly thought.

"That's my bunk," Keid said.

"Ah, right. My mistake. I'd so hoped Reilly would be under me."

"You're sick, Tab," Maia said.

A telsar lamp flickered. The other kids were settling onto their mattresses. Commander Shen called out for everyone to go to sleep, then slid into a sleeping sac in a lower bunk on the girls' side.

After several minutes of silence, Tab began to snore. Reilly wrapped his mother's pillow over his ears. He thought about his parents. Once again, he saw his parents' scooter glinting in the sun, the empty cockpit, the punctured water bottle, the empty meal wrapper, the fire pit. Once again, the urge to search for them rose and crested. This time, he let it propel him into action.

He waited until the room murmured with slow breaths and soft snores and the occasional dreamy whimper. Then he slipped out of his bunk and gathered his shoes. He stood, waiting for someone to ask him what he was doing. No one did. Holding his breath, he tiptoed toward Commander Shen. She lay curled on her side, her back to him, her hair curtaining her eyes.

Outside, the cold prickled his eyes and nose. He slipped like a shadow behind the guard shack. Ensign Rabin was on duty. He would probably be facing the opposite way, watching the world beyond the base. If the ensign happened to see Reilly, he would say he had to go to the latrine.

He crossed the yard, past the musky-smelling barn, to the back fence and peered between the wires. All quiet. Reilly looked over his shoulder at the small barracks he had shared with his parents. He could barely make out the silhouette of the cat-shaped weathervane. Nevertheless, the sight of that feline weighted him with a sadness so dense he felt his legs were filling with sand.

A squeal broke the stillness. Reilly snapped his head in that direction, but he saw nothing unusual, heard no other sound, except the brief grousing of a turkey. Far above, a pinpoint of light blinked. Either the *Romulus* or the *Remus* in orbit. He wished himself back on board, back to a place that was contained, clean, and climate-controlled, a place where music played softly from hidden speakers, a place where he lived with his parents.

Instead he had this unnerving expanse of rocky desert, the infinity of sky. And he was going to have to go out there if he were to find his parents.

On the far side of the fence, a white bloom reflected the moonlight. It was a flower. He had seen this plant before. Nova sometimes tucked the flowers into her hair. The petals, which opened fully at night, were white as goat's milk. The smell was hard to describe, particularly for Reilly, whose only experience with flowers was the buds beginning to appear on the broccoli and zucchini that grew in the greenhouse.

He closed his eyes. His mother smelled a bit like this flower. He leaned forward, inhaling. He wanted to cup this flower in his hands, bury his face in its petals.

A shushing sound caused him to open his eyes. A large, dark shape glided a mere two meters above him. He thought to crouch and cover his head with his hands, but his knees wouldn't bend. His eyes tracked the creature. It banked and made a second, beckoning pass. Reilly made out four limbs tucked to a torso twice as massive as a man's. A barbed tail floated behind the creature. Wings with scalloped borders beat once, twice, and the animal disappeared into darkness.

His heart beat in his ears. A-way, a-way, a-way. *Run away,* he thought. *Runaway, runaway.* He faced the inverted silver Vs of the airscouters lined up to his right.

∞

Feeling like a thief, Reilly snuck into barracks he had shared with his parents and grabbed a pack, night goggles, sun goggles, canteen, and telsar headlamp. In the mess hall, he snatched several nutritional bars, then opened the pharmacy cabinet and removed a pouch of first-aid supplies. The light from his headlamp illuminated the blue drug gun. Reilly palmed it, along with a vial of Anaral, which he carefully packed. If he found his parents in pain, he could eliminate the symptom if not the cause. After a moment's hesitation, he snatched a vial of Harmonal, and hands shaking, loaded it into the gun and slid the gun into his pocket.

Next, he inserted a heating coil into two cups and waited impatiently for the 20 seconds it took the water to boil. Just as he was stirring in the green tea concentrate, something scuffled behind him. He whirled, and his headlamp caught one of the pink rodents sitting on a table, one paw shielding its eyes from the light, the other clutching a broken biscuit. Reilly kept his distance, and the creature crammed the food into its mouth, hopped to the floor, and darted behind the meds cabinet.

Reilly picked up the tea mugs, his unsteady hands sloshing hot liquid, and went out into the yard. He scanned the sky for catdragons, saw only the cold glitter of stars against a dome of blackness and, off to the east, the blue moon. He approached the guard tower, which was two-floors high, and no wider than the latrine. A ladder on the outside wall led to the observation deck. Reilly tucked his pack out of sight and removed his night goggles.

"Ensign Rabin?" he called in a cracked whisper.

A chair scraped the floor overhead. "Who's there?"

"It's me, Reilly."

The second-story door slid open and Ensign Rabin leaned out, goggle-eyed, laser gun in hand. "Reilly," he said, "you about gave me a start. What are you doing up?"

Reilly wished the ensign would whisper. If another adult came out to investigate, he'd never get away. "Couldn't sleep."

"Ah." Ensign Rabin regarded him. His dark hair sprung out from the edges of his cap.

"Cold night," Reilly said. His strategy was to play off the ensign's sincere offer from the previous afternoon: *If you feel like talking, I'm here.*

Reilly cleared his throat, "I made us both some tea. I thought we could sit and, you know, talk." He felt fraudulent, devious, deceitful. He was betraying a kind man's trust. But he had to do it.

Ensign Rabin smiled. "Sure. Why not? Something hot would be nice. Warm me up and help you get back to sleep."

Reilly handed up the mugs, then scaled the ladder. All four of the narrow walls and the roof were windowed. There was a small table and one chair. Ensign Rabin apologized about the lack of a second chair. Reilly said he didn't mind standing. The ensign insisted Reilly sit on the table. Reilly didn't know what to say, but the ensign, who couldn't stand silence, began to talk about his brother.

"You know, Reilly," he said, "just before we left Earth, right about the time I wasn't sure I could leave my loved ones behind, my brother died."

"Oh."

"He was walking the last block to work. He was a systems analyst for a big computer tech firm. A suicide bomber circumvented security, climbed the police fire escape, detonated the bomb. Took out a passing rail car packed with school children and nearby pedestrians."

"Including your brother."

"Including my brother." Ensign Rabin rested his broad forehead on a gloved hand.

He fingered the cold, smooth surface of the drug gun in his pocket, and turned his mind to his task. The ensign began talking about things he and his brother did as boys—building model space ships, scavenging parts from the dump to make an aircycle, pelting neighborhood kids with the fruits from a tree. Clutching his mug, Reilly made occasional noises: Really? Yes. Wow. Uh huh. Despite the cold, sweat slid down his sides. He would have to act soon. The ensign was so bundled the only unexposed skin was on his face. No, that wasn't true. Each time Ensign Rabin bent forward to sip his tea, the back of his neck was briefly exposed.

Reilly set his mug on the table and slid the drug gun from his jacket pocket. Again, the ensign leaned toward his mug. Reilly stood, pressed the drug gun to the ensign's neck. The ensign gave a startled cry. His arm flew out and knocked the gun against the wall. But the drug was in.

His brown eyes wild, Ensign Rabin touched his neck. "Reilly," he said, "what was that? Was that you? Did one of those arachnids—" He switched on his headlamp, turned his head till the light caught the drug gun, which Reilly still gripped in his paralyzed, guilty hand. "Reilly? Why?"

Reilly slid open the door and backed out. "Sorry," he said. "I'm so sorry. It's just a little Harmonal. You'll wake up soon. I have to go look for my parents."

"Reilly—" Ensign Rabin began, the two syllables freighted with disappointment. He slumped back in his chair. His elbow knocked over a mug and tea spilled onto the ground. Reilly slid the ensign's small *yridium* gun out of the holster but left the L4-50 leaning against the tower.

Reilly scrambled down the ladder, snatched up his pack, and ran to the closest of the four airscouters. The solar panels lay open across the wings. He shut them and fastened the latch. He scrambled into the cockpit and lowered the dome. It occurred to him that he was leaving the base unguarded. Why hadn't he thought of this? What if a catdragon attacked? Who would sound the alarm?

Then he thought of his parents, lips cracked with thirst, lying in a cave or under a bush somewhere, clinging to life, hoping he would arrive in time.

And if they died, so would he. He checked the throttle position, depressed a red switch. The sound of the engine was barely audible. The liftoff and forward acceleration would make a whining noise. Nothing terribly loud. Still, Captain Baca was a notoriously light sleeper. At least Reilly had a head start.

He checked that the engine nozzles were angled down, then eased the throttle forward. The scouter elevated. He eyed the positioning system screen. It was black, nonfunctional, which was good and bad. No one could easily follow him, and, if he became lost or unable to fly, no one could easily find him. Also, whereas his flight course would normally show up on the map, the map no longer displayed. At least, the compass worked. Cinnabar did have a magnetic field. So he would navigate by dead reckoning, using visual landmarks, stars, moons, and instinct, whatever that was. He turned off the radio. It was working again. But he didn't want to be in communication. Not now.

Without a backward glance, he throttled forward.

PART II

FLIGHT

FIFTEEN

Once airborne, Reilly experienced the euphoria of doing something. The engine hummed a low, monotonous lullaby. The control panel glowed aquamarine. Encapsulated within galvanized metal he felt immune from microbes, heat, cold, claws, fangs, fiery breath, venom, and vicious children. His sweat dried, his breathing quieted, and his hands became steady and reliable. He felt impervious to sobering facts, facts such as that he had never before flown solo, had never flown at night, had never flown without the aid of instruments.

He focused his senses on his parents. With the night-vision goggles, he could see fairly well. Thinking he might hear better, he slid back the dome, but the rush of air overwhelmed him. Also, the idea that a flying predator might attack from above made him nervous, so he closed the dome. In the quiet, he could concentrate better. He imagined he had invisible antennae attuned to his parents. *Where are you?* For a second, he closed his eyes, sensing which way to go. His mind filled with the silver shape of his parents' airscouter abandoned on the mesa top. He would start there.

He turned toward the mesa and put the scouter into a climb. The altimeter clicked off the meters—150, 225, 300, 305. He crested the top and hovered the craft while he got his bearings. The high plateau stretched so far he couldn't see the other side, though he knew it was roughly 60 kilometers away. The terrain below was pretty monotonous territory. The *Kestrel* was back at the base, no longer there to mark the spot where his parents had once been. He would have to be systematic; he would have to memorize every detail.

Below, the rocky surface unscrolled, sporadically knobbed with a shrub or boulder. Depressions pocked the rock. Reilly wondered if rain ever turned them to ponds. He flew the length of a crevice about two meters deep and perhaps a kilometer long. A half hour later, he came upon a canyon cut so deeply into the mesa's steep side he couldn't see to the bottom. As he cautiously approached the abyss, he thought he saw a shape pass underneath him, a shadow floating in darkness. Accelerating, he swerved away from the canyon.

Before an hour had passed, his eye caught a familiar-looking boulder. He banked for a closer look. The rock resembled the formation that was near his parents' abandoned airscouter—nearly three meters high and with an overhang big enough to shelter two people sitting close together. This rock formed the hub of his hunt. He would fly along ten-kilometer radii from that boulder, gradually working his way around the entire 360 degrees.

On his fifth foray from the boulder, the low-battery light came on. Reilly cursed. He had assumed that the open solar panels had meant the battery was charged the previous afternoon. In his rush, he hadn't checked the reading. He flipped on the indicator light. Low. Five percent remaining. The fuel packs were small and intended for lift-off and quick acceleration.

Reilly's heart dropped. The mesa was a bad place to be stranded. The sides were so steep he might never find a way down on foot. His options were few: head toward the base and hope he made it, or continue his quest till the battery gave out completely. The latter choice meant remaining on the mesa for some time. He checked his watch: four hours till sunrise, two hours of full sunlight to recharge the battery.

He didn't want to go back to the base. What would he say to Ensign Rabin? To the captain? If he returned with his parents, no one would be angry, not for long. He would be a hero. But if he returned alone...

Yet, what choice did have? If he died up here, he wouldn't do anyone any good. He would just take whatever disciplinary action was meted out—extra duty mucking out the barn, weeding the crops, whatever. Then he would escape again.

Furiously gripping the controls, Reilly swore. He used traditional four-letter oaths, words invented by the in vitros, the curses in Chinese and French he'd picked up from Commander Shen. Minje, merdre, ta ma de, shit, fuck.

He piloted the scouter down into the desert and turned south. In this area, before the landscape gave way to flat, featureless sand, there was a cluster of rock formations. At some time, huge chunks of rock had broken away from the mesa's side and the elements had sculpted them.

The battery charge light flashed red. One percent remaining.

Ahead of him was Camel Rock. Ensign Rabin had named it, saying it resembled a kneeling camel enlarged times five. Just as Reilly passed it, the airscouter began to lilt. Reilly glanced at the battery light. Depleted. He pulled up the throttle. He stretched up his neck, tightened his face, arms, and shoulders, as though he could keep the scouter going through force of posture and will. Despite his efforts, the scouter descended, tail first. Reilly made a last-minute attempt to straighten the machine. The ground rushed up at him, then smacked the underside of the fuselage. The restraining harness squeezed his shoulders and ribcage. The scouter skidded along the sand, rammed into brush, and jerked to a stop.

Mixed in with the rasping sound of his breathing were faint squeaking noises. Reilly looked out the dome in time to see a half dozen of the pink rodents, spines inflated, dart from the base of the bush and into a neighboring burrow.

He gently probed his neck with his fingers. It was a bit sore, but otherwise seemed okay. He released the safety harness. His whole body trembled. *It's just the adrenaline,* he told himself. He took slow, steadying breaths. Then he slid back the airscouter's dome, climbed out, and inspected the damage. There was a small fracture in the tail and a dent in the nose—nothing Ensign Rabin couldn't fix. He would help, make his penance.

What now? Set out on foot? And which way? In the direction of the base, or in another direction? How could he possibly find his parents by roaming the desert? He would be alone and vulnerable in the dark, like one of those the creek mollusks, minus its shell. His mother's voice, whispered, *Stay with the scouter.* Good advice. Eventually the crew would find him, if he turned on the tracking system. He could turn on the radio. If anyone was awake and near a receiver, he could tell them to come now. How the vitros would gloat when he was flown back in shame.

An evil smell distracted him. It was like beans gone putrid. He looked about. Despite his night goggles, he couldn't make out anything but the silhouettes of boulders. Something clattered. Spinning toward the sound, he spotted a beast creeping down the bottom of Camel Rock. It was huge, at least three times the bulk of a man, with four squat legs, a barrel torso, not much neck, and a long horn curving up from its prominent brow. It was the type of animal they had seen galloping in the distance, their first night on Cinnabar.

Reilly froze. The animal froze. For a long, heart-pounding moment, they stood like two mismatched statues. Then the beast snarled. Another animal answered, its voice higher in pitch. Reilly strained to see what had made it. Something moved at the top of the rock formation, in the spot that formed the rock-camel's hump. Wings fanned the air. A catdragon.

Reilly flashed on the *yridium* gun he had taken from Ensign Rabin. He patted his pockets. No gun. Then he remembered he'd moved it to a pocket of his pack.

The other beast—the colossal quadruped—clattered down to the sand and began galloping on thick legs toward Reilly. Reilly heard himself scream. *Run, run, run,* his mind shouted, but his legs locked in place.

Lights filled his vision. Not a migraine, not now, he thought. He rubbed his eyes, squinted, resolved the lights into two orbs. The wing lights of an approaching airscouter. It glided lower and lower, hovered, wings tipping right and left, then set down a dozen meters away.

The beast halted, studied the newly arrived scouter, and pawed the ground. At closer range, Reilly could see the twin canine sabers protruding from both upper and lower jaws. He could hear the thing taking snorting breaths.

Reilly couldn't make out the pilot and prayed it was Ensign Morten or Commander Shen or anyone who could shoot straight. He began to run toward the airscouter, bending at the waist to stay clear of the machine's laser gun. Why didn't the pilot fire?

The scouter's dome slid back, and a head popped up—a many-braided, Medusa-like head.

Maia? "No!" Reilly shouted, still running. "Stay inside! Use the scouter's laser."

"Can't," Maia said. "The power browned out when I landed. Come on. Run!"

He was already running.

"Hurry, Reilly!" Maia shouted.

The beast changed course to cut off the angle. Spraying sand, it halted between Reilly and Maia's airscouter. Its great head swung slowly as it looked from Reilly to Maia. Reilly was close enough to smell its malodorous breath, and see the tough hide, the beady orange eyes on either side of the bluish horn, the drool glistening on the long curving canines.

Nostrils quivering, the beast shuffled closer to Maia's airscouter.

"Get down," Reilly told Maia. The calm in his voice surprised him. "Close the dome."

For once, she took his advice.

Reilly glanced over his shoulder to his own airscouter. It was about ten meters away. If the beast hesitated before charging after him, he might make it. He took off. The beast roared. Reilly heard a *thwack* and looked back. The creature must have butted the side of Maia's scouter. It stood there, shaking its grotesque head and staring dully at the dent it had made.

There was a yeowling noise above him. A catdragon soared directly overhead, wings spanning a good three meters. It called out in a cascade of watery syllables. The other beast made a grunting reply. Were they conspiring on how to snatch both humans?

The dome opened a crack. Maia said something about finding a *yrdium* gun. Reilly shook his head, pointed urgently overhead. Hadn't she seen the catdragon?

The beast swung his head Reilly's way, swiveled its hips in line, and began bounding toward Reilly. Reilly accelerated, his feet pounding, his pistoning arms thrusting him forward. He tripped, sprawled on the sand, got up, kept running. He glimpsed the red beam of a laser gun, saw it connect with the beast's armored rump. The beast bellowed, but the pain only goaded it toward Reilly. The distance between them closed.

With the beast close behind, Reilly reached his airscouter. As he clambered up the wing, he slipped. With a dull *thunk,* his head struck metal.

SIXTEEN

A cold wind roused him. Something pinched his shoulders. He had an odd dangling sensation in his legs, pain over his right eye. Reilly regained awareness by degrees. He blinked, saw nothing but sky. He looked down. Far below, rocky ground zipped past. Something moved in his peripheral vision. Wings, big ones, beating up and down. One on each side. Pulses of warm, tangy air rhythmically fanned his face. Harsh breathing sounded. He craned upward and saw a muscular chest and neck, the triangular underside of a jaw, a flash of sharp white teeth.

Catdragon. Carrying him. Flying him off to its den, where it would rip him apart.

He writhed, kicked his legs, thrashed his arms. Something—talons?—tightened around his shoulders, dug into his flesh. He yelped.

The creature made a noise, a two-part vocalization. He had no idea why or how, but he thought he understood. The creature had commanded him to be still. Be still. It was as though the words lit up in his mind, as though etched by comets. Then he had an image of himself hanging motionless from this creature. That's what the animal wanted of him. He complied. His other choice was no better: wriggle free and break his body against rocks. When the creature set him down, he would at least have the chance to fight.

A cliff face loomed into view, then the dark maw of a cave. As the black oval enlarged, Reilly closed his eyes. He felt ground under his feet. The creature released his shoulders. He crumpled to his knees, then pushed himself back to his feet, his fists clenched before him. His head ached. Dazed, he blinked at the catdragon. It folded its wings to its scaled back and watched him with amber eyes.

The creature turned its head and made a series of noises. From the cave's interior, a second creature answered, the cadence the same, but the pitch higher.

I'm surrounded, Reilly thought as he whirled to face the second speaker. He couldn't see anything in the blackness. He groped for his night goggles, which had fallen around his neck, and slid them back over his eyes.

Another exchange followed, this one much longer. The sounds—a lilting series of sharp *k*'s, sibilant *s*'s, and lisping *th*'s—were like water shushing from the garden pump, the creek burbling along its banks.

"It's okay. You're safe." The voice was human, a woman's voice.

Reilly's brain spun to make sense of the sound. Surely he was hallucinating. Maybe the creature had injected him with venom. Something moved toward him. It was carrying a light. Reilly squinted. He saw sandaled feet, two legs in baggy pants, hands holding a crude lamp.

He raised his eyes. A woman stood before him. Slung about her shoulders was an animal skin tufted with white fur. A tunic of indeterminate color topped her loose, ragged pants. Her posture was erect, almost proud. Dark hair hung to her waist. Her face was not young—Reilly guessed mid-forties— but it was handsome. Her wide brow tapered to a narrow dirt-smudged chin. There was a scrape at the bridge of her straight nose. Dark eyebrows arched over deep-set eyes. It was her eyes that got Reilly. They held him in place, as surely as a pin held fastened an insect to a specimen board. Even by moonlight and lamplight, Reilly could see they were green. She was a desert queen. Salvation incarnate. He wanted to throw his arms around her ankles.

She smiled. "Are you alright?" Her voice sounded rusty.

Reilly's head throbbed. He sat cross-legged on the ground, gingerly touched his brow, and felt a lump above his right eye.

The woman leaned closer with the lantern. "You're going to have quite a bruise there." She pulled a clay pot from a pocket, unstoppered it, dipped in her finger, and reached toward his face. "Hold still," she said when he shrank away. "It's just some salve for your injury."

Her fingers were cool against his forehead, and a pungent scent recalled to him a thorny plant that gave off this aroma in the midday heat.

"You're one of the first colonists," he said. "What happened to the others?"

"Yes," she said and looked away.

"Where am I?" He seemed to be in a dark, domed space.

Someone else said, "Cave of Kailani."

Reilly turned toward the sound and beheld a catdragon. It sat on its haunches not two meters away.

The creature nodded toward the woman and said, "Thith Kailani."

"Kailani Knight," the woman said, as though the addition of a surname would clarify things.

"I'm Reilly. Reilly Landreth."

"Your last name sounds Mirnan."

"What?"

"It's the ending. The Mirnan language is full of diphthongs. Anyway, why were you traveling alone in the middle of the night?"

"I was looking for my parents," he said. "They're missing." The words felt barbed in his throat, and he swallowed painfully.

Kailani looked away. "Oh," she said.

Reilly was about to ask why this woman was living in a cave, why hadn't she contacted them, but the catdragon stepped forward. His head came only as high the catdragon's shoulder. Up close, the creature really did look something like a huge cat with wings. In the moonlight, its body was a silvered gray, the wings a shade darker. Its muscular tail, which was twitching side to side, ended in an arrow-shaped point. The animal stopped and extended its neck, such that its whispered nose and its flaring nostrils were centimeters from Reilly's neck. Reilly cringed away.

"Nydea is smelling you," Kailani said. "She gets a lot of information that way. Don't be surprised if she licks you too."

At the thought of a large, wet tongue lapping his face, Reilly shuffled backward.

"Mind the edge," Kailani said, catching his sleeve. "It's a ten-meter drop to the rocks below."

Reilly craned his neck. His backside was a meter from nothing but air. He stepped farther into the cave.

"No need to be afraid," Kailani said. "Nydea won't hurt you. In fact, it seems she saved your life."

"What are you talking about?"

"Nydea. Apparently she rescued you from a *witnaw.*"

The woman gestured at the creature, and it nodded its feline head. Its eyes glowed gold around diamond-shaped pupils, the gaze curious rather than predatory. The left eye was half closed, as though frozen in the act of winking.

Reilly revised his recent history. *Witnaw* must be the name of the lumbering, horned behemoth. This catdragon had snatched him out of the way. It had acted in an altruistic manner. He thought of the catdragons that had attacked Ensign Rabin, killed their animals. He couldn't reconcile these contradictory behaviors.

"You're very lucky," Kailani said. "*Witnaws* are stupid, but dangerous."

"Wit-what? That's what you call the saber-toothed-rhino-thing that attacked me?"

"Yes."

The catdragon bobbed its head and made a series of sounds. The mouth was not feline, lacking the central cleft that went clear to the nostrils. Rather, the shape of the lips and the way they moved were almost human. However, the teeth revealed by the moving lips were the white, pointy teeth of a carnivore.

"I can't believe it talks," Reilly said.

"Many of the creatures on Mirna do," Kailani said. "None so well as the *wyomes.*"

"Mirna?" he said.

"The name of this planet."

"We call it Cinnabar."

"At one time, so did I."

"The creature spoke in English a minute ago."

"I've taught her a few words. Mostly, she and I speak Mirnan."

"Oh. What kind of creature is it?"

"She is a *wyome,*" Kailani said. "*Wyomes* are the reigning species on Mirna."

"We call them catdragons. Some call them catbats. Anyway, they've been attacking us, taking our livestock, killing our dogs." Listing these offenses made Reilly sound and feel angry.

Kailani's brows drew together. "Was anyone injured? Any humans?"

"No. Not yet."

Kailani exhaled wearily. "Sadly, most *wyomes* are unfriendly or downright hostile toward humans. That's because of their leader. Nydea, however, is my friend."

Nydea, who had been licking her right shoulder, stopped and blinked her long lashes. *"Frenth,"* she affirmed.

"Huh," Reilly said skeptically. In the depths of the cave, he could make out a fire pit, pots, some sort of rug on the ground. Did the woman really live here? Did she keep the catdragon as some kind of pet? The bump on his head throbbed, and his thoughts seemed scrambled. "What happened to the others in your group—" *Others,* he thought and sprang to his feet. "Oh, no. Maia. Where's Maia?"

"Who?" Kailani said.

"An *in vitro* kid," Reilly said. "She followed me. My airscouter ran out of solar charge. I think hers did too. I don't know what happened to her." *And I don't want to be responsible for another kid's death.* "Ask what it—what she saw." He nodded toward Nydea.

Speaking in Mirnan, Kailani phrased what sounded like a question. Nydea replied, occasionally gesturing with a fingery paw. Kailani listened with closed eyes. Then Nydea closed her eyes, and there was silence.

"Nydea is pointing," Reilly said urgently. "Why don't you open your eyes?" Reilly asked, but she didn't move a muscle. "What are you doing?"

"Mind communicating," Kailani said. "Shh."

Reilly's apprehension about Maia trumped his curiosity about this speechless communication. *Hurry, hurry, hurry,* he thought.

Kailani rubbed her temples. "The girl's probably still in her airscouter at the base of Kirsna Rock. She'll be safe there."

"But if her scouter's out of charge, she can't get away." He clenched his hands so tightly his ragged fingernails cut into his palms.

"Won't the others come looking for her?" Kailani said.

"Eventually," Reilly faltered. "Maybe not soon enough."

"They don't know you left, do they?" Kailani narrowed her eyes.

"What about the wit—what did you call it"

"A *witnaw.*"

"Could its horn punch open Maia's airscouter?"

"I once saw a *witnaw* ram down a *chagala* tree just to get at a baby *mantalya*. So, yes, I guess it's possible."

Reilly moved to the ledge. The cave was in a small canyon in the mesa. The blue moon was out of sight. By the position of the red moon, he judged he was east of the base. No landmarks looked familiar. He looked down. It was a long way to the rocks below, maybe ten meters, definitely too far to jump. "How do I get down?"

Kailani put up her palm. "Let me think."

"You don't know how to descend your own cave?" Reilly said, but Kailani ignored him.

A debate ensued between Nydea and Kailani. Nydea's claws retracted in and out of her front paws as she spoke, as though she were anxious or agitated.

Reilly interrupted. "I don't know what you two are saying, but I have to go. Just tell me how to get down and which direction I should go. Please." He paced the ledge, adjusted his night goggles, and at last saw the rope ladder that had been drawn up and piled in a basket.

"You can't go alone. Too dangerous. I'll have to go with you," Kailani said. Nydea murmured something, then Kailani continued, "Nydea has offered to carry you on her back. She does so at some risk."

"What risk?"

"Never mind. This way, you'll return to your friend faster. I'll follow on foot."

"Are you saying I'm going to fly on her back?"

"She'll do the flying. You just have to hang on."

SEVENTEEN

"W" ait a minute," Kailani said. She disappeared into the blackness of the cave. A moment later she reemerged with what appeared to be a forked stick. "Just in case," she said, handing it to Reilly.

"In case of what? What is this?" Reilly examined the Y-shaped object. It was harder than wood, smooth, pale yellow, and about as long as his forearm. Perhaps some kind of animal horn. A strip of rubber was tied to each of the forked ends. It looked liked a tourniquet from a first aid kit. Inserted midway along the length of rubber was a rectangle of leather.

"In case you need to defend yourself."

Reilly blinked. "What do I do with it? Throw it?"

"It's a slingshot. Haven't you been taught how to use one?"

Reilly shook his head. "I've read about them in stories."

"You must have been born on the ship. Still, you're supposed to learn about slingshots in survival class." She took the thing from him. "Here," she said. "I'll show you." She snatched up a rock. With her left hand, she grasped the horn and held it at arm's length. With her right hand, she centered the rock in the leather rest and pulled back.

"Sight between the forks." She let loose with her right hand, and the rock sprang into the darkness. A moment later, there was a clattering sound.

"It's easy," she said and returned the slingshot to him. "You try."

"Not now. I'll figure it out. I have to go."

"Try it now. You don't want your first attempt to be in a combat situation."

Combat? Reilly swallowed his frustration. After he scooped a rock from the ground, held the horn with his right hand and pulled the elastic thong with his left. When he released, the rock dropped at his feet. Nydea made a snuffling sound. Was she laughing at him?

"Ah, you're left handed," Kailani observed. "Anyway, try again. It takes practice."

"Look, I don't mean to seem ungrateful or disrespectful, but I've got to find Maia. I don't have time for Primitive Weapons 101."

"You appear to be weaponless. You don't have any idea what you might encounter, do you?"

"Don't you have a spare laser gun?"

"I ran out of *yridium* over a year ago. With a slingshot, there's no end of ammunition." She handed him three rocks. "Once you're good with the slingshot, I'll teach you how to use a bow and arrow." When he widened his eyes, she added, "Not tonight, obviously."

If he didn't leave soon, Kailani would suggest he paint his face and don a loincloth. He thought of Maia, thought of the horned behemoth ramming the side of her airscouter. He concentrated on shooting well enough to get going. The three rocks made progressively larger arcs into the night. Whether he could hit a target, not to mention a moving target, remained to be seen. He slid the slingshot inside his jacket.

Kailani unfastened a leather pouch from her belt, reached in, and held up a wedge-shaped stone. "These are dipped with *shaggoth* venom. I only have a half dozen. Getting the venom is tricky. If you pierce your enemy's hide, he or she will likely die within ten minutes." As she handed over the pouch, she looked Reilly in the eye and said, "Do not let these rocks touch an open wound on your own body."

Shaggoth, Reilly thought as he tucked the pouch into his pocket. No time to ask for a description now. Mention of venom recalled the many-legged reptile that bit Nash and the boy writhing in agony and bleeding from a dozen places. For the hundredth time, guilt at not preventing that death twisted his gut. He had to rescue Maia.

Go now," Kailani said. "Good luck."

Nydea said something to Kailani. They locked eyes. Reilly's head buzzed faintly, as though listening to faint, garbled radio communications.

Nydea took a step closer to Reilly and crouched beside him, making her just a head taller than him. Her amber eyes regarded him, the left partially covered by the scarred eyelid. Hesitantly, he touched her side. He had expected the scales to feel cool and rough, like those of a palm-sized reptile Ensign Morten had once caught near the mess hall. Instead they were warm and smooth. Nydea's left ear flickered.

"Climb onto her back," Kailani told him. "Put your left foot on her elbow." She touched the spot. "Good. Now step, grab her wing base, and swing your right leg over. Mind you don't kick her."

Reilly planted his left foot, hopped to reach the wing base. His hands slipped the first time, then caught. He heaved himself up. Nydea grunted.

"Good," Kailani said. "Scoot forward so that you're sitting between her neck and her wings. Careful you don't kick her wings."

Reilly moved awkwardly, settled himself. His feet dangled below her shoulders.

"When she flies, hook your feet in her—well, her armpits. Press in with your knees."

He looked down at Kailani. "Thank you."

Kailani shrugged. "Thank Nydea."

"How do I say that in her language?"

"Icantha," Kailani said.

Reilly leaned closer to Nydea's ear. *"Icantha,"* he whispered.

Nydea looked over her shoulder at him. *"Parnea."* Her breath was hot and peppery. She moved to the ledge, and Reilly slid his clammy hands lower down her neck. His heart started hammering so hard he didn't think he could say another word.

"Hold onto Nydea's neck," Kailani called. "Once you recover the girl, head back here."

Reilly nodded, checked that his night goggles were on tight. He regained his grip on Nydea's neck just as she spread her wings and pushed off. As she sprang, Reilly's torso lagged, and he pitched himself forward to keep from somersaulting backwards.

"Be careful," Kailani called, her words hushed by the sudden rush of air across Reilly's ears.

Twisting round to look, he could just make out Kailani standing on the ledge, the cave yawning blackly behind her. Nydea's wings sliced up and down through his view. He had an absurd urge to wave. One wing caught his jutting elbow, sending a jolt of pain up to his shoulder and nearly knocking him into space. He clutched at a skin fold at her neck, pressed his knees into her upper ribs, and curled his whole body against hers, eyes squeezed shut.

In the last few days, he'd had thoughts that, if his parents were dead, he may as well die too. But now, he didn't want to die. He clung to Nydea with a fierce will to persist.

Once he felt steady, he looked down. With Nydea's shoulder muscles rolling underneath him, his vision of the landscape below jerked back and forth—tiny bushes, rocks, sand. Feeling lightheaded, he huddled in the space just in front of Nydea's wings, arms clasping her neck. Wind whipped his hair, froze his nose and ears. Each wing beat whisked cold air down his collar. He crouched lower, so that Nydea's head blocked the wind a bit. Nevertheless, cold stiffened and numbed his fingers. Anxious he'd lose his grasp, he clutched harder.

His legs followed Nydea's respiration, cinching in on the inhalation, out on the exhalation. Her breaths sounded harsh, as though carrying him was an effort. Fueled by a mix of exhilaration and terror, his own breathing was rapid.

Rapid breathing feeds fear, his mother often said. *Control your breath; master your fear.* His face near the nape of Nydea's neck, he inhaled deeply and slowly. Her scales smelled like sun on sand. He counted wing beats. There was a pattern—five beats, then a long glide; five beats, glide.

After a time, Nydea uttered a few, clipped words. She paused, spoke again. The words sounded the same, the tone more urgent. He felt a strange buzzing in his head. As she repeated the words, she jerked her head up and down. Understanding flooded him. He lessened his grip on the nape of her neck, eased the vise of his legs. Nydea's relaxing and contracting muscles rocked his torso forward and back. He realized he felt more secure if he let his spine loosen, let his torso move with Nydea. His pelvis tipped forward and back, forward and back.

He noticed that she exhaled as her wings swept in front of her chest and inhaled as she pulled them up again. He began to breathe in the same rhythm. Up and down, inhale and exhale.

In the moonlight, he could see the pattern of scales on her skin. The sleekness reminded him of his father's leather gloves, and the way the scales overlapped made him think of his mother's silver necklace. Sometimes his mother asked him to unclasp the necklace. Once free of her neck, the silver links were, for a moment, still warm from her skin. Nydea's scales felt something like that.

The two moons slid down the bowl of the sky toward the mesa. The red moon was a perfect circle; the blue moon was three-quarters full. Below, strange rock formations, arroyos, and clumps of brush scrolled quickly past. Reilly estimated their velocity at 110 kilometers per hour, which was the fastest he'd ever flown an airscouter.

As they passed over the meager creek lined with spindly trees, a single bough swayed and something let out a long, lonely sound that tensed the skin along Reilly's spine.

Camel Rock loomed into view. Down below, light beams raked the ground. Reilly squinted, made out a total of four parked air scouters. Two men with telsar torches moved about. The shorter, leaner man with the brisk stride was Captain Baca. The brawnier man with more swagger to his step was Ensign Morten. They circled one of the airscouters, shone their lights on a dark shape on the ground. *Maia's body?* A surprising pain jackknifed in Reilly's chest.

Captain Baca and Ensign Morten turned their backs on the scouters and walked toward the creek. Nydea swooped low. The motionless body was three times the size of any human. It was the huge, horned creature. What had Kailani had called it? A *witnaw.* He wrinkled his nose against its foul stench. Who had killed it? Did Captain Baca and Ensign Morten arrive in time to save Maia? If so, where was Maia? Or did Maia kill it? Could she have done such a thing? Probably. But where was she?

With a hissing noise, Nydea banked away from the dead creature. Reilly, who had been leaning out for a better view, let out a cry, and grabbed her neck to keep from falling. After he righted himself, he heard his own hammering heart, followed by startled male voices from below. As he glanced down, a cone of torchlight crossed Nydea's belly, and he hid his face against her shoulder while she veered right.

A second later, a thin, red beam of *yridium* laser sliced past Nydea's right shoulder, narrowly missing his leg. Reilly opened his mouth to shout, *No! Don't shoot! It's me up here!* But Nydea stretched out her neck and flapped higher, her body perilously close to vertical. It was all Reilly could do to hang on.

EIGHTEEN

At this loftier altitude, the air was colder and also thinner in oxygen. Nydea's breathing quickened. She flew a wide semicircle, then gradually descended. Reilly began shivering. He pressed his chest against Nydea's warm shoulders, his cheek against her neck. He could feel her pulse in his jaw, the steadiness a comfort. He was no longer afraid. He looked down. They were paralleling the creek. In this spot, the water had cut deeply into the sand and underlying rock.

A line of trees and shrubs hugged the arroyo's rim. Nydea swooped low and slow enough that Reilly could see into the scrawny canopy. The strange birds that nested in those trees were, for once, silent. He made out a bulge in the branches that might be a nest—or some animal curled there, waiting to spring on an unsuspecting creature walking below.

He heard an unfamiliar sound—something not unlike a child's giggle. A branch bobbed just ahead. A figure hung by its tail over the water. The body was as small as a toddler's, the arms long and limber. The creature swung to a higher branch. There was enough light for Reilly to see that, instead of legs, the animal had two tails—one hung onto a branch while the second swung out for the next branch. The animal chattered and bounced. From behind Reilly came a jabbering response. He craned over his shoulder. In the next tree, one of the same creatures stood on a branch, anchored by two tails. The tails flexed up and down so that the creature bounced.

Gliding a few meters above the canopy, Nydea passed the animal, swaying in the treetop. With one of its two arms, it made a throwing motion. A small, oblong object hit the water a mere three meters below Nydea's glide. Toothy jaws emerged from the dark water, snapped up the object, then fell back under the surface. Reilly blinked. Had he really seen teeth, or merely the chop of water from the impact of the thrown object?

Something small and hard struck Reilly's shoulder. Leaves rustled. A half dozen creatures hooted and hopped about on their tails. The mocking sound traveled down the line of trees. How many were there? Nydea called out to them indignantly and rose out of range.

A few minutes later, Nydea murmured something and circled a boulder. She must of have seen something, Reilly thought. He squinted. Extending from the boulder was a pair of legs—human legs—bent at the knees. His heart rebounded against his ribs. One of his parents?

No. Leaning against the boulder, arms hugging her sides, was Maia.

Reilly opened his mouth to shout. Before he'd uttered her name, she sprang to her feet and began swatting at her shoulder. Nydea glided lower. Reilly craned to see. Something dark and fist-sized detached from Maia and fell to the ground. Even in the dark, Reilly recognized the form, remembered the arachnids that had plagued their early days at camp. It moved away from Maia, swiveled, then charged her. Maia kicked at it, drew her gun. The arachnid attached itself to her boot. Maia stamped, grunting with the effort. The thing fell off, scrambled up a boulder. Reilly assumed it was running away, but, as the creature reached the summit, it pivoted and sprang at Maia.

Reilly let out a wordless shout.

The laser from Maia's *yridium* gun connected with the thing in midair, less then a meter in front of her face.

"Great shot, Maia!" he called, waving madly. "Up here!"

Maia looked up, then suddenly cried out, and began clawing at her face. Reilly remembering how the bodily fluids of the arachnid had eaten away Commander Shen's pants. Maia ripped off her night goggles and scrubbed her face with her shirttail. She stumbled toward the creek, somersaulted down the arroyo, and sprawled face first into the water.

"Land, Nydea," Reilly cried. "I have to help her."

For a moment, Nydea hovered a couple meters off the ground. Reilly was about to swing a leg over her side and drop to the ground, when Nydea tilted backward, and Reilly, understanding her intention, counterbalanced with a forward lurch. Nydea landed smoothly at the top of the arroyo. Reilly jumped down and ran to the edge of the embankment.

"Maia!" he called. "Hey! Are you okay?"

Maia rose to her knees and turned toward him, blinking, water streaming from her hair and face. The creek winked moonlight. Suddenly, the surface drew itself into a single wave. The wave became a long-snouted head. Jaws hinged open.

Nydea keened.

"Behind you!" Reilly yelled.

Maia whirled and scooped up the gun from the water's edge. Reilly groped inside his jacket for his slingshot. He felt a stirring of air; saw Nydea rising into the night. Was she abandoning them? Maia scooted backward. The jaws lunged toward her and snapped shut. The body followed, belly smacking the bank. Maia screamed and got to her feet. She aimed her dripping gun. No laser beam shot forth. With a frustrated shriek, Maia hurled the gun at the creature. The animal hissed and came forward on legs so stubby its belly grazed bottom.

"Reilly!" Maia screamed.

Reilly had already snatched a rock from the ground and fitted it to the slingshot. He pulled back. The shot went long and splashed into the creek. The animal was now completely out of the water. A ridge of spikes ran down its spine. A flipper-shaped tail helped propel the body. Each time the tail thrust, the body flopped forward a half meter. Reilly carefully extracted a venom-tipped rock from Kailani's pouch, loaded the slingshot, pulled back, sighted, released. The rock struck the amphibian's side and lodged there. The beast stopped.

Reilly hoped the point had penetrated the hide deeply enough for the venom to enter the creature's veins. He willed the long body to begin convulsing the way Nash's had. But Kailani had said it might take ten minutes for the venom to work. The thing could swallow Maia in less than that time.

After a beat, the creature shook its head and galumphed forward. Maia clawed her way up the arroyo's steep sides. Reilly got on his belly, extended his arm toward her. Their fingertips were centimeters apart. Sand gave way and she slid back down. The creature's six legs lengthened like telescopes and it trotted forward. Reilly scooped up a rock as big as his skull and heaved it. It landed on the animal's back, close to the head, but did nothing to stop the creature. Maia kicked sand in the amphibian's face.

Reilly released another venomous stone. This one hit the creature's leathery neck. The animal turned baleful, bulbous eyes on him and growled open its long snout, exposing row upon row of jagged teeth. The muscles over its powerful shoulders began to twitch, a sign that the venom was working. Nevertheless, the beast heaved itself another half meter. It quivered and drooled. Maia pulled up her feet, which were a mere meter from the massive jaws. Again, Reilly tried to grab her hand, but couldn't quite reach.

From above came the sound of Nydea's voice. Reilly looked up. She hadn't left them. She had flown above them. Now, wings pulled in to her sides, Nydea rocketed toward the amphibian.

"Maia, move!" Reilly shouted. "Get out of the way."

Maia dove sideways. An orange plume emitted from Nydea's mouth and engulfed the crocodilian animal. The creature, now aflame, roared. It fell to its belly, flopped side to side, got back onto its legs. Its scales smoked and yellow flames rose from the dorsal spikes like candles. Bellowing, the creature scurried into the creek and, with a sizzle, collapsed half in and half out of the water.

Maia screamed. The sleeve of her jacket was burning. Reilly skidded down the embankment. Maia threw herself on the ground and rolled down the bank. Reilly guided her to an area several meters away from the motionless monster, yanked off her smoldering jacket, and scooped water at her.

"Stop!" Maia said. "Reilly, stop." She got to her knees and cradled her left arm against her chest. "I'm cold," she said through chattering teeth. "Only my arm got burned, not my whole body."

"Here," Reilly said. He took off his jacket and pulled it around her shoulders

There was a gurgling sound.

Both kids jumped. The amphibian lay a couple meters to the left, its front half in the water. Its back was burned black. The rest was gray and scaly. A bubble rose from its mouth. Then another. Then nothing.

"I think it's dead," Maia said. She began to walk toward the beast.

"What if it's not?" Reilly called. He paused and carefully took her left arm into his hands.

Maia yanked back her arm. "Ouch! What are you doing?"

"I want to see how badly you're burned," Reilly said. "I'll be careful."

"It's too dark."

"I can see well enough with the night goggles."

Maia gingerly held out her arm. There was a scorched hole in her shirtsleeve.

"Your skin is intact," he said. "You're right handed, aren't you?

"I'm flattered that you noticed," she said. "Don't worry. I'll live."

Reilly let go her arm. "That," he said, "is what I was worried about."

Maia smiled. "Just to annoy you, I'll live a long time. Hundreds of years."

"Probably so. You're too mean to die." His voice clutched at the word "die."

Maia shivered. "Shut up and hand me my jacket."

Reilly picked up the garment and shook out the sand. There was a ragged hole in the left sleeve. He gave it to Maia.

"Here's yours," she said. "And thanks."

As Reilly retrieved it, his head tingled. It was the feeling of having a word on the tip of your tongue, or of trying to recall a dream you'd had only moments ago. He looked for Nydea. He had nearly forgotten about her. She sat at the arroyo's lip. The hunch of her shoulders bespoke nervousness. She said something.

Maia grabbed Reilly's arm. "Get down," she whispered. She had retrieved her waterlogged gun and was pointing it at Nydea, who made a sound like a long, low note on the flute.

Reilly pushed down her arm. "Put the gun away"

"What are you going to do, throw rocks at it?"

"Her name is Nydea. She's friendly."

"Right. Just like the catdragons that carried off our animals."

Reilly walked toward Nydea. "Didn't you see me on her back?"

"I was sort of busy." Maia frowned at him. "You were on her back?"

"Yes."

"Voluntarily?"

"Yes. She was bringing me to you."

"Right. You just said, "Take me to Maia,' you climbed on, and the creature brought you here?"

"Something like that." Using all fours, Reilly climbed the side of the arroyo.

"Come up here and thank her."

"For what?"

"For saving your life."

Her injured arm tucked into her jacket, Maia attacked the embankment, but began slipping backwards. Positioned below her, Reilly put a hand on her butt and pushed.

"Hey," she called. "Watch your hands."

"Just trying to help."

When they were both at the top, Maia panted, "So this catdragon breathed the fire that killed the reptilian creature?"

"Apparently so." Reilly walked over to Nydea, touched her side, and said, *"Icantha."*

"Parnea," Nydea replied.

Maia hung back. "Did you just talk to it?"

"I said 'thank you.' The word is *icantha."*

"Icantha," Maia said.

"Parnea," Nydea repeated.

"Wicked phenomenal." Maia frowned. "Wait. How did you learn those words? And how did you get the catdragon to carry you?"

Nydea narrowed her eyes at Reilly. His head buzzed. Was she trying to communicate? If so, he wasn't getting it. She spoke aloud. He held up his hands in a gesture of helplessness. Nydea repeated the words and pointed a forepaw up the creek. She began walking, her barbed tail swaying over her back.

"I think she wants us to follow her," Reilly said. "We're supposed to meet Kailani."

"What the minje are you talking about?"

"Tell you later. Let's get going."

NINETEEN

They traveled parallel to the creek, but in the opposite direction of camp. While Reilly and Maia walked, Nydea flew slow ellipses, sometimes touching down and waiting for the humans to catch up.

The moonlight was now so bright that Reilly pushed his night goggles atop his head. The shadows of the skeletal trees formed an ancient script against the sand. Every object had two shadows, one darker and squatter, the other longer and more attenuated. A glance at the sky told him the orange moon, which was higher in the sky, cast the short shadow, and the blue moon, soon to set behind the mesa, cast the long, thin shadow.

They passed under the trees until Reilly remembered the many-legged serpent that had dropped from the branches onto Nash. For the hundredth time, he heard the boy's screams; saw the convulsions, the bruised skin, the blood running from nose and mouth.

He looked up nervously, but could see nothing more than branches and leaves. He imagined serpents hanging by their tails, double-tailed animals armed with rocks, birds laughing in celebration of the death of two more humans. He steered Maia a few meters away from the canopy.

His parents had now been out eight nights. He wondered whether Nydea had seen them, perhaps befriended them. He wished he knew how to ask her. As soon as he could get Maia safely back to the base, he would resume his search. Maybe Nydea would carry him. She alighted on a tree up ahead. The branch swayed wildly under her weight. Something in the canopy voiced a high-pitched objection, but Nydea growled a rebuke and the thing fell silent.

In the next tree, a creature popped up, two long arms grasping the branch overhead.

Maia grabbed his forearm. "What was that?"

"I think it's an animal I saw while flying with Nydea. They throw things at you."

She let go his arm. "Oh," she said. "Two tails, right? I've seen them. Harlan says they're harmless."

After a moment's silence, she said, "Why don't you tell me how you came to ride on the catdragon's back and where we're going."

Reilly told her about Nydea taking him to Kailani's cave, about his brief encounter with Kailani, about riding on Nydea's back.

"Wow," Maia said. "I want to fly like that. Do you think she would carry me now?"

Reilly looked at Nydea, who was gliding just ahead. Again, she alighted on a tree branch. Each time they caught up with her, she glided to the next tree. Sometimes she flew a short distance, then circled back. Either she was scouting the route, or she didn't like to walk. For all Reilly knew, she also disliked carrying humans on her back. "I don't know," he said. "And I don't know how to ask her either. It's not like I speak Mirnan."

"Speak what?"

"Mirnan. Mirna is the name of the planet. And Mirnan is the language the animals speak—those species capable of speech."

"I thought we were on Cinnabar."

"It's not what the natives call it."

"Aren't you the know-it-all? You're also saying that the animals can talk?"

Nydea soared low overhead and made a shushing noise.

Maia startled.

Reilly felt surprisingly calm. "I think she wants us to be quiet."

"How do you know?"

Reilly shrugged. It seemed obvious. "Just whisper, okay?"

"Okay," she whispered.

After a few minutes, Reilly said quietly, "Why did you follow me?"

"I heard you leave, but thought you were just making a trip to the latrine. When you didn't come back, I looked out the window, saw you running from the guard tower to the airscouters, saw you lift off. At first, it blistered me that you—I don't know—escaped. That you were having an adventure without me. That you felt so filthin' *entitled* to take one of the airscouters." She blew out her breath. "And I was sort of worried about you."

"Worried about me?"

"Yeah. The collective survival depends upon no one person taking undue risks," Maia said, perfectly parroting protocol.

Reilly looked at her. "I've heard it before. Never thought you were paying attention."

"How would you know? As far as you're concerned, we *in vitro* kids are practically invisible."

Reilly didn't know what to say.

"Given how few of us are left. It's selfish of you to run off into the night."

"Selfish?" He thought he was brave to go search for his parents.

"If you die," Maia said, "everyone else's chance of survival diminishes."

Shame stung Reilly's face. He knew she was right, but her saying so made him angry. "*You* certainly took a risk by following me. Our collective survival might have been better served if you had sounded the alarm. That way, the adults would have come after me. A much better plan, that one." He paused. "Did you sound the alarm?"

Nydea banked overhead and made a shushing sound not unlike a human quieting a fractious child.

"No." Maia sighed. "I know, I know, my logic was flawed. I just wanted to… go."

"You know what your problem is?" Reilly whispered.

"I'm sure you'll tell me."

"You're impulsive. And what were you doing walking around alone? You should have stayed with your craft. The crew would have come eventually."

"Look who's talking about impulsiveness and recklessness," she hissed.

"I planned my escape." He didn't add that the conscious planning had taken under an hour.

Maia made a humphing sound. "Anyway, I wasn't going to walk forever. I'd made a pact with myself. I was going to follow the creek north until the red moon was three palms from the horizon." She held up hands, fingers pointed toward each other, then stacked her left palm atop her right. "If you hadn't come, I'd already be on my way back."

"If I hadn't come, you'd be in the belly of that creek reptile."

"The catdragon saved me, not you."

"Nydea is her name," he reminded her. "And she's a *wyome* not a catdragon."

About 15 meters ahead was a rock formation reminiscent of an enormous spoon standing on end. A knife balanced beside it. Only the fork was missing.

"Apparently someone saw you leave," he said.

Maia looked at him. "No way. I was quiet as a dream."

"Yeah, well, Captain Baca and Ensign Morten were looking around the area where we left the scooters. I saw them from Nydea's back."

"Minje."

"I was hoping to have more time before they came looking."

"Both of us are going to get in a lot of trouble." Maia stopped herself and laughed. "The least of our problems."

Reilly held a finger in front of his lips. "If we return alive, the crew will mostly be relieved."

Maia looked over her shoulder. "Maybe we should go back now. Deal with the consequences. I'd rather scoop goat poop for a month straight than encounter any more monsters."

"Kailani said to meet her. I think we're safer if we stick to that plan." He stole a sidelong glance at Maia. She looked remarkably calm. "Maia?"

"What?"

"When Nydea circled our scouters, I saw the body of that creature that had come after me, the one with the horns. Kailani says it's called a *witnaw.*"

"Whatever."

"Did you kill it?"

"Yeah. While it was ramming the scooter, I ransacked the storage compartment and found a laser gun. Just then, its horn tore through the scouter's side, right near my right thigh. I stood, opened the dome, and shot it through the top of its head. It stank. Smelled worse after it was dead."

"Yeah," Reilly said. He almost congratulated her, but his lips clamped down on the words. She'd been genetically engineered to be brave. It wasn't like she had to battle her fear.

A chorus of yips interrupted the conversation. Reilly and Maia halted and looked toward the sound. Seven meters away loomed a rock formation shaped like a squat, neckless man. A canine head poked out from the side of the boulder, then ducked back.

Without a word, both Maia and Reilly yanked down their night goggles and gathered a handful of rocks. Reilly grabbed his slingshot. When the head appeared again, mouth opened in a snarl, he hurled a rock at it, catching a glancing blow. With a yelp, the creature streaked from the boulder to another. It was twice as big as Beau. Large, rounded ears stuck out from the sides of its head. Spikes protruded from the end of its thick tail.

Nydea circled back. As she glided overhead, she uttered what sounded like a reproach.

"What do you suppose she said?" Maia asked.

"She sounded irritated. Maybe those animals are her friends. Maybe she doesn't want us throwing rocks at them." He cast backward glances toward the rock formations. Nothing moved. Nothing followed them. He returned the slingshot to his back pocket and released the rocks.

They kept walking. The creek bent to follow the base of the mesa.

"Reilly," Maia said, "what makes you think you can find your parents? No one else has been able to."

Reilly shook his head. How could he explain that he could *sense* them, that their love would draw them together? She would laugh. Worse, he might cry. Then she'd really have something to gloat over.

"You don't even have a pack. You have no gun, no food, no nothing. What were you going to do—eat bugs?"

"Shut up. Anyway, I had a pack. And a gun. It's all in the scouter. I didn't intend to leave it behind."

Just ahead of them, Nydea hovered in the air, head lifted and her wings fanning slowly. She sensed something. Neck prickling, Reilly scanned the landscape, took in the creek bending northwest to follow the curve of the mesa, the red moon hovering over the top of the mesa.

Straight ahead, something moved along the ground. The shape was dark, narrow, and vertical. It was about twenty meters ahead and traveling briskly their way.

TWENTY

Within moments it became clear that the advancing creature was bipedal and solitary. A heartbeat later, Reilly recognized Kailani. Nydea flew to her, then looped back behind Reilly and Maia as though herding them.

Reilly started to walk toward her, but Maia held his sleeve and whispered, "Please tell me that's the woman—the one you met, the one from the cave."

Reilly pulled free of her grasp. "Yes. It's Kailani," he said. "I think you'll like her."

As they hurried forward, Maia said, "What in the cosmos is she wearing?"

Reilly squinted. Atop the tunic and baggy pants, she wore a weird cloak—a piece of hide with a hole for her head and a rope to cinch it to her waist. Her hair was now plaited into a long braid that hung over one shoulder. On her back was a crude pack, in her right hand, a staff. She gave the impression of height. Yet when she reached them, she was a hair shorter than Maia.

Reilly pushed his goggles atop his head. "Hello, Kailani," He supposed he should be calling her by some title, but she hadn't told him what it was. He had to struggle to remember her last name. Night or perhaps Knight. "This is Maia."

"Reilly told me he met an old lady who lives in a cave."

Reilly cringed.

"How about you call me Lani instead of 'old lady'," Kailani said. "Full name is Kailani Knight. But Lani will do."

"I'm Maia."

"So I gathered. What's your last name?"

Maia drew back her shoulders. "Just Maia."

"Vitros aren't given last names," Reilly said.

"A shameful practice," Kailani said. "We'll have to give you one." She said something to Nydea. Nydea responded and Kailani gave a short laugh. "How about Maia Halatha? In Mirnan, *halatha* means bold-hearted."

Maia beamed.

Kailani momentarily locked gazes with Nydea. Reilly's head hummed a moment. They were doing that mind communication thing. He rubbed his forehead, the humming ceased, and Kailani spoke in a low voice.

"You've been worrying Nydea," she said. "No wonder. So careless and noisy. I could hear your voices a half kilometer away. By now, all the locals must know you're wandering out here, defenseless and ignorant."

Maia pulled back her shoulders and said, "I have a gun. I've already killed one of those smelly, horned things." Her words lacked their usual conviction and cockiness.

"A *witnaw*." Kailani's eyes assessed Maia.

Maia removed her goggles, returned Kailani's unblinking gaze, and said "yes."

Reilly felt the need to interrupt the energy that streamed between the two women. "Don't forget that crocodile thing that almost got you."

Kailani shook her head. "You encountered a *dilcroth* too?"

"Nydea killed it," Reilly said. "She breathed fire at it."

"How does she do that?" Maia asked.

"You two have stirred up all kinds of trouble," Kailani muttered. "Let me see that arm."

Maia obediently extended her arm, and Kailani leaned her staff against her shoulder so she could use both her hands to investigate Maia's wound. Kailani spoke Mirnan to Nydea. Reilly didn't hear Nydea speak, yet Kailani nodded, as though she had received an answer.

"So," Maia said, "You can communicate with the aliens?"

"We are the aliens," Kailani said. She parted the scorched holes in Maia's sleeves and peered inside.

"A few blisters. Second-degree burn. Nothing serious," Kailani said. "Count yourself lucky."

"How can you see that well? You're not wearing night goggles," Maia said accusingly.

The blue moon had just set, the red moon hung low in the sky, and the sun wasn't up yet.

"My night vision improved. Yours probably will too."

"Mine already has, I think," said Maia.

Kailani swung off her pack, extracted the small pot, removed the stopper, dipped in her finger, and rubbed salve on the wound. Maia winced, but held her arm still. "My place isn't far. We can dress your wound better there. And you can eat and rest."

Kailani unhooked a soft bag with a narrow neck from her belt. There was a sloshing sound as she handed it to Maia.

Maia dangled the bag by its narrow neck, as though she were holding a dead chicken. "What's this?"

"A water bag," Kailani said. "Go ahead, drink."

Maia held the bag at eye level. "But what is it?"

"It's made from the bladder of an *erzala,* an ungulate that lives on the mesa."

"Grotty," Maia said. With a shrug, she loosened the thong that held the neck shut and drank. Wiping her chin with the back of her sleeve, she said, "at least it doesn't taste like piss."

Kailani took the bag and passed it to Reilly, who drank without comment and returned the bag to Kailani.

"Let's go," Kailani said.

Just as they began walking, the sky lit up. Curtains of colored light glowed bright, flickered, danced. A wavering green hugged the horizon, layered above with purple. An ellipse of bright pink bloomed in the middle.

"Phenomenal," Maia breathed.

Reilly recalled watching these lights not long ago with Ensign Morten.

"An aurora," Kailani said. "It happens on Earth too, mostly at the north and south poles, though I never saw those lights. The cause here is the same—electrically charged particles from the sun, either from solar winds or solar flares. The particles become trapped by the planet's magnetic field and strike atoms in the atmosphere, releasing the energy that causes this light show."

"Amazing," Maia breathed, her eyes riveted to the shifting colors.

"Isn't that bad?" Reilly asked. "I mean solar flares disrupt the magnetic field."

"Bad for radio and satellite communications. When the flares are strong, they play havoc with the computers, maybe with our cellular functions. Are yours still working?"

"Our bodies? Or our computers?" Maia asked.

"Computers," Kailani said.

"Most of them are down," Reilly said.

Kailani nodded, as though his words confirmed her suspicions.

"And what about the health effects?" Reilly asked.

"Gamma radiation levels spike," Kailani said. "I suspect the periodic irradiation has something to do with—well, certain changes."

"Changes in what?" Maia asked.

"Hush," Kailani said. "Enough talking for now."

They walked on. Down by the creek, something glinted. Reilly's mind matched the size and shape to something his parents might have left—a gun, an e-scope, a camera. Heart and legs working double time, he hurried toward it.

"What are you doing?" Kailani said sharply.

"I see something. There, by the water."

"It's a dead *wapesh*," Kailani said. "Any minute, a *dilcroth* will be along to eat it."

Using his sleeve, Reilly wiped the lens of his fogged night goggles. He was grateful that the lenses hid his tears. He could now see that the shiny thing was oblong with multiple pointed projections. Something splashed in the creek.

Reilly stumbled backward. "What was that?"

"Another *wapesh*," Kailani said. "Completely harmless. Good to eat too. Mostly, they live on the creek's bottom. Sometimes they crawl out at night to feed on the banks. They have a row of mouth-like suckers on their bellies that take in tiny plants, insects, and the droppings of other animals."

Nydea dropped from her perch in a tree, skimmed the creek's surface, and rose with something wiggling in her front paws. She popped it into her mouth.

"What you need to worry about," Kailani said, "are the animals that feed on *wapesh.*"

After they walked for a while, Maia whispered, "Lani, what's our plan?'

"Well," Kailani said. "We'll rest a bit. At first light, before it gets hot, I'll walk you to the base."

"You know where the base is?" Maia said.

"Of course she does," Reilly said. "She's one of the first colonists."

"You must have seen the lights of our ship in orbit," Maia said. "Why haven't you come to see us?"

Kailani walked, head down, hood concealing her face. "Why is it so hard for you to be quiet?"

"What happened to the other colonists?" Reilly said.

"Not now," Kailani said. "I'll explain once we're safe in my cave."

"Okay. But I'm not going back to the base, not until I find my parents," Reilly said.

Kailani didn't answer. Nydea swooped within two meters of their heads. Kailani stopped, touched her temple, and looked up with alarm.

Someone spoke. Reilly recognized the sounds as Mirnan. But the voice was low-pitched and grinding, like a rockslide.

They all turned toward the sound. A stone's throw away, a second *wyome* crouched on a boulder. It was larger than Nydea. Its folded wings rose from its back like knives, and its barbed tail flicked side to side.

TWENTY-ONE

Maia pulled the *yridium* gun from her pocket. The big *wyome* pulled back his lips over yellow canines and snarled.

"Maia," Kailani whispered, "put it away. This is Hyssel, Nydea's uncle. He knows what a gun can do. Don't move or speak unless I say so."

Maia slid the gun and her hand into her pocket. Reilly wished he knew whether, once the *yridium* cartridge dried, her gun might work again.

Nydea faced the big *wyome*, folded tight her wings, tucked her legs under her, and pulled in her head. Reilly couldn't tell whether she was showing respect, communicating her subdominant status, or protecting tender body parts from potential attack. One thing was clear: She was afraid.

Nydea and Hyssel locked eyes. Reilly felt as though something deep within his brain was vibrating. He tried to suppress the sensation, but the vibration became a sound. First the sound was a sweet alto. A brief silence followed, then a bass rumble. For a minute or two, the two pitches alternated. He remembered when his father had taken out an old-fashioned tuning fork, struck the tines against the base of his palm, and placed the base of the tuning fork on the top of his skull. A pleasant hum collected in the middle of his head, equidistant between his ears. "That's the sound of A," his father had said. It was as though Nydea and Hyssel vibrated strings in his head. Nydea's dominant tone was pure A; Hyssel came in at low E flat. The alternating tones seemed like a conversation, like two instruments playing together out of tune.

"Are they communicating?" Reilly whispered to Kailani.

Kailani gave him an appraising look, then nodded.

"What are they saying?" Maia asked.

Kailani shook her head. "I can only read Nydea's thoughts, and only when she directs them at me."

Hyssel rotated his head, which was as large as Reilly's entire torso, and growled at Kailani. Kailani replied in Mirnan. Hyssel gave a terse response. Reilly's scalp prickled. Kailani touched her temple, then shook her head. The humming in Reilly's head made him want to knock his head with the heel of his hand.

Both *wyomes* looked at him. *They're talking about me,* Reilly thought. Hyssel glared and curled his upper lip. The base of Reilly's spine burned. Sweat dampened his armpits.

One of the pink rodents darted out from under the boulder Hyssel perched upon. As though realizing its mistake, the creature rose on its hind legs, double ears pricked, and looked back at Hyssel. Its spines inflated. As it dove for a burrow, Hyssel exhaled fire at it. The animal screeched and ran in flaming circles. Hyssel watched dispassionately.

"That's cruel!" Reilly took a step forward.

Kailani put a hand on his shoulder. "Be still."

The small animal tunneled into the sand, its back still smoking.

"Someone should put it out of its misery," Maia said. She took out her gun and aimed it at the smoldering creature.

Hyssel growled.

"Maia," Kailani cautioned.

Tight-jawed, Maia dropped her gun hand. The charred creature flopped onto its side and lay there. For a moment, its sides fanned in and out, then went still.

Hyssel sat tall on his back haunches. "Nydea," he boomed.

Nydea's shoulders hunched, and the three humans clustered closer.

Hyssel eyed Maia and licked his leathery chops. The low buzzing in Reilly's head intensified. He stepped in front of Maia. From his back pocket, he pulled the slingshot.

"I'm the one with the gun," Maia whispered.

Reilly pulled a venom-coated stone loose from the pouch. Nydea's ears flattened against her head. Hyssel craned his neck toward Reilly. His nostrils quivered and saliva dropped from his muzzle to the boulder upon which he stood. Nydea spoke aloud, her tone pleading. Hyssel roared and fire flickered from his mouth. Nydea tucked into a ball, and the three humans threw arms before faces. The flames stopped short of Reilly.

Hyssel sat back on his haunches and pulled back his lips into a menacing smile. Kailani stepped forward and spoke in Mirnan.

The big *wyome* blew a fireball in her direction. Kailani ducked. Just to her right, a bush burst into flame. Hyssel hopped off the boulder and advanced.

Reilly fitted the rock into the slingshot, pulled back the sling, aimed, released. The rock glanced off Hyssel's shoulder. With a snarl, Hyssel lunged toward Reilly. Reilly staggered backward, knocking Maia to her knees. She swore and scrambled to her feet.

Kailani's body appeared to elongate. "Leave us, Hyssel," she said. She raised her rock-tipped staff. Her outline shimmered, as though distorted by heat waves.

Reilly wondered if an incipient migraine had affected his vision. He reached under his night goggles and rubbed his eyes. Everything looked normal except for Kailani.

Hyssel stiffened and cocked his head. He said something in a goading tone.

Nydea crept backwards to crouch to Kailani's left. Kailani whispered to Nydea, then lowered her staff. She still didn't look quite solid to Reilly.

Hyssel leapt back up on the boulder. Reilly anticipated he would take flight. Instead, the *wyome* twisted and sprang toward Reilly and Maia. Nydea yeowled. Reilly crouched. Maia remained standing, gun pointed at Hyssel's chest. She pressed the trigger, but nothing happened. Kailani threw herself at Maia, knocking her to the ground and covering Maia's body with her own.

Reilly felt warm breath against his back. Hyssel gave a laugh that sounded like boulders cracking. The laughter grew fainter. Reilly looked up to see Hyssel ascending. He growled Nydea's name. Nydea remained on the ground, head high, chest puffed defiantly.

Hyssel paused in the air and spoke. Nydea's ears drooped and she let out a despairing sound. After a sorrowful glance at the humans, she raised her head resignedly, flapped her wings, and flew off behind her uncle. The two forms dissolved into darkness.

∞

A minute later, Maia punctured the stunned silence. "You're squashing me," she protested, her voice muffled by Kailani's body.

"Sorry," Kailani said. "Better squashed than scorched." She examined her leggings, which were torn at the knee.

"Yes, Maia," Reilly said, "you might thank—" He struggled to remember her title. "Captain Kailani for her trouble."

"Forget it," Kailani said. "Anyway it's Commander Knight."

Reilly gaped. "You were second in command?"

Kailani didn't answer. Instead, she threw handfuls of sand onto the bush Hyssel had burned to quench the last flames. The air smelled of the plant's resin and the charred flesh of the rodent Hyssel had killed.

Kailani glanced at the band of yellow light rimming the horizon. "We'd better hurry," she said.

Kailani's staff lay on the ground. Maia picked it up and touched the mauve-colored stone at the tip. "What did you just do?"

Kailani took the staff from her and ran her fingers along the smooth wood of its shaft. "I don't know," she mused. "It's only happened once before."

Reilly had expected a different answer. He wanted her to say that her staff had always possessed magical powers. He wanted her to say she had killed scores of predators with this awesome weapon. He wanted her to say that nothing could possibly harm them.

"Does this…energy, or whatever it is, have to do with the staff?" Maia asked

"The staff is made from *chagala,* the tree that grows along the creek. The rock on the tip is the kind you find all around the mesa. I've had other staffs made of the same materials without this effect."

"What is the effect, exactly?" Reilly said. "Is it something coming out of you?"

"When I figure it out, I'll let you know." Kailani turned and began striding toward the west. Reilly and Maia followed.

"What was that big catdragon saying to you?" Maia asked.

"First," Kailani said, "Hyssel insulted you and me and Reilly and all human-kind. A scourge upon Mirna is what he called us. We use too much water and cut down the *chagala* trees, which leaves the *boola*—the savory birds that nest there—no place to live. We harm his kind with our laser guns. He should kill all *nakkoths*—the Mirnan word for humans—before we breed like *shekraks.*"

"What are *shekraks?*" Maia asked.

"The little pink creature Hyssel just burned was a *shekrak.*"

"What else did Hyssel say?" Reilly asked.

Kailani took a deep breath. "He reminded Nydea that she was not supposed to associate with *nakkoths.* He said she was starting to stink like us, a smell as bad as the goat-like creatures called *erzalas.* He wondered if that meant we tasted as succulent. He proposed a three-course meal, beginning with Reilly."

"Filthin' bitter," Maia muttered. "Good thing you had that laser spear, Commander Knight."

"I'd rather you call me Kailani or Lani. The title seems ridiculous now."

"Why didn't he kill us?" asked Reilly. Now that the adrenaline was wearing off, his legs felt wobbly and his stomach empty. He wished Kailani would walk a bit slower.

"I'm sure he would have, were Nydea not there to intervene," Kailani said.

"What did she say to stop him?" Maia asked.

Off to their right, one of the creekside birds made a sleepy, cooing sound.

"She threatened to tell the Council—the group of *wyome* elders that offers advice to the High Leader—about the way he treats his mate."

"Who is the High Leader?" Maia said.

"Hyssel."

Reilly let out a rough laugh. "Then the Council is toothless."

"Ah, but the Council could depose him. There's a network of *wyome* colonies on Mirna. Hyssel is a local clan leader. More like a duke from the days of the British monarchy. Other clans live in canyons on the north side

Linda B. White

of Methna Mesa. Further north, the terrain becomes hilly, then mountainous. I'm told the Supreme Leader lives in the foothills. She's equivalent to the king. If a High Leader defies recommendations, the Clan Council can bring the matter before the Supreme Leader."

They had turned away from the creek, and the babble of water tapered to nothing.

Maia spoke. "You said Hyssel abuses his mate. Who is she? Or he? Are *wyomes* heterosexual?"

"Mostly. Sheeda is Hyssel's mate. She's Nydea's aunt, sister to Nydea's mother. Sheeda has taken care of Nydea since her parents died. Until a few years ago, Nydea's parents acted jointly as High Leader of the Ledera Canyon Clan. They died tragically and somewhat mysteriously before I arrived. Hyssel was next in line."

"You sound suspicious," Maia said.

"Well," Kailani said, "you've met Hyssel."

"Hmm," Reilly mused. "If Hyssel is such a tyrant, why doesn't he kill Nydea?"

"Nydea is noble born and will succeed Hyssel as leader," Kailani said. "Nydea's murder would raise a few hackles amongst the *wyome* clan."

"What will happen to Nydea now?" Maia asked.

"I suspect her uncle will punish her."

"How?" Maia asked. "I mean, what will he do to her?"

"Strike her, burn her."

"Oh!" Maia said. "Worse than the Electroprod."

Kailani looked sharply at her. "The crew uses the Prod on you kids?"

"Mostly Reba, the android, used it. But she malfunctioned soon after we landed."

Kailani grunted.

"Will Nydea be okay?" Reilly asked.

Kailani shook her head, "I hope so."

TWENTY-TWO

Within a half hour, they had entered a shallow canyon in the mesa's side and were standing at the base of a cliff. The light of dawn had just reached the rock face, creating a palette of peach, rose, and lavender.

"Home, sweet home," Kailani said and pointed out the opening to her cave, a dark oval halfway up the stone face.

"Wow," Maia said admiringly.

Reilly knew that Maia loved to climb things. On the ship, she was always scaling shelves, scaffolds, struts, girders, and beams. When she was a toddler, she had tried to climb up the back of a chair in the ship's mess hall, and the chair had toppled over onto her. Reilly remembered the blood that had cascaded from a cut on her head and his mother saying not to worry, that the scalp tended to bleed a lot when cut, that the wound wasn't serious. His mother had been the one to hold Maia in her lap, murmuring words of comfort. She asked Reilly to hold the gauze firmly over the cut till the bleeding stopped. Reilly vaguely recalled feeling proud when Maya was up and about again.

A ladder bridged the ten meters between flat ground and the cave's wide ledge. Kailani ascended first, then Maia, then Reilly. He was not about to admit that heights made him nervous. Looking only as far as the next rung, he climbed hand over hand, foot over foot. The coarse rope bit into his palms. At the top, he threw himself onto the ledge. As Kailani pulled up the ladder, Reilly wondered which other species were capable of climbing it. The two-tailed creatures that swung in the *chagala* trees came to mind, but they didn't seem particularly dangerous. Besides, how would they travel from the creek? Walk on their hands?

Kailani invited Maia and Reilly to go inside the cave and wrap up in one of the *erzala* skins while she prepared a breakfast. Maia plunged into the dim interior. Reilly entered more cautiously. It was more spacious than he had imagined, nearly as big as the mess hall at the base. The ceiling was about two and a half meters high at the entrance, opening up to twice that height at the domed center.

Toward the back, the skins were stacked atop a rough mattress, which appeared to be woven of the plant stems. Reilly picked up a skin. The hide was a pale gray with silky white fur. It smelled musky, but not foul. He put it down. He had never worn anything that came from an animal. Maia grabbed a skin, tossed it across her shoulders, and wandered off.

On the floor near the mattress was a computer scroll so deep in dust it took Reilly a moment to make out what it was. Next to it stood a stack of tattered books. He glanced over his shoulder at Kailani. She was stirring something in a pot, her back to him. Reilly tried to make out the titles on the book spines but there wasn't enough light.

Maia was examining a rack made of peeled branches. On this wooden frame, orange-brown threads ran vertically and horizontally. Maia fingered a thread.

"You shouldn't touch her stuff," Reilly said.

Maia pulled back her hand.

Kailani looked up from stirring embers to life in a pit near the cave's mouth. "Touch away," she said. "I'm setting up the loom to weave a new shirt. What do you think of the colors?"

"I like the orange," Maia said. "Does the dye come from a flower?"

Kailani nodded. "For other colors, I use berries and roots."

"Ensign Rabin is going to show us how to use a loom soon."

"Your people are still using titles?" Kailani said.

"Reilly does," Maia said. "We vitros call the lower-ranking crew by their first names."

"Ah," Kailani said.

Reilly pursed his lips. Aside from his parents, no adult had ever invited him to omit his or her title. He pictured Ensign Morten in the dorm with Maia and the other kids, teaching them things, joking, having pillow fights.

Reilly moved closer to Kailani. By the pale light, he could see that her clothing was woven from rust-colored, brown, and red threads. "What materials do you use? To make your clothes, I mean."

"I get the fibers from *guya* root. I use it to make rope too. The leaves have bayonet-like stalks that can be converted to needle and thread."

"Can you teach me how?" Maia asked.

"I suppose so," Kailani said. "Can't say I'm very good at it."

Reilly wondered whether this is what they would come to—wearing crude garments like Kailani's. On the ship, when he needed new clothes, he told the computer the item he needed then walked into a booth. Lasers scanned his body to calibrate dimensions. A minute later, nozzles sprayed out ChemSilk, which quickly congealed into a microfiber membrane, a seamless garment. If you wanted a looser fitting garment—say, a shirt—the CompuTailor spun ChemSilk of the prescribed thickness, then cut, and adhered the pieces together.

The CompuTailor remained on the ship, but Ensign Rabin and Commander Shen had begun building a new one. The goats were genetically modified to secrete spider-silk protein into their milk. Once the ewes started lactating, they could extract the protein from the milk and spin it into fabric— if the goats survived long enough to give birth.

Kailani coughed and fanned smoke away from her face.

Reilly continued to look around. A dusty telsar lamp sat in a rocky niche in the cave's mouth, its small solar panel angled toward the rising sun. On the walls hung bundles of upside-down plants. Some had pods that were variously winged, clawed, or fringed with small barbs. A half dozen pots sat on the ground along one wall. Two held water, others contained strips of what looked to be dried meat, yellow roots, tiny red berries (he'd seen such fruit growing on a spiny plant with thick leaves), leaves from the same plant, and brown leathery things about the size and shape of eyeballs. On the ground was a pile of plants with finger-shaped pods, and another pile with the same pods opened and empty. Between lay a bowl half full of elliptical, spotted beans.

"Come sit by the fire," Kailani said. She gestured toward woven mats beside the stone fire pit.

Atop a metal stand over the fire was a metal cook pot, inside of which bubbled something viscous. Reilly recognized the stand as a piece of the modular shelving used on the ship. Underneath it was a heap of glowing nuggets roughly the size and shape of his thumb. The eye-watering smoke was pleasantly pungent.

"What do you use for fuel?" he asked.

"*Erzala* droppings," Kailani said. She had removed her worn boots and was massaging her feet. Her right big toe poked through a hole in the sock. It was crooked, as though it had been broken. With a jolt, Reilly remembered his mother saying that Captain Baca had frantically checked the feet of the dead first colonists, as though searching for a deformity.

"We've been burning goat shit. You dry it first, right?" Maia asked.

Kailani smiled, which made her look less exhausted. "Right."

"That water sack," he said, "didn't you say it came from an *erzala?*"

"The bladder," Maia put in.

"Right," Kailani told her. "That hide over your shoulder comes from the same animal."

"What do they look like?" Maia asked.

"In many ways, they're similar to Earth's mountain goats."

"We have goats at the base," Maia said.

"*Erzalas* are much bigger. And, they're the only Mirnan animal I've seen that has fur rather than scales."

"Do you eat them?" Maia asked.

"When I can catch one. The meat's a bit tough, but makes a decent stew."

"How do you hunt them?"

"Bow and arrow."

"Don't you have a gun?" Maia asked.

Kailani shook her head. "I ran out of *yridium* over a year ago. I'm working on a way to focus sunlight through an optical fiber to power a gun and other tools. The problem is storing the photons."

Reilly looked around. He didn't see evidence of mirrors to concentrate light, nor fiberoptics. Of course, it was dark in the cave. Maybe she had a lab somewhere else.

"You should talk to Oren about that. Oren Rabin. He's been experimenting with different types of batteries."

Kailani shoved her feet back into her boots and began gathering utensils and scooping things from pots. She was a compact package of muscle and bone—lean, but not emaciated. Reilly marveled that she'd found enough to eat on this parched planet to stay alive.

What about his parents? What had they been eating? They had laser guns, and plenty of *yridium*. Maybe they had killed an *erzala*. Maybe they had eaten plants, using their portable chromatograph to screen for toxins. What if they were too injured to forage? He had to resume searching for them. Now that Kailani was around to return Maia to the base, he could go. A quick bite to eat, and he'd be off. If Kailani or Maia tried to talk him out of it, he'd toss down the ladder and scramble down.

"Keep that fire going," Kailani called.

Reilly poked the embers with the stick Kailani had used, then realized the thing was actually the rib of some animal. Using an empty gourd of some kind, Maia scooped animal droppings from a battered bucket into the fire. The low flames danced. Reilly held his hands to the warmth.

Nearby lay a knife with a broken handle and, beside it, a stone with a deep depression. Inside it rested a smaller, blunt-nosed stone and ground seeds. In a recent survival class, Ensign Morten had taught them about this kind of tool. It was called a mortar and pestle, but Reilly couldn't remember which stone was which.

Kailani returned with three stacked bowls. She stirred the pot, tasted its contents, and set down the wooden spoon. "Breakfast is almost ready," she said.

She ladled steaming porridge from the pot into the bowls and handed Reilly and Maia each a bowl. The grayish pink substance reminded Reilly of something you might hawk up if you had pneumonia. His grandfather had died of pneumonia. The memory of him coughing and gasping made Reilly sad and nauseated. He shifted his focus to the outside of the bowl, which was made from blue clay and bore the indentations of Kailani's fingertips. Reilly glanced at Maia, who had placed her fingers in the depressions along the rim of her bowl.

He cast about for a spoon and saw none, other than the one Kailani had used for cooking. Kailani held her bowl close to her mouth and scooped in food with her index and middle fingers. Maia did the same. Reilly tried to drink his from the bowl, but the thick cereal plopped onto his upper lip and the tip of his nose. He licked. It was gluey, but pleasantly sweet.

"Use your fingers, Prince Reilly," Maia said. "It won't hurt you."

Reilly wiped his face with the cuff of his jacket.

"Sorry," Kailani said. "I'm short on silverware. Had I known I would be having guests, I'd have whittled more spoons. I only have one mug, so we'll have to share." She handed it to Maia.

"What is this?" Maia asked.

"Tea, or, more correctly, a *tisane,*" Kailani said. "I could tell you the names of the plants, but they won't mean much until you see them growing."

They had had tea on the ship. Tea and coffee. First the coffee ran out, then the tea. Reilly remembered sitting in someone's lap. His father's maybe. Maia toddled in and stood for a minute, looking at him. Then she walked to Fari, a dark-haired, dark-eyed woman with big hips and a loud voice, now long dead. She was one of the four developmental psychologists in charge of the *in vitros*. Fari had scooped Maia into her lap, then resumed drinking from her cup. Maia's small hands darted out for the cup's rim, splashing liquid over them both. Fari had exclaimed angrily in a foreign language and pried a screaming, clinging Maia loose.

Now, Maia thrust the mug at him. "It's not bad. Try it."

The mug warmed his palms. Bits of leaves swirled in the brownish water, and the vapors smelled like the desert baking in the mid-day sun. The beverage tasted tangy and slightly bitter—nothing like the astringent beverage he'd had on the ship. "Thanks," he said and returned the mug to Kailani. He put the bowl to his lips and pushed cereal into his mouth with his fingers until it was all gone.

Maia sucked cereal off her fingers, wiped her mouth on her sleeve, and said, "You said you would tell us what happened to the first colonists."

For a moment, Reilly didn't think Kailani would answer. Then she took a deep breath and said, "They all died, except me."

"How?" Maia said. "What happened?"

"One day, I went out on a plant-gathering expedition—"

"Alone?" Reilly said.

Kailani nodded. "Stupid, I know. Suffice it to say that I disliked the crewmember assigned to go with me. I've had years to regret that decision." She gazed into the fire. "Anyway, I followed a dry creek up the north side of Methna Mesa. I came to a place where water had eroded the rock, creating a long, steep slide down to what, during the wet season—"

"It really does rain here?" Reilly asked.

"Yes. For a few weeks each year. You won't believe how the rain transforms this place. Water cascades down the mesa. The creek overflows its banks and fills arroyos that are otherwise bone dry. Plants bloom. The flowers are spectacular. Insects, amphibians, and small mammals come out of hibernation, mate, and multiply.

"Anyway, water had pooled at the bottom of this basin. I was thirsty, and my water bottles were low. As I climbed down, I lost my footing, fell, and broke my wrist."

Maia guffawed. "You're wandering alone, surrounded by predators, and you hurt yourself getting a drink of water?"

Kailani nodded. "I didn't even realize my predicament until, after I had splinted my wrist and quenched my thirst, I tried to climb back out—and couldn't."

She rubbed a bony knot on her right wrist. "Days passed. I ran out of food, then water. *Pakitoks,* this planet's version of vultures, began to circle overhead."

"What's a vulture?" Maia asked.

"A large Earth bird that eats carrion," Reilly said. The memory of the gray birds lurking the day his parents departed chilled him.

Kailani went on. "Whereas vultures have feathers, *pakitoks* have scales. They also have a single eye, rather than two, and curved orange beaks. Anyway, as they circled, I began to drift in and out of consciousness. Suddenly a huge winged creature drove off the *pakitoks,* blowing fire."

"A catdragon," Maia said. "It was Nydea, wasn't it?"

Kailani nodded. "It was. But at the time, I thought I was either hallucinating or had gone from the frying pan to the fire."

Maia and Reilly both looked puzzled.

"The expression means things are getting worse." She took a sip of tea. "I tried to sit up, but I was too weak. Nydea picked me up and carried me to this cave. All night, she lay beside me, covering me with her wing to keep me warm."

"Why didn't she just eat you?" Maia said.

"*Wyomes* might kill humans. But they only eat species incapable of speech. I also think Nydea was curious about me, and also angry with her uncle for what he had done."

"What was that?" Maia asked.

Reilly frowned. "If you'd quit interrupting, Kailani might tell us."

Kailani said, "That's another story. Anyway, at dawn, Nydea flew me to the creek. While I drank, Nydea caught a small reptile, roasted it with a flaming exhalation, and shared it with me. She took me back to the cave and flew away. I was frightened. I thought she had abandoned me. Without a ladder, I couldn't get down."

"But she came back," Maia said.

"Yes, and brought food. Again, I slept under her wing. The following day, I felt strong enough to hike back to the base. After Nydea carried me to the creek, I set off."

"Did Nydea go with you?" Maia asked, rubbing shadowed eyes.

"No." Kailani stared into the depths of her mug. "I couldn't communicate with her then. But she seemed nervous. I thought she might be afraid of being shot on sight. So I signaled for her not to follow."

Kailani was quiet a moment, then cleared her throat and went on. "When I got back to camp, I found the other colonists dead in their beds, not a mark on them." Her voice was sad, but steady. "I didn't know whether it was safe to stay, so I gathered my belongings and returned to the cave."

"How did you get up here?"

Kailani smiled faintly. "Nydea must have anticipated my return, because she was hovering overhead when I arrived. She gave me a lift. I had packed webbing, enough to make a ladder. Nydea came every day. Usually she brought meat to share. Bit by bit, she taught me to speak her language. Finally, I understood enough for her to tell me how the others died...and about *thystam* rock."

Maia's eyebrows went up. "What kind of rock?"

"It's something like coal, a soft, black rock people used to burn for fuel on Earth. *Thystam* is purple and, when burned, emits a toxic but odorless gas. If you breathe enough of it, you suffocate."

"If it's so dangerous, why did the colonists burn it?" Reilly asked.

"We'd been looking for likely fuel. According to Nydea, Hyssel's minions brought *thystam* rock to the colonists. They pretended to be goodwill ambassadors. They lit the rocks and left the people to marvel at the resultant warmth." She paused. "People built fires in the barracks, which trapped the fumes inside." She shook her head sadly. "When I came back, I found pits full of ash in the middle of each room."

"We saw the fire pits," Reilly said softly, staring into the fire that burned before him. "Our analyses didn't show anything toxic."

"The toxin is released into the air. Chances are slim you would find residues in the ashes."

"How horrible!" Maia said. "So you've been alone, how long?"

"Two Mirnan years," Kailani said. "Four hundred sixty-four days, give or take a few."

"You must have been lonely," Reilly said, then immediately regretted stating the obvious.

Kailani picked at a loose thread on her pants.

"Why didn't you come right away when you saw us land?" Maia asked softly.

"It's complicated." Kailani twisted a silver band on her right ring finger, as though trying to remove it. She turned her hand over, revealing a calloused palm.

"We would have been glad to see you," Maia said. "You could have told us what you know about this planet. You could have warned us about this rock, so that none of us made the same mistake."

Reilly pinned Maia with a look and shook his head. Couldn't she sense Kailani's agitation? He could feel her distress as a juddering under his breastbone.

"A week after you landed, I set out for your base. I made two attempts. Once at night and once just after dawn," Kailani said.

"What happened?"

"The first time, Hyssel's right-hand man, Comox, attacked me when I was halfway to your base. I was able to hide in a cleft in a huge boulder. The second time, four *garthans*—sort of like huge, hairless hyenas—ganged up on me. Nydea rescued me."

"That's awful," Maia said. "Why didn't Nydea fly you to the base?"

"Hyssel had forbidden her to go near the place."

"What makes you think the three of us would have more success walking to the base?" Reilly asked.

"We're a pack. And I've recently developed—that is, I've gotten better at self-defense."

The sun crested the cliffs opposite the cave. Maia shrugged off her jacket and winced.

"I nearly forgot about your arm," Kailani said. "Let me see."

Maia peeled back her sleeve to reveal a red, blistered forearm.

"Only second degree," Kailani said. She tipped her water bag and let water stream over the area. Maia didn't move a muscle. "But I'll bet it hurts."

Maia shrugged.

Kailani dipped her index finger into the small pot and gently applied a lavender-colored salve. Maia pressed her lips together.

"You're not a complainer, are you?" Kailani said and stoppered the pot.

"Whining doesn't do any good," Maia said. She nodded at the tiny pot. "What is that stuff? The pain's already gone."

"A salve made from a plant that grows on top of the mesa. I've found it heals burns and has anesthetic properties."

"Herbal medicine, huh?" Maia enthused. "I did some reading on the subject on the ship."

Great, Reilly thought. *Soon we'll be wearing skins, hunting with spears, and digging roots.*

Kailani handed him the salve. "Rub some on your face and neck. You're a bit sunburned."

"Do the herbs have anything to do with that thing you did when Hyssel was bothering us?" Maia said.

"What a ridiculous theory, Maia," Reilly said, smearing the slippery salve across his cheeks. He hadn't noticed the sunburn till he touched his skin. The balm felt cool and tingly and absorbed immediately.

"I don't think so," Kailani said. "But something on this planet has changed me. I can also see pretty well in the dark. With the solar flares that barrage this planet and the strange things I've been eating—perhaps something has changed my biochemistry. Maybe the electromagnetic radiation has sparked beneficial mutations." She smiled, which made her look younger. "Either that, or I have a brain tumor."

Reilly thought of videos of cells floating in earth's primordial soup—dividing, merging, sprouting cilia, budding fins, fins blossoming into legs, legs scrabbling the ever-changing organism onto dry land.

"These changes," Maia said, "they could be happening to all of us."

Reilly snorted. "Don't expect to repel predators with your offensive energy anytime soon."

"And don't assume you're immune," Kailani said. "No matter where we live, the environment shapes us. We are the sum of our experiences."

Chastened, Reilly looked away. The sun was now a palm's breadth above the top of the mesa, and the temperature had risen appreciably.

Reilly thought, *my parents are my world. They made me who I am.* "I'd better go before it gets too hot."

"Go where?" Kailani said. "To the base? You can't go wandering off alone."

"Yeah," Maia said, "look what happened to Lani."

"I'm not returning to the base till I find my parents." Reilly swallowed hard. "If they're dead, I want to at least find their bodies."

Kailani waved away smoke from embers smoldering in the fire pit. "We all could use a few hours sleep. After that, I'll help you."

Now that his belly was full, Reilly felt exhaustion bearing down on him. But every minute counted. "I've already spent too much time resting," Reilly said and stood. "I'm going now. Anyway, I was hoping you could take Maia back to the base. I—"

Kailani raised her emerald eyes to his. "They are dead, Reilly."

They are dead, they are dead, they are dead. Reilly's brain reverberated, as though his skull was a metal pot struck by Kailani's words. "Why do you say that?"

"Nydea brought them to my cave," Kailani said. "Your mother first, then your father." She looked at her sun-browned, calloused hands. "I tried to save your mother, but it was too late. Your father—well, he was already dead when Nydea set him down."

Reilly looked around. Their bodies had lain here, maybe right where he sat. He sprang to his feet. "I don't believe you!"

Maia moved to stand beside him, her face so full of concern that Reilly wanted to shove her off the ledge. Fortunately, she didn't speak or try to touch him.

Kailani went to a natural shelf in the wall of the cave. When she came back, she opened her palm to reveal his mother's silver necklace. Reilly snatched it, felt the oval locket against his palm. "What killed them?" he whispered. He could scarcely hear himself speak over the *ka-room, ka-room, ka-room* of his heart.

"Same thing as the first colonists. The *thystam* rock."

"How? How did this happen?" Reilly said.

"Nydea told me two *wyomes* led them to an outcropping of this rock atop the mesa and lit it for them." Kailani's voice was rigid with anger.

Reilly fisted his hands to stop them from shaking. "I hate *wyomes*. I will kill them. All of them."

"Even Nydea?" Maia said. "She saved your life. She tried to save your parents."

Reilly turned on Kailani. "You should have told us about this rock," he said. "If you had told us, my parents would still be alive."

Kailani looked as though she'd been punched. "I'm sorry, Reilly. I'm so—"

"Where are they now?" Reilly asked belligerently. "Where did you put their—" His voice cracked.

"I buried them," Kailani said. "Nydea helped me. I'll show you the place. It's not far."

"That's not right! I should have buried them. You should have brought them to the base. Or you should have contacted Captain Baca to tell him where they were."

"Maybe so," Kailani said.

"Hyssel is responsible," Reilly said.

Kailani said nothing.

"I'll kill him first."

With a sob, Reilly spun away from Kailani and Maia and sat with his knees hugged to his chest. His lips trembled, and he pressed his mouth so hard against his bony knees that he tasted blood. The necklace was tight in his fist, and he worried about bending the silver links. He opened his hand. The chain was kinked in two places. With trembling, ineffectual fingers, he tried to smooth the spots. His back began to make jerky movements as he wailed without sound.

"He's crying," Maia whispered.

Someone knelt beside him. Reilly hugged his legs tighter and willed the person to go away. He felt a hand on his shoulder, the weight of it firm and confident. He hunkered there and tried to control his breathing, which had become wild and fast. Migraine pain, abrupt and unwelcome, lanced his left cheek and eye.

Kailani began to sing, "White coral bells upon a slender stalk…" Her voice started out husky and cracked, then grew more sure. Reilly thought he knew this song. He tried to remember, then it came to him: his grandmother had sung it to him. He lifted his face. Still singing, she wrapped her arms around him. He leaned into her. As she stroked his hair, he laid his head on her shoulder and wept, loud and unashamed, like a baby.

TWENTY-THREE

When Reilly opened his eyes, he was inside the cave, lying on the mattress and half covered by an *erzala* hide. Hearing low voices, he pushed to his elbow. Kailani and Maia sat side by side near the ledge. As he brushed sand from his cheek, something shiny dropped to the ground. His mother's necklace. He fastened it around his neck and tucked it inside his shirt. He stood stiffly, mindful of the rocky roof that slanted low toward the rear of the cave. His left cheek ached dully, a reminder of his grief-induced migraine.

As he approached the two women, Kailani appraised him with unblinking green eyes. "How are you feeling?"

He felt dull, empty, and sluggish, like an android running out of battery, like a human emerging from the hibernation tank. None of this seemed worth saying.

The light was about the same intensity as when he had fallen asleep, but he couldn't see the sun, which meant it was now behind the cliff, which meant it was afternoon.

"What time is it?" he asked.

Kailani nodded at the oval of blue sky framed by the cave's mouth. "Mid-afternoon. My timepiece quit working months ago."

"You're wearing a watch," he pointed out.

Kailani looked at her left wrist, which was encircled by an old-fashioned timepiece—a black leather band interrupted by a round, white clock face. The crystal and the minute hand were missing. The hour hand pointed to five. "Strictly ornamental," she said. "It was my grandmother's."

"We've all been sleeping," Maia said cheerfully. "Kailani has become

218

nocturnal, just like most other Mirnan animals, which makes sense, when you consider how hot it gets during the day. Maybe we will, too—become nocturnal, once we can see in the dark."

Reilly gaped at her. How could she chatter on as though nothing had happened, as though his parents were alive and well, as though she and every other human on this dreadful planet weren't in mortal danger?

"Have a seat," Kailani said and patted the ground between her and Maia.

Reilly sat. His sinuses felt waterlogged and his eyelids puffy.

Maia passed him a basket, inside of which were wizened red berries the size of his thumbnail. *"Skeeba* berries," she said. "They're a little chewy, but good. Try them."

Reilly put a couple berries in his mouth. The tartness made him salivate. A minute later, the taste went sweet. His stomach rumbled, and he felt ashamed of his hunger. How could he have an appetite?

"Go ahead, Reilly," Kailani said. "The living have to eat."

"How did you find out what's safe to eat on this planet?" Maia asked.

"After we landed, I was able to use the Chemalyzer. But someone broke it about the same time everyone died."

"You mean a *wyome* broke it," Reilly said.

"Possibly. After that, I relied mostly on trial and error," Kailani said. "I also took cues from Nydea. Although *wyomes* are primarily carnivores, they sometimes graze on the vegetation. However, I once tried to eat a plant Nydea favors and was sick for days afterward. Ironically, it's the same herb that works so well as a burn salve. I guess *wyomes* have a different physiology—"

"No kidding," Maia said around a mouthful of berries. "Breathing fire is definitely different. How can they do that?" Using her sleeve, she wiped red juice off her chin.

"Some trick with their digestive gases," Kailani said. "I think *anosote,* the plant that made me sick and heals burns, might contribute to these gases. They belch this gas, click their teeth, which causes a spark, which ignites the gas as it's exhaled."

"Wicked phenomenal," Maia said. "They must have a fire-proof lining in their mouths."

"The fire only burns outside their mouths," Kailani said.

Reilly thought he'd smack Maia if she didn't shut up. He moved to the edge, put his back to the two women, and clapped his hands over his ears. He heard murmurs but no words. After a few minutes, the voices ceased, and he lowered his hands and looked at the ground below. Nothing moved down there. The only sign of life was a prostrate rust-colored plant. He didn't feel anxious about falling. He didn't feel much of anything.

"Come back from the edge, Reilly," Kailani said quietly.

Reilly's shoulders tightened.

Kailani moved closer and passed him a water bag. He took a sip of water, thought he could taste the muscle that the bag was made from, made himself swallow. The water dropped into the hollowness inside him. He could drink a gallon of the stuff and still feel empty.

"My mother—did she say anything?" he whispered.

"Yes."

Kailani drew a deep breath. "She said to give you the necklace. She said she loves you. She said, 'Tell him he's stronger than he thinks.'"

"Anything else?" Reilly sniffled.

"She thanked me."

"That's it?"

"Yes. She was having trouble breathing. She died soon after that."

"Did she—" Reilly's throat constricted painfully. "Did she feel pain?"

"I don't think so. At first, suffocation makes a person feel panicked. But soon, there is peace, like going to sleep."

Reilly curled onto his side, right there in the dirt and the ashes from the *erzala* poop that had spilled over the side of the fire pit. Tears ran down his cheeks. He shouldn't have let them go. He should have saved them. He couldn't believe they were dead, couldn't believe he would never see or hear or touch them again. He had never imagined a future where he went on without them.

For a while, he lay still, the afternoon sun on his face, warming his tears as they puddled the orange sand below his cheek.

Maia called Kailani's name, her voice sharp with alarm.

Reilly raised his head. Maia stood on the ledge, shading her eyes with one hand and pointing with the other. "Something's coming," she said.

∞

At first Reilly couldn't see what Maia was talking about. Scrubby hills stretched into arms of crimson soil that embraced an amber desert plain corrugated by arroyos. Magenta trees snaked along the thin creek. A flock of birds, their long tail feathers streaming behind them, broke out of these trees. Their wings, ridiculously short compared to their tails, flapped furiously.

A larger bird glided like a missile into their midst, scattering the flock. Their cries were faint and eerie, like wind whistling under a door. The big bird chased one of the long-tails and drove it away from the others. It winged high, then plummeted, front legs outstretched.

Legs, Reilly thought. Four of them. This predator was no bird.

With its front paws, the animal seized the bird by the neck. The bird's feathers fluttered then went still. The predator rose and turned. He watched it grow bigger and bigger. A *wyome*. And it wasn't Nydea.

Kailani darted into the cave and came out holding her staff. "Go inside the cave and stay out of sight. Don't do anything unless I tell you to first."

"Lani?" Maia asked, as she moved behind her.

The *wyome* was so close now that Reilly could see the purple tail feathers of the bird that dangled from its right foreleg.

"What?"

"Are any of the *wyomes* friendly, aside from Nydea?"

"Not so far. And this one's Hyssel."

∞

Reilly snatched up his slingshot from the sleeping mat. He didn't know what had happened to the pouch of venom-tipped rocks. There were only two left and there wasn't time to search, so he scraped together a handful of rocks from the cave's floor. He caught a silver glint as Maia slid her gun under the waistband of her pants. He remembered how useless both weapons had last proven against this *wyome*.

The air stirred as Hyssel drew near. Hind legs extended, he touched down so close to Kailani that she was forced to stumble back. He made a snuffling sound something like a chuckle and loosened his grip on the dead bird, which flopped limply to the ground, the small teal head bouncing once.

Maia grabbed his arm and pulled him behind the loom. "Get down," she whispered.

Reilly felt rage boiling up from his gut. "Murderer!" he cried. He pulled free of Maia and rushed forward.

Kailani grabbed his arm and shoved him behind her.

"Stop it," Reilly protested. "I'm going to kill him."

"With what, nannobrain?" Maia hissed from behind the loom. "A stick? A rock? Your bare hands?"

"Shut up," Kailani snapped. In a more controlled tone, she addressed Hyssel in Mirnan.

Feigning indifference, Hyssel leaned over the bird, and, with a click of his teeth, exhaled. His breath ignited. Purple feathers burst into flames, then shriveled to ashes that floated into the air. The scaly red breast blackened. With one deft motion, Hyssel clawed open the charred skin. Retracting his claws, he plucked a bite of pink flesh between first and sixth digits. Aside from the scales, claws, and extra digit, the forepaw functioned like a human hand—opposable thumb and all.

Hyssel spoke, his mouth half full. Despite the low register of his voice, his tone was bizarrely affable.

Kailani responded with a shake of her head.

Hyssel snorted, then tore off more flesh and chewed hugely, his mouth gaping between bites, the better to display his sharp, glistening teeth.

A conversation ensued. Nydea's name came up a lot. Ignorant of the language, Reilly nevertheless caught the ominous tone, the short declarative statements, the inflections that indicated questions. Kailani asked most of the questions, her tone taut with anger. Hyssel answered leisurely, as he made a display of dissecting and eating the bird. At one point, Hyssel extended his neck toward her and sniffed. Kailani leaned away from him, and Hyssel exploded with a staccato sound akin to derisive laughter.

Reilly opened all his senses, as though sheer concentration might yield a translation of this conversation. The tension between Kailani and Hyssel chafed the air.

Hyssel said something that caused Kailani to stamp the end of her staff against the ground and exclaim in English, "You evil bastard!"

For an instant, Reilly perceived a different scene than the one unfolding before him. He saw three *wyomes*—Nydea, Hyssel, and one other. Hyssel attacked the other two with fire, claws, and the arrow-head tip of his tail. He heard yeowls and roars, smelled charred flesh, saw orange blood. Hyssel held Nydea down. He had something in his hand—perhaps a long, sharp stick. The third *wyome*—a female—leapt at him. Hyssel flamed her face and chest, and she fell back. Squatting on Nydea's back, Hyssel plunged the sharp object through her wings. She screamed.

Something grabbed his arm, and he recoiled.

"Reilly," Maia whispered hoarsely. "It's okay. Don't be scared."

"I'm not," Reilly retorted. "Hyssel hurt Nydea, hurt her badly. I saw it happen." He kept his eyes on Hyssel. The *wyome* caught his gaze and stared back, his diamond pupils pulsating. Reilly felt a pain behind his eyes, and pressed his fingertips to the sockets.

He was only half aware of Maia muttering, "You sound weird. Did you take some Harmonal?"

Meantime, Kailani continued speaking in Mirnan, her words still heavy with the punch of curses.

Maia edged closer to Kailani and whispered, "What's he saying?"

Hyssel glared at Maia and roared a command, smoke curling around the words. The atmosphere around them curdled.

Without taking her eyes off Hyssel, Kailani said, "Hyssel is explaining that leaders must demand obedience. When subjects disobey, consequences ensue. And he just ordered you two to retreat."

Reilly hesitated until Maia yanked him back two paces.

Hyssel took a long breath, as though trying to contain an urge to annihilate them. His front claws moved in and out of their sheaths. In a low, menacing tone, he spoke to Kailani, then paused to pick up a thighbone in his forepaw, crunch it open, and suck the marrow. He licked his lips and added another few words.

Reilly's skin prickled as the hair rose at his neck and scalp. "What did he say?"

"You don't want to know."

"Tell me. Otherwise I will imagine the worst."

"He said that *boola* is delicious, but not as good as the miniature *garthan-like* creatures." Before Reilly could ask for clarification, Kailani added, "He ate your dogs."

"Asswipe," Maia spat.

Hyssel snarled and advanced a step.

Kailani glanced back at them. Her eyes were a paler shade of green and her skin glowed. Reilly pulled the slingshot from his back pocket. Kailani nodded, then turned back to Hyssel and spoke Mirnan in a low voice.

"Hah!" Hyssel said, expelling fire along with the sound.

The flames stopped just short of Kailani, who didn't flinch. Reilly fitted a stone to his slingshot, sighted between the forked piece of wood, and let loose. As the stone struck Hyssel's right ear, he roared and crouched to pounce. Maia aimed her *yridium* gun. A weak laser beam extended a meter from the barrel and dissolved harmlessly into air. Hyssel made a snickering sound. Maia scooped a rock from the ground and, with a fierce cry, heaved it. Hyssel ducked, and the rock skimmed the top of his head and clattered off the ledge.

Hyssel sprang forward. Kailani, Reilly, and Maia scattered inside the cave. Maia stumbled, landing in a heap just inside. Hyssel lunged, but his wingtips scraped the top of the cave's mouth, and his front claws closed inches from Maia. Reilly stretched out his arm to Maia, but she was already scrambling to her feet and moving deeper into the cave. Kailani moved to stand before the two children.

Hyssel grinned horribly. Kailani pointed her staff at him. The air around her took on substance, as though it contained whirling dust particles. Reilly put out his hand and felt a pulse extending from her back. Hyssel gnashed his teeth, releasing sparks that ignited his breath into a stream of orange fire, a stream that halted and lapped at an invisible barrier between him and Kailani. After a pause, the flames curled back toward Hyssel.

The edges of Hyssel's wings flickered orange. He flapped them, which only fanned the fire. Smoke billowed into the cave, carrying the stench of singed flesh. With a roar, Hyssel staggered toward the ledge and dove, winging furiously.

He did not rise.

TWENTY-FOUR

Kailani lowered her staff and leaned her weight against it. Reilly and Maia ran to the ledge. Kailani followed more slowly. The three of them silently watched as Hyssel, trailing smoke, swooped unsteadily toward the creek then disappeared behind a rocky outcropping.

"Do you think he's dead?" Maia asked. She squinted in the direction Hyssel had careened.

Kailani sank to her knees. "Probably not." She set down her staff, which now looked like ordinary wood.

"Let's go see," Maia said.

"If he isn't, I'll finish him off," Reilly said. Minutes ago, he had felt as inert as stone. Now revenge galvanized him.

"You continue to amaze. I didn't think you had it in you," Maia said.

"Had what?"

"The ability to act. The ability to do more than sit around and read."

If his parents were alive, Reilly would want nothing more than a quiet place and a good book.

Kailani gathered bow, arrows, and backpack.

"What's the plan?" Maia asked.

"I must hurry to Ledera Canyon, the place where Nydea lives."

"First we'll find Hyssel, right?" Reilly said.

"I'll check the spot where he would have landed. If he's there and still alive, I'll do my best to kill him. Otherwise, I'll continue to the canyon. I want to arrive before Hyssel does."

"But—"

"Listen, Reilly. Helping Nydea and Sheeda is a greater priority than revenge against Hyssel. Believe me, you're not the only being who'd like to take him down."

Maia looked from Reilly to Kailani. "So something bad did happen to Nydea. What exactly did Hyssel do?"

"He pinioned her." Kailani's voice sounded dull, dry.

"He what?" Maia said.

The earlier image of Hyssel brutalizing Nydea swamped Reilly's senses. He squeezed his eyes, then opened them and was relieved to see Kailani's concerned face, rather than the nightmare of Hyssel and Nydea.

Reilly nodded. "He put a stake through her wings so she can't fly, after he beat up her and another *wyome.*"

"Sheeda, Nydea's aunt." Kailani paused, looking hard at Reilly. "Have you always been able to receive? No, or you would have—"

Kailani shut her mouth, but Reilly knew what she thought. If he had always been able to pick up another's thoughts, he would have been able to find his parents, would have known what befell them. What exactly did it mean to receive? Where had the transmission come from? How did his brain turn that energy into sensory information?

"I thought only *wyomes* had that power," Kailani said. "I'm only recently getting the knack."

"What power?" Maia demanded.

"To mind communicate."

Maia looked at him with genuine curiosity. "No kidding. Like mind-read? Okay, so, what am I thinking right now?" She scrunched her forehead and touched her temple, as though such action would amplify and beam her thoughts his way.

"I think the thoughts have to be more…intense." He turned to Kailani. "Do you know how it works?"

"I don't understand much. Thoughts can be shielded. For mind communication to work, one sentient being has to want his or her thoughts to be received by someone with the ability to do so. Nydea tells me she receives not so much words but sensory impressions—visual images, sounds, smells. For more complicated communications, *wyomes* speak aloud."

"Fascinating," Maia said. "I want to do that."

"Nydea was reaching out to you, Reilly," Kailani said.

Reilly looked away. Why would she do that? It wasn't like he could fly off and rescue her. He blinked. The visions had never been so real, so graphic. A few times before, he'd registered colors and emotions and a strange vibration, as though he could hear the base notes of a song but not the lyrics. Something had changed.

Maia shrugged. "Whatever. So why did Hyssel come here? To brag about his evil deed?"

"That," Kailani said, "and to kill the three of us. He plans to get rid of all *nakkoths*. He views us as the root of all evil. Or at least the cause of all his problems."

"Merde, scheisse, caca, kuso," Maia said. Reilly knew she'd said shit in French, German, Spanish, and Japanese.

Maia began pacing. "How far is it to this canyon where Nydea lives?"

"Too far and too dangerous for you to go there."

"But we have to do something," Maia cried.

"I will do something. You and Reilly, on the other hand, will stay here till tomorrow morning. Then I'll accompany you back to the base."

Maia frowned. "And if you don't return?"

"You'll have to find your way alone."

"But we can help you," Maia said.

The adrenaline rush over, Reilly suddenly felt too drained to help anyone. He sat. His eyelid twitched, and he covered the spot with his hand, felt the spasm of the tiny muscle. He still wanted to kill Hyssel. But he wasn't sure how to feel about Nydea, wasn't sure about saving her.

On the other hand, he didn't want to return to the base. He thought of the barracks he had shared with his parents. He saw his father playing the flute, his mother studying her biological specimens, the three of them playing cards and laughing. He swiped a dirty hand across his eyes. He couldn't go back.

Kailani was speaking to Maia. "Absolutely not. It will be dark in a few hours. You do not want to be in Ledera Canyon after sundown."

Maia took up her protest again. Kailani bent her head and pressed her palms to her eyes.

"You looked tired," Maia said and took a step closer to her. "In stories, when wizards work spells, they're exhausted afterward. It's the price of the magic."

Her face was serious. Did she actually believe those fairytales? Reilly wondered. Maybe she took stories at face value, the same way she accepted scientific facts. If he weren't so tired, he would have made fun of her.

"Headache?" Reilly asked Kailani.

Kailani nodded.

"I get migraines," he said.

Kailani squinted at him. "Me too. Do either of you have an Anaral patch?"

Maia shook her head.

"I had some in my pack, but it got left in the scooter," Reilly said.

"Doesn't matter," Kailani said, "I have something that will help." She went to her row of baskets, pulled out a root, broke off a piece, and began chewing it. She gathered things—small, stoppered clay pots, leather pouches of dried food, scraps of material, food, a knife, and a battered case with *First Aid* in faded red letters—and stuffed them into her pack.

Maia put on her jacket. "It won't be easy getting to Nydea," she said. "If Hyssel's the ruler, the other catdragons will be on his side, right? How many live in the canyon? No matter. I say we hurry to the base and get scouters and guns. Maybe ask Harlan to come along. He was the International Space Academy's best marksman. I'm sure the captain will support—"

"Oh, right," Reilly said. He fake-smiled and waved. "Hi there, Captain. We just came by to see if you'd like to risk life and limb—and possibly another scouter—in order to save a member of the same species that's been killing our livestock."

Maia glowered at him.

Kailani turned her back and began lacing her boots. Her great toe showed through a hole in the right boot. "Going back to the base is an excellent idea—for you two. If I don't return by morning, wait till full daylight. Mirnans hunt till dawn, then den up once the temperature climbs." She pointed. "Go south.

When you reach the creek, turn west, or right. Carlos—Commander Baca—will probably be out looking for you." She went to the ledge and lowered the ladder.

"It's Captain Baca now," Maia said. "The other captain—Captain Bergen—died." When Reilly looked up, Maia added, "Captain Bergen was Reilly's grandmother."

Reilly said, "She and my grandfather and a lot of other people died of the Dagnar virus. We picked it up at a refueling station."

Kailani looked at him. "You're Twyla Bergen's grandson."

"You knew her?"

"She was one of my favorite instructors at the Academy."

All my relatives are dead. He saw himself back on the ship, imagined the docking door opening and his body hurling into the frozen blackness of space.

Maia squinted at Kailani. "How do you know our captain's name—Carlos Baca?"

A flush enlivened Kailani's haggard face. She spoke rapidly. "I met him at the Academy too. I had heard he was second in command of the second ship." She brushed her hands together, as though shucking off the topic. "Time to go."

Maia pressed her fists into her hips. "I'm going with you."

"Me too," Reilly said. He slipped his hand into his pocket and fingered his mother's locket, one side smooth, the other engraved with a heart. Fighting *wyomes* seemed no worse than spending more time with Tab in the *in vitro* dorm. So what if he died in Ledera Canyon? He would die somewhere on this planet and probably relatively soon.

"I refuse to risk your lives," Kailani said.

Reilly stood. "I'm not going back to the base." His voice cracked, and he cleared his throat. "And I don't see how you can make me."

"Right," Maia said. "So you may as well take us both."

Reilly glanced at Maia, who stood resolute as steel at his side. "And if you don't take us," he added, "We'll follow you."

"Right," Maia said, "you'd have to tie us up to make us stay. Which would be hard because we'd fight you, and there are two of us, and Reilly is taller. And if you tied us up and didn't come back..."

Reilly completed the sentence, "We'd starve, which would be a terrible thing to have on your conscience. Along with not warning us about the *thystam* rock and Hyssel."

Reilly remembered the vision of Nydea's wings bloodied and mutilated. He recalled the trusting look she gave him as he climbed onto her back, her reference to Kailani as a friend. *Frenth,* she had said. "You're not the only one who owes Nydea a life, Commander Knight."

Kailani hesitated.

Maia walked to the cave's ledge, aimed, and pressed the trigger. A thin, but steady red line beamed from the gun's bore, connected with a boulder, and split it. "My gun must have dried out."

"My gun's in the scooter," Reilly said. "But I have your slingshot."

Maia snorted.

"Hey," Kailani said to Maia. "David slew Goliath with a sling."

"Huh?" Maia said.

"It's from the Bible," Reilly said. "Old Testament."

"That was a confusing book," Maia said. "The language was weird."

Kailani sighed. "My point is if you place your shot right, the humble slingshot is a worthy weapon. Especially when loaded with rocks dipped in *shaggoth* venom."

"What happened to that pouch?" Reilly said, referring to the leather bag of rocks.

"What are *shaggoths?*" Maia asked.

"The many-legged snake-like creatures that live along the creek," Kailani said.

Maia shivered. "I hate those things. One killed Nash."

My fault, my fault, my fault. He could have prevented Nash's death. And if he had pleaded with the captain not to let his parents leave together, he might have saved his parents.

Kailani retrieved the leather pouch from a nook in the cave wall and gave it to Reilly. The weight in his hand told him she had replenished the supply. She tore a strip from some fabric piled in a basket and threaded it through the leather thong that closed the pouch. "Tie this around your waist," she said.

"Don't handle the rocks any longer than necessary. Aim for the neck, just to the side of the windpipe. A sharp stone into the artery could bring down a *wyome,* especially if it's venom-tipped."

Reilly touched his own neck. Under his fingers, his pulse throbbed. He picked the slingshot off the ground and tucked it under his belt. He hoped his aim had miraculously improved. He wondered what Kailani had had to kill to survive on this planet.

∞

After they descended the ladder, Kailani pointed toward the ridge above. "Look," she said. *"Erzalas."*

A half dozen scrawny beasts clambered up a steep rock face, scattering rocks in their wake. Reaching over his shoulder, Reilly fingered the furred hide of the pack slung on his back. He was getting used to its musky smell.

"Wicked phenomenal. They must have suction cups instead of hooves," Maia said. "They do sort of look like huge goats."

"Huge goats with one horn instead of two and a longer, thicker tail," Reilly added. That tail, he noticed, looked stout enough to serve as an extra leg. Just then, one of the *erzalas* used that muscular tail to thrust itself upward.

"What you can't see is the third eye atop their heads. It helps them watch for *wyomes,* their chief predator."

Reilly glanced up and saw only azure sky devoid of *wyomes.*

"Have you ever tried riding one?" Maia asked. "They look big enough."

"They'd be hard to domesticate," Kailani said. "That horn can be deadly."

"Do they talk?" Maia asked.

"No," Kailani said. "If they could, I'd have a harder time eating them." She began walking briskly. Reilly and Maia followed.

"You said *wyomes* don't eat species that speak. What happens when they kill a talking Mirnan?" Maia asked. "Is the carcass left to rot?"

"That hasn't happened in the time I've been here. Different species have gotten into territorial disputes. But there's a hierarchy, with the *wyomes* on top. It's a crime for one *wyome* to kill another."

"What if there's just cause?" Reilly asked.

"They have rules. I believe the Council resolves such cases."

"What about crimes of passion?" Maia asked.

Reilly lifted his eyebrows.

"Well, there's certainly enough of that sort of thing in fiction," Maia said. "Anyway, so that's why nothing ate the first colonists. I thought perhaps a toxin lingered in the system that might poison a predator."

"Enough talking," Kailani said. "We need to move quickly."

Kailani walked faster than anyone Reilly knew, including his mother who was notorious for her rapid stride. She used her spear as a walking staff. The bow slung over her shoulder shifted side to side. A dozen arrows stuck out of a leather sheath sewn to the outside of her pack, which was so worn the International Space Academy logo had nearly rubbed off.

Reilly kept looking for places where the ground was disturbed or mounded. "Where are they?" he blurted.

"Where are who?" Kailani said.

"My parents. Where did you bury them?"

Kailani turned and pointed to a small rise with a scattering of scrubby bushes. "Over there." She glanced at Reilly. "We'll go later. Right now, we need to head the other direction."

Reilly looked down at his shoes; they were dusty and his little toes bulged the sides of the fabric.

"We'll return," Kailani said softly. "We can move them if you want. Cremate them, create headstones and cover the area with slabs of rock, whatever you wish, but not now. Nydea needs us. A proper ceremony requires you gather your community."

Reilly bit his lip. His parents were beyond help; Nydea wasn't. So what if he died trying to save Nydea? The dead, as far as he knew, didn't grieve.

Kailani sighed. "Okay," she said. "It's only a few minutes out of our way."

Near the top of the hill, they came to an oblong spot where the orange dirt was darker and devoid of plant life. Nobody spoke, not even Maia.

Staring at the patch of turned earth, Reilly thought, *they're under there.* So close. Did Kailani lay them side-by-side? Were they facing each other?

233

They would have wanted that. He wanted to ask Kailani, but his throat felt bruised. He wanted to fling himself down and press his chest into the ground. He wanted to claw away the earth and curl up between his parents.

Nearby, an insect clicked its wings—probably one of the green insects that made quick work of all dead creatures. Despite the afternoon heat, Reilly felt cold and clammy. He turned away and vomited.

Maia pulled a water bag from a utility belt Kailani had loaned her and handed it to Reilly. He rinsed his mouth and spat.

"Come," Kailani said. She held her arms away from her sides. "Each of you take my hand."

Maia did so without hesitation. "Go on, Reilly."

Kailani's hand was warm and dry. Reilly hoped she wouldn't spout platitudes. Life goes on. Time heals all. It was crap. Time did not diminish tragedy.

"A long time ago, a wise woman named Mary Oliver wrote a poem called 'In Blackwater Woods.' Over the years, I've said it to myself so many times it's like a 'Hail, Mary.'"

"Because her name is Mary?" Maia asked.

"Religious education wasn't part of your curriculum, I see. Anyway, part of the poem goes like this:

"Every year everything
I have ever learned
in my lifetime
leads back to this: the fires
and the black river of loss
whose other side is salvation...
To live in this world
You must be able to do three things:
to love what is mortal;
and to hold it
against your bones knowing
your life depends on it;
and, when the time comes to let it go,
to let it go."

Reilly released Kailani's hand. "I'll never let go, never forget them."

"I understand," Kailani said mildly.

"If I die—" Reilly's voice broke and he took a steadying breath. "If I do, bury me here, beside my parents."

"All right," Maia said solemnly. "You'll die sometime. Me, too. But not anytime soon. I won't let you."

One hand on his shoulder Kailani turned him away from the grave. As they walked, Reilly wondered what she meant by "a proper ceremony." On the ship, the captain had given a eulogy and, afterwards, two adults slid the body into the incinerator and the ashes drifted into space. When his grandparents had died, several people eulogized. His mother tried to give a speech. Partway through a story about her own mother's habit of adopting stray cats, she looked over, saw Reilly cradling Cosmic, and erupted in sobs.

"Reilly," Maia called. "Come on!"

Reilly didn't realize he'd fallen behind. A stone's throw away, Maia and Kailani stood silhouetted in twilight. He walked toward them, his heart overflowing with longing and regret. He wished that his parents formed those silhouettes, wished that he could move toward them until they pulled him into a double embrace. *I'll never see them again. I'll never smell or touch or hear them.* Pressure built from his chest to his forehead, and liquid leaked from his eyes and nose. He paused, wiped his sleeve across his face, pressed his lips together, and trudged on.

TWENTY-FIVE

When they reached the creek, Kailani tracked back and forth along the bank until she found the spot Hyssel had entered. The three of them examined the disturbed sand and the floating filmy gray tatters that Kailani said were singed wing.

"Looks like he climbed out here," Maia said.

Kailani nodded. Her eyes followed the course Hyssel had taken. "He's headed back for Ledera Canyon. No surprise there. But he's on foot, which means his wings are too damaged to fly." She smiled ruefully. "An eye for an eye."

∞

For nearly two hours, they walked due north along the creek's banks, about 30 degrees away from Hyssel's tracks. The water, which moved swiftly at this point, had carved a channel at least two meters deep. To avoid *dilcroths,* they stayed to the banks, occasionally skirting the dry streambeds that radiated perpendicularly from the creek.

Twice, Kailani led them down to the water to drink and refill their water bags. Before descending the steep banks, she heaved a boulder into the water to scare away any *dilcroth* that might be camouflaged on the muddy bottom. Since nothing stirred, they skidded down the shoulder-high, crumbling bank to drink from the creek. The water, though murky, tasted sweet.

As the light faded, the first animals began to stir. The humans' footfalls scattered fist-sized electric-green insects on diaphanous wings. Small khaki-colored amphibians of similar size floated the water and occasionally hopped

236

along the shore. Their bodies were thin and flat as leaves, but with a membrane rising from the spine like a small sail. By changing the angle of their vertical membranes, the creatures could switch direction.

Reilly was wondering whether the amphibians preyed upon the large insects or vice versa when something struck his shoulder. Clutching the spot, he whirled. A purple, conical object about four centimeters long bounced off onto the ground. Chattering noises overhead caused him to look up. The boughs of the creek trees swayed. About a dozen pale creatures not much larger than domestic cats hopped about. Reilly had seen such animals on his flight with Nydea the previous night. In the waning daylight, he could see that they were scaled, not furred. The two tails and two arms were incredibly mobile.

One creature snatched a large insect out of the air and clapped it into its mouth. Its teeth were short and yellow. Another purple object—a tree pod, Reilly realized—grazed Maia's head, causing her to crouch and whip out her gun.

"Oh, for goodness sake," Kailani said. *"Mantalyas* are mischievous and irritating, but certainly not dangerous—not to beings your size, unless you were sleeping under the trees. An exposed jugular vein might be too tempting."

Reilly rubbed his sweaty neck. "They bite?"

As if in response, one mantalya jabbered, exposing teeth sharp enough to pierce human flesh.

Kailani rebuked them in Mirnan.

The *mantalyas* chorused back.

"They speak Mirnan?"

"Not fluently. *Mantalyas* have the mental capacity of human toddlers. They say things like: go away, you stink, beware *witnaw,* more *viats. "* Maia opened her mouth, but Kailani preempted her. *"Viats* are the lime-green insects *mantalyas* like to eat."

It was nearly dusk when Kailani led them into a yawning canyon that broke the mesa's smooth, almost vertical side. The cleft was so deep Reilly couldn't see the end.

"This is Ledera Canyon," Kailani said in a low voice. "Whispers only. Keep your wits about you."

The shadowed canyon floor sloped upward as they hiked. Down the middle trickled a turbid, blue-gray stream. The cliff, a mottled yellow at the base, gathered reds and blues to become violet at the top. Dark ellipses of caves pocked the higher strata. They twice had to scramble over boulders that had sheered away from the cliff face.

The stream thinned to a ribbon, then to a line of damp sand, then nothing. Meanwhile, the bushes that had bordered the stream gave way to a sparse mix of dusty shrubs with tiny, fragrant leaves and the occasional shoulder-high thorny plant whose two lone branches created the shape of a human standing with legs together and arms outstretched.

High above, two *wyomes* glided back and forth in the shaft of canyon air.

"Sentinels," Kailani whispered. "The others will be resting in their caves, but not for long."

"What do we do now?" Reilly asked.

"Keep going."

"But won't those catdragons come down once they see us?" Maia asked, gun in hand.

"Yes," Kailani said, her eyes scanning the slot of sky overhead. "And since most *wyomes* know about guns, I suggest you keep yours hidden until I advise otherwise. If the sentinels think we've come as warriors, we're cooked. Literally."

Maia pocketed her gun. Kailani draped her cloak over her quiver, concealing the arrows. They continued single file. Kailani was in the lead, then Maia, then Reilly.

Overhead, one of the two *wyomes* let out a piping call. A third emerged from a cave. The trio flew in a circle, heads toward the center, as though conferring with one another. After a moment, one of them descended in a slow spiral and touched down five meters from the humans.

"Be still and be quiet," Kailani said in a low voice.

Using her staff as a walking stick, she took several paces toward the *wyome*. He was large, even bigger than Hyssel. Reilly figured his head would come to the top of the *wyome's* front leg. Though his ears flickered, he remained otherwise motionless. Kailani called out what sounded like a brief, but cordial greeting.

In a deep, resonant voice, the *wyome* responded with similar shushing sounds.

Kailani said something that ended in her own name. The *wyome* pointed to his chest and said one word—Granock, or something like that. Kailani managed a few steps closer before the *wyome* laid back its ears and uttered a warning. The other two *wyomes* descended several meters. They were close enough that Reilly could see the venation in their wings.

Kailani continued speaking to the third *wyome*. Reilly couldn't have understood the words, even if she had been speaking in English. She was too far away and she had lowered her voice. The increasing urgency of her tone, however, came through.

From time to time, the *wyome* interjected. More than once, he looked upward and spoke to his compatriots. One of them looped lower to respond in a clipped, tetchy voice.

Within five minutes, the conversation ended. The *wyome* rose from the ground and joined the other two, who, Reilly now realized, were smaller in size. For a moment all three fluttered their wings, so that they hung in the air, facing one another. Then the largest of them stroked the air, flew up the canyon, and disappeared from view. The other two resumed rotating overhead. Kailani returned to Maia and Reilly, her expression solemn.

"What happened?" Maia said.

Kailani wiped her face with the loose end of her head cloth. "I told this *wyome,* whose name is Granos, that Hyssel came to us and boasted of injuring Nydea and Sheeda. I said we came out of concern for their welfare. I said we possessed healing powers."

Maia twisted one of her braids. "So what's going to happen now?"

"Granos flew to Hyssel's cave to see for himself."

"Do you think we can trust this Granos?" Maia said.

"I do." Kailani glanced upward. "I got the sense of some contention between him and one of the other sentries."

"Which one?" Reilly asked.

"The male. His name is Comox. He's the one Hyssel sent to attack me when I tried to come to your encampment. The female's name is Locatha."

Reilly shaded his eyes with his hand and looked. On the walk here, Kailani had explained that male *wyomes* are relatively larger, with broader heads and narrower pelvises than the females. One of the *wyomes* guarding them was a bit larger. From this perspective, he couldn't really tell much about the relative width of body parts.

"Might they be reading our minds?" Maia asked.

"I doubt it," Kailani said. "You'd have to try to send your thoughts and emotions. And I suspect there has to be a connection between sender and receiver."

Soon, the *wyome* named Granos came winging down the canyon. The other *wyomes* met him halfway, hovered, spoke feverishly, pivoted, and flew toward the humans. They landed and, almost in unison, folded their wings snug to their backs. Dusty air fanned Reilly's face and neck.

Comox, the smaller of the two males slunk behind the humans, his shoulder level with Reilly's head. Reilly felt the electricity of the *wyome's* stare against his back. The animal's breath felt hot against his neck and smelled of decaying meat.

Kailani bowed her head, spoke a greeting, introduced herself and Reilly. Before she finished, Maia said, "Maia Halatha."

Her raised tail swaying, the female bowed her head and said, "Locatha." The male posted behind them emitted only a snarl.

Reilly remembered his father telling him that many Earth animals could detect a person's fear. A sign of weakness could, furthermore, trigger aggression. He uncurled his fingers, and let his hands hang loosely at his sides. He steadied his breathing, felt his ribs slide rhythmically under his backpack. He focused on the diamond-shaped pupils of the two *wyomes* sitting in front of him. Granos's pupils pulsed, but Locatha's remained reassuringly steady. Her irises were the blushing gold color of the morning sun, when it delivered a welcome heat. His head buzzed, and he wondered if she might be probing his thoughts. He imagined a steel curtain veiling his mind.

Granos spoke at length, his voice low and sonorous. Reilly concentrated, as though sheer effort would help him translate Mirnan to English. Comox interjected with indignant-sounding outbursts that sounded more like bits of broken bones than words. Upon the third interruption, Granos silenced him with a growl. Granos seemed older than the other two. Dark ridges of scar tissue ran in four parallel lines down his right shoulder.

Locatha said something, her voice melodious, her mouth near Granos's ear in a gesture of intimacy. Kailani asked a question. Heads close, Locatha and Granos conversed quietly. Comox grumbled, saying the word *Hyssel* more than once.

A rapid four-way conversation ensued. Comox went on a tirade. Eyes closed against the grating of this *wyome's* voice, Reilly's mind began to reel with jagged disjointed images. He saw humans cutting down the creek trees, gunning down *wyomes,* becoming more numerous until they swarmed over the planet. When Kailani spoke, he saw Nydea saving Kailani and himself. He saw Hyssel breathing fire at Nydea and another female. He shook his head to banish the scenes, but when Granos took over the discussion, the visuals crowded back, along with sounds and smells. Nydea and another *wyome* whimpered in a cave that smelled of blood and burning flesh.

When Comox burst into another torrent of malediction, Reilly pressed his hands to his temples and his mind went mercifully blank.

Maia whispered, "Another migraine?"

He shook his head.

Kailani turned to them. "I need to go see about Nydea." Her eyes were bloodshot.

"What did the big *wyome* see?" Maia asked.

"Granos confirmed my worst fears. Hyssel burned and clawed Nydea and her aunt. He indeed pinioned Nydea, which is the worst punishment possible. Granos and Locatha seem to be outraged. Comox insists Hyssel had just cause."

Comox moved to stand with the other two *wyomes.* At the sound of his name, he pulled back his lips over ochre fangs. The tip of the left incisor was broken off.

Kailani added, "Locatha allowed that she had seen Sheeda with unexplained injuries other times."

Locatha's tail twitched. Granos sheathed and unsheathed his claws.

"So, are we going to help Nydea and Sheeda?" Maia asked.

"Granos agreed to take me to Nydea and Sheeda," Kailani said. "Locatha and Comox will watch you two."

"Nuh uh. We're way better off with you. Tell them that we're your assistants," Maia said. "I have medical training, and I'm good at bossing Reilly around."

Reilly looked uneasily at Comox. "Whatever. Also, three can do the work of one in a third of the time. We could be done and gone before the other *wyomes* wake up, maybe before Hyssel returns."

Kailani sighed. "And to think once I longed for children." She squared her shoulders and addressed the *wyomes*.

Granos and Locatha exchanged glances, and Comox made a scoffing sound. Again, the three *wyomes* conversed in the heated, broken manner of an argument. Reilly worried that their rising voices would rouse slumbering *wyomes*. Finally, Granos silenced a stream of invective from Comox with a single word.

TWENTY-SIX

Locatha lowered her belly to the ground and tipped her head toward Maia.

"There's your chance," Kailani told Maia. "Her name is Locatha. She has invited you to climb onto her back."

Maia needed no encouragement. She hurried toward Locatha, whose tail twitched back and forth.

"Slow down," Kailani said. "You're scaring her. You'll want to sit in front of her wings."

Moving more sedately, Maia closed the distance, braced her left foot on the bend in Locatha's left foreleg, grabbed a shoulder blade, and threw her right leg over, nearly kicking the *wyome's* left wing.

Granos swung his broad head toward Comox and gave an order. Comox snarled a response. Locatha hissed at him, and his ears flattened against his skull.

Grumbling to himself, Comox crouched and rhythmically sheathed and unsheathed his claws.

"Get on," Kailani told Reilly. "Hang on tightly. I don't trust this one."

Reilly wondered why he should get stuck riding Comox. As he approached, the *wyome* gave him a surly look. As he climbed up, Reilly wondered if Comox smelled his fear and loathing. Comox's scales were rougher and cooler than Nydea's, more like weathered gardening gloves than sun-warmed silver, and he stank like moldering soybeans.

Settling herself onto Granos's back, Kailani managed to look stately, as though she rode *wyomes* every day. *"Icantha,* Granos," she said.

"Parnea, Kailani," Granos answered.

243

Reilly remembered that those words meant "thank you" and "you're welcome."

Kailani bade Reilly and Maia to remain silent and to hug close to their *wyomes'* backs. "They're only taking us to Hyssel's cave because they're worried about Nydea and Sheeda," she said. "They care nothing for us. One false move, and you'll likely find yourself in a broken heap on the canyon floor."

Reilly needed no such admonition. Maia ceased grinning and patting Locatha's neck and chattering at her.

With a glance at the waning light, Kailani leaned forward and spoke a word to Granos. The great *wyome* pulled himself to his full height, bent back his great head, beat his wings, and lifted off.

Locatha took flight in one graceful movement. Comox reared on his hind legs and rose along a steep trajectory. Reilly's torso tipped backward, but he righted himself, squeezed the creature's upper chest with his legs, and gripped a skinfold at the base of the neck.

As the *wyomes* winged upward, the boulders down below shrank to pebbles. Without apparent cause, Comox banked hard to the right, and Reilly cried out involuntarily.

Granos growled a warning, and Comox straightened his course. Reilly's heart smacked his rib cage, as though trying to eject itself. Just as it seemed Comox had settled down, he arched and executed a backward roll. Reilly found himself dangling from the *wyome's* back, his hands miraculously clutching the wing bases. His fingers slipped a centimeter on the scaly surface. A strip of cloth that he'd tied turban-style around his head came loose and floated down. Something slipped from his backpack and, long seconds later, clunked faintly against the far-away ground. He glimpsed Granos a couple meters underneath him, Kailani looking up in horror.

Comox righted himself, and Reilly clamped his knees into the *wyome's* sides. His heart worked so hard it rocked his whole body. He couldn't pull himself to the spot in front of the wings. So he fitted himself between the beating wings and gripped with his whole body. Comox's ears flicked back and away, back and away.

Granos pulled alongside and bared his teeth at Comox. Kailani said something to Reilly, but the blood roaring in his ears prevented him from hearing. A cold sweat slicked his face, his stomach contracted, and corrosive vomit spewed onto Comox's neck. The *wyome's* growl vibrated Reilly's entire body.

The whoosh of flight faded as the three *wyomes* hovered outside the dark maw of a cave. Locatha called out a greeting to Hyssel, Sheeda, and Nydea. When no sound emanated from within, Locatha tucked her wings and slipped into the cave. Granos and Comox followed.

All three *wyomes* stood uncertainly at the cave's opening. Kailani peered at Reilly and mouthed, "Are you okay?" Reilly nodded, even though his whole body shook, and he had to clamp his jaw tight to stop his teeth rattling. Comox shrugged his shoulders, as though trying to unseat his cargo. Reilly swung one leg off the *wyome's* back.

"No," Kailani whispered, "don't dismount till I say so."

Comox twisted his head and sniffed, then drew together his nostrils in an expression of disgust. Sickened by the smell of his own vomit, Reilly longed to jump down, scurry away from this horrible creature, and burrow into the back of the cave.

With Maia atop, Locatha padded deeper inside, making soft, inquiring noises. Comox stood his ground, his muscles taunt and his breathing shallow. He called, "Paterth Hyssel." Reilly assumed the first word was a title. No reply followed. The cave was so deep in shadow, Reilly couldn't see to the back of it, couldn't even see Locatha and Maia.

A moment later, there was a mewling noise, followed by a dismayed cry from Locatha. The way the sounds echoed suggested the space was cavernous.

"Kailani," Maia called. "You'd better come."

Kailani was already on the ground. Granos strode after her into blackness. As Reilly began to dismount, Comox tossed him off with a swing of his hips. Reilly landed on his hands and knees, got shakily to his feet, exchanged glares with Comox, and ventured deeper into the cave. To Reilly's relief, Comox hung back.

Bones lay in a heap to his right—long bones, ribs, vertebrae, skulls of various sizes. The air smelled smoky and dankly metallic. He heard a whimper.

"Nydea?" Kailani called.

No answer.

"Oh my god." Kailani again.

Reilly hurried toward her voice, stumbling over stones. Once he fell, catching himself on his hands, and realized the stones were skulls.

By now, Reilly approached shapes blacker than their dim surroundings and saw Locatha standing above a large lump. The lump shifted and spoke.

Locatha asked a question, and Reilly heard a mumbled response and had a fleeting vision of Hyssel attacking a smaller *wyome*. Something touched his shoulder, and he whirled.

"It's me," Maia whispered.

As Reilly's eyes adjusted to the darkness, Sheeda came into sharper focus. She resembled a map with continents of scorched scales and islands of burned, weeping flesh. Locatha extended her head and licked the margins of one of these burns. Sheeda's closed eyelids flickered.

"Minjen shit," Maia muttered.

Sheeda raised her head and cried, *"Nakkoths!"*

Reilly marveled at Sheeda's look of terror. Had she learned to fear humans? Or did she worry their presence would bring down the wrath of Hyssel?

Granos lowered his head until his nose touched Sheeda's. He spoke calmly, using the words *nakkoths* and *Kailani*. No images came to Reilly, just the sense of reassurance.

Off to the left, a shape Reilly had mistaken for a boulder elongated and there stood Kailani. She uttered respectful-sounding words, took a few paces, and knelt. Reilly couldn't see what she was doing.

Granos phrased a question that contained the word 'Hyssel' and Sheeda's answer was agitated. Again, Reilly pictured Hyssel coming at the two females, smacking them with clawed forepaws, thumping them with his tail, breathing fire at them, piercing Nydea's wings. Granos' ears went forward and his tail twitched, nearly striking Reilly.

"Where's Nydea?" Reilly asked.

Maia pointed to where Kailani crouched, muttering, "Oh, Lord, sweet

Jesus, son of a bitch, what has the bastard done to you?"

Reilly went over and squatted beside Kailani, who fingered a stake that appeared to be thrust into black crepe. It took him a moment to recognize the black, frangible stuff as Nydea's wings. His eyes sought to make out the rest of Nydea in the darkness. Her head was close to him, her tail curled protectively around her shivering body.

Kailani tugged at the stake and Nydea cried without tears. Sheeda hissed, smoke curling from her nostrils.

"Nydea?" Reilly groped forward and went down on one knee.

Sheeda was talking rapidly now.

"What is she saying?" Maia asked.

"Sheeda is blaming herself for not being able to protect Nydea," Kailani said.

"It's my fault," Reilly said. "If Nydea had been home rather than rescuing me and Maia, none of this would have happened."

"Give up the guilt," Kailani said. "Useless emotion. And you didn't ask for rescue."

Kailani rummaged in her backpack and switched on a telsar torch. Everyone, except Nydea, made startled noises—the *wyomes* at the spectacle of artificial light (which Kailani explained was harmless) and the humans at the horror of Nydea's injuries.

Her burns were more extensive than Sheeda's. Blood the color of deep amber pooled in the wounds. In most places, Reilly could make out the plates of individual scales, and he hoped that meant the damage was superficial. The worst of it was her wings. The stick ran through two jagged holes, one at the top of each wing, and was twisted together at the top to form a loop.

"Hold this," Kailani said, handing Reilly the torch. "Shine it where I tell you."

With Maia's help, Kailani cut the stick to release the loop. Then she tugged on one end, but the wing tissue stuck to the wood. Twisting didn't loosen it either. Nydea's wings quivered.

"Damn you to hell, Hyssel," Kailani muttered.

"Hyssel," Granos repeated in a bass echo, exhaling hot, spicy-smelling breath against Reilly's cheek.

From her pack, Kailani withdrew clean cloths, a water bag, small stopped pots, a knife, and the packet of surgical instruments and set them on the ground beside her. She handed a cloth and a clay jar to Maia. "Go to Sheeda," she said. "Wash her wounds and dress them with salve."

Maia took the proffered things and hesitated.

"You know more than you think, Maia Halatha."

Maia nodded and made her way to Sheeda. Kailani called out what Reilly imagined was an explanation of Maia's mission. Locatha, who remained beside Sheeda, made a brief reply.

Kailani faced Reilly. "We'll need your water too."

Holding the lamp aloft with one hand, Reilly opened his pack with the other. "The water skin's gone," he said. "Must have fallen when Comox turned upside down."

Kailani sighed. "Never mind. Just hold the light steady and direct the beam to wherever my hands are working."

Maia began chattering in English. "Okay, now. Just hold still. I'm not going to hurt you..."

Granos lowered his head level with Kailani's and asked a question. Kailani answered and gestured at the stick. She took a ceramic bowl and a battered canteen from her pack, filled the bowl with a brownish fluid, handed it to Reilly, and said, "Give this tea to Nydea to drink. It will ease her pain."

As Reilly put the bowl near Nydea's face, she raised her head a few centimeters, sniffed at the fluid, lapped it up, and, with a sigh, lowered her head onto her front paws.

"Reilly, hold the stick steady, will you? Granos and I are going to do a little surgery."

Using a solution that smelled sharply of disinfectant, Kailani washed forceps and a pair of tiny, curved scissors. For a moment, Reilly wondered why she didn't have a laser scalpel or an electrocautery knife, then remembered both required *yridium*. Next, Kailani swabbed the tips of Granos's right front digits.

Kailani leaned her mouth to Nydea's ear and murmured an explanation.

Nydea blinked an assent.

Then they set to work. Using a fore claw as a scalpel Granos delicately liberated the wings from the stick. Kailani pulled free the stick, then, using forceps and scissors, nipped away ragged bits of flesh around the wing holes. She said clean margins healed better. Nydea whimpered and her back muscles clenched, but she held her wings still. Kailani squeezed water from her bag onto the wounds, allowed the tissue to dry, then daubed on salve.

Reilly reached out, and tentatively stroked an unscathed patch between Nydea's ears He cleared his throat and began humming "White Coral Bells," the song his grandmother sang to him so long ago, the song Kailani had earlier that day sung to him while he wept for his dead parents. The words caught in his constricted throat, but not before Nydea's matted eyelashes closed, and under his hands, her breathing slowed.

Reilly paused, wiped his eyes. Nydea raised her head, looked at Reilly, then spoke to Kailani. Reilly heard Hyssel's name, and had a brief image of him flying.

Kailani responded with a rueful laugh.

"What?" Reilly said.

"Nydea urged us to leave. She said we weren't safe because Hyssel would return at any minute and kill us."

"Why did you laugh?"

"I told her Hyssel wouldn't be back soon, and he certainly wouldn't be flying nor in any mood for a fight. I told her I beat fire with fire, and she said that perhaps I was part *wyome*."

When she was finished, Kailani sat back on her heels. "Where's Comox?" she said, then directed what seemed a Mirnan translation to Granos. *"Dethena Comox?"*

Granos turned toward the mouth of the cave, which framed an oval of late afternoon light. He shrugged. *"Phuay."* The word sounded like wind over wings.

Fly away, fly away, Reilly thought. At first he felt glad. Then an icy thought lodged in his brain. Wherever he had gone, his mission wouldn't be to help them.

TWENTY-SEVEN

Reilly didn't have to wonder long about Comox's whereabouts. He and Kailani had just finished bandaging Nydea's most serious wounds when a *wyome* scream rent the night. Reilly faced the cave's mouth and detected murky shapes against the ash-gray evening light. Gradually those shapes assumed the form of Comox and another *wyome* hovering outside the cave, Hyssel balanced atop their backs—right fore and hind feet on Comox, left appendages gripping the other *wyome*.

"Kanapapiki!" Kailani said.

"What does that mean?" Maia asked.

"Son of a bitch in Hawaiian. Both of you, stand behind me."

Granos and Locatha paired up in front of the humans. Reilly craned to see around Locatha. Comox and the other *wyome* hovered with shoulders level to the cave's ledge until Hyssel stepped precariously into the cave. Fatigue and pain darkened his eyes and tensed his massive jaw muscles. His wings, rather than folding neatly to his back, stood in a halfway position, bent and ragged.

For a startled moment, Reilly almost laughed.

"Looks like shit, doesn't he?" Maia said.

"Why is he here at all?" Reilly said. "He's pretty vulnerable."

"Quiet," Kailani said. "He's still dangerous. And he's still the leader."

Hyssel took another step into the cave, creating space for Comox and the other *wyome* to land and flank him. Granos and Locatha held their positions a fiery breath from their new enemies. Behind Reilly, Sheeda crept to lie directly in front of Nydea, who curled into a fetal position. The acrid smell of fear and fury freighted the air.

250

Kailani stepped toward her staff, which lay on the ground just to Locatha's right.

Hyssel uttered a clipped word. Kailani halted, her empty hand outstretched. "Locatha," he said, followed by a string of Mirnan. Reilly got a mental image of Locatha passing Kailani's staff to Hyssel.

Locatha turned to look at Kailani. Kailani gazed steadily back. Comox growled his impatience. Hyssel repeated the command.

Locatha faced Hyssel. Kailani bent toward her staff. Hyssel snarled, and Locatha's fingery right paw shot out and snatched the staff.

Hyssel purred the next order.

"*Diss,*" Nydea hissed. "*Diss,* Locatha."

"*Zak,* Locatha," hissed Comox.

Locatha laid the staff on the ground and balanced her front paw atop it.

Hyssel roared a word, and attempted to unfurl his wings. Twilight leaked through the ragged holes. One wing tip scraped the low ceiling at the cave's entrance. With a half-suppressed cry of pain, he lowered his wings.

Granos didn't so much as twitch. He said something that, to Reilly's ear, carried a sarcastic edge.

Comox muttered something to the *wyome* who had helped carry Hyssel. He used the word "Frethana" twice. Reilly assumed it was her name.

Hyssel glanced over his shoulder. One of the moons must have risen, silvering the *wyomes* that circled outside the cave.

"Locatha," Kailani called.

Locatha glanced at Granos, whose tail swept the ground, raising dust. Reilly sneezed. Locatha flipped the staff toward Kailani, who caught it. Comox and Frethana advanced a pace. Maia drew her gun. Reilly slid the slingshot from his belt.

Outside, two *wyomes* peeled off from the group and alighted on the ledge. The cave was now too crowded for a *wyome* to unfurl his or her wings.

With a curt order, Hyssel stepped aside. Comox sprang at Granos, who deftly flipped him onto his back. Locatha and Frethana exchanged words. Reilly wondered what bonds of kinship had just been broken.

Frethana lunged. Locatha clawed the side of her face. Both pairs of *wyomes* bit and scratched and wrestled. Dust and harsh breathing thickened the air.

The two newcomers—both females—crept toward the humans. Kailani stood erect, gleaming eyes focused on her opponents, her skin glowing as though a lantern burned within her. The dust around her glittered and swirled. In unison, the *wyomes* exhaled a burning plume. Reilly crouched, arms over his head. Kailani held her ground. The fire stopped two meters from Kailani, then curved backwards. With twin yeowls, the *wyomes* leapt sideways. One of them dropped to the ground, rolled to smother a burning shoulder, lurched to the cave's mouth, and sprang into the night. The other, unscathed, turned vengeful eyes on Kailani.

"Move back," Kailani said to Reilly and Maia. "Stay close to the walls."

Head lowered, the *wyome* slunk toward Kailani. She stood still, brows furrowed, as though trying to work out a complicated mathematical formula. Her outline was solid. Reilly felt no energetic pulse from her. Maybe he was too far away.

Growling, the opponent took another step.

"Kailani!" Maia cried.

Kailani's expression sharpened. She hefted her staff like a spear and hurled it. The tip penetrated the *wyome's* chest. With rasping breaths, the *wyome* wrapped her fingery forepaws around the shaft and pulled ineffectually, blood pumping from the wound. When she collapsed, Kailani darted forward, planted her foot on the *wyome's* ribcage and yanked the staff free.

Out of his peripheral vision, Reilly caught another *wyome* charging them. Before he could load a venom-coated rock into the slingshot, Maia lasered the big male in the forehead. Blank-eyed, he teetered, fell onto his side, and took a final breath.

Reilly looked up just as Granos shoved Comox over the ledge. Reilly didn't see Comox rise and hoped him dead. Chest heaving, Granos shouted a jagged word at Hyssel, who sneeringly slipped past Granos and, without attempting to open his wings, stepped out onto air. As Reilly listened for the thump of a body hitting the ground, he heard *wyomes* calling and the woosh of wings stirring the air.

Locatha and Frethana fought on. Frethana pinned Locatha to the ground and lowered her open mouth to Locatha's throat. Before she could bite, Granos swung the spiked end of his tail into her neck. Frethana reared onto her hind legs, paw pressed to the wound, blood pulsing between her digits. Locatha got to her feet and watched Frethana crumple.

Maia shouted, "Reilly! Look left."

A *wyome* was lunging toward him. Reilly raised his slingshot, aimed, and released. The rock burrowed into the flesh left of the windpipe. If *wyome* anatomy resembled that of earth animals, he had hit the carotid artery, or close to it. With an annoyed look, the *wyome* yanked out the rock, releasing a stream of blood. Muttering something, it took two steps toward Reilly and keeled over.

Yet another *wyome* entered the cave and bolted toward Kailani. She threw her staff, but the tip glanced off the creature's shoulder and clattered to the ground. The *wyome* threw itself on Kailani, knocking her flat. Maia shrieked, "No!" and ran forward, gun-arm locked before her. A red laser beam hit the *wyome* just below the jaw. The creature swayed, one huge paw on Kailani's belly. Reilly shot a stone that smacked the creature between the eyes. The *wyome* fell over backward. Maia kneeled beside Kailani, whose cheek was scratched and bleeding.

Reilly gestured toward a dead *wyome* lying less than two meters away. "We can use the body as a shield."

He and Maia grabbed Kailani under the armpits and started to drag her.

"I'm not dead," Kailani said indignantly. "Ow!"

Maia's eyes went to a dark spot blooming high on Kailani's tunic. Maia lifted the cloth to reveal three parallel claw marks, just below Kailani's left collarbone.

Kailani raised her head. "It's superficial," she said. Her gaze shifted and she cried, "Nydea!"

Reilly turned. A *wyome* slunk toward Nydea, who stood with her back to the cave wall.

"Maia, get my pack," Kailani said, gesturing toward a crevice in the cave wall.

Maia dashed over, scooped up the pack, and returned. Grimacing, Kailani sat, unhooked the bow, and drew an arrow from the quiver. Reilly fired a venomous rock. Nydea's attacker halted and batted an ear. An arrow whistled through the air and sunk into the animal's chest. The creature yelped, staggered backward to the cave's ledge, and disappeared.

Movement within the cave stilled. Locatha and Granos stood on the right side of the cave, panting and bleeding from numerous gashes. To the left, Nydea and Sheeda huddled together, weeping. Five enemy *wyomes* lay dead.

A long minute later, *wyome* shouts rose up to them, Hyssel's rough voice among them.

"Is that Hyssel?" Reilly asked. "What is he saying?"

Kailani cocked her head. "He's yelling, 'You are dead and your children are dead and all humans are dead.'" She sighed. "It seems someone caught him. Damn! He's hard to kill."

A strange noise muffled Hyssel's rantings. Reilly drew closer to the ledge. Outside the cave, dozens of *wyomes* flapped against a sudden wind, which wailed through the canyon.

"Devil wind," Kailani called.

The wind gusted to a gale. *Wyomes* dove from the canyon into various caves. The air outside became opaque with sand. Reilly could not see what had happened to Hyssel.

Kailani yelled over the roar, "Reilly, Maia, move to the back of cave! Cover your face with cloth and keep your eyes closed."

Inside the cave was blind dark. Reilly lurched along until he tripped over a large object that cried out. Sprawling, he felt smooth, warm scales. His head hummed with a sweet, but unintelligible voice.

"Nydea?" He shifted so he no longer lay across her.

Something wet and raspy slid up the side of his cheek. Nydea's tongue. After his grandparents died, leaving Reilly their cat, he would awaken each morning with Cosmic licking his head. Nydea's tongue was bigger and more leathery, but just as comforting. And her spicy breath smelled nicer. Mindful of her wounds Reilly reached out gingerly and rested his hand on her forepaw.

"Frenth," Nydea whispered.

"Friends," Reilly agreed. With his jacket hiked over his face, he laid his head on the crook of his arm, and settled down to wait.

As the wind moaned through the canyon, Reilly wondered about the others. He pictured Kailani kneeling near Maia, the grooves in Maia's braid filling with sand, Kailani's arm crossing protectively over her back. He imagined Granos, and Locatha nestled on either side of Sheeda, their outstretched wings meeting above her to shield her wounds. He thought of Captain Baca in his barracks, possibly worrying about Reilly and Maia. He saw the wind sweeping away the sand over his parents' grave; saw them curled on their sides, heads bowed toward each other. His eyes opened and he took a jagged breath.

"Ookay," Nydea whispered, drawing out the O. "You okay."

Her words echoed in Reilly's head. Gradually, his aching body relaxed against her hip. His breathing rate doubled hers, every other inhalation dipping between hers like a grace note. From where he lay, no escape seemed plausible save for sleep.

TWENTY-EIGHT

V oices—both human and the lower register of *wyomes*—roused Reilly. His mouth was dry and gritty. He pushed up on his elbow and opened his eyes, which stung. His nose ran, expelling orange snot. He reached up to wipe his eyes, which only resulted in rubbing more sand into them. After a few minutes, tears cleared his vision.

Hazy daylight filtered into the cave. The space was perhaps ten meters high at the tallest point and large enough to park a half dozen air scouters. Ancient winds had sculpted the walls into arcs, buttresses, and natural ledges. Along those more horizontal spaces someone had arranged skulls and pelvises from large to small, rocks of various colors and sizes, dried flowers, and shells. Some of the displays had been disturbed, presumably by the fighting. Harder to overlook were the five dead *wyomes* piled up in a mound on the ground. Reddish dust covered everything, making it look as though the place had rusted overnight.

Reilly and Nydea were in a small cave that budded off the back. Nydea lay curled on her side upon a jumble of *erzala* hides, the end of her tail touching her nose. As Reilly pushed up on his elbow, Nydea opened one eye—first the outer lid, then semi-transparent inner lid. Sand-flecked yellowish fluid glued shut the other eyelid—the one already scarred.

"I should wash your wounds," Reilly said. Nearby, he found an empty pot distinguished from those Kailani made by the indentations of narrow digits and etchings of flying *wyomes*. Turning, he saw that the back wall was full of carvings, some of which had been brought to life with smears of pigment. He walked along the wall. It was a map of Nydea's world: Ledera Canyon with *wyomes* standing at cave mouths and flying; another canyon with *witnaws* and *garthans; erzalas* grazing atop the mesa; the creek with birds in the trees and the swinging animals with two tails and a *dilcroth* lounging on the bank. The humans were there too. There was Kailani in her cave in the small canyon. The two bases were there. One showed buildings with no people about. The other was Reilly's base. Crosshatches represented the garden plants. Chickens and turkeys pecked the ground. A boy stood at the gate looking out.

Reilly looked at Nydea. "You did this?"

She nodded.

"You were the one watching me."

"Yeth," she said. "I watch."

Reilly felt both the lightness of gratitude and the heaviness of grief.

Sheeda shuffled into the space and raised her scorched head, revealing a constellation of old scars and fresh scratches on her neck. After a wary look at Reilly, she sat and began licking a wound on Nydea's shoulder.

Suddenly aware of his full bladder, Reilly stood and edged into the main cave. He steered around a dead *wyome* lying in a puddle of congealed orange blood with a hole in its chest. Kailani's staff must have pierced this one. Nearby, another dead *wyome* lay on its side with a neck wound. As Reilly passed, he saw spotted a triangular rock in the creature's front paw. He picked it up and began to put it in his pouch.

"We'll need to coat that one with venom again," Kailani said. She sat with her back against the side of the cave, facing Granos and Locatha. The two *wyomes* blinked at him.

Reilly slipped the rock into his pocket.

"*Ganeth vinden,*" Granos said.

"Pleasant breezes. Short for 'pleasant breezes beneath your wings.' It's a standard Mirnan greeting," Kailani said.

"*Ganeth vinden.*" Reilly repeated.

Maia slept on her side, her head in Kailani's lap. Reilly bent his head near Kailani's to ask where he should pee. Maia stirred, rubbed her eyes, and sat. "Hey," she said. "We're all alive. Wicked phenomenal, eh?"

"Not unless we're able to get out of this canyon alive," Reilly said. "That would be, as you say, wicked phenomenal."

Maia yawned. Her teeth shone white against her pink tongue. "How did you get to be so negative?"

Let me count the ways, Reilly thought, but held his tongue.

Kailani looked at Reilly and inclined her head toward the mouth of the cave. "Just try to avoid being killed," she added.

Maia scooted back to lean against the wall beside Kailani. She crossed her ankles in the same way, right over left.

Reilly edged toward the cave's opening. The sky was azure. Mauve and lavender striated the opposite canyon wall, which was about 200 meters away. Caves of various sizes pocked its face. No creature stirred. He stood at the far left of the ledge and, with his back to the others, managed to start a stream of urine.

A shrill call pulled his gaze to the silvered underside of a *wyome* flying overhead. Deeper in the canyon, a second *wyome* answered. *Sentries,* Reilly thought as he melted inside the cave.

"I wish I had a penis," Maia said. "More efficient. Less vulnerable."

"Guess I'm just lucky." His foot struck something hard. A skull. He bent to examine it. "This looks suspiciously dog-like."

In an instant, Maia was beside him. "I think you're right." She moved a meter away and knelt. "Here's the pelvis and most of the tail." She sighed, fingering the fur still clinging to the tail. "If Erik were here, he could tell us whether the bones belonged to Xena or Beau. Mangy-headed bastard." She looked at Reilly. "Hyssel, not Erik."

"Got it," he said.

"Come sit," Kailani said, "patting the ground on both sides of her." She looked strangely inert. "Sorry about your dogs."

"Let's hope we avoid the same end," Maia said.

"*Wyomes* are more reluctant to eat any species capable of speech."

"Right," Reilly said. "If you can talk, they poison you and leave you to rot." No one spoke for a moment.

Reilly cleared his throat. "Anyway, how will we get out of here?"

"Granos, Locatha, and I have been discussing that," Kailani said. "They are willing to fly the two of you out of here."

Maia frowned. "What about you?"

"I'll catch up with you later."

"How's that?" Reilly asked.

"Perhaps Granos will return for me," Kailani said. The dawn light cast deep shadows under her eyes and cheeks.

Reilly shifted his gaze to Granos, who watched Kailani with what appeared to be concern. "Will it be safe for him to return here? Now that he—" Reilly searched for the right words to express his betrayal of Hyssel. "That is, some *wyomes* will view Granos and Locatha as traitors."

Granos and Locatha both turned golden eyes his way. How much did they understand, he wondered.

"I have a better idea," Maia said. "We come back for Lani in airscouters."

Reilly tried to imagine two airscouters flying into Ledera Canyon, dodging irate *wyomes*. It seemed improbable, though no more far-fetched than sending Granos alone. He disliked the idea of leaving Kailani behind. "What about Sheeda and Nydea?" he asked. "How will they escape? They can't stay—not with Hyssel at large. Sheeda might be able to fly, but Nydea can't."

Sheeda emerged from Nydea's small cave, her hide a mosaic of normal blue-gray scales and livid pink. She gave him a doleful look and said something to Granos and Locatha.

Locatha replied. Reilly tried to eke some meaning from the exchange, but couldn't.

"What?" Maia asked.

Kailani sighed. "Sheeda said that she could deal with Hyssel. Locatha more or less told her she was nuts."

Nydea made a mewling sound. Sheeda padded back to her.

Maia pressed her hands to her temples, then looked up. "Here's a plan: We come back in airscouters to rescue Kailani. Granos carries Nydea. Sheeda flies alongside."

Reilly wondered who "we" might be. He couldn't fathom rejoining the crew. What would Captain Baca do to him and Maia? After all, they had run away, grounding two airscouters in the process. Surely, they wouldn't be allowed the use of airscouters in the near future. Plus, how would the crew react to the appearance of Granos and Locatha, two members of the species that had aggressively threatened them? Why would the adult crew risk flying into a canyon full of enemy *wyomes?*

"Most *wyomes* are sleeping now," Kailani said. "The sooner you leave the better." Addressing Granos and Locatha, she switched to Mirnan. Fatigue coarsened her voice.

Granos looked at Locatha and nodded.

Reilly stood. "But who will protect you, Sheeda, and Nydea while we're gone?"

Kailani gave a weak laugh. "You doubt my military prowess?"

Granos said something to Locatha, who addressed Sheeda, who spoke to Nydea, who called, "Reilly, Kailani no okay. Kailani *cranph.* Kailani *hilthin noth.* Reilly, Kailani *cranph.*"

Reilly closed his eyes and struggled to understand. He pictured Kailani, saw her clutch her belly. Something was wrong. *Cranph.* Sick. He remembered the injury she'd sustained last night, the blood seeping through the rough material of her shirt. He looked at the spot now, which was covered by tunic and cloak.

Locatha stretched out her long neck and sniffed at Kailani, who leaned against the cave wall with eyes closed. She exchanged a look with Granos.

"Lani?" Maia said. "Are you all right?"

"I'm fine," Kailani said, without opening her eyes.

Maia laid two fingers across Kailani's wrist. "Your pulse is rapid and thready." Without asking permission, she peered down Kailani's top. "The shoulder wound isn't bleeding. Does anything else hurt?"

Kailani hesitated. "I think I'm tired from using the staff."

"Someday I hope you'll tell me how you do the thing with the light," Maia said.

"But not now," Reilly said.

"No," Maia said. "Now you should lie down."

To Reilly's surprise, she complied. He peeled off his jacket and folded it to make a pillow

Maia peeled back Kailani's cloak and tunic. "I should wash this wound and apply some of your salve."

"Later. It's too cold now," Kailani protested.

But it wasn't cold. The sun angling into the cave was quite warm.

Maia whispered to Reilly, "Shock. We need blankets."

"I'll look." The morning light had yet to illuminate the back of the cave. There he found a jumble of bones—ribs, legs, pelvises, vertebrae, hooves, and paws. Different species, none human. In far corner, he found a pile of *erzala* hides. He hurried back with two.

Kailani lay on her back, her head propped on Reilly's jacket. She shivered. Maia was spreading her own jacket over Kailani's chest. She looked up at Reilly. "Pish, Reilly. Those things reek. Take them away."

"No one has ever died of bad smells," he said.

"Not true. It can indicate pathogenic bacteria."

"Would you rather she shivered?" He laid the stiff hides across Kailani's legs. "If malodor was so deadly, anyone sleeping in kids' dorm would perish."

"Pish off," Maia said and began working the shirt loose from the scab.

Kailani grimaced.

"I need water," Maia ordered.

Reilly looked up at Granos and Locatha. Surely *wyomes* kept water in their caves. "Water?" he asked. He concentrated on an image of the creek with the lavender trees and *boola* birds. The two *wyomes* stared at him. He crossed to Nydea and pictured oceans, streams, creeks, rivers, humans and animals drinking. "Water," he repeated.

Nydea raised her head. "Water?"

She must have learned the word from Kailani. Reilly felt foolish for trying to mentally project the concept.

Nydea struggled to stand, pushing straight her forelegs then her hind legs. Her tattered wings quivered against her back. Sheeda, who hovered nearby, made a protesting noise. Nydea said something to Sheeda and carefully resettled herself on the dusty hide. Sheeda motioned with her fingery forepaw for Reilly to follow to an adjoining cave twice as big as the one he and Nydea had slept in.

In the new space, the *erzala* hides didn't stink. And they had been connected like a quilt to form two layers stuffed in the middle with something. It was, Reilly realized, a large mattress, big enough for Hyssel and Sheeda. An intricate latticework of bones, dried flowers, and feathers arced over the head of the bed. In the corner stood a hollow stone pillar full of water.

"*Icantha,*" Reilly said.

"*Parnea*" Sheeda said.

Reilly looked back at the arbor over the bed. Feathers. There were the long purple feathers of the *boola*. But there were also black and white striped feathers, much like those belonging to a tom turkey. And rust-colored chicken feathers. He turned to confront Sheeda, but the glint of metal arrested his gaze. Four meters away, an array of wires, computer parts, *yridium* guns, and scientific equipment littered a stone bench. Sitting in the middle was a portable microscope—his mother's microscope. Reilly looked sharply at Sheeda, who watched him with unblinking eyes.

"Hyssel," she said, followed by a sentence or two Reilly couldn't understand.

Hyssel had collected these things, from the first colonists and his parents. The way things were taken apart, it seemed Hyssel wanted to know how they worked.

Sheeda walked over and plucked at his sleeve with her forefingers. "*Khattan,*" she insisted.

"What was Hyssel doing with these things?" Reilly demanded. He picked up the microscope. "This was my mother's."

Sheeda shook her head sadly. She picked up the water bag, which Reilly had dropped, and began to fill it.

Reilly grabbed the bag from her. "I'll do that," he said, clamping the microscope under his arm. On the wall behind the water pillar was pinned a hide. It was brown and white.

"That's one of our dogs," Reilly said.

Sheeda backed out of the room.

Reilly shook with anger. He waited for the feeling to abate. No point in mentioning what he saw. Not now. On the way back to Maia, he stashed the microscope in his pack. Together they washed and dressed the wound, which didn't look infected.

"Lani?" Maia said. "Do *wyome* claws carry a poison or something? Did the scratch make you sick?"

Kailani shook her head. "Thirsty," she said.

Reilly poured water into a water sack, lifted Kailani's head, and said, "Take a few sips."

Kailani cried out.

Reilly lowered her. "What?"

Kailani shook her head.

Reilly gently touched her abdomen. Her skin felt cool, and the muscles underneath taut. Maia depressed the area around Kailani's navel and quickly released her hand.

"Shit!" Kailani said. "Don't do that again."

"Internal injuries," Maia said. "The blood irritating the abdominal lining causes pain. That filthin' *wyome* must have injured her spleen or something."

"I don't think it's that serious," Kailani said. "I'm fine. Really."

Maia narrowed her eyes.

Reilly, whose grasp of medicine was limited to basic first aid, tried to remember what a spleen was. He pictured a spongy organ tucked under the ribs on the right or perhaps the left. He had no idea what it did. "We should transfer her to the base. I'll stay here. She can ride Granos."

"I'll fall off," Kailani murmured.

"We'll tie you on," Reilly said.

Reilly turned at a scuffing noise. Nydea hobbled toward them. The burned spots oozed a golden fluid. Her ruined wings mounded her back. Her face looked longer, older. Her injured eye opened only a slit. The good eye held an ocean of despair.

Nose twitching, Nydea sniffed Kailani. She said something to Granos and Locatha, who sat shoulder to shoulder, watching.

Locatha nodded, then walked to the cave's ledge and crouched.

Maia looked at Reilly. "What is she doing?"

Nydea nudged Reilly's thigh with her nose and uttered a string of sibilant prose. Reilly closed his eyes and saw himself atop Granos and Maia atop Locatha, flying out of the canyon. He said to Maia, "Locatha wants you to climb on her back. The *wyomes* think I should ride Granos. Kailani will need an airscouter to get out of here."

He looked at Nydea, whose vulnerability pained his heart. "You and Sheeda need help too," he said. "I'll be back as soon as I can." He formed a picture in his mind of flying a scouter into the cave.

Nydea nodded.

"Okay," Maia said. "Tell Nydea that she and Sheeda need to drink a lot of water and to keep their wounds clean. And they should make sure Kailani stays hydrated too."

Reilly faced Nydea. "Drink water."

"Water," Nydea repeated.

Maia frowned. "That's not Mirnan."

Reilly smiled, which seemed twisted, considering how horrible everything was. Chances were they'd all be dead before nightfall. Yet he felt so weirdly detached.

Maia put her *yridium* gun in Kailani's hand. "Back soon."

Kailani's fingers closed around the handle. "I'm counting on it," she whispered.

TWENTY-NINE

ompared to Nydea's back, the space between Granos wings was flat as a tabletop. Reilly hoisted himself up and scooted forward until his legs dangled on either side of Granos' massive neck. Whereas Nydea's scale were uniformly smooth, Granos neck scales projected upward to form a ridge, giving Reilly something to grip. As long as Granos didn't try to dump him, he'd be fine. The memory of Comox's homicidal ride raised Reilly's sweat. He peered over the ledge and estimated that the canyon floor lay 50 meters below. About 27 average-sized men could fit head to toe underneath him. If he fell from this height, he wouldn't suffer.

Maia smiled without a trace of nervousness. "Ready, Reilly?"

Reilly nodded and wiped his slick palms down his thighs. He glanced backward at Nydea, Sheeda, and Kailani, who sat together, looking vulnerable.

Locatha pushed off and spread her wings upon the air. Reilly held his breath as the wind bore Locatha and Maia aloft.

Granos's muscles bunched under Reilly's thighs as he crouched and sprang. Reilly cinched his legs and gripped with his fingers. After a slight downward lilt, they leveled. A breeze cooled his face. Granos' wings sculled behind him, fanning his back. Reilly twisted to see the cave's mouth, to memorize its squashed Q shape.

As Granos beat his wings harder, Reilly leaned forward and held on. Though the bottom of the canyon was still in shadow, at their height, the sun cast a buttery glow. No other creatures stirred. Granos flew beside Locatha. Maia waved. Reilly waved back.

A keening sound rose behind them. Granos looked back, his breath hot against Reilly's left thigh. A quarter kilometer behind, two *wyomes* gave chase.

Granos and Locatha flew faster, lengthening the distance between them and the sentries.

Calls echoed up and down the canyon. *Wyomes* appeared at the mouths of their caves, sometimes alone, sometimes in twos or threes. Sunlight illuminated the cliff on Reilly's left, glinting off scales and causing the residents to raise forepaws or maneuver wing tips to shield their eyes.

Several *wyomes* swooped in to join the hunt. Two plunged from a cave directly overhead, claws daggering toward them. Granos veered sideways and swung his tail sideways, slicing open his attacker's shoulder. The injured *wyome* drifted to the cave's bottom.

Locatha's opponent met her head on. Locatha exhaled fire, but the *wyome* flitted out of range. Reilly glimpsed Maia's face, her lips set and her eyes wide. The enemy *wyome* reared and opened its mouth. Head lowered, Locatha swerved, claws unsheathed, managed a swipe at the exposed underbelly, raising orange blood. Granos closed in, causing the attacker to tread air and allowing Locatha to deliver a fiery blast to the haunch. With a hiss, the creature winged away.

"If you can't stand the heat, stay out of the kitchen!" Maia called after it. "Keksa!"

Reilly swiveled to see four *wyomes* in pursuit. The canyon's exit was about fifty meters away. Neck outstretched, Granos powered in that direction, his harsh breath drowning out all other sound. Reilly didn't permit himself another backward glance until they were through the gap, and out into the wide expanse of the desert. They flew onward for a minute or two. Reilly looked over his shoulder. No *wyomes* followed. Locatha pulled up beside Granos and exchanged a few words.

Maia grinned at Reilly. "We made it!"

"That's the good news," Reilly shouted into the wind. "The bad news is the *wyomes* now know Kailani, Sheeda, and Nydea are alone."

∞

About half an hour later, Camel Rock came into view. The squat gray buildings of the base shimmered in the distance. Reilly's breath caught in his throat. He'd only been gone three days, but it seemed ages. During that time, so much had happened. He felt older, sadder, and wearier.

Reilly searched the sky for airscouters and saw none. It was only a matter of time before one of the crew spotted them. Time to get the *wyomes* out of sight. He was about to call to Maia, when Locatha dove behind the half dome of a rock formation. Granos followed and landed beside her. Maia and Reilly dismounted.

"We'll have to go the rest of the way on foot," Maia said.

"My thought exactly."

She frowned. "Hold on a minute." She slipped into a crevice in the side of the rock. Reilly heard liquid hitting sand and realized she was peeing. "I wonder what Kailani told Granos and Locatha to do once we got to the base," Maia called.

Reilly cleared his throat. Granos and Locatha were looking at him. He shifted his eyes to his dusty boots. "Um. I don't know. We should probably try to get them to stay behind the rock—at least until we explain things to everyone. Otherwise, they might get shot."

Maia emerged, her shirt half tucked into her pants. "They look tired. They must be hungry and thirsty. I sure am." She put a hand on Locatha's shoulder. *"Icantha,"* she said.

"Parnea," Locatha replied.

Reilly thanked Granos. "Could you wait here for us?" he asked. He formed an image of them lying behind the rock.

Granos and Locatha looked at each other. Locatha nodded once and said, *"Zak."*

"I'll take that as a yes," Reilly said.

"We'll get some airscouters and go back with you," Maia said. "We can cover each other."

The *wyomes* stared.

"Do you think they understood?" Maia said.

"Did you form a mental image?"

Maia squinted at him. "So that's what you've been doing. Anyway, we'd better hurry. It's wicked hot and this rock formation won't provide shade much longer."

∞

Maia and Reilly jogged the 200 meters to the base. Two figures moved in the garden—skinny Keid and ponytailed Tally. Both were hoeing between the rows of beans. Beyond them, sunflowers nodded their big heads. Spear-like heads of pearl millet grew almost as tall at the sunflowers.

A shadow shifted in the guard tower. The alarm sounded. Ensign Morten leaned out the high window and waved.

Her face glistening with sweat, Maia cupped her hands around her mouth and hallooed. Tally and Keid dropped their gardening tools and began shouting and waving. Captain Baca emerged from the goat pen, pushing a wheelbarrow.

The gate slid open. Ensign Morten clambered down the guard tower ladder.

Wearing a broad smile and a broader hat, Commander Shen ran to them. "Where have you been?" she asked. Her expression tipped toward anger. "We thought you were dead."

Before Maia and Reilly could explain, Tally, Keid, and Nova rushed forward and engulfed Maia with hugs. For a moment, Reilly felt alone. Then Tab turned, thumped Reilly on the shoulder, and mumbled, "Glad to have you back, man." Ensign Morten fist-bumped him. Keid threw his arms around Reilly.

Once released, Reilly found himself face-to-face with Ensign Rabin, who reached a dirty finger under his sun goggles to wipe his eyes. Then he folded his hairy arms over his chest. "You slipped me some Harmonal."

"I'm sorry," Reilly said. "I had to."

"And why was that?" Captain Baca stood apart from the rest, one hand shading his eyes, which stared in the direction of Camel Rock. Had he seen Granos and Locatha?

"So that I could go look for my parents." His parched throat ached.

"So you could steal an airscouter for an unauthorized and unnecessary mission?"

Reilly felt his lips wobble. He nodded and hoped he wouldn't cry.

Maia pointed to an A-shaped structure formed by BioFuerte hung over a steel cable. Slit-like openings ran at eye level across the side facing them. "What is that?" she asked.

"A pillbox," Ensign Rabin said. "A defensive structure we can shoot from."

Maia frowned. "Why is it called a pillbox?"

"Nice try, Maia," the captain said. "Give me one good reason you followed Reilly."

Maia pulled back her shoulders. "I had to protect Reilly."

Ensign Morten had appeared, his sun-bleached hair held back with a thong. He laughed. "You thought you were most qualified for that job?"

Maia's gazed shifted from one adult to another. "Are we in huge trouble?"

"I reserve judgment until we hear more." the captain said. "I'm glad you're alive. It's getting hot and you both look like you could use some water. Let's conclude this debriefing in the mess hall."

They crossed the yard, past four airscouters parked in a line. One had a hole in its side from the *witnaw* that had attacked Maia. Reilly blinked. Four scouters. That meant the crew had been able to fix the one he grounded. And they had retrieved his parents' scouter.

The inside of the mess hall was only a few degrees cooler. Ensign Rabin disappeared into the pantry and returned with crackers, a canister of nut butter, a bag of dried fruit, and a stack of plastic glasses, all of which he set on the table. Commander Shen followed with two pitchers of water.

Nova handed Reilly and Maia glasses of water and a bowl of radishes and snap peas. "Our first harvest," she said.

Reilly gulped the water and popped a radish into his mouth. It was smaller and tangier than those grown on the ship. He suddenly realized how hungry he was.

Lieutenant Schuler loped in, smelling like he'd just come from the barn.

"Okay," Captain Baca said, "let's hear your story."

Reilly swallowed. "We'll have to give you an abridged version. We have two Mirnan allies waiting on the other side of Camel Rock. And we have to go rescue somebody."

"Mirnan? Allies? Rescue somebody?" Lieutenant Schuler asked. "You've connected with the resident species?"

Everyone started talking at once.

Captain Baca held up his hand. "Is the individual we need to rescue human?"

"Yes," Maia said. "One of the first colonists. Kailani Knight. She was wounded in battle with the bad *wyomes.*"

Everyone except Captain Baca and Reilly looked at Maia with consternation.

The group started talking. "Wyo—what?" "First colonist?" "One is still alive?"

Captain Baca rose from his seat. "Silence! Tell me what happened."

"There isn't time to tell you everything," Maia insisted.

Reilly downed another glass of water and stood. "First of all, I'm sorry for taking the airscouter and worrying everyone."

"You have no idea how many hours we spent looking for you two," Ensign Morten muttered.

"Go on," Captain Baca said.

Reilly compressed the tale to the essentials. When he mentioned Kailani, he said her whole name, including title.

Commander Shen nodded. "I know her. So does Carlos," she said, shooting him a glance.

The captain kept his eyes on Reilly. "Continue."

"She found my parents." Reilly's voice cracked.

Maia stood beside him and took up the narrative. "They died. The bad *wyomes* brought them *thystam* rock to burn. And the toxic fumes killed them." She glanced at Reilly. "But that's another story. Right now, we have to go help Nydea, Sheeda, and Kailani."

"Who are the other people?" Captain Baca asked.

"Nydea and Sheeda are *wyomes*," Maia said. "You know, those huge flying creatures."

"The animals that have killed half our livestock?" Ensign Morten asked.

"And our dogs." Lieutenant Schuler added.

"The monsters that attacked me?" Ensign Rabin said, running a hand over the stubble resurfacing his scalp.

Captain Baca held up his hand for order and the room quieted.

"They're not all monsters," Maia said. "They're a highly intelligent species. Some are good, especially Nydea. She rescued Kailani after all the other first colonists had died. She also saved Reilly's life and mine. But her uncle—his name is Hyssel—is evil. He's responsible for killing the first colonists. And he hurt Nydea and Sheeda—that's Nydea's aunt. Anyway, we had to go to their cave in Ledera Canyon, which is where the *wyomes* live—"

"Who's we?" Captain Baca asked.

"Maia, Kailani, and I," Reilly said. "We went to the cave where Nydea and Sheeda live. They were badly hurt. While we were taking care of them, other *wyomes* attacked—"

"Except for Granos and Locatha, two *wyomes* who defended us. They brought us here. They're waiting for us by Camel Rock. We were afraid you would shoot them."

The group gaped at them. Ensign Morten folded his arms over his chest. Ensign Rabin ran his fingers over the stubble popping through his healing scalp. Nova leaned to whisper in Tab's ear. He smiled and shook his head.

"They'll accompany us back to Ledera Canyon to rescue Kailani," Reilly said.

"Why didn't Lani—Commander Knight—come with you?" Captain Baca asked.

"She's hurt," Maia said. "An enemy *wyome* wounded her. She has lacerations to the upper chest and, I think, internal bleeding."

Captain Baca's face tensed and his brown eyes darkened. "How far away is this canyon?

"It took about a half hour flying on Locatha and Granos," Reilly said. "So maybe eight to ten kilometers to the northeast."

"Wicked phenom," Tab said. "I want to fly on one."

Reilly ignored him. "Anyway, Kailani's with Nydea and Sheeda."

"And all three of them injured," Lieutenant Schuler said. "Who's protecting them?"

Maia shrugged. "That's our job."

Commander Shen looked hard at Captain Baca. "We'd better hurry," she said.

Captain Baca began giving orders to pack food and water, to gather emergency medical supplies, to put fresh *yridium* cartridges in the handguns and the scouter's guns.

Commander Shen unrolled a computer scroll on the table. The monitor came dimly on, revealing a topographic map. "Show me where we're going," she said.

"The computers are working again?" Reilly asked.

"Not the mainframe. We can access some files from the scrolls, but it's hard to input much."

Maia frowned at the map, then pointed. "There's the canyon. That is, I'm pretty sure. You'll have to take me along to point out the correct cave."

"You'll need me too," Reilly said, though he couldn't think of a great reason why. In fact, Granos and Locatha were the best guides back to the canyon.

"I'm only risking two scouters," Captain Baca called. "I need an empty copilot's seat for Commander Knight. So only one of you can come."

"How many enemy catbats are we talking about?" Ensign Morten said. He was loading four guns with *yridium* cartridges.

"About fifty," Maia said. "Lani told me this morning. She said other clans live in canyons on the far side of the mesa—Methna Mesa they call it. Generally clans don't have much to do with each other, unless they come together for ceremonies and big meetings."

The captain pulled down his cap. "Lian, I'm leaving you in charge."

Commander Shen nodded. "Don't worry about us. I'll set up a surgical unit. In case we need one."

"Good," the captain said. "Harlan, you'll pilot one airscouter. I'll take the other."

Harlan grunted his assent.

Lieutenant Schuler said, "Carlos, you shouldn't lead this mission. It sounds dangerous. Let me take your place."

The captain's brown eyes narrowed to slits. "Thank you for your concern, Erik," he said stiffly, "but I'm going. You can assist Lian in prepping the medical supplies." He looked at Ensign Rabin. "Oren, you keep watch. Don't let the kids roam. As soon as you see anything approach the base—even if it's us, send the kids into the vegetable cellar. You, Erik, and Lian will go into the pillbox."

"Got it," Ensign Rabin said.

The captain dismissed everyone except Ensign Morten, Maia, and Reilly. "One of you can help navigate."

"Take me," Maia said. "I'm a better navigator, a better shot."

"Hey," Reilly said, "I can do those things too."

"But I know medicine," Maia insisted. "What if I rode Granos or Locatha?"

Reilly shook his head. "The *wyomes* can't fight as well while carrying someone. You might fall off."

"How about the kids draw straws?" Ensign Morten said.

"Do what?" Maia asked. Reilly couldn't imagine how drawing figured into the plan.

Outside, Ensign Morten grabbed two twigs from the ground, closed his hand around them, and said, "Pick one, Maia."

Maia pulled free a twig. Reilly chose the other. His was longer.

"You win, Reilly," Ensign Morten said.

"That's it?" Maia said. "He draws a longer stick and wins?"

"Yep."

"That reeks," she grumbled, arms folded over her chest.

"As you pointed out, you have the medical background," Captain Baca said. "Help Commander Shen set up an operating suite. She'll need an assistant."

"Yes, sir," Maia said resignedly.

Captain Baca and Ensign Morten strode toward the airscouters.

Reilly hesitated. Maia's face sagged with disappointment and fatigue. "Hey," he said, "I'm sorry. I wish we both could go."

Maia's eyes narrowed, as though gauging his sincerity. "Humpf," she said. "Friends still?"

"I guess."

Reilly turned.

"Be careful," Maia called. "Keep Lani, Nydea, and Sheeda safe."

"I'll do my best," Reilly said. He reached into his pack, drew out the microscope, and thrust it at her. "Keep this for me, okay?" Before she could ask questions, he hurried toward the airscouters.

THIRTY

Reilly rode shotgun to Captain Baca. In seconds, they reached Camel Rock. Granos and Locatha crouched side by side in the shadow. As the airscouters set down, Granos fanned his wings, as though readying for flight.

Ensign Morten spoke into the radio. "Captain, I don't like this."

"It's fine," Reilly insisted. "We need allies."

The scouter's dome slid back. Reilly stood in his seat, waved, and hoped his behavior came across as reassuring.

Locatha's nostrils flared and her golden eyes shifted from Captain Baca to Ensign Morten. The remains of a *dilcroth* lay at her feet, the head with its beady eyes and narrow toothy snout still intact.

Reilly made introductions and hoped Granos and Locatha would understand.

In a low voice, Granos said something to Locatha.

"Holy shit," Ensign Morten said. "They talk."

"I don't suppose they speak English," Captain Baca said, not taking his eyes off the *wyomes*.

"Not these two. They speak Mirnan. But they seem to be able to decipher thoughts and emotions, especially if you want them too."

"I'm not even going to ask what that means," Ensign Morten said through the radio. He remained in his seat, dome closed. "I don't want any damn catbat reading my mind."

Captain Baca said, "Time to go. No time to talk strategy. Useless with the language barrier. Feel free to send thoughts to your friends about taking us to Lani."

"To Nydea, Sheeda, and Kailani," Reilly called to the *wyomes*.

275

Locatha sprang into the air. Granos followed. The two airscouters fell in behind them.

Ensign Morten flew close enough that Reilly could see him casually popping food into his mouth.

The sun was directly overhead, which meant they had several hours until darkness roused the *wyomes* en masse. If they were lucky, they'd only have to contend with the sentries—at least until one of them screamed an alarm.

The captain cleared his throat and asked, "How serious is Kailani's condition? Is she conscious?"

"She was in pain, but trying hard not to show it," Reilly said. "She was conscious when we left."

"Does she have a weapon?"

"A staff. And Maia left her gun."

"A staff doesn't sound lethal. How much *yridium* was left in the gun?"

"I didn't check. Probably not a lot."

"Jesus."

"How do you know Kailani?"

"The Academy."

Reilly waited for more, but the captain only said. "How much farther?"

Reilly scanned the mesa. A cleft running vertically through the cliff became visible. "There," Reilly said. "A kilometer away."

"I see it. Keep your hand on the laser gun."

There were two guns: one that fired out of the scouter's nose; and one that was mounted on a disc at the scouter's base, allowing it to swivel three hundred sixty degrees. Reilly had control of the latter. The captain slowed the pace of the scouter to coast on battery power and gave the order to Ensign Morten to do the same. Without the thrusters, their progress was nearly silent.

They followed Granos and Locatha into the canyon. The canyon floor remained in shadow, but sunlight illuminated the lavender, mauve, and orange striations along the western wall.

Reilly looked for sentries, but saw none. That seemed wrong. The Q-shaped cave entrance came into view. "There!" he cried, his arm extended over the captain's shoulder and pointing. "At two o'clock."

Below lay four dead *wyomes*. The body of one arced over a shrub as though embracing it.

Just ahead, a *wyome* flitted out of a cave and swooped toward Sheeda and Nydea's cave. It extended its hind legs to land on the ledge just as fire plumed from the entrance, causing the intruder to fall back. Granos rocketed toward it and swiped one of its wings with his tail. The *wyome* screamed and winged lopsidedly up the canyon.

Ensign Morten's voice came over the radio. "Shit on a shingle."

The captain said to Reilly. "The clearance at the opening is adequate. How much room is inside?" he asked Reilly.

"The cave is about twice as big as the mess hall. Big enough for both scouters. Just watch out for a few dead *wyomes* on the ground."

"Harlan," the captain said. "Hover outside the cave. We'll attempt to land inside. If enemies appear, defend yourself. And try not to shoot our allies."

"How do I tell them apart?"

Without answering, the captain nosed the scouter into the cave. Reilly's eyes worked to distinguish shapes in the dim interior. He saw Sheeda step backward to make room. The captain landed between two dead *wyomes*, opened the dome, and hopped out. Reilly scrambled after him.

Sheeda stood uncertainly, tail twitching, ears cocked forward. The right ear was torn nearly in half, and fresh scratches crosshatched her chest.

Captain Baca stood before Kailani. She sat propped against the wall, *erzala* hides covering her legs, the staff balanced across her thighs. One hand clutched Maia's gun; the other lifted in greeting.

"Took you long enough," she said with a wan smile.

The captain knelt and touched her face. "I thought I'd never see you again. We found the other first colonists. When you didn't appear at our camp, I imagined—Why didn't you come?"

Kailani reached up and laid her index finger over his lips. "We left Earth long ago. Many things have changed."

"I know. We'll talk later. First, let's get you out of here."

Sheeda made a murmuring sound.

Reilly went over to her. A fresh cut on her chest glistened with ocher blood. "Thank you for protecting Kailani and Nydea," he said. "Where is Nydea?"

Sheeda pointed toward the adjoining smaller cave. Nydea appeared to be sleeping, but when he squatted beside her, her good eye opened.

"Reilly," Nydea said. She didn't raise her head.

Reilly's heart jumped at the sound of her saying his name. As he stroked an uninjured patch on her head, he heard the hum of an airscouter engine.

"I'll be right back," he said.

Ensign Morten landed the scouter and stepped out onto the body of a dead *wyome*. "Christ Almighty," he muttered. "How many did you kill?"

Captain Baca had a first-aid box open beside him. He had already applied a bandage to Kailani's chest and slipped inflatable pants over her legs. Inflation would squeeze blood from the lower limbs into the rest of the circulation. A MedGauge blinked on her wrist.

"How's she doing?" the ensign asked.

"Blood pressure is low. Pulse high. Consistent with internal hemorrhage. She just lost consciousness. What's the situation outside?"

"Reilly's two catbats are holding off attackers. Not sure how long they can last." He nodded at Kailani. "Let's move her into the copilot's seat and get out of here."

Reilly grabbed a pile of gauze, returned to Sheeda, and pressed the bandage to her chest laceration. Warm liquid wet his fingers. With a low growl, Sheeda backed away. Nydea limped over.

"Pressure will stop the bleeding," Reilly explained as he came slowly toward her.

Nydea murmured something to her. Sheeda quieted, but Reilly kept talking, more to calm himself than to communicate. "The gauze contains synthetic spider silk, which binds to the wound and stops bleeding." After a moment, he withdrew his hand. The bandage held. He used another piece to bind a split in her right ear together.

"On the count of three," the captain said.

Reilly looked up to see Captain Baca and Ensign Morten lift Kailani and begin walking toward the scouters. Kailani moaned as they bent her into the copilot seat of the captain's scouter.

The captain called, "Reilly, you go with Ensign Morten."

Outside a *wyome* roared and swooped near the cave. Ensign Morten swiveled and fired his *yridium* handgun, connecting with the spot just under the *wyome's* jaw. The *wyome* shuddered and dropped from sight.

"Time to go," Captain Baca called.

"I say we rise above the canyon," Ensign Morten said. "Atop the mesa, we'll have more room to maneuver. And we can make a beeline for the base."

"What about Sheeda and Nydea?" Reilly asked.

"What about them?" Ensign Morten said.

"We can't leave them here. They're not safe. Nydea might die without medical care. And Locatha and Granos can't stay behind either. I don't know what happens to traitors, but it can't be pleasant."

Captain Baca said, "What do you propose?"

"I think Sheeda can fly. Nydea's wings are too damaged. Granos can carry her."

"They'll slow us down," Ensign Morten said. He was already sitting in the pilot's seat.

Reilly looked hard at Captain Baca. He wanted to say that he couldn't lose anyone else. But he didn't trust his voice, didn't expect the captain to understand the bond he felt with Nydea.

Captain Baca's eye moved from Reilly's face to the back of the cave. Sheeda approached, Nydea hobbling behind her. "Okay," he said, exhaling. "Harlan, you and I will fly behind the—the *wyomes*. Do your best to shield them."

Ensign Morten shook his head, but said nothing.

"All right, Reilly," the captain said. "I don't know how you're going to relay the plan to your friends."

Reilly moved toward the mouth of the cave and motioned Sheeda and Nydea to follow. Just overhead, Granos and Locatha circled in an updraft. No other *wyomes* were in sight. "Granos!" he called.

The big *wyome* dropped to his level.

Reilly formed an image of Granos flying with Nydea held to his chest. He pictured Sheeda, Locatha, and the airscouters in formation around them. "Carry Nydea," he said. "Nydea come closer." He pointed to the ledge.

The pupil of Nydea's good eye pulsed. She took two paces forward.

Granos uttered a command.

Nydea turned her back to the ledge. Reilly thought she was refusing. Then she rose onto her hind legs and tipped backwards into the canyon.

Reilly sucked in his breath.

Nydea plummeted. Granos dove after her, scooping her up between his forelegs. Sheeda moved to the ledge and pushed off. Her wings opened slowly, causing her to lose altitude before she began rowing her self upward and forward. Locatha fell in beside her.

Reilly scrambled into the seat behind Ensign Morten. The dome of Captain Baca's scouter was down. Kailani's head drooped to the right. The captain lifted off, filling the cave with dust, and shot out of the cave. Reilly hadn't even fastened his harness before the ensign rocketed after him.

Within seconds, they had pulled into formation with the four *wyomes*. Locatha flew just ahead of Sheeda and Granos. Nydea looked like a bundle of gray rags between Granos' forelegs. Sheeda's mouth hung open with the exertion of flying.

"Hell," Ensign Morten said, "that catbat doesn't look like it's going to make it."

Orange flashed behind them. Reilly checked the mirror and saw fire arcing from the mouth of a *wyome* near the scouter's right wing. Ensign Morten throttled forward. Another *wyome* cut in front of them, barely missing the nose of Captain Baca's scouter and causing him to veer dangerously close to the cliff's face. Ensign Morten fired the laser gun at this attacker, the red beam boring a hole into a wing tip. He lifted the craft straight up. A *wyome* slipped underneath, neck stretched toward Sheeda.

"Hit it, Reilly," he said.

Reilly depressed the button and fired down on the enemy, striking it squarely between the shoulder blades. The *wyome* floated a few seconds, then dropped out of sight behind them. For a moment, regret twisted Reilly's gut. How quickly he'd become a killer. If he had kill to defend his friends, he would. And if he had Hyssel in his sights, he would depress the trigger with electric elation.

"Elevate," Captain Baca radioed.

The two airscouters ascended. Locatha followed, Granos more slowly. Sheeda looked up, but couldn't seem to muscle herself higher.

"Wait for Sheeda," Reilly begged.

The airscouters slowed. Five enemy *wyome* formed a net above.

"Looks like we'll have to run the canyon," Ensign Morten said into the radio.

"Agreed," came the captain's voice.

They pressed forward. The canyon widened, giving them more room to maneuver. Granos flew just ahead and to the left, his forelimbs wrapped around Nydea, all four of her limbs clinging to Granos's middle, her battered wings dangling.

From a cave above, a *wyome* dropped toward the scouter. Ensign Morten banked hard to the right. The view out the cockpit rotated. Reilly's vision filled with the left-hand cliff, caves, *wyomes* popping out of them, the canyon floor, lavender sand, mauve boulders. He closed his eyes against a wave of nausea.

"Jesus," the ensign said. "Everyone in Dodge knows we're here. They were waiting for us to emerge. They'll try to box us in. An alien version of shooting fish in a barrel."

A fiery blast swept toward Locatha, but she was able to rear up and fan it away with her wings. Up ahead, the exit to the canyon and the rim of the mesa framed the lilac light of afternoon. In a minute or two, they'd be there. Dark shapes swarmed in the exit.

A flare made him swivel. *Wyome* fire licked the cockpit's dome, which darkened at one edge. Reilly angled the laser gun and shot. The *wyome* made a bucking motion.

"Got him in the backside," crowed the ensign. "You're not such a bad shot after all."

They flew a dodging course. Ensign Morten maneuvered; Reilly shot. Reilly glanced at the captain's scouter. Kailani remained slumped in the co-pilot's seat, leaving Captain Baca to act as both pilot and gunner.

Ahead of them, a *wyome* pivoted and winged straight for the captain's scouter.

Ensign Morten accelerated toward it. "Captain, take a bow. I got this one."

They intercepted the *wyome*, causing it to career sideways into Sheeda. The two creatures seemed to hang in the air a moment, claws grappling at each other's bodies, before they began to sink. Sheeda beat her wings, but the other *wyome* acted as dead weight. Sheeda swung her tail. The barbed end caught in her attacker's wing, lodged, then ripped free. Still the other hung on.

"That one's a suicide bomber." Ensign Morten shifted the scouter into hover, then into a straight descent. "Aim carefully, Reilly."

The ground grew quickly nearer, but Reilly focused on the twisting *wyomes*. He waited until the enemy's back was to him, then pressed the button. After the laser beam vectored to its chest, the creature flipped backward. Sheeda righted herself, wings slowly stroking the air. Fresh scratches and a few deep gouges crisscrossed her belly. The bandage had fallen off her chest wound.

Her mouth moved, but Reilly couldn't hear. She began to lose elevation. Locatha descended toward her.

"Do something," Reilly said.

"Like what?" the ensign said.

"Fly under her. Lift her up!" Emotion clogged his voice.

"Are you nuts? We wouldn't be able to see. Our first turn would knock her off."

Seemingly out of nowhere, three *wyomes* tore after Sheeda. Locatha followed, exhaling fire. But she could only take on one attacker at a time. The other two *wyomes* pursued Sheeda, who had no chance of outpacing them.

"No!" Reilly wailed.

"We can't help her," Ensign Morten said.

"Harlan," the captain said over the radio. "Get out of there. You're about to be mobbed."

The airscouter ascended, accelerated, and zigzagged around enemy *wyome*. Blinking away tears, Reilly craned to look behind them. Sheeda lay on the ground. The two *wyomes* stood on either side of her. Keening eerily, Locatha batted away a pursuer and followed the humans.

"Hold it together, Reilly," Ensign Morten said. "Heavy traffic ahead."

Twenty meters distant, a dozen *wyomes* clouded the mouth of the canyon.

"We're leaving Granos and Locatha behind," Reilly said.

The ensign spoke into the radio, "Let's sweep a path for the cat—for our allies."

"Copy that," the captain said.

"Reilly, keep your finger on the trigger. First get rid of the two on our tail. Release your chair and swivel."

Rage crowded out sorrow as Reilly spun his seat 180 degrees. He aimed and shot, the beam connecting with the belly of one *wyome*. Its wings beat once more then stalled. The other *wyome* whirled away. Reilly spun forward and began strafing the *wyomes* blocking the exit. Bodies fell. Others darted into side canyons and caves.

The airscouters held their positions until Locatha and Granos slipped into the relative safety of the open desert. Reilly never thought the flat expanse of orange sand would look so good to him. No enemy followed. Two hovered at the entrance to Ledera Canyon, then turned back.

In his earpiece, Reilly heard Captain Baca say, "Mobile one to base, come in."

Lieutenant Schuler answered. The captain said they had Kailani. He said to expect them in approximately eleven minutes and to have *yridium* guns loaded in case of attack.

"Lieutenant Schuler," the captain added, "we have three *wyomes* with us that you're not to shoot."

THIRTY-ONE

Minutes later, the base was close enough that Reilly could see the snout of the mounted laser rifle swivel in the slit-like opening at the top of the guard tower. Commander Shen waved from the small window.

Captain Baca radioed an order to open the gates and deactivate the shield, which meant that, in Reilly's absence, Ensign Rabin had finished the process of running a dome of current over the base.

For a moment, the yard was empty. The animals must have been shut in the barn. No kids could be seen.

The door to the subterranean cold storage area opened. Maia's head, then whole body emerged. She shaded her eyes with her hand. Her mouth moved, but Reilly could only hear the hum of the airscouter's engine winding down. One at a time, Tab, Tally, Nova, and Keid climbed out.

"Home sweet home," Ensign Morten said as he slid back the scouter's dome.

Reilly stood, hopped to the ground, and turned toward Ledera Canyon. The western horizon, now crimson with sunset, was clear. He had expected an approaching horde of *wyomes*. His shoulders sagged with relief and exhaustion.

Locatha landed. Still hugging Nydea to his chest with his front legs, Granos touched down on his hind legs. Locatha helped rotate Nydea so that her paws met the ground.

Tab ran toward Ensign Morten. When their paths intersected in the middle of the yard, they exchanged high fives, low ten, and a brief hug. To Reilly's surprise, Tab approached him and held high his palm. Reilly clapped it. Tab caught his hand and gripped, but, contrary to custom, not so hard as to inflict pain.

"Stout work, hume," Tab said. "Totally solid."

"Thanks."

Tab grinned. "I only wish I had been in your place. My aim is better. And not much scares me."

Reilly shrugged and decided not to take offense.

Tab gestured toward Granos, Locatha, and Nydea, who sat shoulder to shoulder, Nydea in the middle, all three looking near collapse. Locatha began licking Nydea's wounds. Nydea sank to the ground and curled her tail around her body.

"Those your friends?" Tab asked.

"Yes."

"Wicked phenom."

Maia hurried past. "I'm going to help with Lani," she said.

"Okay," Reilly said. "The *wyomes* probably need water."

"I'll help," Tab said. "We can fill the water trough in the corral."

"Why are you being nice?" Reilly asked.

Tab shrugged. "I've always been a nice guy. You're just less of a grothead. Plus, I almost missed you. Not many humes left. And only 3 boys, if you can count Keid."

Reilly didn't know what to say. This was probably the closest he'd come to acceptance. He glanced toward the captain's scouter. Ensign Rabin and Lieutenant Schuler were helping Captain Baca lift Kailani's limp body from the copilot's seat. Tally stood beside the scouter. After the lieutenant said something to her, she hurried up the guard tower.

Tab pulled his sleeve. "Come on, Reilly. The captain doesn't need our help. We'd just be in the way." He picked up a rock and started walking toward the *wyomes*.

Granos moved to stand in front of Nydea. Reilly hurried after Tab, who walked right up to Locatha, his empty hand extended as though to touch her. She hunched her shoulders and showed her teeth. Tab gripped the rock and cocked his arm.

"Drop the rock, Tab."

Tab scowled.

"I said drop it."

To Reilly's surprise, Tab did.

"How do you know they won't attack?" Tab said.

Granos made a rumbling sound in his throat.

"I just do. Take a couple steps back. You're making them nervous." Reilly looked at the *wyomes* and pointed to Tab. "This is Tab. He is a friend."

"Frenth," Nydea repeated.

Tab blinked. "Did it just say, 'friend?'"

"Yes."

"Minje me," Tab said. "I can't wait to ride one of them."

"I doubt they want to make a habit of it," Reilly said. He turned to the *wyomes*. "We'll take you to water."

"Water," Nydea said. *"Zak. Dakith."*

"What else did it say?" Tab asked.

"My guess is she thanked us in Mirnan,"

"Mirnan," Tab repeated.

Gesturing to the *wyomes* with a broad arm motion, Reilly started walking toward the water pump in the garden. After a moment's hesitation, the *wyomes* followed, Nydea barely able to shuffle along.

"After they drink, we should get them food," Tab said. "What do they eat?"

Reilly shrugged. "Smaller animals."

"Phenom," Tab breathed.

Keid and Nova watched from a safe distance. Nova wrapped and unwrapped a lock of dark hair around her index finger. Keid thoughtfully chewed the neck of his T-shirt.

"Stop eating your clothes," Nova said.

Keid opened his mouth and the shirt fell back into place. Saliva darkened a semicircle of cloth.

Tab said in a low voice, "He's been doing that lately, chewing his cuticles, his lip, his nails, the cuffs and collars of his shirts."

Keid's wide blue eyes watched Tab. His lower lip was red, the skin underneath a raw pink.

Reilly gave Tab a sharp look. "Might years of teasing have anything to do with it?"

Tab pursed his lips. "Having people die and disappear doesn't help. Catbats firestorming the base panics the pee out of him. And now he's supposed to believe these three won't kill him."

Reilly registered that this conversation was the longest he'd ever had with Tab and one of the few devoid of taunting.

Tally leaned out the guard tower window. "I want to help with the catdragons," she called.

Keid cupped his palms around his mouth. "Tally, I'll trade with you."

Reilly wondered when the kids had started keeping watch. Keid scanned the yard. No adults in sight. He waited for Tally to descend the ladder then climbed up. Reilly suspected he felt safer up there.

Tab and Nova ran ahead and began pumping water.

"I'll fetch first-aid supplies," Tally said as she ran past Reilly.

Reilly led the three *wyomes* to the trough and gestured for them to drink. Locatha went first, her tongue, the pale orange of sunrise, lapping the purple-tinged water. Granos and Nydea followed suit.

"Their tongues are so long," Nova said. "They sort of curl them to scoop water to their mouths."

Tally puffed back, spread a tarp on the ground, and set down the first-aid box. "I brought BioGlue. As well as bandages, adhesive strips, antibiotic ointment, burn cream, an injection gun for SynPlasma. Pretty much everything we need." She paused. "Except fresh water for cleaning the wounds. Tab, bring another bucket of water, okay?"

"I just finished filling the trough. Why not use that water?"

"Because it's now laden with mouth bacteria," Tally said.

"Well, they've been licking their wounds. Just like dogs. Maybe whatever's in their mouths helps with the healing."

"That may be true," Tally said. "But I'd still like to use fresh water. Please."

"Women," Tab grumbled. "Nova, help me, okay?"

"After you just insulted women?" Nova said.

"Sorry," Tab said. "Nova, please help me."

"When did everyone become so polite?" Reilly asked.

Tally squinted her blue-green eyes. "You're saying we're usually rude?"

"Of course not," Reilly said. He squatted beside Granos. There were no new wounds. The others had crusted with ocher scabs. Nydea didn't have any fresh injuries either. Now that he thought about it, enemy *wyomes* had harassed them, but had never actually attacked.

He looked into Granos' golden eyes and said, "We need to clean the sand out of those cuts, which will hurt a bit."

Granos' ears flickered. He turned to Locatha and Nydea, as though hoping for a translation.

Tally gently examined two gaping cuts at the base of Granos' neck. "BioGlue should hold those together." Her gaze shifted to Nydea. "Glad I brought the SynPlasma. The little one will need extra fluids. Burns that extensive can lead to dehydration."

Nydea wearily lowered her head to her front paws. A sighing exhalation swirled the dust. She looked defeated. Her sorrow gave off a cloyingly sweet smell. Closing his eyes, he saw a shimmering indigo sphere, felt the weight and chill of it in his chest. When he opened his eyes, she was watching him. "Sheeda," she whispered.

Reilly's eyes welled. Nydea's were dry. She didn't sweat and didn't cry. Probably desert animals couldn't afford such extravagance. "I'm sorry," he whispered. "I wish we could have saved her."

"The small one just said something," Tally said.

"Yes," Reilly said. "Her aunt didn't make it out of the canyon. We had to leave her behind."

"Oh," Tally said and stroked Nydea. "What's this one's name?"

Nova and Tab lurched over with sloshing buckets. Reilly took that moment to introduce the *wyomes* and the kids.

Tally produced three sponges still in their wrappers. "Get them wet and squeeze to release the antimicrobial soap inside the sponge." She kept one, handed the other two to Nova and Reilly. Making soft, reassuring sounds, Tally walked to Granos and began washing a wound on his flank. The underlying muscles quivered, but he otherwise sat still.

"What about me?" Tab said, red-faced with some combination of heat, exertion, and indignation. "Am I good for nothing but fetching water?"

"You're good for a couple other things," Nova said coyly. She held out her hand to Nydea, who sniffed tentatively. "I won't hurt you," Nova cooed. She plunged the sponge in the bucket and squeezed soapy water down Nydea's spine.

"Here," Reilly said, handing his sponge to Tab. "You work on Locatha."

Tab grunted. Locatha watched him warily, but relaxed as Tab spoke to her in surprisingly gentle tones and carefully wiped her wounds.

Reilly stood by Nydea. "Careful not to break the blisters," he said to Nova.

"I know that," Nova retorted. "Good catbat," she murmured to Nydea. "We'll make you better."

"Why-o-mees," Reilly corrected. "They're called *wyomes.*"

"Fine," Nova said. "Good wyoming."

"Do you have any idea how we can fix Nydea's wings?" Reilly asked Tally.

Tally squinted at Granos' wings. "Double epidermal layer with a little connective tissue between. The tissue is thin enough to see the blood vessels. I think we should take a small piece of normal tissue from Nydea, put it in a sterile tank, add epidermal growth stimulating factors, and grow some grafts."

"How long will that take?" Reilly asked.

"About 24 hours to create pieces long enough to patch the holes. We'll have to stimulate new capillary growth to supply the area. Meantime, we need to keep the intact but injured tissue from contracting, which would distort her wing structure. Erik will know what to do."

Erik. Not Lieutenant Schuler, Reilly thought. Was he the only kid still using full titles? And how had he failed to realize how much Tally knew about veterinary medicine? Would Nova start spouting complex mathematical formulas describing aerodynamic wing design?

Maia walked up, looking sweaty and tired.

"How is Kailani?" Reilly asked her.

"She's stable. I was right about her spleen—ruptured. We gave her another liter of SynPlasma and a unit of SynRBCs. Commander Shen managed the blood pressure and anesthesia. I closed the superficial wounds."

"What about her spleen?" Reilly asked.

"What's a spleen?" Tab asked.

"It's an immune system organ that filters and stores blood."

"What was wrong with this woman's spleen?" Nova asked.

"A *wyome* crushed it, causing it to bleed. Anyway," Maia said, "Captain Baca removed most of it with fiberoptic surgery, left a little bit of viable spleen for immune purposes."

"The captain performed surgery?"

Maia smiled. "I was surprised too. Remember how he sometimes assisted his wife in surgery?"

"Doctor Mbaake?"

"Right. Well, after she died, rather than relax by playing computer games, he practiced on the surgery simulator. Just in case."

"I didn't know that," Tally said. "Erik and I practiced on a simulator for various animals."

For a moment, Reilly imagined not Kailani, but his mother lying on the operating table, her pulse still throbbing in her neck, her skin still warm. A sob rose in his throat. He swallowed hard.

Maia handed him her canteen. He shifted his gaze toward the wind turbine slowly turning in the breeze, and drank. The sun had dropped to a hand's width above the mesa.

When he looked back at Maia, her face was wet.

"What?" he said.

Maia shook her head and walked away from the others.

Reilly followed. Tally began giving Nova and Tab instructions about proper bandaging technique. "Let me handle the BioGlue," she said.

"You want to talk," Reilly asked Maia.

Maia sniffed. "I know Lani will be fine. But I was worried, you know?"

"I know." He lifted his hand to comfort her, felt the veneer of his composure crack, and let his arm drop.

"I'm okay now," Maia said. "Let's figure out what to do with the *wyomes.*"

Sunlight glimmered on Nydea's blisters. Reilly felt like that, like he was a walking blister. Nova was daubing cream onto a large burned area on Nydea's rump. She began shivering.

Maia drew closer. "We'll need to move her indoors for the night. With so much surface area burned, she'll have trouble staying warm."

"Where? The barn?"

"Crazy idea," Tally said. "The other animals would go wild with terror."

Tab's head appeared over Locatha's shoulder. "We have extra BioFuerte and cables. It wouldn't take long to rig up a tent."

At that moment, the alarm sounded. "*Wyomes* flying our way," Keid shouted into the speaker. "Five of them. They're in some kind of weird formation."

A cluster of dark objects moved through the air from the direction of Ledera Canyon. Reilly wished he had binoculars. The other kids had enhanced visual processing systems. "What do you see?" he asked them.

"Four *wyomes,*" Maia said. "No five. A big male carries another, smaller *wyome.*"

"Where will we hide Nydea?" Reilly asked.

Nydea, Locatha, and Granos had turned to watch. Bandages covered larger wounds. BioGlue glistened where it held lacerations together. Granos growled. Locatha said something.

"Sheeda!" Nydea cried and pushed to her feet. "Sheeda!"

Reilly squinted. He thought he caught movement in the dangling body. If that was Sheeda, were the other *wyomes* using her as a shield?

Captain Baca, Ensign Rabin, Ensign Morten, and Lieutenant Schuler came barreling out of the mess hall.

"All you kids in the bunker," the captain shouted.

Bunker? Reilly thought.

"Keid!" called the lieutenant. "Come down."

Keid jumped the last four rungs of the ladder and raced after Nova and Tally, who were already climbing into the vegetable cellar.

Reilly could now distinguish the five approaching *wyomes.*

"Reilly, Maia, Tab!" Ensign Rabin said. "Take cover."

"I'm going with you to the pillbox," Tab said.

The captain, Ensign Morten, and Lieutenant Schuler had already disappeared inside the structure. The muzzles of two LR-50 rifles appeared in the slits in the walls.

"Me too," said Maia.

"Someone bring me a gun," Reilly said. "I'm not leaving Nydea."

At that moment, Granos reared onto his hind legs as though to take flight.

The shield! Reilly thought. *Granos would be electrocuted.* He sprinted toward the guard tower. Found the switch for the electric fence, which he didn't touch. Below it was another button, presumably for the invisible shield overhead. He depressed it just as Granos cleared the height of the fence, Locatha trailing after. His heart thrumming in his neck, he reactivated the shield watched them close the distance to Sheeda and the other *wyomes*.

Clucking, chirping, and bleating sounds turned his head. Nydea had crept to the barn and was crouched against the outside wall. He opened the barn door and motioned her inside, but she refused.

"I know it smells bad in there, but at least you'll be hidden," he said.

"Diss," she said, her expression stubborn.

"No? What? You want the enemy to see you?"

"Reilly," Captain Baca bellowed. "Take cover."

Reilly frantically scanned the area. The only other structure big enough to accommodate Nydea was the mess hall.

"Let's go," he said. "You can be with Lani."

Nydea hesitated, then followed him. Reilly stopped outside the mess hall door, looked from the door to Nydea. Her wings stuck out at odd angles. If only she could fold them to her back, she could duck through the entrance.

"Fuck," Reilly said. He'd seen the word in literature and had occasionally heard adults—mainly Ensign Morten—utter it. "Fuck, fuck, fuck."

"Reilly!" Commander Shen called. "Get in here and stop swearing. Your parents would—I could use your help."

He lifted the flap. "Nydea won't fit through the door."

The commander finished injecting a small bag of SynPlasma into Kailani's arm. "That's a bad thing?"

"I can't leave her alone and unprotected."

"Then take that gun and post yourself by the window." She nodded her head at the *yridium* handgun lying on a nearby table.

The door pushed open. The commander snatched her gun from a back pocket. Nydea's head poked inside, nostrils flaring, no doubt detecting the burnt flesh smell left by the cautery pen, as well as scents beyond human detection. Kailani lay on a green surgical drape atop the table. A foil thermal blanket covered her. Her chest rose and fell. Her color looked healthier.

"Kailani," Nydea said. "Lani okay."

Reilly couldn't tell whether Nydea was posing a question or stating fact.

"Yes," the commander said, removing a pair of surgical gloves. "Lani is much better."

"Okay. Good," Nydea said, drawing out the double O sound. Then she backed out the door.

The commander sighed and peeled off a piece of cloth wound about her head. Damp, dark hair spilled about her face. "How much stranger will this life get?"

Reilly grabbed a gun and crossed to the window. Nydea sat on her haunches, watching the sky. The five *wyomes* were nearly within firing range of the LR-50s. Granos and Locatha faced them. The assemblage formed a circle and hovered, as though having an aerial conversation. No fighting ensued. After a moment, Granos, Sheeda, and her four escorts descended to the ground. Locatha winged toward the base.

Reilly spoke into the com. "It's Locatha. Don't shoot. I'm going to deactivate the shield."

Ensign Morten radioed back. "Could be a trap."

"No," Reilly said. "I can tell by Nydea's reaction."

"Right," Ensign Morten said. "Now that you're the great catbat whisperer."

Nydea hobbled toward Locatha, who landed just outside the fence. Reilly ran after. Behind him, Commander Shen ordered him not to go.

"Don't touch the fence," Reilly said. To underscore the point, he pictured himself touching the fence and jumping backward in pain.

Nydea looked at him, alarmed. "Why would you build something that hurts?"

Though she spoke in Mirnan, he understood. "To keep out enemies," Reilly said.

"I will warn the others," Nydea said.

Heads bowed, Locatha and Nydea exchanged greetings. Locatha, if Reilly could judge *wyome* expressions, looked happy. Her eyes and vocal tone had brightened. She smelled pleasantly spicy. Sheeda's name was repeated. Reilly closed his eyes, saw warm colors—tangerine, butter, honey.

Nydea faced him and spoke. He heard words he knew: Sheeda, Granos, friends. Images of *wyomes* filled his mind, their gestures benevolent. The strangers were not enemies.

Locatha turned, pushed off the ground, and winged toward the waiting *wyomes*.

Reilly opened the gate.

Captain Baca strode out of the pillbox. "Might I trouble you for an explanation?"

Reilly smiled. "Get ready to welcome Nydea's Aunt Sheeda and our new allies. It seems we have sparked a rebellion."

PART III

MIGRATION

THIRTY-TWO

Nova and Tab Lay two dead *boolas* at the feet of Nydea and Sheeda. Reilly translated as Sheeda thanked the bearers by name. Nydea sniffed appreciatively at the birds.

"Stand back," Reilly said to Tab and Nova.

"Why?" Tab demanded just as Sheeda clicked her teeth and blew flame over the birds.

Nova shrieked and hopped backward. Tab grinned and said, "Minjin' astral."

They watched the two *wyomes* devour the meat. Sheeda's wounds had been cleaned, closed with BioGlue, smeared with surgical ointment, and covered with gauze. Nydea wore so many bandages that little skin remained visible. Lieutenant Schuler had given her an Anaral patch, which seemed to diminish her discomfort but had the paradoxical effect of making her agitated rather than calm. When Nydea started pacing around and breaking open her wounds, Locatha left the base and returned with the leaves of a small, gray-blue succulent plant that, at least in *wyomes,* had a sedating effect. The plant-drug combination worked well. Now, with a sort of drowsy euphoria, Nydea was devouring the first meal she had had in days.

Behind them, Tally was making protesting noises. Reilly turned to see her tagging after Ensign Morten and Lieutenant Schuler, who carried *yridium* guns in their belts.

"The dogs weren't vegetarians either," Ensign Morten said as he strode past. He and Lieutenant Schuler left through the gate and called to Tally to shut it behind them.

"Where are they going?" Reilly asked Tally, who paused to stare with dismay at the charred, half-eaten *boolas.*

"To hunt those cute pink creatures," she said.

"The *wyomes* call them *shekraks*," Reilly said.

Tally sighed and pushed her honey-colored bangs out of eyes. "I don't think we should kill them."

"That's how the food chain works," Tab said. "Apparently the catbats are at the top of that cycle on this planet."

That evening, Nova and Ensign Rabin prepared a dinner of green beans and dark leafy vegetables, topped with raw, sliced radishes and thyme leaves. It was their first meal created entirely from fresh garden plants. The vegetables from the ship's greenhouse had been bigger and juicier, but, as the captain pointed out, they lacked the flavor of plants that grew in dirt, fresh water, and sunlight.

Lieutenant Schuler shoveled dried goat dung into the outdoor fire pit and lit it with a sparker. Captain Baca, Reilly, and Maia transferred Kailani from the mess hall table onto the futon and bore her outside. The Anaral had worn off enough that she was alert, but not in pain. Her back propped on pillows, she thanked Captain Baca, Commander Shen, and Maia for "the great repair job." The captain introduced her to the other adult and kids. She repeated each new name as it was given. Afterward, Nova served her a mug of tea and a bowl of soup.

Under the blue glow of telsar lanterns, humans and *wyomes* feasted in the yard. Ensign Morten grumbled about the *wyomes* getting all the meat. Tally pointed out that the hens would soon lay eggs, which would provide plenty of protein. Keid and Nova joined Tally in a vow never to eat *shekraks*. Tally began talking about how the some of the juveniles had been eating grain out of her hands.

"Need I remind you why feeding those creatures is a bad idea?" Captain Baca said. "Now that the millet is ripening, it's almost impossible to keep them out of the garden. Fences are useless. They just burrow underneath."

"Drop poison bait in the burrows," Ensign Morten said. "Better yet, the little buggers would make good target practice for the kids."

Tab cheered. Nova swatted at him and called him an insensitive pixelhead. He caught her wrist in his hand and held it for a long moment, finally letting go when Nova outstared him. Reilly marveled that no adult told Tab and Nova to stop flirting and that neither Tab nor Nova blushed or otherwise looked uncomfortable.

"Lani," Commander Shen said, "I have so many questions. I know you've been through an ordeal. But could you please tell us what happened to the rest of your group?"

Kailani set down her mug and explained, as she had to Reilly and Maia, about the "gift" of *thystam* rocks from Hyssel, about the mistaken belief that these rocks provided an energy source not unlike Earth's coal, about the toxic fumes that killed everyone but her. She paused and said, "The same thing happened to Reilly's parents."

People began talking at once. Reilly wanted to run weeping into the night. He wrapped his arms around himself, as though to keep himself from flying apart, and tried not to listen. Maia moved to sit beside him. She didn't say anything, didn't touch him. Something inside him unwound enough that he could breathe.

Captain Baca held up his hand. "A thorough debriefing can happen later. Kailani, do you have enough energy to translate for the *wyomes?* We need to understand the current situation, need to assess our threat of repeat attacks."

Kailani nodded and addressed the *wyomes,* who sat on the other side of the fire, facing the humans.

Locatha made introductions. The newcomers were Pashtak, a male older and more scarred than Granos, Pashtak's son Abath, Zedena, a female with white patches on her nose, and Jannatz, a young female friend of Nydea.

Zedena and Pashtak had close ties to Sheeda and Nydea. Zedena had cared for Sheeda after her three miscarriages. Pashtak was a boyhood friend of Nydea's father Ocasso. He had long been suspicious about the deaths of Ocasso and Nydea's mother Pacha, but feared challenging Hyssel.

When Hyssel had ordered them to capture or kill Sheeda before she escaped Ledera Canyon, Pashtak and Zedena publicly assented. Privately, they formed a counterplan. To avoid immediate suspicion, they chased Sheeda to the canyon floor. Rather than harm her, they ushered her into a side canyon.

Sheeda spoke and Kailani translated. "I told them what Hyssel had done. And they could see my injuries. I told them it wasn't the first time, but it was the worst. If Nydea didn't escape, he would kill her. Now that she had reached adulthood, she posed too great a risk to his rule."

Nydea raised her head. A thermal blanket covered the rest of her body.

Pashtak added in a rumbling voice, "I believed Sheeda. Right after the humans arrived, I intercepted Pashtak, who had long distrusted Hyssel. He spread the word to allow Nydea and Granos to leave the canyon unharmed."

"Too bad you couldn't do the same for me," Locatha muttered as she licked a swollen hind foot.

"I hid Sheeda in an abandoned cave," Zedena said. "Later, Pashtak and I planned our escape. We took Abath and Jannatz with us—Abath because it was dangerous to leave him behind, Jannatz because she insisted."

Jannatz sat beside Nydea and made a throaty noise much like purring. Nydea parted her lips in what might have been a smile. Using his teeth, Abdath cracked open a *boola* bone and began sucking out the marrow.

Pashtak took up the story. "A dozen *wyomes* ensured our safe escape. If Hyssel learns of their betrayal, they must flee or face death."

"What will happen now?" Kailani asked.

Pashtak hunched his shoulders. "War."

"Phenom," Tab said.

Ensign Morten stopped picking his teeth with the quill of a *boola* feather. "I hate to be a sourpuss, but we're vastly outnumbered."

A few minutes passed in silence.

"Thanks for interpreting, Lani," Captain Baca said.

Reilly realized he had stopped listening to the translation. There was no need. The more Reilly relaxed into listening, the more he understood. In fact, hearing Kailani repeat the conversation had begun to annoy him.

Kailani dropped her head onto the pillows. "Hyssel will retaliate." Her voice was husky with exhaustion. "He won't allow factions that undermine his power."

"If he's smart, he won't attack tonight," Commander Shen said. "He'll rest his fighters and strategize. We will do the same."

"Where will we all sleep?" Tally asked. "I can help watch over the *wyomes.*"

Lieutenant Schuler smiled. "You will sleep in the dorm, as usual."

Tab stood. "I had an idea to create a tent with BioFuerte and cables for the cat—for the *wyomes.*"

"I'll help you," Ensign Morten said. "That okay with you, Captain?"

"As good a plan as any." Captain Baca removed his hat and ran his right hand over his balding head. "Everyone else to bed."

Reilly stood awkwardly on legs that had gone numb from sitting cross-legged. As people drifted away, he felt paralyzed with the reminder that his parents were gone, with the reality that the three of them would never again sleep together in the barracks, that he would never again fall asleep to his parents murmuring in the darkness, never again feel their goodnight kisses on his cheek.

"Reilly."

He looked up, wiped his face.

Maia was watching him. "Come bunk with us."

Reilly looked at Nydea. Her eyes were closed. The thermal blanket covering her reflected the moonlight. Jannatz curled next to her rump; Sheeda lay behind her.

"Nydea will be fine," Maia said.

"Maybe I'd rather sleep with Nydea and the other *wyomes,*" Reilly said.

"Suit yourself," Maia said, turning away.

"Wait," Reilly said. "I didn't mean—" He didn't know how to explain. Was it that Nydea was also an orphan? That she was also injured and bereft? Maia would just retort that she'd never had parents, like that made him comparatively fortunate. The night swallowed her retreating form.

Nydea was watching him. He stepped among the other *wyomes,* knelt before her, and stroked her head. She sighed and lowered her head to her paws. As he adjusted her blanket, he heard the thumping of beams self-inflating. He trudged to the place where Tab, Nova, Tally, and Lieutenant Schuler were tugging a huge section of BioFuerte into position. Each staked down a corner.

Since they didn't appear to need help, Reilly kept walking. He paused in front of his barracks. The cat weathervane cut a pattern against the star-sequined sky. The windows were dark. Inside the kids' dorm, the blue light of a telsar torch flickered. He moved toward it, hesitated at the threshold, pushed open the door.

Maia lay on her bunk, her back to him. She didn't turn as he entered.

Keid sat up, his neck bent to avoid hitting his head on the beam above. "I have your spot ready," he said, pointing to the bunk below his.

"Thanks," Reilly whispered.

On his pillow was a white night-blooming flower. He slid into the sleeping sac, inhaled the sweet scent, and tried not to think of his mother leaning down to kiss him goodnight.

∞

When Reilly awoke the next morning, the dorm was empty and the sun had already risen two palms above the horizon. He hurried to the *wyomes'* tent and peered inside. All seven *wyomes* lay in a circle. In the center was a dead *erzala,* the bones picked clean except for the head and lower legs. Green insects swarmed over the carcass. The air was hot and smelled of meat and the minty aroma of burn cream. Granos and Locatha blinked at him sleepily. Nydea's eyes remained closed; her sides moved in and out. The other *wyomes* also appeared to be sleeping. Reilly slipped away and replenished the water trough, which someone had moved closer to the tent.

Inside the mess hall, Tab and Ensign Morten were cleaning up from breakfast. Tab thrust a cold bowl of porridge into his hands. "You'll have to wash it yourself," he said. "I'm done here."

Only Commander Shen, who looked tired, was still eating. After Reilly sat beside her, she said Kailani had slept in her barracks.

"How is she?" Reilly asked.

"Better." The commander stuck a loose piece of black hair into her ponytail. "Her vital signs were stable all night. No sign of fever. And her red blood cell count is creeping back up. How are your patients?"

"Nydea and Sheeda? They're sleeping now. At least one of the *wyomes* went hunting last night."

"I wonder how he or she asked Erik to turn off the shield."

"Sign language maybe." Reilly also thought it quite possible that the *wyomes* had already figured out how to turn the shield off and on.

"The lieutenant is good at understanding animals."

Animals, Reilly thought. We're all animals, just different species.

∞

Kailani sat in a chair in Lian Shen's barracks, a vital signs monitor encircling her right wrist. She wore a clean blue regulation shirt and pants rolled up at the ankles. Maia stood behind her, brushing her hair. Both women looked up as Reilly entered.

"How do you feel?" he asked.

"Bored of lying around. Tired of being inside. Grateful to be alive. Thank you for coming back for me."

Reilly shrugged. "It must be weird to have so many people around—after so much time alone."

"Yes, but it's good. I've spent too long alone."

"How do you want your hair?" Maia asked.

"What do you suggest?" Kailani said.

"I only know braids and ponytails. If you want more, ask Nova."

"A braid is perfect. Just one. Afterward, I'm going to do something about your hair."

Maia patted her head. Tendrils of brown hair corkscrewed around her face. What had once been a half dozen braids had become so matted they reminded Reilly of the hairballs Cosmic had occasionally hacked up.

The door flapped open and Captain Baca leaned inside. "Am I disturbing you?" he said to Kailani.

"I've been disturbed for years," she replied coolly.

Reilly couldn't tell if she was serious, but thought he detected a slight upward curve of her lips.

Maia jumped into the conversational void. "We were talking about dropping titles and going by first names. Except us kids need last names. Kailani gave me one."

"Oh?" the captain said.

Maia drew back her shoulders. "I'm now Maia Halatha. Halatha means bold-hearted in Mirnan."

"Good choice," the captain said. "We'll need surnames once the next generation begins."

Reilly's thoughts snagged on the notion of a second generation. That meant kids, which meant parents, which meant sex.

"So," Maia said, "you can either call me Ms. Halatha, or I get to call you Carlos."

The captain smiled. "Call me Carlos then."

Maia smiled. "Carlos."

Reilly gaped at the suddenness of this shift.

Carlos removed his hat and stood awkwardly.

Kailani let out a breath and said, "I hear I should thank you. I didn't realize you moonlighted as a surgeon."

"Captain Baca—Carlos—was married to the ship's physician," Maia said.

Reilly flinched.

Kailani twisted the tarnished silver ring around her finger. "Yes. We got the happy news mid-flight."

"I thought your radio had failed," Carlos said.

"The transmitter did. But, for a time, we could still receive."

"Did you hear any of my transmissions to you?"

Kailani nodded.

"Anyway," Reilly blurted. "Dr. Mbaake died. During the virus epidemic."

Kailani pressed together her lips together then said, "I'm sorry."

Emotion played under the tight muscles of Carlos' face. He touched the green stone that hung around his neck. After a moment he said, "You realize you put Maia and Reilly at risk when you took them to that canyon. You should have brought them to the base."

"There wasn't time," Reilly said. "And I refused to go back till I—till I knew what happened to my parents."

"Then we found out they were dead," Maia said. "By then, Nydea was in trouble—"

Reilly's lips started to tremble. Hand pressed to his mouth, he bolted from the room. He stopped half blinded by the sunlight, and wondered where he could go for solace. Nydea. He would find Nydea.

Behind him, the door to Lian's barracks slapped shut.

"Reilly," Maia said.

Reilly kept walking.

"Reilly! Don't you dare walk away from me."

He turned. He must look ugly, his eyes red, his face balled up. "When will it stop?" he demanded.

"What?" She hurried to catch up.

"The pain," he sobbed. "I miss them so much."

She put her arm around his waist and led him into the shade cast by the outdoor shower. He slid down the rough wall. The sand was damp and relatively cool.

He pulled up his knees and rested his head on their knobby surface.

Maia rubbed his back. "I don't think it's supposed to stop for a while. Not if you loved the person—the people. I'm sad about Nash every day."

"Yeah, but you don't cry all the time." His knees smelled like dirt.

"I cried at first. Tab still cries."

Reilly looked up. "Tab?"

"At night, when he thinks no one can hear him."

"I thought he didn't feel—"

"He has a very high threshold for fear. But he has other emotions. It wouldn't make sense to genetically engineer away love. Love is what drives us to protect each other."

He returned his head to the tops of his knees.

Maia stroked the back of his neck, which was something his mother did when he was sad. "Go ahead and cry. Your father told me crying was normal."

"He did?"

"Sure," Maia said. "Your parents were nice to us kids. When I was little, if I got hurt, your mother or father would pick me up. Your father would sing.

Your mother might tell a story. If I was upset or sick, she rubbed my back. I—I miss them too."

Something splashed against his jaw. Reilly sat up straight. Maia was wiping her eyes.

"I'm glad," he said and hugged her awkwardly.

They moved apart and sat in silence for several minutes. Two types of plants had taken advantage of the moisture around the shower. One had a fleshy octagonal stalk with tiny pink flowers clustered on top. Reilly had learned that the fine hairs projecting from the stalk stung. The other had a slender yellow stalk with teal-colored leaves that smelled minty.

"What do you think is going on between Carlos and Lani?" Maia asked.

"Well, they must have been more than friends."

"Why weren't they put on the same ship?"

"I wonder that too."

"And why did Carlos marry Dr. Mbaake? What was her first name? I'm not sure I ever knew."

"Me neither." Reilly cast a sideways glance at Maia. "I can't believe you didn't insist she either tell you her first name or call you Ms. Maia."

Maia flicked his arm with her index finger. "Anyway, back to your earlier question. Fifteen years is a long wait."

"Seventeen years. The *Romulus* left two years before the *Remus*. After we lost radio com with the *Romulus,* Carlos might have thought she was dead."

The door to the shower scraped open. They sat on the opposite side, out of sight.

The small reservoir above the shower began to gurgle as water sluiced down the pipe to the showerhead. The back of Reilly's shorts grew wet as the sand sopped up the water.

A man's voice broke into song. "I'm a goin' fishin'. Yeah, I'm goin' fishin'. And my baby's goin' fishin' too."

Maia snickered. "It's Harlan."

Reilly became aware of the spot where Maia's hip contacted his own. His attention lost track of the sound of running water, the smell of soap, the singing, the drone of insects, the heat shimmering outside the dwindling shadow cast by the shower. Instead his focus rested on that contact point, the thin bit of clothing separating his hip from hers. He wondered if he could receive her thoughts and immediately closed his mind to that possibility. Not now. If his penis grew any bigger, she wouldn't need any special powers to know what was on his mind.

"Reilly," Maia said.

It took him a moment to realize she spoke aloud. "What?"

"Harlan's gone."

"Oh." Sunlight had replaced shadow, heating his legs.

"I think I'm overdue for a shower. Afterward, I'll try to pull a brush through my hair."

"Let me know if you need help. I mean, with—"

Maia stood. "Reilly, I didn't realize you're such a flirt."

A blush warmed his neck as he watched her round the corner. He had to move. Either that, or he'd sit there imagining her naked in the shower.

∞

Late that afternoon, after Nydea had awakened, Reilly led her to a shady spot near the mess hall. Erik was there, holding a tray on which lay scalpel and forceps. Reilly faced Nydea and tried to explain what would happen and why. Though he was beginning to understand Mirnan, he only knew how to say a handful of words. So he conjured images of her wings looking normal again, images of her flying.

"Understand?" he said.

"Oh kayee," Nydea said.

Erik blinked. "What? Did she just say *okay?*"

Reilly smiled. "Yes."

Erik's blue eyes were calm and his hands steady as he stroked the space between Nydea's ears. "Well then, Nydea. I only need a tiny piece of your wing. The snipping only takes a second. It shouldn't hurt much. But I need you to hold very still."

Her breathing quickened and her ears flattened, but she held still as Erik quickly nipped off a piece of wing and dropped it into a tray layered with fluid. "All done," he said.

Nydea bent to look, her spice-scented breath rippling the liquid.

"What's in there?" Reilly asked.

"Nutrients, epidermal growth factor, and some other proteins isolated from goat's milk. Within twenty-four hours, we'll have a sizeable sheet of cells. Then we cut strips to match the size of the holes in Nydea's wings, lay them down, and BioGlue them in place." Erik looked into Nydea's eyes. "You'll have to rest your wings afterward, give the grafts time to heal."

Nydea looked from Erik to Reilly.

"Soon, your wings will be healed." He visualized Nydea circling in an air current, her wings whole. *"Ganeth vinden."*

Nydea stretched out her neck and licked his ear. He stroked her neck and felt the wetness slowly evaporate.

"What did you say?" Erik asked.

"Pleasant breezes, which is short for pleasant breezes beneath your wings. It's *wyome* greeting. I hoped Nydea would know what I meant."

"Ganeth vinden," Nydea said.

Beaming like he'd just won a prize, Erik repeated the words.

A sudden pinging made the three of them flinch.

Erik pointed. "Target practice."

Harlan stood near the back fence and aimed a remote control. A silver disk arced upward from a grey box.

"Go!" Harlan shouted.

Tab aimed a gun and a red laser beam shot out and connected with the disk. The other kids lined up behind him.

"Next," Harlan barked.

Keid stepped forward. Reilly cringed at the thought of him missing and Harlan yelling at him. Another target disk launched. Before it was even two meters off the ground, Keid hit it, causing the disk to skitter sideways.

"The artist's eye," Erik said. "I wonder how long we have to prepare?"

Nydea turned her head and gazed toward Ledera Canyon. Shadows stretched from the base of the mesa. Nothing moved in the dusky sky. Nevertheless, Reilly felt Nydea's anxiety as something cold and damp in his gut.

∞

In the middle of that night, a small pack of *garthans* and three *witnaws* attacked. A single *wyome* gave orders from above. As Reilly ran to the pillbox, he recognized the sharp voice of Comox.

The *witnaws* lined up, lowered their big heads, charged forward, and rammed the fence. Buzzing with electricity, the fence buckled slightly then rebounded. One *witnaw* shoved its face into the sand to cool the burns. The other two seemed unfazed by the charge in the fence.

Comox called out, what seemed to Reilly, a string of insults. The *witnaws* lined up to charge again.

"Nova, Maia, Erik," Carlos said. "Get ready. Fire."

Maia and Erik hit the beasts squarely in the chests. Nova's beam caught the third *witnaw's* shoulder. It was enough to send the animal bellowing away.

Keid, who was stationed on the south side of the pillbox, cried out. "Big dogs coming this way."

Reilly moved to a slit in the BioFuerte and squinted. Six *garthans* slunk into view; saucer ears cupped forward, heads oscillating side to side. Two jumped onto the fence, began to scale it, then yelped and fell backwards. Three dug furiously at the base of the fence, as though to tunnel beneath it. One hung back and seemed to shout orders.

Keid fired and hit two *garthans* in quick succession.

Harlan slipped into position and killed the leader. Reilly managed a shot to a retreating *garthan's* hindquarters. Keid took down the sixth.

Granos rose into the air and chased after Comox, who fled. Then it was over.

"That's it?" Keid asked. His eyes had a feverish look.

"For now," Harlan said. "They're just hassling us. Something bigger will come."

∞

The next afternoon, Erik applied the skin grafts to Nydea's wings. Tally and Lian assisted. Reilly was there to reassure Nydea and explain, as best he could, what was happening. After Tally and Erik moved the animals into the corral, Reilly led Nydea into the barn to an area covered by a clean tarp. That morning, Reilly and Tally had spent the morning mucking out the barn and sprinkling disinfectant on the packed ground. But even with the windows open, the sun made the inside like an oven—an oven wherein old turds baked.

While Reilly visualized the procedure to Nydea, Lian gave her a handful of the sedating plant and dose of Anaral, and waited for her eyelids to droop. Reilly talked to Nydea and stroked her face.

At Erik's prompting, Reilly asked her to unfold her wing as far as she could. The day before, Tally had created wing-shaped splints to keep Nydea's wings outstretched. As she and Lian strapped the splints in place, Nydea jolted fully alert. Her diamond pupils devoured her irises and she reared onto her back legs, knocking Tally to the ground and nearly tipping over the tray containing the strips of graft material.

"Easy, Nydea," Reilly said. "It's okay. They need to hold your wings still to repair them. No one will hurt you. Not ever again. Not as long as I'm around."

Nydea lowered her front legs and stood panting.

"Okay?" he said.

Nydea nodded.

"You can sleep now. I'll sing to you."

"Ookay," she said sleepily.

Reilly sang nursery rhymes until the transparent membrane closed over Nydea's eyes and then the long-lashed outer eyelids.

"Why does she have two sets of eyelids?" Tally whispered behind her surgical mask.

Erik slipped on his surgical gloves. "The inner translucent one is called a nictitating membrane. On earth, birds and reptiles have them to protect the eye from dust."

Using forceps and tiny scissors, Erik nipped away dead wing tissue, sized the grafts to fit the holes, and lay down the grafts, which looked like Nydea's wings except that pink tinged the usual silver coloring. Tally followed with a tube of BioGlue, applying thin lines of the gel to the edges of the graft. Sweat beading her brow, Lian injected a syringe of epidermal and capillary growth factors.

Erik, Tally, and Lian removed their surgical attire. Nydea slept on. Tally ran her fingers down Nydea's back.

"I hope the grafts take," she said.

Erik mopped his face on his disposable gown. "They will."

Reilly wondered how Erik could be so confident, this being the first time anyone had performed plastic surgery on a *wyome*. "I'll stay with Nydea till she wakes," he said.

"You can untie the splints in an hour," Erik said. "Just don't let her try to fly."

Reilly didn't bother Erik with the fact that no timepieces worked since the last solar flares. The sun glared in through the window. He noted the position and waited until it descended a good hand's width. By then, the grafts had already conformed almost seamlessly to fill out the wounds. He untied the splints and slid them out from under Nydea's wings. She looked at him blearily.

"No flying," he said. He lay beside her on the tarp. Nydea made a contented throaty noise. They slept until Maia woke them for dinner.

∞

In the middle of the night, the alarm sounded as Reilly dreamt that he lay in his bunk on the ship, still weak from the Dagnar virus. Cosmic curled against the small of his back. His father sat in a chair, reading to him. His mother entered and laid a cool hand on his brow.

The second alarm dispersed the dream. The dorm was already empty. Reilly pulled on his pants and stumbled outside just as Granos, Locatha, Pashtak, and Zedena took flight. A *wyome* dropped from the sky and exhaled fire at the guard tower, the one structure built of wood. Someone jumped screaming from the tower, clothes aflame. A second *wyome* scorched Reilly's old barracks and the roof of the barn. The flame-resistant exterior smoked but didn't catch fire. Frantic bleating and squawking followed.

Reilly raced toward the person rolling on the ground. Erik was ahead of him. He whipped off his jacket and began smothering the flames. Reilly did the same.

Oren Rabin lay on the ground, his head and face blackened. He coughed. "It doesn't hurt too much," he said.

"That's a bad sign."

Reilly turned to see Kailani, her expression fierce, her limping gait the only outward sign of her injuries.

"I'll take care of him," she said. "Fight the bastards."

Erik streaked toward the barn.

Laser beams stitched the sky. One *wyome* fell heavily into the garden. The second intruder began to ascend, wings sizzling upon contact with the now-restored electric field. As it hovered, a red beam struck its chest and the body tumbled to the ground three meters from Reilly.

He bolted for the pillbox, from which red rays of *yridium* laser angled low at the pack of *garthans* melting in and out of darkness at the edge of the fence.

As he entered, Harlan tossed him a gun and turned to shoot out the rifle slot. "The hell took you so long?"

"Oren's hurt," he said.

"Badly?" Lian asked.

"Yes," Reilly said. "*Wyome* fire. Kailani's with him."

"Where are they?" Carlos asked.

"Near the guard tower."

"Out in the open? Damn it," Carlos said. "Let's finish this. Reilly, take a position and don't shoot upward. Can't tell friend from foe. Focus on the canines."

Every couple of seconds, two or three *garthans* would dart forward and start digging at the fence. Beyond Reilly's sight, other *garthans* yipped and shouted. Whereas the *wyomes* spoke in long, fluid sentences, *garthan* speech was clipped. He heard a *witnaw's* bellow.

"I can't see around the barn," Harlan said. "Fuckers could be tunneling on that side of the fence."

"Go," Carlos said.

"I'm taking Tab with me."

Tab turned from his position at a rifle slot. Carlos nodded.

Nova whispered, "Be careful."

Tab gave an upward jerk of his head and followed Harlan outside.

Reilly and the others picked off one *garthan* after another. A *witnaw* charged out of the darkness and smacked the fence, sending out sparks.

Reilly took aim. "I got it."

As the *witnaw's* legs folded, Reilly felt a momentary triumph. Then Maia said, "Like hitting the side of the barn, right?"

Soon a half dozen bodies lay motionless on the other side of the fence.

"I think that's all of them," Carlos said.

"Those big animals really stink," Keid said.

"Yeah. It's worse than the latrine," Nova said. She peered out. "Where are Tab and Harlan?"

Reilly craned to see the sky through his slot and made out the occasional plume of *wyome* fire. "They're still fighting up there."

"I'm going out," Carlos said. "The rest of you stay here."

After they left, Reilly moved from porthole to porthole, but it was difficult to get a sense of the aerial battle.

As he went to the door, Maia said, "What do you think you're doing?"

"I need a better view."

"Reilly!" Lian said. "I order you to—"

Outside, Reilly scanned the sky, counted six *wyomes* darting back and forth. Even with night goggles, he couldn't recognize anyone. He dashed to the *wyome* shelter and found it empty.

"Nydea!" he called. He feared that she had tried to fly, tearing apart the grafts in the process. He tore around the yard, tripped over something, and paused to see that the thing was the cat weathervane, which the enemy *wyome* must have knocked off the roof. Nydea's sibilant voice sounded in his head, but he couldn't decipher the meaning. He set the weathervane against the side of his old barracks and scanned the area until he saw four *wyomes* silhouetted against the starry night. Nydea, Sheeda, Jannatz, and Abdath sat by the water trough, watching the sky.

Nydea bobbed her head in greeting. Reilly squatted close enough to feel her warmth. Sheeda, crouched on the other side of Nydea, glanced at him.

"Can you see what's going on? Granos? Locatha?"

"All okay," Nydea said. "Granos, Locatha okay. Zedena, Pashtak okay."

The cacophonous chorus of distressed goats, turkeys, and chickens swelled.

Jannatz stretched, her front legs extended, her hind end lifted. Abdath paced, his young body elastic, his wings partially extending and flexing in a gesture akin to a man cracking his knuckles. He spoke urgently. Sheeda uttered what sounded like a rebuke.

Reilly understood that Pashtak wanted to join the fight, but that Sheeda denied him. He was too young. Furthermore, he was needed within the compound.

"Pashtak, you can't leave." Reilly pointed overhead. "The shield is on. It would hurt you."

Nydea said something to Pashtak about a barrier that burned. Pashtak frowned at the fence and the space above it. Jannatz rubbed her head against his shoulder; Pashtak exhaled impatiently through his nose.

Nydea spoke to Reilly, "It will soon be over. Only three enemies remain." Though she spoke Mirnan, Reilly's brain quickly translated.

Two *wyomes* grappled four meters overhead. One yowled and veered westward. It stopped abruptly. Reilly strained to see, realized that the *wyome* must have collided with the cable tethering the high-altitude wind turbine. The creature grabbed the cable with all four paws. One wing beat, the other flailed as though broken. Scaly digits loosing traction, the *wyome* slid down the cable, intersected the electric field, jerked, made futile scrabbling movements, and fell sizzling to the ground a stone's throw from where Reilly watched.

Jannatz moaned. Pashtak exclaimed sharply, like someone cursing.

Nydea said, "That was Stiphel. He was not much older than me. Too young to die."

Four *wyomes* hovered overhead. Granos' deep voice called down, "It is over. Ready to descend."

Sheeda nudged Reilly. "Make the hot energy stop. Let them return."

Reilly ran to the guard tower. The lookout platform had burned and collapsed onto the base. Reilly found the button that turned the electric field off and on. He deactivated it, and shouted to the *wyomes,* circling his arm in a downward motion.

They descended.

Locatha landed near him. She moved toward an oblong shape covered with a tarp, sniffed, and stepped back. Reilly squatted and lifted the corner of the tarp. He saw a boot, smelt burnt hair and flesh. His stomach rolled; he dropped the tarp.

Kailani and Carlos materialized out of the shadows.

"Oren is dead," she said. "His airway was burned."

Furious tears stung Reilly's eyes. "You couldn't save him?"

"If we had a critical care unit and a ventilator—"

An anguished noise escaped Reilly's throat. On the ship they had such a unit. They just hadn't been able to shuttle all medical supplies to the surface.

Carlos put a hand on his shoulder. "He wouldn't have wanted to live that way. He had third-degree burns over most of his body."

Nova, Tally, and Keid clustered around. The sound of their weeping gave Reilly license to cry. He wondered if he would ever run out of tears.

THIRTY-THREE

In the gentle glow of dawn, they buried Oren beyond the garden. Reilly and Erik made a grave marker out of a piece of polychiton into which they etched *Oren David Rabin, 2144 to 2189.* Lian and Nova stitched the body into a shroud of BioFuerte. Maia, Tally, and Carlos began digging a grave. Abdath must have understood what they were doing because he walked over and, with a few strong strokes of his front legs excavated a hole 3 meters deep. The other *wyomes* stood nearby, watching.

After they lowered Oren in, Carlos cleared his throat and said, "I grew up in the New Mexican desert. My grandmother had a saying about death. *Dust makes us. We walk in dust. When we die, the wind blows away our footsteps and sails our souls to the stars.* The wind may erase your footsteps, Oren, but not our memories of you."

Each person shared one thing about Oren. Most people had stories that exemplified his kindness. Harlan remarked that he was the best-looking guy in a tonsure since Friar Tuck, which made people laugh and required an explanation to some of the kids about Robin Hood and his followers and about how monks of the time shaved bare the crowns of their heads.

When it came Reilly's turn, he was lost in speculation about what people would say about his parents and when they would hold a memorial. He worried that, with all the fighting, his parents would be largely forgotten.

Carlos said, "Reilly? Anything you want to add before we fill in the grave?"

"Um, yes. Oren was—" He fought down the grief that would rob him of coherent speech. "He could fix anything. He could even fix a meal from practically nothing." People smiled, which bolstered him. "He tried hard to repair the communication and tracking systems after—after the solar flares, after my parents disappeared. I'm sorry I yelled at him when he couldn't." Then the tears won. But he wasn't the only one. The only dry eyes belonged to Harlan.

Carlos dropped a fistful of sand over the body. Then they each took a turn. Carlos turned to Abdath, said his name, and gestured to the hole. The young male turned his back to the hole, and began pushing sand between his back legs with his forepaws. The humans back away to avoid getting flying bits of dirt in their eyes.

Harlan grumbled that *wyomes* killed Oren, that allowing a *wyome* to participate in the burial rite was "unholy." No one replied. Reilly thought of his history lessons about the great wars on Earth, when humans divided by creed, skin color, or nationality killed other humans, when people buried those whom others had killed. But he held his tongue. Erik settled the grave marker into place and tamped down the area with his feet.

∞

Humans and *wyomes* dozed the rest of the day. Harlan took the first watch; Reilly took the second. As the sun sank toward the mesa, Nydea ventured out of the *wyome* shelter to sit with Reilly.

She thought at him, *"When will I fly"*

He thought back, *"Soon. Perhaps a few days."*

"We must leave this place."

"And go where"

"To a canyon. Not far from here is Standea Canyon. It has caves. Witnaws live in the lower caves. We can remove them. Pakitoks roost higher up. These we can kill and eat."

"What are pakitoks?"

Nydea sent him an image of the carrion-eating birds he despised. He remembered the three *pakitoks* hanging about the morning his parents left, recalled the sinister single saucer-shaped eye set above the curved orange beak.

Something tapped his shoulder, causing him to jump to his feet. It was Maia. Her hair was arranged in a single, tidy braid down the back, her teeth white in her brown face.

"What are you two doing?"

"Talking."

Maia frowned. "I didn't hear anything." She cocked her head and stared him in the eye. "You can do the mind thing now? Just like that? Carry on a conversation?"

Reilly shrugged. He hadn't realized he was doing it till she startled him.

"I only get snatches of thought," Maia said. "More like blurry images than actual language."

Reilly smiled. "That's how it started for me, too. It gets easier."

"Maybe so. You know, I really resent it when you do things before me. Someday, I'll surprise you. I'll sprout wings and fly over our head and taunt you with my superior powers."

Reilly suppressed a smile. Maia was so earnest; he didn't want to appear to make light of her honesty. "How long have you felt like this?"

"I've adored and hated you my whole life."

"Oh. I just knew half the equation." He felt himself blush.

"Which half?"

"The dislike. I thought all you, uh, kids—"

"Vitros? Admit it. That's how you thought of us. Like manufactured parts. Something subhuman."

"No. I didn't." What had he said to unleash such scorn? "I only thought you all detested me."

"You didn't do much to make yourself likeable. You kept yourself apart. Only socialized with the other wombers."

"Wombers? That's what you called kids born the old-fashioned way?"

"What else? After your privileged pals died from the Dagnar virus, I thought you'd deign to hang around the rest of us. But, no…you'd rather be alone."

"You all scared me." There, he'd finally stated the truth.

Maia released a short laugh. "Seriously? All of us? Even Keid and Tally?"

"Not them. Not so much."

"So I scared you." She threw her hands in the air. "Anyway, we're having a strategy meeting—"

"But I'm on watch."

"Great job. You didn't even hear me coming." She shook her head when Reilly opened his mouth to speak. "Anyway, we're gathering outside the mess hall, so everyone can keep watch and so the *wyomes* can participate." She began to walk away. "I'll do my best to act in a demure, nonthreatening manner."

"Maia!" he said to her back. When she didn't turn around, he became aware of Nydea's presence. She watched him, the way someone might watch a foreign film, trying to figure out what all the words and actions signified.

"What?" he said. "Did I do something wrong?"

Nydea bobbled her head side to side. *"Diss.* Maia *kairenth* Reilly. Reilly *kairenth* Maia."

"What?" Reilly said in halting Mirnan. "Didn't you hear how she spoke to me?"

Nydea shook her head, as if to say he was just another foolish boy.

It was getting dark and chilly. Reilly frisked his arms with his hands. "Let's go to the meeting," he said. "We'll discuss your ideas there."

When they arrived, a fire already danced in the stone-lined pit. Carlos was praising everyone's bravery, including the *wyomes*. Reilly stole glances at Maia. She sat a quarter of the way around the circle, her face in profile. She did not look his way.

Carlos paused and said, "Oren's death was tragic. We can't afford to lose another life. For that reason, we must sharpen our defenses."

"Our offense could use improvement, too," Harlan said.

Lian stood and Carlos acknowledged her. "Before we talk war strategy, we need more information," she said. "Kailani, what do you understand about the enemy's resources? How many *wyomes* are there? How many species want to destroy us?"

"Three species: the *wyomes, garthans,* and *witnaws.* The local clans, at any rate. As you probably noticed, the *wyomes* are the most intelligent."

Kailani nodded at the *wyomes,* who sat on the other side of the circle—except for Nydea, who curled beside Reilly. "As you know," Kailani continued, "Methna Mesa is huge—93 kilometers long and 64 kilometers wide. Other rocky formations dot the Zakara Desert, which stretches along the 15th latitude, across the entire continent of Adocalendra. Most animal species cluster at the edge of rocky geologic features that provide shade, water, and shelter. At this point, I defer to a *wyome* to explain more about the politics governing the species capable of speech."

"What about the species that can't talk?" Tally asked. "Don't they count?"

"They count, but they don't form complex alliances."

"They are eaten by the smarter, stronger species," Harlan said.

"That's not fair," Tally said.

"It's how it worked on Earth," Harlan said.

"Not exactly," Erik said. "Many cultures had taboos against eating certain species. Case in point being cats and dogs."

"Does that mean some people ate cats and dogs?" Tally asked.

Erik nodded.

Nova and Keid muttered words of disgust.

Carlos clapped his hands for order. "Back to the subject." He turned to the *wyomes.* "Can one of you tell us more about the enemy?"

Kailani translated.

Locatha sat up straighter. Kailani translated as she said, "Four clans live in canyons at the perimeter of Methna Mesa. Except in emergency, the clans gather twice a year—once at the start of Dry Season, once at the start of Wet Season."

"Wet season?" Nova asked. "It rains?"

Maia shushed her and whispered, "We learned that on the ship, remember?"

Locatha continued. "My mother's family is of the Compuwl Clan. Granos' mother came from the Integha Clan."

"Are these clans against us?" Carlos asked.

"I don't think so. Not yet. Hyssel has no doubt sent emissaries."

"We must send our own," Lian said.

Locatha nodded. "We *wyomes* have already discussed this. I will go."

"And I," Sheeda said. "My father was born in Asmina Canyon. I am strong enough to travel."

Locatha looked at Sheeda for a long moment, as exchanging thoughts. "Yes," Locatha said. "We will visit all the other clans. Sheeda can tell her story. Her scars may help convince them."

"Can't you just send thoughts and images to the other clans?" Maia asked.

"What is she talking about?" Nova whispered loudly to Tab.

"Beats me," Tab said, parroting a typical Harlan response.

Reilly noticed how much Tab had come to look like Harlan—the belligerent jaw, the gray-blue eyes, the flushed cheeks, the light brown hair sun-streaked with blonde. Tab even had the beginnings of a beard the same copper-color as Harlan's. The main difference was that Harlan didn't have acne.

Kailani translated Maia's question and Nydea's response. "It is too far," Nydea said. "Also, mind communication happens only when sender and receiver want to be read."

"Fascinating," Erik said.

"I don't get it," Nova said, zipping her jacket to her neck. Tab scooted closer to her. Harlan who sat on the other side of the circle, looked at Tab and Nova sitting hip to hip, then returned his gaze to the *wyomes*.

"What about the other species?" Erik asked. "How do we form alliances with them?"

Granos rumbled, "The *wyomes* rule the *garthans* and *witnaws*. If we assemble a sizable *wyome* army, some of the other species will follow us. The *garthans* may require coaxing. What they lack in loyalty, they make up for with guile. The *witnaws* are stupider than fledgling *wyomes*, and they're easily bribed with food."

"In the meantime, we should move," Reilly said.

Everyone looked at him.

"Why? Where?" Tab asked.

"Nydea says all of us should move to Standea Canyon."

Harlan snorted. "You and the crippled catbat have been talking strategy?"

Reilly felt his jaw tighten. "Actually, yes."

Nydea stirred beside him. She sat straight, which made her a head taller than Erik, the tallest of the humans. She explained her plan as she had to Reilly. Kailani translated.

"Why is this canyon any better than our base?" Carlos asked.

"Caves are easier to defend," Kailani said.

"What if we get boxed in?" Harlan said.

"That's unlikely as long as humans have airscouters and *wyomes* have wings."

"What about the livestock?" Erik asked.

Kailani repeated to question in Mirnan. Abdath muttered something to the effect that it might be better to eat them now—a statement Kailani didn't translate, but Reilly understood. Nydea assured Kailani that they could secure one or two of the lower caves.

Lian said, "But we have to leave behind the garden and the wind turbine. And the barracks. And the energy created by the solar cells in the fabric of the barracks." She sighed. "I wish Oren were here. He'd have ideas about our energy systems."

Carlos suggested there might be a way to hang solar-cell embedded BioFuerte on a south-facing wall of the canyon. *Wyome* fire had damaged some of the cells, but enough usable material remained. The wind turbine would, for now, be left behind.

"As for the garden," he added, "presumably we'll resolve this conflict and either return to the base or move someplace more temperate. We've already talked about relocating to the hills to the north within a year. Crops will grow more easily and the livestock could forage. Meantime, we'll harvest what we can from our garden here."

"And don't forget about the native edible plants," Kailani said.

Maia sat up straighter. "You'll teach us about them?"

"Is that how you grew so plump?" Carlos said as he encircled one of her wrists with his thumb and forefinger. "Eating roots and berries?"

Kailani pulled her arm free, but allowed a small smile to curve her lips.

"I plan to hunt," Harlan said.

"I propose that everyone think over the idea of moving camp," Carlos said. "We'll have a final discussion tomorrow."

∞

That evening, three enemy *wyomes* harried Abnath and Pashtak as they returned to the base with a freshly killed *dilcroth*. On his way to the mess hall, Reilly passed the *wyomes*. They clustered together, eating and talking. Granos sat facing Locatha, their heads so close their foreheads nearly touched. Reilly wondered if they were reevaluating the plan for Sheeda and Locatha to depart that night for the clans on the northern side of Methna Mesa. Their palpable anxiety recalled the dread he felt when his parents left. His parents had faced an uncertain danger. Sheeda and Locatha knew their enemies all too well.

An hour later, Reilly stepped out of the mess hall to see three female *wyomes* lifting into the air. Once they were well clear of the fence, the electric field buzzed back on.

Nydea, Abnath, and Pashtak sat together and watched till the trio vanished into the dusk. Granos paced, his tail arced over his back.

"Zedena went with Sheeda and Locatha," Reilly said. "Why?"

Nydea opened and closed her wings, exposing the healing patchwork of grafted tissue. "Better protection," she said. "Sheeda isn't strong enough to fight. Also Zedena has relatives in the Integha Clan."

They spoke for a few moments longer, Reilly in English, Nydea in Mirnan. They understood one another well enough. But Reilly vowed that, once they were free of imminent attack, he would learn to speak Mirnan fluently. As it was, his understanding far outstripped, his ability to negotiate the diphthongs and to mimic the sibilant, lilting speech.

∞

In the morning, the humans assembled in the mess hall. The consensus was that, in light of the attack on Abdath and Pashtak and the flurry of attacks on the base, they would move.

Within an hour, a scouting party comprised of Pashtak and Abdath with Lian and Harlan in an airscouter flew to Standea Canyon. Reilly heard later that the *wyomes* negotiated with the *witnaws* living in the low caves to move to a more easterly canyon in exchange for four *erzalas*. Two *witnaws* who refused were smoked out. Lian piloted the airscouter in and out of the upper caves while Harlan shot fleeing *pakitoks*. The *wyomes* collected the bodies for later consumption.

The following day, people and *wyomes* began to transport gear to the canyon. The humans ferried possessions by airscouter; the *wyomes* conveyed objects in their paws, flying in formation to transport larger items such as rolls of BioFuerte, air tubes, an air pump, webbing, cables, fencing material, and sheets of polychiton. The colonists would use these supplies to secure the livestock, block the mouth of the canyon, erect solar arrays, and create crude weapons such as catapults. The *wyomes* also carried crated chickens, turkeys, and goats, much to the consternation of the domesticated animals and some of the people, particularly Tally and Erik.

Each person was allowed to bring one duffel. Most people had fewer personal belongings than they had upon arriving on the planet. Clothes had been outgrown and hardware had ceased to function. Keid, however, had created art projects—primarily rock sculptures—that he hated to leave behind. Nova and Tally each stowed one of Keid's smaller creations in their bags.

Reilly didn't have room for anything extra because of his father's flute and grandmother's books, which he wasn't about to leave behind for the enemy to burn. He also packed some of his father's clothes since he was outgrowing his own.

After he finished packing, he approached Keid, who stood outside the kids' dorm, trying to close his duffel. "I have bad news for you," Reilly said, his arms behind his back.

Keid turned, anxiety bunching his brow. "What?"

Reilly held out a small bag. "Something else for you to carry."

Keid took the bag and extracted a tablet of art paper, a tray of watercolor paints, and five brushes. "Oh! Are you letting me borrow these?" He turned shining blue eyes on Reilly.

"They're yours."

"Really?" He beamed, then looked serious. "What do you want from me?"

"Nothing."

"I've never used paints."

"I'm not very good, but I can show you the basics." Reilly nodded at Keid's bulging duffel. "You might have to leave a couple rocks behind. I'm sure there are more where we're going."

Keid laughed. It was a childlike laugh that inspired hope. It made Reilly want to give away everything he owned to the other kids—or at least to share his things. So what if a book became smudged, its pages dog-eared?

At that moment, Maia trudged up, set down her duffle, and pulled out the microscope. "Here," she said, thrusting it at him.

"Why don't you keep it?"

She narrowed her eyes. "It's your mother's."

"Yes. But you're the scientist."

Maia looked at the compact microscope. It was white with black eye pieces. "It's stereoscopic."

Reilly shrugged.

"That means you can see in three dimensions."

"All the more reason you should have it."

"If you ever want to, you know, look at it or anything…"

"I'll know where to find it." He smiled. He could get used to being more generous. "Hey, do you want any of my books?"

Maia looked up from zipping her duffel. "Now? Are they weighing you down? Your bag a bit too heavy?"

"No, I just thought—"

"You're just Mr. Magnanimous today. But, as you know, I have already read them all."

Reilly stood, hands hanging useless at his sides, and watched her go. One minute his actions pleased her; the next, they offended.

Someone came up behind him.

"Women."

Reilly turned to see Tab grinning at him. "As Harlan says, 'Can't live with 'em; can't live without 'em.'"

Reilly managed a faint smile.

"Probably her time of the month. Give her a couple days. At any rate, it's not like she has many choices." Tab stuck out his chest. "I'm handsomer and stronger. But I'm already taken."

Nova, who had caught up with him, elbowed him in the ribs.

"Ow! What did I say?"

She shook her head, which caused her long dark hair to ripple across her back. "If you ever make another comment about a woman's menstrual cycle, I'll—"

"You'll what?" Tab fluttered his eyelashes.

Nova gave Reilly a slow smile. "I'll find another man."

Reilly looked at Tab helplessly. "I wouldn't—"

"You wouldn't dare," Tab said, his tone still friendly.

Reilly waited for them to walk past before heading to the airscouters. As he rounded the corner of his old barracks, he saw the weathervane leaning against one wall. He picked it up, blew off the dust, and ran his fingers over the contours of the black cat. Although he could think of no use for it, he needed a reminder of happier times. So he strapped it to his duffel and hoped no adult objected.

After the last of the supplies had been transported, Carlos, Erik, Lian, and Harlan took Kailani, Nova, Keid, and Tab in the four airscouters. Pashtak, Abdath, and Jannatz consented to fly Reilly, Maia, and Tally. Granos would carry Nydea, who wasn't yet allowed to use her wings.

When the kids assigned to airscouters protested, Carlos interrupted, saying, "Now is not a good time to try something new."

"But, sir," Nova said. "Tally's never ridden a *wyoming* either."

"At least, I know how to pronounce *wyome*," Tally said, her teal eyes calm as she stroked, Jannatz's neck. "And I know all their names. You can't even tell the difference—"

"That will do," Lian said. "Time to check out our new home."

Tab swiveled his head toward Reilly, who stood a short distance away beside Pashtak. Sun goggles hid Tab's eyes, but didn't shield Reilly from the heat of his glare.

As Tab lowered himself into the copilot seat behind Harlan, he said, "I can't believe this! I'm the one who's been dying to ride a catbat. Why does Reilly always get—"

"You're preaching to the choir, pal," Harlan said as the airscouter dome shut.

Carlos helped Kailani into the copilot's seat of the *Kestrel;* the airscouter Reilly's parents had flown.

Reilly sighed, as though to expunge Tab and Harlan's animosity. He faced Pashtak. "May I?"

"Zak," Pashtak said.

Maia began to tell Tally how to climb onto Jannatz's shoulders. But Tally was atop the *wyome's* back in an instant. Jannatz's ears swiveled backward as Tally whispered to her. Then, in one liquid movement, the two took to the air.

Reilly waited for Maia to settle herself on Abdath. Flicking his tail, Abdath exchanged a look with his father. Reilly held onto a roll of skin at Pashtak's neck. His legs felt the *wyome* exhale, crouch, and spring. The beating of wings fanned Reilly's back. Granos lifted up, cradling Nydea between his forelegs. Because her wings could now fold smoothly shut, she flew with her back to Granos's chest.

The airscouters rose last, so that Carlos could remotely reactivate the shield that, with any luck, would deter attacks on the remains of their compound and gardens.

Midway through the twenty-minute trip to Standea Canyon, five *wyomes* peeled off the edge of the mesa and dove toward them. Pashtak growled a command and moved to the top of a triangular formation with Abdath and Jannatz forming the other two corners and Granos and Nydea in the center. The airscouters split, with two craft on either side of the *wyome* allies.

As the enemy approached, Harlan accelerated forward. Reilly saw Tab through the cockpit dome as he aimed and fired a *yridium* beam at the heart of the lead *wyome*. The animal stalled, eyes wide open, then plunged.

Reilly held on tight as Pashtak swerved around another enemy. A jet of fire came toward them. Reilly ducked his head, felt heat along the right side of his body. He glimpsed Pashtak's tail whipping around to slash the edge of the opponent's wing.

A slender *wyome* slipped below Granos and Nydea then corkscrewed up to face them. To avoid collision, Granos reared, inadvertently putting Nydea between him and his attacker. Nydea cried out, *"Diss!"* and a name. She was telling the attacker, No.

The slim, young *wyome* beat her wings tentatively.

As though in warning, Nydea click her teeth but didn't ignite her exhalation. The other *wyome* ducked, streamed beneath them, and appeared to be departing. But Carlos' airscouter was directly behind. Reilly saw Kailani's mouth open as Carlos depressed the trigger. The beam sliced the young *wyome's* neck. A cry tore from Nydea.

A beat later, Maia yelped. A *wyome* flew a meter above her head, clawed hind feet outstretched. Abdath's best option was to roll.

"No, no, no," Reilly said into the wind. He knew from his hellacious ride on Comox how difficult it would be for Maia to hang on.

Abdath stretched out his neck and flapped harder. He banked sharply left and right, but his pursuer stuck close. Maia wrapped her entire body around Abdath. Opening his mouth wide, the enemy *wyome* emitted a tongue of flame then drew his breath inward, nearly pulling the fire to his lips.

Reilly looked up to see Lian's airscouter bearing down and Keid's steady gaze as he shot the *wyome* in the back. Maia glanced backward. Abdath raced on. The attacker flipped in the air.

The two remaining enemies sprinted toward Standea Canyon, the airscouters close behind, the laden *wyome* allies lagging. A minute later, Reilly could see the canyon, a scarf of smoke wafting from its mouth.

The *wyome* foe flew above the canyon, calling shrilly. Two other *wyomes* rose into view above the edge of the cliffs. One carried a box. Reilly strained his eyes, saw movement within the box. It was a crated turkey. The four enemies winged toward Ledera Canyon. No one followed them, the collective goal having shifted from fighting to putting out fires.

Reilly urged Pashtak onward, knowing from Pashtak's labored breathing that he couldn't go much faster. Wind whipped Reilly's hair and stung his eyes.

Upon entering the canyon, Reilly saw smoke billowing from a lower cave and two upper caves along the left-hand cliff. The *Kestrel* slid into one of the upper caves. Carlos climbed out and Kailani handed him a fire extinguisher. Lian piloted her craft into another high cave.

Pashtak descended to the canyon floor. Tally had already hopped off Jannatz's back and was dashing toward whatever burned in the lower cave. The fencing covering the entrance had been bent sideways.

Erik landed his scouter, popped the dome, and jumped down, fire extinguisher in hand. In her haste to deplane, Nova slipped on the wing and landed on her backside in the sand. Reilly helped her up as he ran past.

Inside the cave, Tally was screaming and Erik was spraying fire retardant on a crate containing two hens. The flames died quickly. Reilly hoped the chickens had expired that fast too.

∞

All told, the losses included the two chicken hens, the remaining tom turkey, Nova's duffel, and a box containing computer scrolls and components of the radio tower.

"Now that we have no male turkeys, what will we do with the hens?" Lian asked as people gathered in one of the larger, upper caves. Her dark hair was pulled into an untidy ponytail, and soot smudged her left cheek.

"Eat them," Harlan said. He sounded downright cheerful and had already volunteered to pluck, clean, and cook the two dead chickens.

"Not so fast," Erik said. "Two of them are pregnant."

"I wonder if the other one could mate with any of the native birds?" Kailani said. "Turkeys are about the same size as *boolas.*"

"The birds with the long tails?" Maia asked.

Kailani nodded and pulled her cloak around her.

Erik said, "Getting two closely related species from the same planet to breed is one thing. But two species from different planets?"

"Yah. Their blood isn't even the same color. And who knows what kind of sex organs those *boolas* have." He looked thoughtful. "Turkey toms don't have tiny penises do they?"

"No, silly. They have cloaca." Before Tab could respond, Tally said. "What's the matter with Nova?"

Nova sat against a wall, knees hugged to her chest, her head resting on her forearms. She raised her tear-tracked face. "What about my clothes?"

"They're just clothes," Tally said impatiently. "No big deal compared to our animals."

"They're a big deal to me," Nova said, her voice thick with tears. "I made most of them."

"I have a spare shirt and top," said Maia, who sat between Nova and Kailani.

Nova looked at the ceiling. "You have no style. You wouldn't understand."

Maia looked down her body. "It's regulation attire," she retorted. "I didn't design the stuff."

Tab, who sat on Nova's other side, sighed loudly.

Kailani reached over to touch Nova's knee. "When it's safe, we can retrieve the loom I made from my cave. *Guya* leaves contain a fiber that's good for weaving. Other plants have flowers for dyes. You can help me figure out how to spin *erzala* fur—"

"Really?" Nova said. Her smile wobbled and she began to cry again.

"Now what?" Maia snapped.

"I'm pregnant," Nova wailed.

A stunned silence followed. People looked from Nova to Tab, who picked at a scab exposed by a hole in the knee of his pants. Reilly's thoughts spun. How old were the kids now? How old was he? Almost fifteen when they landed. His parents had told him his birthday was July 31, 2174, which seemed meaningless in space, meaningless on Mirna with its longer orbit around the sun, meaningless in the desert, where every day seemed the same. Maybe he was fifteen. The vitros seemed to have caught up with him, in terms of development. No, at least two of them had surpassed him. When and where had Nova and Tab had sex? There was so little privacy. Had Tally and Keid had sex too? Maia? He glanced at her, caught her watching him. Her eyes skittered away. She probably thought him hopeless and immature. He hadn't even kissed anyone, aside from pecking his parents' and grandparents' cheeks.

"Who is the father?" Carlos asked.

Nova elbowed Tab. He looked up, face flushed. "That would be me."

Harlan stood, walked to a stack of polychiton crates, and began sorting through a charred box.

"Congratulations!" Kailani said. She raised her water cup. "A toast."

Carlos lifted his cup, followed by everyone but Harlan, who fiddled with an antenna.

Kailani rose to her feet. She had regained so much of her strength Reilly half expected her to project a flickering aura. "May the tribe grow and prosper," she said.

"To the tribe!" Keid said. After he swallowed, he added. "Our tribe needs a name."

"You work on that," Carlos said.

"The tribe has to include our *wyome* friends," Tally said adamantly. "And the goats, turkeys, and chickens."

Carlos held up his hand. "In the meantime, we should discuss the fact that we have lost our radio transmitter."

"The receiver too," Harlan muttered as he opened the back of a small, black box.

"Oren could have fixed them," Tally said sadly.

"Yes," Harlan said. "Eventually, we'll repair or rebuild them."

Nova stopped whispering to Tab and snapped to attention. "I did well in physics and electronic engineering. If I reread the communications modules in the computer databases, I'm sure I could figure out how to make repairs."

Carlos nodded. "That would be helpful, Nova." He rubbed his neck. "Except the scrolls seem to have been damaged."

Harlan held up a scroll. The edges had melted together. "Scorched, I'd say. The catbats are either lucky or spookily strategic."

THIRTY-FOUR

Reilly spent an uneasy night in a cave with Carlos, Kailani, and Maia. Before their meeting had adjourned, Carlos assigned each kid to an adult. He paired Erik and Keid, Harlan and Tab, Kailani and Maia, himself and Reilly, and, because two girls remained, Lian with both Tally and Nova. Tab looked uncomfortable at being assigned to Harlan, which surprised Reilly. Nova protested that, since she and Tab were, as she put it, "a mating pair," they should get to sleep together. Carlos said the adults would discuss the matter in the morning.

There were only two upper caves large enough for a *wyome* to open his or her wings. Granos, Nydea, and Jannatz took one, Abdath and Pashtak the other. That left three caves for the humans. Erik, Keid, Harlan, and Tab claimed one as "the man cave." Nova grudgingly bunked with Lian and Tally.

"Well," Carlos said to Kailani, "that leaves the last for us."

Kailani pressed her lips together. But Reilly thought she seemed to be suppressing a smile rather than expressing displeasure.

The scouts had already mounted ladders made from webbing at the mouth of each human cave. Jannatz and Abdath lowered the ladders for them. Reilly climbed up behind Maia, conscious even in the twilight of his proximity to her buttocks.

When he hauled himself over the top, Maia said, "You need to get yourself in shape."

"What do you mean?"

"Your breathing rate. It's fast." She sat cross-legged, watching him, her breasts rising and falling slowly.

Reilly's face and neck flared so hot he felt must glow in the dark. "Whatever." He bent and dusted off his knees, a futile gesture since dust covered everything.

Maia yawned luxuriously. "I'm going to sleep."

Their cave was no bigger than Reilly's old barracks, which had had just enough room for three inflatable futons and a crude lab bench for his parents. Now, the four of them arranged their air mattresses and sleeping sacs side by side. Carlos and Kailani lay in the middle with him and Maia on the outside. Reilly detected tension, as though they were strangers forced into unwanted intimacy. Carlos whispered something to Kailani. Reilly felt like an intruder with no place else to go. He'd much rather have slept beside Nydea. Were he capable of flight, he would have flitted over to her cave and curled himself under her wing. With the image of her warm wing sheltering him, he fell asleep.

∞

Keid's suggestion for the name of their group was the Mearth Tribe. He liked it as a pleasing melding of the words Mirna and Earth. "Plus," he said, "it sounds like 'mirth'."

"I don't find our circumstances the least bit cheerful," Harlan groused.

"What name would you propose?" Kailani asked him.

Harlan thought a moment. "Tribe Jinxed."

What followed was a chorus of boos and nos. Tab threw a millet cake at Harlan. Harlan tossed the biggest piece of it back at Tab. Carlos declared a ceasefire before they wasted any more of their breakfast.

The next several days saw the Mearth Tribe shoring up defenses. Using a large swath of BioFuerte and steel cables, Lian, Erik, Abdath, and Jannatz erected a four-meter high barricade that spanned the mouth of the cave. Abdath tested its strength by dropping boulders on it. It held. In theory, the wall was strong enough and high enough to keep out *garthans* and *witnaws*. It also extended two meters underground, to deter animals from tunneling underneath. For now, the only way for humans to leave the canyon was via airscouter.

"We should all learn to ride the catbats," Harlan said. Sweat darkened his underarms and made a track down his chest. He, Tab, and Nova had just finished creating two catapults made from inflatable tubes reinforced with polychiton. They were too long to fit in any of the humans' caves, but the *wyomes'* caves were tall enough to accommodate them.

Kailani had been in the process of explaining to Nydea, Pashtak, and Granos how to install the catapults. Kailani couldn't both speak Mirnan aloud and send mental images, so Reilly formed pictures to help get the idea across. They stood on the canyon floor, the late-afternoon sun lighting the red, violet, and yellow striations of the cliffs.

Kailani turned to Harlan and said, *"Wyomes* are not horses."

Nydea cocked her ears and eyed Harlan warily.

"They've carried humans before," Tab said, shooting a glance at Reilly, who stood beside Nydea.

"And the airscouters will eventually give out," Harlan said.

"When that happens, we'll repair them," Kailani said. She shoved a stray lock of brown hair under a green and orange headscarf.

"Maybe not, if they're damaged in battle," Harlan said.

"Especially not without Oren," Nova said. "No one is as good of a mechanic. I know a little but—"

"The *wyomes* fight better without a passenger," Reilly said. "They can't maneuver much without a human falling off."

Granos and Pashtak looked from Reilly to Harlan, their long lashes lowered against the sun's glare. They had only recently awakened to help with the day's projects.

"We could make saddles," said Harlan.

"That's enough, cowboy," Kailani said coldly. "You only ride with a *wyome's* expressed consent." With that, she turned to the three *wyomes* and, switching to Mirnan, continued to describe how the catapults worked.

Harlan, Nova, and Tab strode off. Tab stopped at a water bucket, unclipped his water cup from his waist, dipped it in, and took a long, slow drink, watching Reilly the whole while. The look didn't contain malice. But it certainly wasn't friendly.

"What does that one want?" Granos asked, his eyes following Harlan.

"He wants you to fly with him on your back," Kailani said in Mirnan.

Granos gave a sharp exhalation through his nostrils. "Never," he said.

∞

Early the next morning, Reilly and Nydea watched Granos and Pashtak fly off alongside an airscouter. Kailani sat in the pilot seat; Carlos rode copilot. The destination was Kailani's cave.

Jannatz drifted down from her cave and landed beside Nydea.

Nydea hopped from hind foot to hind foot. "I want to fly. It's been long enough." She stretched open her wings. The grafts were still held a pinker hue than the normal tissue. Otherwise, the wings looked normal.

"Maybe you should wait," Reilly said.

"Erik and Tally check them every day. They say my wings look good."

"You could try a short glide," Jannatz said and pointed to a nearby boulder. "Just hop up there and spring off."

Reilly thought he should go find Tally and Erik. But before he had gone five paces, Nydea had done just as Jannatz suggested. She crouched on the boulder, spread her wings, and jumped. The wings spread on the air. She touched down beside Reilly and Jannatz.

"They work! They work!" Nydea's amber eyes glowed. "I'm going to do it again." She and Jannatz curled together their tails in the equivalent of a handshake.

This time, Nydea pushed off from the boulder and flapped her wings. When she reached the opposite canyon wall, she somersaulted and flew higher.

"Okay," Reilly said. "That's high enough. Jannatz, please go get her. I don't want the grafts to break."

Jannatz winged up beside Nydea, flew with her a short distance, then coaxed her back down to the canyon floor. By then, Erik, Tally, and Lian had emerged from the livestock cave and were standing, faces upturned, to catch the final few moments of flight.

For a moment, all of them were jumping around congratulating Nydea and praising the humans' surgical skills. Then Harlan looked down from an overhead cave and announced that Granos, Pashtak, Kailani, and Carlos had returned. Better yet, no enemy tailed them.

After they landed, Carlos and Kailani began unpacking the airscouter and handing things to the other humans with instructions on where to store them. Items included a bow, arrows, arrowheads, strips of cloth, scraps of *erzala* hide, a sac of dried berries and beans as long as Reilly's thumb, and a clay pot of cooking oil. Nova had hoped one of the *wyomes* would carry back Kailani's loom, but this, along with most of her *erzala* hides and food stores, Hyssel's minions had burned.

Two *wyomes* followed them back. They didn't attack, but circled in the currents high above the canyon.

"What are they doing?" Reilly asked Nydea.

"Watching," she said. "After, they will report to Hyssel. I have seen others spying on us."

Later that day, Harlan assembled a flamethrower from a hand-pump, hose, and Kailani's oil. "Fight fire with fire," he said. "We need such a stunning victory that the fuckers won't dare bother us again."

Near bedtime, Maia asked Kailani, "Aren't you going to make a new staff?" The one she had used to defend Nydea and Sheeda had been left in that cave.

Reilly, who was brushing his teeth with the frayed end of a stick, paused to hear the answer.

"That's not necessary," Kailani said.

"Don't you need it for—you know, for that energy thing you do?" Reilly asked.

Carlos looked up sharply, his face all angles in the bluish glow of a telsar lamp.

"I don't think the staff is important."

Maia began to press her to explain, but Carlos said, "Time for bed."

Carlos and Kailani moved their mattresses farther away from Reilly and Maia. About a half hour later, Reilly heard Carlos and Kailani whispering in the dark but couldn't make out the words.

∞

In anticipation of the laser guns running out of *yridium,* Maia, Tally, Kailani, and Nova made slingshots, bows, and arrow shafts from a bush that grew in the canyon's shadow. They spun bowstring from both *guya* fibers and *erzala* wool by rolling strands of fiber against a piece of *erzala* leather laid over the knee. Maia complained to Reilly that she lacked the patience for handicrafts, even if they had a martial purpose. She imitated Nova's near rapture at the notion that eventually she could weave these strands into clothing.

Keid and Erik hunted rocks, some of which they chiseled into arrowheads with the help of *erzala* horns, some of which they piled for use in the slingshots. Keid quickly caught on to the art of shaping the arrowheads. Reilly too often broke the rock flake in the final stages.

Kailani sorted the rocks collected for use in slingshots, putting aside the sharper ones to tip with venom. Granos and Nydea flew the short distance to the creek and returned with four dead *shaggoths.*

Reilly stood back, fighting visions of Nash's final moments—the sudden bruises, the violent seizures. The yellow, orange, and purple of the creature's lengthwise stripes glistened in the morning sun. The hundreds of tiny legs were motionless. Beady orange eyes protruded from scaly yellow heads.

"How did you kill them?" Reilly asked Nydea.

"It's not hard." She yawned extravagantly. "While they're sleeping, you knock them from the tree, grab them behind the head, and squeeze till they stop moving."

Kailani positioned the *shaggoths'* upper bodies across a slab of polychiton, raised a cleaver, and cut off the heads. Erik took two of the long bodies and called out to Tally to help him skin and cook them. Granos took the other two, blew fire over them, and, once the skin had crisped, passed one to Nydea.

Maia stood by with a hypodermic needle. Kailani reached for it, slid the needle into bulges on each side of the *shaggoth's* cheek, and pulled back the plunger. As she repeated the process, the syringe filled with a bilious fluid. With gloved hands, Reilly held out a rock and waited while Kailani squeezed out a few lethal drops onto the tip. He set the rock onto a flat boulder to dry. At the end, they had 19 venom-tipped rocks.

"Can they inject venom after they're dead?" Reilly asked, staring down at a vile head with its paired fangs.

"If you scratched yourself with the fangs, yes," Kailani said.

To insure no one contacted the toxin, Kailani guarded the stones while the venom dried then placed them in a metal box. Now the venom would only kill if it entered the body through an open wound.

Later, under Kailani's tutelage, people practiced using slingshots and bows. Harlan, already skilled with all manner of weapons, could launch a rock with a slingshot farthest and with the most accuracy. Maia rivaled Kailani in her skill with bow and arrow. Reilly preferred a slingshot to a bow. Too often his inner arm got in the way of the recoiling bowstring, which resulted in welts and bruises. Kailani loaned him her leather bracer to protect his arm. Nova complained that her breasts got in the way. Maia told her that, according to myth, a race of ancient female warriors removed their right breasts to fix that problem. All the while, Nydea, happy to be able to fly short distances, retrieved arrows and gathered more rocks.

After Granos and Jannatz brought clay from the creek bed, Kailani taught Keid and Reilly to shape small, narrow-necked pots. The clay felt deliciously cool and moist. Carlos dried the pots in a fire pit. Once the pots cooled, Tally and Nova filled them with oil and stuffed a rag into the top. These would serve as primitive grenades.

Humming as he worked, Keid also created bowls and mugs and small sculptures shaped like *boolas* and *wyomes*. Nydea joined him. She flattened clay against a rock and, with a single extended claw, etched into it images of running *erzalas*. Reilly watched, relishing the rare moment of serenity. He remembered the carvings on the wall in Nydea's cave, the small image of himself looking out the fence, waiting for his parents to return.

Meantime, Abdath and Pashtak draped reams of BioFuerte embedded with solar cells along the highest, sunniest reaches of the canyon walls. The energy generated powered the telsar lamps and created an electric current in the fence Erik and Tally fitted into the mouth of the cave housing the turkeys, chickens, and goats. The animals were allowed into the canyon to graze the stunted shrubbery and peck up the green insects called *viats,* but only when a *wyome* watched while perched on one of the cliff's ledges. The humans learned right away that the guard *wyome* couldn't soar back and forth, as the passing shadow roused an instinctual fear of raptors in the livestock.

Granos stood watch more than the others. Reilly guessed he hoped to see Locatha, Sheeda, and Zedena winging home. When he asked Nydea whether she had received any images or thoughts from Locatha, she replied that the distance separating them was too great.

∞

When five days passed without attack, Kailani and Maia flew an airscouter to the top of the mesa to forage. Pashtak and Abdath hunted *erzalas* nearby. Reilly and Carlos stayed behind to sharpen arrowheads. By now, Reilly had learned which rocks chipped easily by the ringing sound made when struck with a harder stone.

Carlos broke more arrowheads than he made. Each time, he cursed and looked anxiously at the sky, relaxing only when the airscouter descended into the canyon and parked in a lower cave. Pashtak and Abdath followed. Each carried a limp *erzala,* the hoofed feet dangling.

That night, the humans feasted on meat seasoned with tart berries, the inner flesh of a gourd, and tea that Kailani swore improved night vision— their first meal comprised entirely of native species. The *wyomes* ate meat and the magenta leaves of a shrub called *anosote.* Nydea explained to Reilly that this plant perpetuated flammable intestinal gases that ignited with a click of the teeth.

"What are you talking about?" Nova asked. "I wish everybody would speak English." She sighed dramatically. "I mean it's rude and, well, exclusive."

Reilly swallowed a bolus of *erzala* meat, which was darker and tangier than chicken. Then he translated what Nydea had told him.

Tab looked at him incredulously. "You mean they're lighting their burps?"

Reilly smiled. "Sounds that way, doesn't it."

"How come they don't burn their mouths?" Keid asked.

"Because they exhale, so the burning gas moves away from their faces," Kailani said.

"What if there's a headwind?" Tally asked.

Tab laughed. "It'd be a lot worse than having your fart blow back at you."

"We could probably ignite your farts," Keid said. "There's enough methane in them."

"Fart eater," Tab began.

Kailani leaned into the conversation. "I don't advise this plant for human consumption."

Maia set down her spork. "Why not? Obviously, you tried it."

"I made tea from it. A half hour later, I vomited and began to see things that weren't there."

Harlan stopped chewing. "Are you saying there's a local hallucinogen?"

"Believe me, it's not an experience I'd want to repeat."

With a grunt, Harlan resumed eating, his eyes on Jannatz as she stripped leaves from a stem and popped them in her mouth.

"Ironically," Kailani said, *"anosote,* when extracted into oil, makes an excellent burn salve."

Reilly and Tab were on cleaning duty. The others continued to sit around the fire.

As Reilly scrubbed a pot with sand, he said, "Still angry with me?"

"Me?"

Reilly waited.

Tab wiped his mouth on his dirty sleeve. "You piss me off sometimes, sure."

"Why?"

"Privilege of the womb-born. You always get what you want."

Reilly took a swallow of tea. The taste changed from sweet to an oddly appealing sourness. "That's hardly true."

"Anyway, I stopped disliking you weeks ago. Too much work. And, after Nash…." Tab took an unnecessary amount of time rinsing a cup in a tub of water.

"We can't afford to be enemies. We have plenty of those."

Tab looked him in the eye. "Right."

Reilly was first to look away. "Well, I don't dislike you either."

Tab elbowed him playfully. "That doesn't mean we like each other."

"We wouldn't want to get carried away," Reilly agreed.

"Look!" It was Tally. "Lights!" She pointed upward. "The aurora."

The strip of night sky visible between the canyon walls flickered green.

Reilly went to stand by Kailani, Carlos, and Maia. The color wavered then flared then shaded into blue. Reilly's neck began to ache from looking up. He cradled the back of his head in his hands until his fingers tingled. He wished he and Nydea could fly to the top of the mesa for a better look.

"Reilly," Maia said urgently. She had her hands tucked into her armpits.

"What? Are you cold?"

She jerked her head toward the shadows outside the campfire. "Follow me."

When they were out of earshot of the others, she held out her hands.

"What?" he said.

"Try to touch me." When Reilly hesitated, she added, "My hands, stupid."

Reilly reached out. A half meter before he made contact, the air turned staticky. Closer still, the air felt thick, almost gelatinous, and charged with electricity. Loose strands of hair began to stand up from Maia's head.

"Wow," he said. "You're like Kailani." He rubbed his hands, which felt like they were being pricked with tiny, hot needles.

Maia's eyes widened. "It's happening to you too."

He raised his arms. Against the darkness, a faint glow wavered near his fingertips. He passed his hands several centimeters in front of his chest and his jacket rippled. He felt a mixture of awe and anxiety. "Now what?"

"I don't know for sure. We can ask Lani if this is how it started for her."

"How what started?"

"Don't be dense, Reilly." Maia held up her hands. "I wonder how I can make the current extend outward." She squeezed shut her eyes, pressed her lips together, and frowned. Nothing changed.

"You look like you're constipated," Reilly remarked. He shoved his stinging hands into his pocket. He couldn't deal with anything new.

Maia gave him an annoyed look. "And you're not helping. Reilly, this is huge. We're like…like a defense system."

"I hate it when you underestimate yourself." Reilly held back from saying he wouldn't mind if Maia switched from being offensive to being defensive. "What's causing this reaction? Does it have to do with the aurora?"

"Maybe. Maybe the accumulated bursts of solar energy altered the genetic code, or at least genetic expression."

"So we're mutating?"

Maia shrugged.

"Mutations cause cancer, Maia."

"I know."

"And you remember what we learned about environmental insults, including solar radiation, increasing cancer rates on Earth."

"Of course."

"I don't want to get cancer."

"Stop being so negative. Party pooper."

Reilly sighed, looked at his hands again. They still tingled, but the intensity had diminished. "Sorry, it's just sort of…overwhelming."

"It's okay to feel scared."

"I didn't say—"

"I'm scared too. But that doesn't change anything."

"I know." He sighed. His body felt heavy, his mind dull. "I'm tired."

"Me too."

"I need to lie down."

Reilly began to climb the ladder to their cave. He felt tension in the webbing and looked back to see Maia following. He grabbed the handhold at the top, hauled himself over the ledge, drank water out of his canteen, slid into his sleeping sac, and lay on his back. He felt an unwelcome throbbing behind his left eye.

Maia dragged her mattress and sleeping sac alongside his. She curled onto her side, facing him, and shivered.

Reilly turned, unzipped his sac, and pulled her toward him.

"I'm cold and my head hurts." Her breath warmed his neck.

"Mine too," he whispered. He couldn't remember Maia disclosing physical discomfort before. "Carlos gave me some Anaral patches to use at the first sign of a migraine." He slid out of his sac, felt for the foil-wrapped patches in a side pocket of his duffel, and returned. "Hold out your arm."

She reminded him of the child she had once been as she sat, shrugged out of her jacket, and dropped her arm into his lap. He tore open the packet, pulled up her sleeve, and pressed the adhesive onto the warm, silky skin of her inner arm. She took the other packet from his hand and did the same for him.

They lay on their backs, his arm under her neck, and waited for the pain to abate. Reilly sensed Maia relax. Her hip settled against his, the latticework of her ribs glided up and down, up and down. He thought about the coming battle, thought about the chance of one or both of them being injured or killed.

"It will be okay, Reilly," Maia whispered. She rolled toward him, and he mirrored her. His lips found hers. He couldn't believe that, not long ago, he thought her mouth annoyingly big. How wrong he'd been. Her lips were warm, plush, generous. Her mouth tasted tart, like the berries she and Kailani had picked.

She let out a husky laugh.

"What?" he said, alarmed that he had so quickly made a fool of himself.

"Your whiskers tickle," she said.

"Do you want me to stop?"

"What? No!"

They kissed and explored one another's contours until they heard Carlos grunt as he hauled himself from the ladder to the cave floor. Kailani followed more quietly.

"Are they asleep?" Carlos asked.

Reilly held his breath.

Kailani murmured something.

Reilly listened as they arranged their sleeping gear and whispered and stopped whispering. Kailani sighed. Maia's breathing became slow and regular.

Reilly wondered how he could capture this feeling of complete contentment. He imagined he could bring down the light of the aurora, great gauzy swaths of greens and reds and blues, and spin the colors together and knit a cocoon around him and Maia and another around Carlos and Kailani. Then they could live inside these sheltering sheaths, dining on the hues that the sun would daily replenish.

THIRTY-FIVE

Reilly awoke with no feeling in his arm. He opened his eyes and saw Maia, curled on her side, her head nestled into the crook of his elbow. He tried to slide his arm free without waking her, but her eyelids parted immediately.

She smiled sleepily. "Good morning."

"Morning."

She sat and looked around. "Carlos and Kailani already gone."

"Yeah," he said. "I hope we haven't missed breakfast." He suddenly felt self-conscious and awkward.

They both busied themselves with brushing their teeth and washing their faces with water in a bucket. The sun was still low, and it was quiet and cool in the canyon.

Maia loosened her hair from her braid and began brushing it.

"Let me," he said.

She smiled in a way that was almost shy and handed him the brush. Reilly sat behind her and began to pull the brush through her hair. A memory of his mother brushing her blonde hair jabbed him, but the pain wasn't fierce. He focused on Maia, whose hair was dark, thick, and curly.

"How do you braid it?" he asked.

She showed him and let him finish the plait, which stopped midway down her back.

"I don't think I got it tight enough," he said.

Maia patted the braid. "It's fine."

"Guess I need to practice."

"Let me know when you're in the mood."

Reilly felt his face flush. He turned his back to her and moved toward the ladder. He smelled smoke from the cook fire. Down below, Kailani ladled something from a pot into Keid's bowl.

"Before you join the rest of society, you need some grooming. Sit," Maia said, gesturing toward a bench-shaped boulder. "You look like you spent the night strapped to the wind turbine."

Reilly obeyed. He closed his eyes and luxuriated in the sensation of the brush against his scalp. She set down the brush, which now contained light and dark strands, and pulled back his hair.

"Not a ponytail," he protested.

"Yes. A low, manly ponytail." She walked around to face him and nodded. "Much better."

They descended the ladder and found they were the last to breakfast. Kailani arced an eyebrow at them. Reilly sat beside Maia and ate, conscious of the furtive glances from the others. When Reilly caught Tab staring, Tab grinned and gave him a thumb's up. Reilly quickly looked down at the pinkish porridge clinging to the side of his bowl.

Before the *wyomes* went to sleep for the day, the two species assembled for a meeting. Kailani asked what news the *wyomes* had of Locatha, Sheeda, and Zedena.

"None," Granos said, exhaling so forcefully dust swirled on the ground before him.

Kailani translated to English, then addressed Granos in Mirnan. "What do you think is keeping them?"

Nydea spoke, "They had to visit four clans. Perhaps it was not easy to make their case. Maybe they have also negotiated with *witnaws* and *garthans*."

"They have been gone eight days," Carlos said. "We expected they would return in—what—two or three days?"

Granos nodded gravely. "I don't know what has happened. But I would know if Locatha had died."

Pashtak flexed his front digits. "I have something to report."

"What?" Reilly asked. He felt bitter dread taking the place of the porridge in his belly.

"Last night, Abdath and I went hunting in the direction of Ledera Canyon. A large group had assembled on the desert near the canyon. We saw *garthans, witnaws,* many *wyomes,* even a small group *of mantalyas.*"

"What?" Keid asked. Reilly noticed he hadn't waited for Kailani's translation. "What are mont—whatever?"

"The creatures that swing in the trees," Reilly said, eyeing Keid closely.

"Oh. The ones with two tails and straw-colored scales."

Tally said in Mirnan, *"Mantalyas* talk?"

"What the—" Tab sputtered. "Does everyone talk Mirnan except me?"

Nova patted his leg. "I only understand a few words."

"And I've been making an effort to learn," Tally said. She switched to Mirnan, "Jannatz teach me."

Abdath yawned, exposing glistening teeth, and said, "The *mantalyas* speak a little, but understand more. However, they are only good warriors if they can fight from trees."

"Well," Lian said, "a large cross-species gathering doesn't bode well, does it?"

Harlan rubbed his stubbled jaw. "Sounds like Hyssel and his gang are rallying the troops for battle."

The scales along Nydea's spine rose. Reilly moved to sit next to her. He felt her agitation as a prickling under his skin, as though sand had penetrated his pores.

Carlos stood and dusted off his hands. "We knew this was coming. We're strong and we're ready. While our numbers are few, we are united and will mount a coordinated defense." He glanced at Kailani, who returned his gaze with steady green eyes. "The enemy is unlikely to attack by day. *Wyomes,* I suggest you sleep. The rest of us will make final preparations."

Nydea was the last *wyome* to leave the group. Reilly stood and rested a hand on her shoulder.

She gave him a mournful look. "He's coming for me. He won't stop till he has captured me and killed all his enemies."

The image of Hyssel's yellow fangs and cruel eyes filled Reilly's head. "I won't let him get you," Reilly said and hoped it wasn't an empty promise. "Sleep now. You need your strength."

Nydea rose, arced her spine, took a few steps away from him, then flapped her patchwork wings and ascended to her cave.

"Hey catbat boy," Harlan said, his loud voice interrupting Reilly's thoughts. "If you want a weapon, get your butt over here."

The other kids were clustered around Harlan, who stood just inside a lower cave they had turned into an arsenal. Maia was already climbing the ladder to their cave, a bow slung over her shoulders. Tab walked past him with a bow, four arrows, and an LR-50, which was distinguished from the shorter ranged *yridium* gun by a scope mounted on top.

"Stay strong, hume," he said.

"You too, Tabman."

Tab grinned and gave him a military salute—stiff right hand to his brow.

Reilly waited his turn. Each person received one yrdium gun and either a slingshot and stones or a bow and arrows.

"Choose your poison, Reilly," Harlan said.

"Slingshot," Reilly said. "But I already have one." He was referring to the slingshot Kailani had first given him.

"Fortunately, it's not a popular choice," Harlan said. "You should have two, in case something happens to the other."

"Like what?" Reilly said.

"Use your imagination."

Reilly didn't have to try hard to picture the slingshot falling as he climbed a ladder or a *wyome's* yanking it from his grasp. "Fine," he said. "An LR-50, too."

"The adults each got one. I gave the remaining two to Keid and Tab. You get a *yridium* handgun."

Reilly shrugged. It no longer bothered him that Keid and Tab were better shots. He wondered how Maia felt about this decision.

Harlan handed him two pouches. "The smaller one has three venom-coated rocks. Save them for sure shots."

"I know that," Reilly said.

"Right," Harlan said, giving him a look. "I forgot your vast experience in armed warfare." He took two stones from another sack and began juggling them. Reilly wondered whether or not they contained venom.

"Glad you're on my team, Harlan," Reilly said.

Harlan snatched the two stones from the air. "Stick with your girlfriend. She's the one you most want on your team." He looked toward Abdath and Pashtak's cave. One of the *wyomes* had lowered a ladder. "Well," he said, "time for me to ready the catapult."

Reilly felt edgy the rest of the day. The shadow of two *pakitoks* gliding overhead made his heart lurch. A small dust storm drove them into their caves. Afterward, when Reilly looked outside, the sky to the west was still dark.

"Clouds," Kailani said. "The rainy season approaches."

Reilly knew about clouds and rain, but hadn't experienced either and couldn't imagine water falling from the sky. Would the rain feel good? Would it be warm or cold? How do you build a cook fire in the rain? Would he live long enough to learn the answers to his questions?

THIRTY-SIX

The attack came just before sunset. The *wyomes* hadn't yet awakened when Erik sounded the alarm. Reilly and Tally had just begun the nightly task of herding the goats, turkeys, and chickens into the lower caves. Reilly felt the ground tremble, heard a dull thud, saw the barricade ripple, and heard the crackling of something hitting the electric field. A moment later, the barricade bowed inward in another spot. An explosion of guttural Mirnan followed. Reilly thought he saw a small rent in the fabric.

"*Witnaws!*" he cried.

Human and *wyome* shouts ricocheted up the canyon.

"To your posts!" Carlos called.

As planned, Carlos, Lian, Erik, and Harlan sprinted for the airscouters parked further up the canyon. The four vehicles lifted off. One was parked in each of the three human caves, the fourth in the larger of the two *wyome* caves.

Reilly pulled a length of webbing from his pocket, looped it around a nanny goat's neck, and began tugging her toward the cave. She leaned back, resisting him.

"Let go, Reilly," Tally said, and smacked the nanny goat on the rump, causing her to bolt for the safety of the cave. The other two goats chased after her.

Out of sight, *garthans* yapped to one another. Reilly understood some of the commands. *Move right. You two stay by the boulder. The rest—forward.*

Showing the whites of their eyes, the goats milled and bleated as Reilly closed their enclosure. The chickens and turkeys squawked and scurried helter-skelter as the shadow of three *wyomes* passed over them. Tally and Reilly shooed them toward shelter.

349

"Forget about the minjin' poultry," Tab said, as he and Nova ran past. "Climb to your caves."

Reilly knew Tally wouldn't take cover until the fowl were safe. He stuffed a chicken under each arm, tossed them into a crate, flushed the last turkey home, and pulled down the flap BioFuerte that covered the mouth of the cave.

Above them, Lian leaned her head over the ledge of a cave and shouted at Tally. Keid was halfway up the ladder, looking down imploringly at Tally.

"Go," Reilly said. "The animals will be fine. You can pick off attackers more safely from above."

Maia screamed his name. Reilly hesitated. Tally had climbed up to Keid, who didn't like heights and appeared frozen in place on the ladder. Tally called encouragement. Movement above caught Reilly's eye. A *wyome* folded its wings and dropped toward Keid and Tally. Reilly didn't remember pulling out his gun. He aimed and depressed the trigger until the red line connected with *wyome's* belly. At the same moment, a laser beam projected from his cave to the *wyome's* skull.

Tally and Keid let out twin screams as the animal fell past them and landed with a heavy thud five meters from where Reilly stood.

Maia leaned out from their cave and yelled, "Reilly, get up here NOW!"

Reilly raced for the ladder and began to scramble up. Another *wyome* barreled down toward him.

"Keep climbing," Carlos shouted. "We'll cover you."

An arrow whistled the air and pierced the *wyome* in the neck. Reilly heaved himself over the top as Kailani fitted another arrow into her bowstring.

"Thanks," he said.

Kailani nodded, her eyes focused on the sky and the flocking *wyomes*.

Maia helped Carlos fasten a long reel of BioFuerte to cover the lower half of the cave's mouth. She crouched behind it, balanced her gun arm atop, and glanced at Reilly. "Took you long enough."

"Nice to know you care." He meant what he said. He grabbed his slingshot, rocks, and gun and knelt near Maia. Carlos and Kailani flanked them.

At this height, they could see over the top of the barricade. A pack of sixteen *garthans* loped in from the southeast, joining the group that was mostly hidden behind the barricade. The dusky gray back of a *witnaw* juddered back and forth. The barricade bowed, recovered. The curved tip of a horn poked through, disappeared.

"So much for the electrified barrier," Kailani muttered. *"Witnaws* have thick hides and thicker skulls."

"What about the catapults? What are our *wyomes* waiting for?" Carlos said. "What I wouldn't give to have the com system back."

Just then, the long arm of the catapult lashed out from Abdath and Pashtak's cave. Because of the angle from there to the barricade, the grenade landed left of center. The subsequent explosion triggered yelps and bellows. A single *garthan* tore away from the canyon. A *witnaw* galloped after. The catapult arm levered back into the cave. With a whoosh, a second grenade arced over the barricade. Sand fanned up. The process repeated, releasing a third grenade. Reilly thought he saw the long foreleg of a *garthan* rise into the air. Another *garthan* shouted orders. The right side of the barricade rippled.

"They've figured out we can't bomb that direction," Kailani said.

"Shouldn't we fly out an airscouter?" Maia asked. "Take care of them before they breach the barrier?"

"Not yet," Carlos said. "We'll wait until our *wyomes* take to the air."

Their strategy was to postpone an aerial battle, to save the *wyomes* and scouters until absolutely necessary. Granos had bridled at the strategy, but admitted to its wisdom.

"Get ready," Kailani said, standing to pull back the bowstring.

Six *wyomes* flew into the canyon. Two peeled off toward the caves occupied by the allied *wyomes;* three beelined for the human caves; and one dove toward the cave housing the livestock. Another half dozen *wyomes* descended and followed the same pattern. Reilly could see a third group assembling overhead.

"Fire down the line," Kailani said. "Me first. Then Maia, Reilly, Carlos."

A *wyome* came at their cave feet first. Kailani loosed an arrow that lodged in the creature's armpit. Maia finished it off with her gun.

Reilly's fingers felt slippery against the gun's grip as he aimed at the next incoming *wyome.*

"Now," Carlos said.

Reilly depressed the trigger, watched the ray drill into the *wyomes* throat, and thought, *that's for my father.*

Carlos shot the fourth attacker in the chest.

The canyon filled with winging *wyomes,* shouts, red lines of *yridium,* arrows, stones, the scarves of fire. A burst of flame yellower than *wyome* fire came from Harlan's cave. He was using his flamethrower. A *wyome* careened away, forepaws over face.

Reilly glanced down to see a *garthan* flowing toward the livestock cave. A *witnaw* muscled through a rent in the barricade. It didn't get far before an arrow stuck into its side. Bellowing, it ran lopsided circles.

"Filthin' *witnaw,*" Maia muttered and shot it in the neck.

The huge animal took a few more paces, fell onto its side, and groaned a last exhalation.

The *garthan* looked over its shoulder and barked a few Mirnan words. Three of its kind slipped through the barricade. Reilly looked down, but couldn't see where the first had gone, couldn't see the entrance to the livestock cave directly underneath. The other *garthans* ran that direction. A sound like crying children swelled.

"The goats," Carlos said. He stood to get a better angle on the *garthans* and made one shot before Kailani cried, "Get down!"

A *wyome* must have dropped straight down their side of the canyon, invisible to the humans until the last moment. Clicking its teeth, it belched fire. Reilly grabbed Carlos's elbow, yanked him back.

Maia aimed but no beam emanated. Screaming, she hurled the gun at the *wyome's* forehead. It bounced back into the cave. The *wyome* stretched unsheathed claws toward Maia, who grabbed an arrow with her hands and brandished it before her. Reilly heard a whap. A rock pierced the *wyome's* yellow eye. Paws to its face, it howled out of sight.

Kailani lowered the arm holding her slingshot and looked at Carlos. "You okay?"

"Just getting warmed up," he said. He looked at the singed bill of his cap, put it back on his head. "Thank you, ma'am."

Turkeys and chicken screeches joined the screaming of the goats. Maia fit the arrow to her bow, stood, sighted down at the milling *garthans*, and released, hitting the hind end of one.

Kailani joined her. "Cover us," she said.

Reilly and Carlos knelt, balanced their gun arms on the barricade, and shot at approaching *witnaws*. Reilly's gun made a clacking noise. No more *yridium*.

An explosion below caused Maia to stumbled backward. Two *garthans* scrabbled toward the barricade, one missing a hind leg.

Harlan hooted from the cave next to theirs.

"He used his grenade launcher," Carlos said.

Reilly knew he was referring to the outsized slingshot Harlan had built.

"What livestock survived will surely be deaf," Maia said.

"Incoming *wyomes,*" Kailani said.

Reilly grabbed his slingshot, slipped a stone from one of the pouches hanging from his belt.

Carlos fired at a *wyome,* but the beam wavered before connecting. Reilly's stone went wide. Kailani hit it with an arrow.

"Sorry," Reilly said.

"No one hits the mark every time," Carlos said, picking up his own slingshot. "Especially not with this gadget." He glanced at Kailani. "How many arrows do you have?"

"Five."

"Maia?"

"Three." She stiffened. "*Wyome* coming."

"Save your arrows," Carlos said. His slingshot stone glanced off the *wyome's* shoulder, causing it to rear. Reilly had already loaded a venomous stone. He waited until the beast was three meters away, sucked in a steadying breath, thought, *This one's for my mother*. The force embedded the stone between two ribs. Treading air with its wings, the *wyome* pulled it free, pressed its paw over the spot. Kailani fitted an arrow, waited. The *wyome* banked away, flapped erratically toward the opposite side of the canyon. Suddenly, its wings spasmed and its legs contracted.

Maia said, "Phenom, Reilly."

Carlos exhaled loudly. "Time for the scouters."

"I'll ride shotgun, fire the guns while they last," Maia said.

Carlos looked from Maia to Kailani to Reilly.

"Let's go."

"Maia," Reilly said, the word snagging in his throat.

She smiled at him. "I'll be back."

Reilly tried to smile back. Kailani rolled the silver ring around her finger and turned her attention back to the sky. Night had fallen. A semicircle of *Tobla,* the name the Mirnans gave the blue moon, had crested the canyon wall.

"Granos is out," Kailani said. She squinted. "There go Abdath and Pashtak."

Reilly turned. Abdath and Pashtak wore white banners—thin strips of fabric running across one shoulder and secured below the wings—to distinguish them from the enemy.

While Carlos and Maia took their seats in the *Kestrel,* Kailani and Reilly rolled aside the reel of BioFuerte half blocking the cave's mouth and stood aside and pressed cloths over their faces to block the dust kicked up as the scouter lifted and glided out into the night.

Two seconds later, a *wyome* darted past and threw a smoldering object into the cave.

Kailani sniffed, ran to the glowing object, grabbed it with her tunic, and flung it outside. *"Thystam!"* she cried.

Another hunk of burning *thystam* rock arced into the cave. Reilly pulled down his night goggles, grabbed the gardening gloves lying atop his duffel, picked up the rock, loaded it clumsily into the ammunition pocket of his slingshot, and sent it across the canyon.

More rocks hailed inside as one *wyome* after another flew by with a toxic payload.

Reilly tried not to breathe, gasping each time he ran to the cave's mouth with another smoldering rock. He saw flickering on the cave's bottom and the silhouettes of *garthans.* "They're building a *thystam* bonfire down there! And another, further up the canyon. The plan must be to suffocate us in our caves or flush us out in the open." He thought but didn't say, *and then kill us.*

Two other airscouters accelerated out of the canyon.

"We need the fourth airscouter," Kailani said.

Reilly nodded. With Abdath's help, they had rigged a narrow rope bridge between this cave and the one housing Jannatz, Nydea, Granos, and the last airscouter.

"I'll get it," Kailani said. "You stay here and cover me."

"No," Reilly said, surprised by his forcefulness. "Too many enemy. I can't pitch out *thystam* and cover you." As if to emphasize his point, another burning rock thudded behind him. He scooped it up, tossed it out. His movements were becoming alarmingly languid. The urge to lie down weighed upon him.

"Nydea will come," he said. "And Jannatz."

"Why is that? And why do we want to risk their lives?"

"They're being smoked too," Reilly said. "Shush. I need to concentrate."

He closed his eyes, leaving the *thystam* chucking to Kailani. *Nydea. Nydea, I need you. Come to me, Nydea. Bring Jannatz.* He repeated his plea, visualized the two females flitting from their cave to his. In a moment, he had his reply. *Yes. We are coming. Watch for us.*

Reilly blinked open his eyelids, which felt like they were made of lead. "They will be here," he said thickly. "Gather your weapons."

He secured his slingshot and slung Maia's bow and the quiver of arrows around his neck. The two females flew, skimming the canyon wall. Kailani shot an arrow into a *wyome* on their tails and stood back from the ledge as Jannatz and Nydea landed on the threshold.

Without a word, Kailani scaled Jannatz's shoulder. Likewise, Reilly scooted into position behind Nydea's neck. He ran his hands over her web of scars.

"Icantha," he whispered. "Sure you can carry me?"

"Zak. No more hiding in caves," Nydea said bravely. "It is time to fight."

Reilly caught the dank smell of fear on her.

A passing *wyome* breathed fire on a hunk of *thystam* and threw it. Jannatz neatly caught it in her front paw and hurled it at the sender's hindquarters. Then she took to the air.

"Ready?" Reilly said.

In answer, Nydea crouched and sprang upward, fanning the air with her wings. Compared to the time he first rode atop her back, Reilly noticed that her movements felt more tentative; her wings seemed to beat faster just to maintain altitude. He wondered how much of her difficulty came from her imperfect wings, how much from the *thystam* fumes. How long did it take for the toxins to dissipate? He pulled the cool night air into his lungs, kept his eyes on her cave, where the airscouter awaited them. It wasn't far. She could practically coast there.

Jannatz stretched out her hind legs to touch down on the cave's entrance. Kailani screamed a warning. Smoke billowed toward them, carrying the cloying smell of *thystam*. Jannatz wheeled. The enemy must have ignited a pile of rocks inside. No way could they get the fourth scouter now.

Nydea banked, flapped, and, after a few agonizing seconds, rose above the canyon walls. A pair of *wyomes* followed. Reilly kept one hand on Nydea's neck and, with the other, pulled free his slingshot, almost dropped it. His head seemed to be clearing, but his movements still felt clumsy.

Not yet, came Nydea's voice in his head. *They may mean no harm.*

Reilly chafed then remembered that, on their escape from Ledera Canyon, no *wyome* had attacked Nydea. But she hadn't been carrying a human, a *nakkoth*. Ahead and to the right, Jannatz and Kailani trailed three *wyomes*. Her bow in one hand, Kailani craned over her shoulder. Neither she nor Reilly could shoot directly behind. Even if they could rotate their torsos 180 degrees, they risked hitting their *wyomes'* beating wings.

Reilly scanned the sky for the airscouters, spotted the lights of two of them flying a quarter kilometer away, saw staccato bursts of *yridium*. The third hovered just outside the canyon's mouth, firing toward the ground. None was close enough to help. If Granos, Abdath, or Pashtak were nearby, he couldn't see them in the dark.

Wyomes now approached from every direction like a living net closing around them. Jannatz drove forward, turned back as two enemies charged. She vectored off but was again repelled. Kailani fired an arrow that disappeared into the blackness. Four arrows remained in her quiver.

The net tightened. Wings blotted out the moon. Nydea and Jannatz were forced to land atop the mesa. Kailani jumped free, loaded an arrow, looked about wildly. Reilly hopped to the ground, nearly fell, recovered.

"It's hopeless," Kailani said. "There are too many of them."

A *wyome* separated from the flapping mass and touched down so close that Reilly had to jump backward.

The *wyome* spoke. "No way out now."

Reilly recognized the narrow eyes, the broken incisor, the foul breath, the grating voice.

"Nydea, dear," Comox said. "Have no fear. We will not harm you. Hyssel wants you safe."

"And the *nakkoths?*" Nydea said, moving to stand beside Reilly. "And Jannatz?"

Comox smirked. "The *nakkoths* will, of course, die. Jannatz and your other friends will be tried as traitors."

Jannatz crept closer to Nydea. Reilly slipped a venomous stone from its sack.

"Stand back. Both of you," Comox said to Nydea and Jannatz. Neither budged.

Two big males descended to flank Comox. Reilly gripped his slingshot in his left hand, the poisoned stone in his right.

"Forward," Comox said.

The males reared onto their hind legs and charged Nydea and Jannatz, who scattered sideways.

Comox turned on Reilly, opened his mouth. In a flash, Reilly yanked back the pad of the slingshot, and released. The stone disappeared into the back of Comox's throat.

Comox doubled over, coughed blood. Jannatz cried out as her attacker pinned her to the ground. With a whoosh, an arrow sank into its side. Before he could pull free the arrow, he toppled over. Jannatz got to all fours and moved to help Nydea just as Kailani loosed another arrow into the second male, hitting it in the low spine and causing it to rear before running crookedly away.

Two arrows remained in Kailani's quiver. Plus the three of Maia's that Reilly carried on his back. Above, *wyomes* called in confusion.

Comox gagged, rolled onto his side. His body trembled, began to jerk. Everyone else seemed to freeze. After several minutes, Comox went still.

Overhead, a *wyome* yelled, "The nakkoth killed Comox. Death to the *nakkoths!*"

A dark mass of *wyomes* descended. Reilly reached back to pull an arrow from Maia's quiver. His hands had started to tingle. His fingers closed clumsily around the arrow shaft.

Nydea stepped in front of Reilly and looked up. "Stop! No more bloodshed."

The *wyomes* paused, hung in the air like so many mobiles.

Nydea continued, her voice calm, commanding. "You see what Hyssel has done to me." She spread her wings. The grafted areas shone palely in the moonlight.

Murmurs vibrated the air.

"You have heard how he burned and clawed his wife, my Aunt Sheeda." Her uplifted face radiant and serene, she waited for the chatter to die down, waited until the only sound was that of wing-stirred air. "The *nakkoths* rescued me and Sheeda. They took care of us. Few of you came to our defense. Why did you stand by? Why did you carry out Hyssel's orders? He murdered my parents, who ruled you with wisdom and justice. Yes, those rumors are true. Hyssel also killed defenseless *nakkoths,* a species that traveled far to live in peace with us. It is Hyssel you should kill."

"*Nakkoths* have killed," a *wyome* shouted. "They killed my mother."

"My son, Brandoth!" another cried.

"And my sister, Sideaka."

Nydea turned a slow circle, looking into the faces overhead. "That is regrettable. But they did so only in defense. Had your loved ones not attacked, they would yet live. Ask yourself who sent them into battle."

The name *Hyssel* repeated like the rustle of leaves.

The *wyomes* drifted downward, save two that flew away. The rest alighted in a circle around Nydea, Jannatz, Reilly, and Kailani, who bunched together and faced outward. Reilly felt Nydea's composure as a cool piece of polished metal.

"You will not hurt us," Nydea said.

"No," came a female voice. "We will not."

A male said, "There lies Comox. These *nakkoths* slew him." He pointed overhead. "And here are more traitors."

Three *wyomes* hovered nearby.

"Nydea," came Granos' deep voice. "Are you harmed?"

"All is well," Nydea said. "I am speaking with our clanspeople."

A *wyome* in the circle scratched the ground with a front paw. "What should we do with the traitors?"

"The only traitors are Hyssel and his followers," Nydea said. "You will now follow me. No longer shall sister fight brother, friend slay friend. We the righteous shall unite. Many flames together make a conflagration."

At this, the *wyomes* cheered.

"Zak," a female with a flute-like voice said. "Nydea is now our leader." She stepped forward and lay on her belly before Nydea.

A large male did likewise. Another half dozen *wyomes* lay prostrate. Four remained standing.

Granos touched down, followed by Abdath and Pashtak.

Reilly felt lightheaded and realized he'd been holding his breath.

"Maybe we won't die," he whispered to Kailani.

"Not this second," Kailani replied.

One of the standing *wyomes* turned. *"Nakkoths* in flying shells!"

The lights of three airscouters grew brighter and larger.

All of the *wyomes* stood. Four took to the air, one of them roaring, "It's a trap!"

"It's not," Reilly protested. But the words came out in English.

"Tell them to stay back," Nydea said to Reilly. "The vessels are scaring my people. We will lose our chance for peace."

"We don't have radios," Reilly said.

Kailani looked at Reilly. "Connect with Maia."

Reilly peered upward. He couldn't distinguish the *Kestrel* from the other two craft. The ships drew closer. More *wyomes* rose into the air.

Reilly closed his eyes and imagined his thoughts forming tentacles. *Maia. Stop. Come no nearer. Tell Carlos.* He repeated variations on the theme. He pictured her beautiful face, her generous lips, her eyes like warm, dark pools. "Come on, Maia!" he found himself saying aloud.

Reilly? Her voice was in his head.

Yes! Reilly formed the thoughts that they must stop, that the scouters upset the *wyomes*. After a pause, he didn't receive actual words, but a sense of her understanding.

"You did it," Kailani said, her voice light with relief.

Reilly opened his eyes. The airscouters hovered. Granos, Pashtak, and Abdath had moved to flank Nydea and Jannatz.

"We must return to the canyon," Kailani said in Mirnan. "People remain in the caves."

The reminder startled Reilly to full awareness. He didn't know who was in the other two scouters. No doubt Harlan and Tab occupied one. That left Lian, Erik, Nova, Tally, and Keid. Two of them occupied the third scouter, leaving three in a cave—one cave or two? If two, who was alone? Nova? And where was Hyssel? Wherever he was, he wasn't alone.

Granos lowered himself to his belly and nodded at Reilly. Reilly thanked him and hauled himself into position behind Granos' noble head. Kailani climbed nimbly atop Pashtak, who rose to full height.

"You will let us pass," Granos said to the assembled *wyomes*. It sounded more a statement of fact than a question.

The ring opened. Reilly cinched in his knees and felt Granos' muscles ripple as the big *wyome* galloped four paces and bounded into the air. The ground pulled away from them. Reilly glanced over his shoulder to see Jannatz, Abdath, Pashtak, and Kailani following. The other *wyomes* stayed on the ground, looking up. Aside from refraining from attacking, they gave no sign that their allegiance had firmly shifted to Nydea.

As they rose level with the airscouters, Reilly saw Maia in the copilot's seat, waving madly. He motioned down to the canyon. She blew him a kiss. He grinned. His mother blew him kisses, did so the last time he saw her. But the reminder didn't make him sad. That his mother had probably blown kisses at Maia too didn't make him jealous. The wind tore at his hair, stole the heat from his skin. But the core of him felt warm, alive, wild, and unafraid.

THIRTY-SEVEN

The exultant feeling vanished when they descended into the canyon. It was eerily still. Smoke blurred the mouths of the upper caves.

One airscouter shot ahead and disappeared inside the cave where Erik, Keid, Lian, and Tally slept.

Reilly asked Granos to fly closer, but wasn't sure he had been heard, much less understood. Nevertheless, Granos slowed his flight.

In less than a minute, the airscouter emerged from the cave, its dome open, Harlan piloting and a hysterical Tab cradling Nova in the copilot's seat. The craft descended to the canyon floor. Reilly scanned the area for *garthans* and *witnaws* and saw motionless bodies, but none that moved. He urged Granos downward. When they landed, Tab and Harlan had already laid Nova on the ground. By the moonlight of *Tobla,* her skin shimmered a bluish gray.

"She's not breathing!" Tab cried. "She was alone. Why was she alone? She was supposed to be with Tally and Erik."

"There's a pulse," said Harlan. He shouldered Tab aside, pinched shut Nova's nostrils, covered her mouth with his own, and blew. He gulped air, blew again into her airway. He repeated the process a dozen times as Tab held Nova's hand and wept and begged her to live.

As Harlan lifted his head for another inhalation, Nova took a shuddering breath of her own.

"Nova!" Tab cried. "Nova!" Simultaneously weeping and laughing, he said her name over and over.

Reilly tasted blood and realized he'd been biting his lip. He scanned the caves overhead. A scouter stopped and hovered outside of each of the humans' caves, then descended. When it landed, Reilly saw Lian and Keid in the cockpit.

The dome opened. Lian stepped down and yanked off her helmet. "Have you seen Tally and Erik?"

Reilly shook his head. "They're not in their cave?"

Lian shook her head. She cupped her hands around her mouth and called their names.

Keid jumped to the ground and raced to the cave that housed the animals. Tally appeared in the doorway, her hair wild, her face smeared with something dark. A goat limped beside her.

Lian and Reilly ran over, wending their way through the bodies of *witnaws, garthans,* and *wyomes.* One *garthan* clenched a dead turkey in its teeth.

Keid was holding both of Tally's hands and talking gently, as though she were a wild animal in need of taming.

Lian switched on a torch. Tears made tracks through the blood crusted on Tally's face. "You're hurt," Lian said.

Tally shook her head slowly. Her eyes were aquamarine wells of grief. "They're all dead. Except Gretta." She reached down and touched the goat's head. The goat butted her leg, then began chewing the hem of her pants.

"What about Erik?" Lian said frantically.

"Not dead," Tally said, her voice almost a whisper. "But hurt. We tried to defend our animals. But there were too many. The *garthans* kept lunging and snarling and biting." Her eyes were unfocused, as though seeing the horror anew. "We shot them until we ran out of *yridium.* Then we used bows and slingshots. We picked up rocks and threw them. Finally, the *garthans* ran away."

"Shhh," Keid said. He removed his jacket and wrapped it around Tally, who had begun to shiver. "It's over. Let's sit."

Reilly followed Lian into the cave, which smelled of blood, shit, and fear. She swept her torch left and right. There were feathers everywhere. "Erik?" she called.

Someone moaned. The torchlight tracked the source. Reilly saw a man curled on his side.

Lian ran to Erik. His right pant leg was bloody to the knee. Lian pulled out a pocketknife and cut away the material, exposing multiple lacerations and punctures. Reilly thought he saw bone glistening white through the blood.

"Reilly," Lian said. "Go find Carlos and Kailani. Tell them to fetch water, blankets, antibiotics, BioGlue, and gauze—the entire emergency kit. And send Maia in here."

Reilly barreled out, narrowly missing collision with Maia, who was already on her way to help.

Out on the canyon floor, Carlos and Kailani had landed and were opening the dome.

"The first aid kit," Reilly called. "Lian needs it for Erik. Also a thermal blanket and water."

Carlos nodded and closed the dome. Kailani piloted the craft to their cave and hovered the craft even with the ledge while Carlos darted in for supplies.

When they returned to the canyon floor, Reilly had a fire crackling. Harlan and Lian carried Erik over and lay him on a sleeping sac. Maia walked with them, pushing against the artery at the back of Erik's knee to slow the blood loss from his wounds. Carlos took over for her. After Lian administered an Anaral patch and a hefty dose of antibiotics, Kailani and Maia cleaned and closed the wounds.

On the other side of the fire, Keid sat with Tally, who rested her head on his shoulder and stared blankly into the flames. Wrapped in a thermal blanket, Nova curled on her side, her eyes closed, her color restored, her head in Tab's lap. Tab stroked her hair. She sniffled and wiped her face on her sleeve.

Maia came over and sat beside Reilly, who had just finished banking the fire.

"How is Erik?" Reilly asked.

"He'll mend. He just needs to stay off that leg for a while. No more fighting."

"Wouldn't that be nice?" Reilly said.

"Nova looks better."

"Nothing like a little oxygen to perk a person up. It's a miracle she's alive."
Maia elbowed him. "Is she crying?"

"Yes. She's been worrying about the effects of *thystam* toxins on her fetus."

"I'd worry too, were I in her shoes."

"What do you think might happen?" Reilly asked.

"Dunno. We've never had a chance to analyze the chemicals released."

"What happened to your face?" He touched a welt on her cheek.

"One of those thrown *thystam* rocks hit me." She yawned. "Are all our *wyomes* in one piece?"

Reilly looked around. Jannatz and Abdath crouched watchfully nearby. Abdath licked a gash crossing her right shoulder. He bore minor burns and several gouges from tail swipes.

Granos and Pashtak flew above, patrolling the canyon. Reilly's eyes sought Nydea, saw her emerge from the darkness with something in her mouth. It was a sprig of a plant.

"What's that?" Maia asked.

Reilly took the plant and listened as Nydea spoke in Mirnan.

Maia looked at Reilly. "I think she said that the plant heals wounds, especially bite wounds. Something about chewing it and putting it on the wound. Sounds like an old-fashioned poultice. Kailani taught me about that."

Reilly nodded. "You got more than I did. I couldn't make sense of the chewing part."

"*Icantha,* Nydea," Maia said. "I'll give it to Kailani. She'll know what to do."

People sat around the fire talking. Everyone looked tired, dirty, and variously bruised and scraped. Because they didn't know how long *thystam* toxins might linger in the caves, they decided to spend the rest of the night on the canyon floor. Lian and Harlan brought down everyone's sleeping sacs. Carlos volunteered to keep watch.

"They let us go," Maia said. "Maybe we're safe now."

Harlan gave a harsh laugh. "Right. We'll see how long this truce lasts."

∞

Screams awoke Reilly. In the dim light of dawn, Tally hopped about, shouting. Still in his sleeping sac, Keid lay rigidly on his back, his huge eyes fixated on a large dark shape that squatted on his chest.

Erik limped slowly toward Tally and Keid. "Shush, Tally. Be still."

"Get it off him," Tally said in a strangled voice.

Reilly stood. His brain resolved the shape—round hairy body that radiated a dozen legs. An *azentak*. He couldn't think of a way to kill the creature without also harming Keid and hoped Erik had a plan.

Maia squeezed Reilly's arm and whispered, "Where is Abdath going?"

Tearing his eyes away from pallid Keid, Reilly glanced up. Abdath walked on his hind legs toward the mouth of the canyon, hopped onto a large boulder, and crouched.

"Are there other *azentaks?*" Kailani asked softly.

"Two," Tally said. "They tunneled into the sand when I stood."

The *azentak* waved its appendages—the ones tipped with compound eyes— toward Keid's face. Keid pressed trembling lips together.

"Move out of the way, Tally," Harlan whispered hoarsely. Both hands wrapped around the end of a meter-long stick, he took a slow backswing.

"Everyone freeze," Kailani said.

Abdath zoomed forward, wing tips nearly brushing the ground. He snatched the *azentak* in his forepaws, tossed it in a high arc. As the *azentak* fell, legs flailing, Abdath engulfed it with fire. Jannatz darted forward, covered the burning creature in sand, then dug it up again.

"What is she doing?" Maia asked.

Reilly shook his head.

Jannatz pulled off one of the *azentak*'s legs and held it toward Keid, who cringed away.

Jannatz spoke two words.

"It's delicious," Kailani said. "Jannatz is offering you the first bite."

Keid got to his knees and wiggled free of the sleeping sac. "No, thank you," he said weakly.

With a puzzled expression, Jannatz set the leg before Keid, ripped off another and threw it to Abdath, who had landed nearby. He caught it in his mouth and chewed crunchily.

"Hell, I'll have it," Harlan said. He stepped toward Keid, picked up the ten-centimeter long appendage, brushed sand off it, and took a bite.

He nodded. "Not bad. Reminds me of soft-shelled crab. Crabs," he said dreamily, seemingly oblivious to Keid crying into Tally's shoulder. "That takes me back. I used to walk out on the sewer line that went into the bay and catch them with bacon-flavored tofu tied to a string. My dad would dredge them in cornmeal and fry them with garlic and lemon."

"Want a bite?" Harlan asked when Tab came to stand beside him.

Tab took a mouthful and began to offer the half-devoured leg to Nova, but Harlan grabbed it back. Nova scowled at Harlan like they were competing over more than an appetizer.

Later that morning, people flew scouters to the caves, collected possessions, and ferried them to the canyon floor. The *wyomes* took on the onerous process of moving dead bodies out of the canyon. Reilly saw Nydea comforting Jannatz, who cried over the body of one *wyome* before Pashtak and Granos gravely flew it to the other side of the barrier.

Reilly pulled his lumpy duffle from the tiny cargo area of the *Kestrel* and began spreading out his clothes to air out any lingering *thystam* toxin. Kailani had assured them the toxin broke down quickly. Maia pointed at the polychiton cat's head poking out of his duffle.

"What do you plan to do with that?" she asked.

Reilly shrugged. "Put it atop our next home."

"Home," Maia said, her eyes focused on the horizon beyond the tattered barrier at the mouth of the cave. "I don't even know what that means."

"What's burning?" Nova called.

Reilly squinted at a column of smoke rising over the desert.

Kailani straightened. She and Lian had been spreading a bolt of BioFuerte atop the area they would sleep that night. *Azentaks* couldn't dig their way through it. "Our *wyomes* are burning the bodies," she said.

Nova wrinkled her nose. "That's grotty. Smells bad too."

"It's traditional," Kailani said.

"Like the funeral pyres of old," Lian added.

"Like incineration on the ship," Maia said. "I'm just glad we're not burning any of our own."

Reilly thought of his parents, still in the ground—if no animals had disturbed them. He pushed the idea of anything nibbling on their flesh from his mind. "We need to have a ceremony for my parents." The words just came out.

Carlos looked up from his task of unfolding the airscouters' solar collectors. He walked over. "Yes, we do."

"When? When will we go to them? I know where they are."

"As soon as it's safe."

He blinked away hot tears. "When will we ever be safe?"

Carlos glanced at Kailani before saying to Reilly, "Soon."

∞

Instead of sleeping that day, Nydea paced up and down the canyon and watched the sky. Reilly had asked her what she saw.

"Air currents," she said. "And many colors."

Reilly looked again, only saw a blue, cloudless sky. "You can see the air move?"

"Of course," Nydea said. "You can't?"

Reilly shook his head. "The wind has different colors?"

Nydea made a scoffing sound. "Of course not. It makes shapes." She pointed. "There is an upward spiral, very nice for soaring. Sometimes the sun releases more energy than usual. This we can see as colors."

The aurora, Reilly thought. *Wyomes* could see bursts of solar energy at a lower threshold than humans.

"I can't see Hyssel," Nydea said sadly. "But I feel him. He's coming."

That night, as they prepared to sleep, Granos roared a warning from his perch overhead. Reilly's eyes sought Nydea. She crouched a few meters from the campfire, Jannatz alert at her side.

"Now what?" Harlan said. His eyes were bloodshot from lack of sleep.

"Hyssel," Reilly said. He peered upward, but couldn't see him yet.

"I knew we couldn't trust those fuckers." Harlan stomped over and began stuffing his sleeping sac and other belongings into a duffel.

The aurora rippled greens, blues, and reds into the blackness. Backlit by that curtain of light flew Hyssel and a squadron of *wyomes*. Reilly counted ten in all. Hyssel's wings had healed enough to allow flight, though scarring had created an asymmetry. With each stroke, he listed to the right, corrected, listed, corrected.

Carlos shouted, "Everyone in place."

Two hours earlier, the humans and *wyomes* had discussed strategy in the event of such an attack. The four airscouters had been fully charged, the solar panels secured. Now, Harlan and Tab, Lian and Nova, Carlos and Keid, and Erik and Tally took their seats. When the enemy had descended to about ten meters from the bottom, the airscouters shot out into the desert, Abdath and Pashtak close behind. As expected, more than half the enemy took the bait and followed.

Jannatz shepherded Nydea into the partial shelter of a rocky outcropping. Reilly dashed to join Maia and Kailani, who crouched behind a nearby boulder with the remaining bows, arrows, slingshots, and a large pile of stones. They had all volunteered to stay in the canyon. When Carlos balked at the arrangement, Reilly argued that the other kids would be more useful as copilots. Also, he had promised he wouldn't let Hyssel come near Nydea—a resolution he shared only with Nydea. Maia's argument for staying on the ground was that Reilly was such a lousy shot he needed her help. She smiled as she said that, which gave Reilly hope that she exaggerated.

Now, watching the enemy draw closer, their scalloped wings almost black in the evening gloom, Reilly felt vulnerable and clammy with dread. He glanced at Maia, who looked back with steady dark eyes.

Kailani shouldered her quiver. She and Maia had three arrows apiece. Reilly had none, since he was better with a slingshot.

Granos winged upward to confront the attackers. Facing one another, he and Hyssel hovered, a task that required Hyssel to beat his wings more rapidly than Granos. Reilly heard their voices and the occasional bellicose rumblings of the *wyomes* clustered around Hyssel.

"What are they saying?" Maia asked, craning her neck to look at the *wyomes*, who were almost straight overhead.

Reilly shook his head. "They're too far."

Nydea spoke. "Granos asked them to leave. He said nothing good could come of further warfare. My uncle laughed and said that killing Granos and the other traitors would be better than good. Granos asked my uncle what he hoped to achieve. Hyssel said he wished only for the return of peace and order. Granos promised Hyssel just that. Granos said that our group would move to the far side of the mesa."

After a pause, Maia said, "Well? What was Hyssel's response?"

Reilly wished he could see Nydea, but the boulder sheltering him blocked his view. Nevertheless, he could feel her presence, her thorny unease interlocked with his own.

Nydea let out a long sigh. "Hyssel said he would consent to such a plan... as long as I returned to him. Perhaps that is a fair exchange."

"No," Reilly said. "That's not negotiable." He stepped sideways in an attempt to see Nydea, but Maia yanked him back.

"I'm sure that's more or less how Granos replied," Kailani said as she pulled an arrow from her quiver and fitted the nock into the bow's string. "Hyssel wouldn't let the rest of us live. Heads up."

Granos peeled away from the other *wyomes* and streaked toward Nydea. Several meters from the ground, he rolled and doubled back, straight for Hyssel. Three *wyomes* intercepted. The *Kestrel,* which carried Carlos and Keid, nipped back into the canyon, fired *yridium* at the enemy, sent two *wyomes* barreling to ground, then slipped back into open country. That left Hyssel and three of his allies in the canyon.

The three *wyomes* dove at them. Maia and Kailani each sank an arrow into one of the attackers. Reilly released two stones at a time from his slingshot, turning back another *wyome* just as it gushed fire at them. Reilly ducked, felt heat along his spine, then a douse of cold water.

"Take off your jacket," Maia yelled as she tossed aside her empty water skin.

He peeled off the smoking thing off and grabbed his slingshot. "Where's Hyssel?" he gasped.

Maia shook her head.

Kailani stood, arched her back, and released an arrow into the belly of a *wyome* passing overhead. It swerved into the canyon wall with bone crunching forced and slid down the side.

Several meters above, Granos fought an attacker. Reilly saw no other *wyomes*.

"Nydea!" he called. He zigged around his boulder and stopped so fast he almost pitched to his knees.

Jannatz sprawled on the ground, holding together a gash in her side. Hyssel loomed over Nydea, forefingers clutching the back of her neck. Nydea stared at Reilly, her eyes black with terror.

"Get away from her," Reilly said. He held a loaded slingshot in front of him and wished he had a venomous stone.

"Or what?" Hyssel said. "You will pelt me with rocks?"

Kailani spoke behind Reilly. "You're outnumbered, Hyssel."

"You might want to count again." Hyssel nodded toward the top of the canyon.

Reilly squinted. Silhouetted against the aurora, *wyomes* lined both rims of the canyon. He wondered what Nydea's speech had accomplished. Were the other *wyomes* still too afraid of Hyssel to switch sides?

"Keksa," Maia said. She stood, one last arrow in her quiver, beside Reilly.

"Wonderful," Hyssel said. "You're learning our language. How fitting that you would first learn the word for excrement."

"Fuck you," Maia said. "Actually, the words are more satisfying in my language."

"I haven't bothered to learn *nakkoth* speak. No point to it. You will soon be extinct."

Reilly's thoughts spun. If he could kill Hyssel, maybe the other *wyomes* would turn back. He wished he had a *yridium* gun—or something more reliably lethal than a slingshot.

Kailani now stood on his other side, her remaining arrow positioned on the bow. "I still have plenty of time to kill you, Hyssel," she said in Mirnan.

"Don't," Nydea cried.

"That's right, Nydea. You're smart enough to know that, in the time it takes Kailani to use her ridiculous weapon, I can scorch your entire body."

Jannatz growled.

"And kill you," Hyssel added, nudging Jannatz's belly with his hind foot. "But you're already dying."

With an anguished cry, Jannatz bit his leg and held on. Hyssel swept back his tail for a strike with the barbed end. Just as he turned, one hand still gripping Nydea, Kailani loosed the arrow, which buried into Hyssel's shoulder.

Shrieking in anger, *wyomes* began streaming down into the canyon.

"I missed his heart," Kailani muttered.

As Reilly stooped to pick up stones, the aurora illuminated the weathervane protruding from his duffel. He sprinted to it.

"Reilly!" Maia cried. "Look out."

His peripheral vision caught a dark shape bearing down on him. He somersaulted, regained his feet, kept running. Hyssel kicked free of Jannatz. She curled around her wound. Hyssel began tugging Nydea into one of the lower caves. Maia and Kailani stood back-to-back, slingshots at the ready.

Reilly barreled toward Hyssel, weathervane tucked under his arm. Hyssel turned, an annoyed expression on his face. Reilly leapt onto his back. Hyssel whirled and fanned open his wings, which smacked Reilly's sides and tossed him to his knees. Nydea tumbled sideways.

"Run!" Reilly called to her. She backed away, then stood mesmerized.

Hyssel bucked. Reilly stretched for a handhold. His fingers closed on Kailani's arrow shaft sticking out of Hyssel's shoulder. Hyssel roared. Reilly twisted the wood, drove it in deeper. Hyssel swiveled his head around. Reilly scrabbled forward, grabbed the weathervane and jammed the arrow end into the crease in Hyssel's neck.

Hyssel's expression changed from anger to disbelief. He swatted at the weathervane, which bent but did not break. Blood began to pump from his neck.

"That's from my father," Reilly said, leaning close to the beast's face.

Hyssel exhaled his meaty breath and clicked his teeth. Reilly flipped off Hyssel's back and threw his arms over his head. No fire came. Hyssel yeowled. Nydea was throwing herself at Hyssel, clawing at his chest and sides.

She stood back and gasped, "That's for my parents and for Sheeda and for me."

Hyssel staggered and fell, which snapped the weathervane in two and drove the arrow deeper into his neck. Blood gurgled in his airway.

Nydea spoke urgently. "Celebrate later. Come!"

Reilly took one last look at Hyssel, who clawed at the ground as though trying to drag himself out of the widening puddle of blood. The weathervane's cat had broken free. With its tail buried in the sand, it appeared to be climbing into the air.

Reilly turned. *Wyomes* darted back and forth in the canyon. He spotted the gleaming silver of the first-aid kit and started for it. A *wyome* cut him off with a tongue of flame. He skittered sideways and another *wyome* dove toward him.

His reached for his slingshot, but it no longer hung from his belt. It must have fallen out while he grappled with Hyssel. He dodged, backpedaled, swerved.

He heard Maia's voice in his head. She was calling his name. He spun, saw her standing beside Kailani, both of them weaponless. Reilly ran to them, momentarily forgetting about the emergency kit, compelled by a fierce protective instinct. He would use his knuckles, his nails, his kicking legs, the force of his own skull.

Maia's eyes stared straight ahead, as though hypnotized. Her lips pressed into a determined line, as though she bore the weight of boulders on her back.

Reilly felt a sharp pain in his shoulder, realized one of the *wyomes* harrying him had swiped him with outstretched claws. Fists up, he whirled and backed toward Maia and Kailani. A pulse seemed to emanate from them. He felt tingling. It was like before, only stronger. The sensation burned up the backs of his legs, up his spine, then down his arms. His head buzzed. He felt as though he were drawing electricity from the ground. He wondered if this is what dying felt like—a jolt of energy and then nothing. The shock-like sensations continued. A *wyome* came at him, so close he could smell its carnivore breath. Its image was warped, as though underwater. He blinked, unfurled his fingers. The air felt thicker, almost gelatinous. The attacker yapped and banked away.

Reilly backed up until he, Maia, and Kailani formed a triangle, a triangle that radiated a vibrating shield. The air around them seemed to glitter. *Wyomes* darted back and forth overhead. He heard their voices. He wondered where Nydea and Jannatz were. The current running through him seemed to waver. He cleared his mind, focused on the charged flow from firmly planted feet to spine to hands. It took everything to keep the fierce energy running down his arms. His body began to tremble. He felt Maia's exhaustion.

"I can't," she gasped. "I can't." She cradled herself in her own arms.

Reilly shook harder. He told himself he couldn't stop, told himself everything depended on his continued effort. But he felt like he was running out of oxygen, running low on blood sugar. His vision began to darken. It was like the world had turned to shades of gray, like everything was made of grains of sand, like a wind was blowing away their vitality grain by grain.

"Sheeda!" It was Nydea's voice. "Sheeda and Locatha and Zedena." She sounded happy. Reilly couldn't understand. He couldn't see anything but dark shapes shifting above him.

A hand shook him. "Stop, Reilly." Kailani? Someone forced down his arms, which felt made of wood, wood that had bleached in the sun, wood that had been pulled from a fire. They were hot and dry and heavy and unyielding.

He closed his eyes. Someone helped him to sit. He was crying, but he didn't know why.

"It's over," Kailani said. "It's over."

So, he was dead. He was dead and so was Kailani and Maia and Nydea and Hyssel.

"Look! Reilly, look." It was Maia.

He opened his leaded eyelids a few millimeters. Maia sat beside him, rocking back and forth and laughing or crying or both. "They came!" she said.

"Who?" Reilly said. His voice seemed to echo inside his skull.

"Sheeda, Locatha, and Zedena," Maia said. "They brought *wyomes* from the other clans. There were so many of them that Hyssel's *wyomes* fled."

His focus widened. He saw a ring of *wyomes* with Locatha standing in the middle. More *wyomes* perched on canyon ledges and watched.

Locatha inclined her head at Maia and Reilly. "Many apologies for our late arrival," she said. "We encountered some…difficulties."

Within the circle, Nydea sat beside Sheeda and Zedena. The three of them leaned over Jannatz, who lay on her side panting. Kailani strode over with the first-aid kit and her pack.

"I should help," Maia said. She took a step and her legs folded underneath her.

Reilly scooted beside her, put a heavy arm around her shoulder, felt amazed that he could move his arm at all. "The *wyomes* can assist Kailani," he said.

Indeed, Zedena held shut the wound while Kailani applied BioGlue. Sheeda covered the wound with gauze. Nydea purred reassurances and stroked Jannatz's face.

Reilly looked up and noticed the aurora had vanished. So had Hyssel's allies.

White headlights pricked the darkness then slowly dilated. Reilly heard the murmur of engines. The four scouters touched down behind the circle of *wyomes*. Locatha turned and disappeared into the darkness beyond.

"What if Harlan or someone doesn't understand these *wyomes* are our allies?"

In a moment, Granos limped into the circle, his hind legs a bloody mass of lacerations, Locatha at his side. Just behind came the humans: Carlos and Keid, Tab and Nova, Harlan and Erik, Lian and Tally. As they passed, the new *wyomes* bent toward them, nostrils quivering. Two young females whispered together. Reilly realized this was their first experience with humans.

Harlan looked around uneasily. "Would someone explain to me what is going on?"

THIRTY-EIGHT

The naming ceremony took place by the light of the campfire. The *wyomes* wanted to be present. In fact, they had provided a list of possible surnames, though the concept of first and last name had to be explained to them. Mirnans, those capable of speech, created a novel first name for each newborn. They were otherwise identified by their clan names, a method complicated by the fact that, to avoid inbreeding, *wyomes* usually pair-bonded with individuals from other clans.

As they sat there, firelight flickering on their faces, Reilly understood that childhood was over. No one giggled or made silly jokes. One by one, each of the kids, who were no longer children, stood with an adult, who announced their new name. Nydea stood before Abdath, Pashtak, Granos, Locatha, Sheeda, Zedena, and a reclining Jannatz and translated English to Mirnan.

Harlan called Tab, who now sported a beard as full and reddish-blonde as Harlan's. "If I had to go into battle and could only bring one other person, I'd choose Tab. He's decisive and brave. You, my right-hand man, are now Tabit Ayten. In Mirnan, *Ayten* means 'pain in my ass.' Is that right, Nydea?"

Nydea gave him a toothy grin. "It meanth 'fiery warrior'." she said.

Harlan smacked his forehead. "Is that right? Well, I'd say that's an apt name for our Tab. What about the rest of you?"

Tab grinned as humans applauded and *wyomes* rapidly clicked their tongues in approval.

Nova went next. She kept a protective arm over her belly, which didn't look much bigger though her breasts certainly did.

Lian hugged her and said, "Nova is smart and warm-hearted and will, in some months time, expand our tribe. We can only hope that, in addition to repairing our communication systems, she will elevate the couture on this planet. It is my pleasure to introduce Nova Sathira, named after the fragrant night-blooming flower."

Nova curtsied as the group acknowledged her new name.

Looking tired but happy, Kailani called upon Keid. His fine hair was pulled into a ponytail. His blue eyes looked enormous in his thin face. His clothes no longer covered his skinny wrists and ankles. He had become a blade of a young man.

"Once we set up a loom, you and Nova will be the first recipients of new clothes," Kailani said. People laughed. "You will henceforth be known as Keid Mikkan. In Mirnan, *mikkan* means 'creative one.'"

Erik stood for Tally. Looking calm and confident, Tally wore her hair in an elegant bun that showed off her long neck.

The dancing light cast shadows under Erik's high cheekbones. "As you all know," he said, "Tally has a way with animals. I could not have done my work without her." He paused, and Reilly thought about the fact that, despite their devotion to the Earth animals, only one goat had survived. "I hereby name her Talitha Cybele, after the Greek Goddess of nature and animals."

Next, Kailani called forth Maia, who had wrapped one of Kailani's shawls around her shoulders. The two women were the same height, both brown skinned, Kailani's eyes emerald to Maia's greenish brown. Kailani had plaited Maia's hair and wound it over her head.

Kailani spoke in her clear, commanding voice. "Nydea gave Maia a surname the night we met. *Halatha* means 'bold-hearted.' When you look beyond the brave—and somewhat cheeky—exterior, you find a loyal, wise, and compassionate woman with a skill at healing all wounds. I give you Maia Halatha."

Reilly clapped enthusiastically, nearly drowning out Tab's comment about Maia the bold-farted. Maia returned to her seat beside him and kissed his cheek.

"You looked like a princess," he whispered.

Mai scowled and fingered her elaborate hairdo. "Too much?"

"No. Not a silly princess, but a warrior princess—the kind who arm wrestles her suitors and saves the townsfolk from ogres."

She smiled. "That's better."

"Can we eat now?" Harlan said loudly.

"One more," Carlos said. "Your turn, Reilly."

Reilly blinked in surprise. "But I already have a last name."

Carlos beamed at him, his teeth white in his black beard. "Stop protesting and stand up."

Reilly did.

Carlos put a hand on his shoulder and looked him in the eye. "Reilly, we have watched you grow from a brilliant, but somewhat insecure and, perhaps a bit arrogant, boy—"

"To an arrogant but kickass hume," Tab interjected, drawing guffaws from the crowd and confused murmurs from the *wyomes*. Unable to translate that bit of dialogue, Nydea simply shook her head.

Reilly smiled sheepishly and hoped Carlos would soon get to the point.

Carlos cleared his throat. "—to a confident, capable, and empathetic young man." He again made eye contact with Reilly. "Granted, you defied authority and broke rules."

"It had to happen," Tab interjected raucously.

"But your motivation was understandable. The end result is you returned Kailani to us and helped forge important alliances." Carlos smiled at Kailani, touched the green stone that now hung outside his shirt, and bowed to the *wyomes*. "Thank you, for supporting us. Without you, we would not have survived."

Lian and Maia hugged Kailani. The *wyomes* nodded and clicked. Locatha rubbed her head against Granos' shoulder. Sheeda came to stand hip to hip with Nydea, who gazed affectionately at Reilly, her left eye in its perpetual half wink.

"Back to Reilly," Carlos said. "Like all of you, he has overcome loss. We still mourn Anika and Skyler. Tomorrow we will memorialize them at their graves."

Reilly felt his face and throat contract. He hadn't imagined Carlos would talk about his parents, hadn't heard of tomorrow's ceremony.

"Anika and Skyler would be proud of you, Reilly Landreth," Carlos said, his voice thick with emotion. "You have shown yourself to be valiant and true."

"Thank you," Reilly managed.

"Carlos, wait," Harlan said, making a show of looking through his pockets. "If you're going to launch into an ol' timey ballad, I need my hankie."

Carlos laughed. "Okay. Enough. I'll finish by saying I'm proud of every one of you. You are my family."

"If that's true," Nova said, twirling a lock of hair, "some of us, you included, are committing incest."

Carlos tossed his hands into the hair. "A tribe then. Okay, let's eat." While the others erupted into conversation, he hugged Reilly. And Reilly hugged him back.

∞

The only *wyomes* to attend the graveside ceremony for Reilly's parents were Nydea, who had carried Anika and Skyler to Kailani and helped with the burial, and Sheeda, who perhaps came to exorcize the evil done by Hyssel.

Nydea had flown Reilly there, which comforted him. Sheeda took Tally, who had asked permission in Mirnan.

Keid and Nova had created crude headstones by etching names and dates into two rock slabs that had sheered off the face of the canyon. These they brought in the airscouter. Tab and Harlan solemnly sank the headstones into the sand at the gravesite.

Apprehension twisted in Reilly's belly. He hadn't been able to eat that morning. The night before, he dreamt that his parents' graves had been excavated, that their bleached bones lay scattered, white against the red sand. Maia had shaken him awake, had promised him she would arrive first to make sure everything looked okay. Good on her word, she had given Reilly a thumb's up as he and Nydea descended.

By the light of early morning, the site looked more or less the same—mounded earth surrounded by a few desiccated bushes. Reilly wished it were greener. His parents, his father especially, would have enjoyed a tree or two.

Maia thrust the box containing his father's flute at him.

"I don't think I can," he said.

"You've been practicing the better part of two days."

"That's not enough. I should have asked Lian to bring her oboe."

"You sound good to me. Either you put the thing together or I will."

Reilly unsnapped the scuffed black case and slid the cool, silver tubes into position, rubbed a tarnished area with his thumb. He looked over at Keid, who had fashioned a drum out of *boola* hide stretched over the rim of a wheel that had once propelled Reba, the android.

Keid nodded. "Ready when you are."

Carlos asked for quiet. The humans, Nydea, and Sheeda formed a circle around the graves.

Reilly stood at his parents' feet. "The headstones look good," he said.

Maia bugged out her eyes and mouthed, *"Go on."*

"Keid and I are going to play one of my father's favorites. It's called "Danny Boy." He swallowed. "I'm afraid I won't do it justice."

"Shut up and play," Tab said. "Remember we're not the most cultured of audiences."

Using the femur of a *boola*, Keid struck a measured beat on his drum. Reilly lifted the flute and played. After one stanza, Erik began to sing in his baritone. Carlos joined in, then Harlan, and then, in a rich alto, Kailani. Lian sang until crying took her voice. The kids hummed and occasionally interjected words, not all of which belonged in the original lyrics. Surprisingly, only German-born Erik knew the words to all four stanzas.

As they did after Nash and Oren died, everyone said a few words about Anika and Skyler. Reilly was surprised that each of the kids had a story of some kindness one or the other of his parents had done.

When it came his turn, he took a deep breath and hoped he could get a sentence or two out without sobbing. "When my parents died, I thought I was the most miserable human alive. Now, I understand that I have been lucky. As some of you have pointed out, I had parents for fifteen years. They were gentle and loving and playful. If they were here," he paused to steady his breathing, which snagged on something sharp in his throat. "If they were here,

I would thank them for teaching me to appreciate literature and music and science. I would thank them for bedtime stories and those kisses that began to embarrass me. I would thank them for their enthusiasm about, well—just living.

"They were so excited to come to Mirna, though they never knew it by its proper name. They—my mother especially—would be thrilled to see that we have *wyome* friends." Reilly swallowed, which caused surprising pain.

"After they died, I felt abandoned and alone." He looked at the people standing before him—the humans in their tattered clothes, Sheeda and Nydea with their scars. They looked back, expectantly, warmly, buoyantly. "But now I understand that, though we may each feel, in our own way, orphaned, we are never alone."

He looked down at his hands, which still held his flute. His nails were dirty and ragged, his skin a network of nicks and callouses.

"Nice job, Reilly," Tab said, then more quietly, "Quit while you're ahead."

People laughed softly, and Reilly found he could smile. He had wanted to say more. He had wanted to thank Maia for bringing him back to life. He wanted to remind people of the particulars of his parents, the way his father's hair spiked up from his forehead in the morning, the times his mother sent all the kids on scavenger hunts on the ship, the times his father—when Reilly pretended not to listen—recited poetry to the cat, the way his mother danced whenever anyone played music and even when no music—not any he could hear—played. He stood there, apart from the others and clutching the flute, until Maia came to his side, slipped her arm through his, and said, "They're not over, your parents. You have your memories. Plus, each of us—you most of all—have incorporated their habits, their values, their songs, their stories."

That was the first time he kissed her in full view of everyone.

THIRTY-NINE

Five days later, after Jannatz was strong enough to travel, they journeyed to Compuwl Canyon on the far side of Methna Mesa. The airscouters and some of the *wyomes* transported the gear. Gretta the goat flew, tethered to the copilots seat, with Erik. Other *wyomes* carried the humans not traveling in airscouters. Everyone was pleased with that situation but Nova, who kept saying things like, "I'm a pregnant woman. What if the *wyome* drops me?"

"Well," Harlan said with a slow smile. "Then you'll both probably die."

Nydea insisted on carrying Reilly. After several kilometers, she wearied and Granos took Reilly.

As he flew, Reilly thought of the last few days, considered what it meant for Nydea and the other Ledera Canyon *wyomes* to abandon their homes. The day before they departed Standea Canyon, four *wyomes* from the Upshala Clan, previously under Hyssel's rule, appeared carrying sprigs of *anosote* as a sign of peace. They apologized for fighting on Hyssel's side, apologized for the harm they had caused. In turn, Nydea, Granos, and Locatha expressed regret for hurting and killing clan members. Then the emissaries asked the refugees from Ledera Canyon to return. They said the Upshala Clan recognized Nydea as their rightful leader. They begged her and the other clan members to return. They promised a heroes' welcome.

Nydea, Sheeda, Locatha, Granos, Pashtak, Abdath, Zedena, and Jannatz deliberated for an hour in an upper cave. They emerged with Nydea as their spokesperson.

"I love my clanspeople," Nydea said in a ringing voice. "And I am honored to be chosen leader. Pacha and Ocasso, my parents, would be pleased."

The emissaries clicked their tongues rapidly as a sign of appreciation and approval.

"However," Nydea continued, pulling herself up even taller, "I decline the offer. My trusted allies and I must leave. The hurt from these past few weeks runs too deep. Perhaps later, when the scars heal, when we have regained the trust of all who live along Ledera Canyon—not just *wyomes,* but also *garthans, witnaws,* and *mantalyas*—we can be reunited. That process will take time."

How much time? Reilly wondered as he sat astride the rolling muscles of Granos' shoulders. Why was happiness too quickly forgotten and sadness so hard to shake? It took a hundred joyful moments to push tragedy into the past.

Into the purpling twilight, Granos flew with strong, steady strokes. Under Reilly's fingers, the big *wyome's* neck was ridged with scars. The changing landscape slid beneath them. The scrubby plants became more numerous. The ground folded into hills and ravines. Clouds dragged themselves across the sky from north to south. Until now, he had only seen the occasional cloud that evaporated in the heat.

As they rounded the northwest corner of the mesa, something wet splashed his nose. A second later, drops splatted his head and back.

Nydea flew on one side of him, Maia and Locatha on the other.

"*Yovay!*" Nydea said.

"What?" Reilly replied.

"It's raining!" Maia whooped. She tilted back her head and lifted both hands into the air.

Reilly held his breath until Maia returned her hands to Locatha's neck.

Maia grinned at him. "I heard you in my head, worrywart."

The rain came down harder. His jacket was waterproof but his pants weren't. As the temperature dropped, his legs grew numb, except where they pressed against Granos' chest. He hoped they would reach their destination soon.

In the last rays of the sun, he saw a creek flowing out of a canyon. Moving as a unit, the group banked that direction. This must be their destination, Compuwl Canyon. As they entered the canyon, Reilly thought he heard wind sheering over rock then realized it was the sound of water rushing down the creek.

Wyomes came to the mouths of caves and called greetings. Some took to the air to meet the group, and some of those reversed course at the sight of the airscouters.

A male *wyome* flew out to meet them, calling Granos and Locatha by name. They peeled off from the group and slowed in front of a large cave. Granos, Locatha, Nydea, and the stranger entered and folded their wings. The ceiling was so high it disappeared into the darkness.

A female *wyome* came from an adjoining cave, trailing the smallest *wyome* Reilly had ever seen. It was larger than their dogs had been, but only half the height of an adult human. It hopped along beside its mother, noticed Reilly and Maia, then, with a squeak, darted behind her.

"It's a baby!" Maia said and slid off Locatha's back. She got to her knees. The little *wyome* peeked under its mother's belly. Maia waggled her fingers. The *wyome* jumped back, peeked out again.

Reilly jumped to the ground and found he had lost feeling in his knees, which buckled underneath him.

The little *wyome* let out a high-pitched cackle.

Locatha and Granos warmly greeted their hosts, rubbing noses and pressing their foreheads together. Then they made introductions. The male was Locatha's brother, Kyget. The female was Kunish. Their daughter was called Sartatha. She crept forward to sniff Nydea's scarred wings, but wouldn't come near the humans.

Reilly creased his frozen face into a smile. He was shivering. Maia, he noticed, was too. Kyget fetched them *erzala* hides. Kunish brought an urn of water and two *boola* legs, fired to perfection.

"This is good," Maia said, scooting closer to him.

They ate and listened to the *wyomes* chattering. The baby climbed onto his father's shoulders, draped its unblemished silver body over his neck, and fell asleep.

Reilly lay back and listened to the rain pelt the canyon walls. Maia curled her back against his hip. For the first time in many weeks, he felt safe.

∞

When Reilly awoke, Maia sat beside him, reading one of his books. She turned the page with a dirty finger.

"Good morning," he said.

"Good afternoon," she corrected.

He looked toward the cave's mouth. Above the cliff opposite was a band of sky scalloped by gray clouds. He pushed onto his elbow. In the adjoining cave, three *wyomes* slept on a hide-covered platform, the baby in the middle.

"Is anyone else up?" he asked.

"Not long ago, I saw Harlan standing at the edge of a cave across from us and peeing."

"That must have been thrilling."

"Hmm," she said her eyes on the page.

It was an anthology of short stories. "Which one are you reading?" he asked.

"A story about a boy and a girl who travel to a distant planet and sleep in a cave with large, flying creatures."

"Does the story have a happy ending?"

She looked at him, her eyes shifting from brown to green as the light caught them. Reilly's mother had a word for that eye color. Hassle. No... hazel. Or something like that.

"We shall see," she said.

"What do we do now?"

"Eat. And soon, I hope." She smiled. "After that, we live long and unremarkable lives."

∞

After five days of rain, the sun broke through and the people gathered on the canyon floor to discuss a plan for a permanent home. There weren't enough unoccupied caves in the canyon for them all. Kailani and Carlos reported that, after scouting the area, they had identified a place in the nearby hills favorable to farming and, if Gretta successfully gave birth, raising goats.

The next day, Lian and Locatha flew to the area to meet with the local *garthan* clan and returned with promises of mutual peace, which Harlan dismissed as a pact with "a bunch of outsized, bloodthirsty coyotes." Locatha swore that the *wyomes* would keep an eye on the *garthans* and punish any transgressions.

The Compuwl Clan *wyomes* prepared a farewell feast. It was a bedtime event for the *wyomes,* breakfast for the humans. Along with several *wyomes,* Harlan, Tab, and Kailani had hunted *erzala.* The other humans had gathered *skeeba* berries, nuts from *coulia* bushes, oniony bulbs, and aromatic herbs.

Reilly, Nydea, and Maia sat with their hosts, Kyget, Kunish, and little Sartatha. Between Nydea's English and Maia and Reilly's rudimentary Mirnan, they were able to carry on a bit of a conversation. Holding an *erzala* rib in one forepaw, Sartatha danced forward to touch Maia's hair. Maia tickled her under the arms. Sartatha shrieked, ran behind Kyget, then tiptoed back for more. She plunked down in Reilly's lap, and he ran his hands over the silver hairs that puffed out between the tiny scales.

"Why does Sartatha have hair?" he asked Nydea.

"All baby *wyomes* do," she said. "Even after maturity, we grow hair during the rainy season." She bowed her head toward Reilly so that he could see the hair sprouting on top.

"Amazing," Reilly said. "I wish I could grow fur when I'm cold." He shifted uncomfortably. Sartatha's weight had cut off the circulation to his legs. The small *wyome* jumped up and began to scale Nydea's back.

"Sheath your claws, little one," Nydea chided.

Sartatha pressed her face into the crook of Nydea's neck. "Nice Nydea," she cooed.

Nydea twisted to lick Sartatha's face, then returned her amber gaze to Maia and Reilly. "I will miss seeing you every day,"

Reilly sighed. "So will I." He'd been dreading their separation for days. He told himself Nydea would be happy with her new clan, and, seeing her with Sartatha, it appeared that she would. But that didn't stop him from feeling sad.

"How long will it take you to reach our new home?" Maia asked.

"Not long," Nydea said. "Only a little longer than it will take this one to fall asleep." She pointed at Sartatha, whose inner eyelids had already begun to droop.

Reilly didn't know how the *wyomes* measured time. He'd heard them describe the passage of time based on nights (which they counted rather than days) and the phases of the moons and the onset of the rainy season. But he had never heard them refer to smaller units equivalent to hours or minutes. Perhaps there was no need.

"I will look for you in the skies," Reilly said.

"You will know when I'm coming," Nydea said. "I will send my thoughts in advance. Expect my first visit three nights hence." She paused, looked over at Sheeda, who chatted with another female *wyome*, then back to Reilly. "I owe you my life."

Reilly stood to face her. "No, you saved my life," he said.

"Mine too," Maia said, a note of protest in her voice. "Anyway, it's not like it's a contest."

Reilly laughed. "Okay, okay."

Nydea bent her head to Reilly, then Maia. After they all touched foreheads, she said, "May our lives always be linked."

∞

The journey to their new home was short enough for the people and Gretta to travel on foot. Carlos, Harlan, Lian, and Erik, whose legs were still healing, went ahead with the airscouters. While Granos and Locatha flew laps above them, the others paralleled a creek upstream into the hills. The day was warm but not hot. The higher they climbed, the lusher the landscape became. Flowers of every imaginable hue popped from the ground. Some plants grew only a few centimeters tall; others reached shoulder height. Gretta kept stopping to browse, and Tally tugged her along so they didn't fall behind.

Flying insects Reilly had never seen zipped from bloom to bloom. Another new species emitted a hiccupping sound and hopped out of the way as they approached. The creatures were thumb-sized, with four eyes bulging from a disc-shaped head, two strong hind legs, and two short forelegs. Tally thought they must survive the dry season in a dormant state, perhaps as fertilized eggs, bursting to life as the first drops hit the earth.

At least three types of tree bordered the water. These were home to *boolas,* two other avian species and small, shorthaired creatures with wing-like extensions under their forearms that caught the wind when the animals leapt from branch to branch. *Mantalyas* lived in the trees as well. Standing on their two tails, some of them clutching infants to their chests, they farted, belched, hooted insults, shook the branches as the humans passed, and occasionally threw woody conical objects and once poop, which nearly hit Keid on the head. The behavior stopped after Granos flew down and growled a reprimand.

After two hours, they reached the spot, a small valley between two hills. There, the creek ended at a lake that reflected blue sky on which sailed white clouds. Granos and Locatha reported that, aside from *wapesh,* which were good to eat, and several types of smaller fish and wormy creatures, no other animals lived in the water. After sharing a lunch with the humans, they made their goodbyes and began the flight back to Compuwl Canyon.

Erik stripped to his underwear, limped into the water, and stroked strongly toward the middle of the lake.

Lian called out in alarm. "How can you be sure there aren't creatures down there? I mean… do they open their eyes under water?"

Erik swam on.

Reilly stood at the edge. The bottom dropped quickly way. After a few meters, he could only see darkness. Do *wyomes* swim? he wondered. If not, how did they know what lived in the lake?

Harlan remained fully clothed the longest. He watched Tab and Nova splash in the shallows, then turned his eyes on Maia, as she entered the water and her bra left little to the imagination. Reilly's skin tightened along his spine.

"Come on, Reilly," Maia called. "It feels wonderful."

"Yeah," Tab said. "And you'll smell better afterward."

The mud squished warmly between Reilly's toes as he waded in. The temperature was refreshing, but not cold. He sank to his chest, smelled decomposing vegetation, saw tiny animals corkscrewing through the water.

He experimented with pushing his arms through the water. He remembered that, soon after they landed on Mirna, his mother had promised to teach him to swim, once they found water deep enough yet safe.

"Over here, Reilly," Carlos called. He and Kailani were treading water a short distance away. Carlos made a couple expert-looking arm strokes back to shallow water.

Silt sucking at his feet and ankles, Reilly lurched over to Carlos, who told him that there was more than one way to move through water.

"This one's called the crawl," Carlos said, which sounded to Reilly like a gawky name for swimming. He showed Reilly how to efficiently kick the water with his legs, while slicing through it with arm strokes that put the shoulder through its full range of motion.

Maia shouted, "Get your hand off my ass!"

Reilly stood in chest-deep water in time to see Maia angrily paddling away from Harlan. Carlos scowled. Harlan shrugged and said, "You said you wanted a swimming lesson."

Reilly followed Maia. His arms seemed to thrash the water rather than cut cleanly, as Carlos's had. His entire head came out of the water each time he breathed. By the time he reached Maia, he was panting and his feet no longer touched bottom.

Maia rolled onto her back. "Look, you can float," she said.

Reilly rotated and enjoyed a few seconds of bliss before his legs began to sink. He inhaled deeply, turned face down, and opened his eyes. The water muffled the sounds of human speech. He heard a distant, vaguely metallic clinking. A *wapesh* oscillated past, sunlight glinting off its green-striped body. Purplish vegetation waved below him. His chest ached for a fresh breath. Just as he began to lift his head, something large, dark, and triangular peeled away from the lake bottom and rose toward him. It's not over, he thought, as he splashed as fast as he could toward Maia.

About The Author

Linda B. White has been a published writer for 30 years. She has written two nonfiction books, coauthored three others, contributed to other titles, and written countless magazine articles on health. She holds an M.D. from the University of California, San Diego and a master's degree in biology from Stanford University. *The Orphans of Mirna* is her first novel.

www.lindabwhite.com

Photo Credit: Ellen Jaskol

ACKNOWLEDGEMENTS

When he was ten years old, my son, Alex White, made drawings of the wyomes. He didn't call them by that name, nor did I, until I was deep into a novel about the relationship between these winged creatures and a group of human colonists. Thank you, Alex, for the inspiration.

The Orphans of Mirna would never have gone anywhere without the encouragement of William Haywood Henderson, a novelist and teacher at Lighthouse Writers in Denver.

Ed Zorensky's critique group fueled the long revision process.

Alex and my daughter, Darcy White, proved to be astute readers of the final draft.

Novelists Jahnna Beecham and Helen Phillips offered timely insight and reassurance.

Maggie McLaughlin designed the book you now hold in your hands.

A friend of my daughter's connected me with the talented Shannon Faber, who created the cover art.

My husband, Barney White, helped me to believe in myself.

ALSO BY LINDA B. WHITE

500 Time-Tested Home Remedies and the Science Behind Them

Health Now: An Integrative Approach to Personal Health

The Herbal Drugstore

Kids, Herbs, and Health

The Grandparent Book

Made in the USA
Coppell, TX
18 October 2021

64269023R00236